James R.. O'F

The History of Dundalk, and its Environs

SALZWASSER
VERLAG

James R.. O'Flanagan, John D'Alton

The History of Dundalk, and its Environs

Reprint of the original, first published in 1864.

1st Edition 2022 | ISBN: 978-3-75259-294-8

Verlag (Publisher): Salzwasser Verlag GmbH, Zeilweg 44, 60439 Frankfurt, Deutschland
Vertretungsberechtigt (Authorized to represent): E. Roepke, Zeilweg 44, 60439 Frankfurt, Deutschland
Druck (Print): Books on Demand GmbH, In de Tarpen 42, 22848 Norderstedt, Deutschland

THE

HISTORY OF DUNDALK,

AND

ITS ENVIRONS;

FROM THE EARLIEST HISTORIC PERIOD TO THE PRESENT TIME;

WITH

MEMOIRS OF ITS EMINENT MEN.

DUNDALK

1864.

Forster & Co. lith. Dublin.

TOWER OF FRANCISCAN FRIARY.

SEATOWN, DUNDALK.

DONORS AND LOCAL SUBSCRIBERS TO THE HISTORY OF DUNDALK.

	£	s.	d.
THE RIGHT HON. THE EARL OF RODEN, K.St.P., *Custos Rotulorum* of the County of Louth, . . .	20	0	0
RIGHT HON. LORD CLERMONT, D.L., . . .	10	0	0
RICHARD MONTESQUIEU BELLEW, Esq, M.P., Co. Louth, .	5	0	0
CHICHESTER SAMUEL FORTESCUE, Esq., M.P., do., .	5	0	0
SIR GEORGE BOWYER, Bart., M.P., Borough of Dundalk, .	3	0	0
HIS GRACE MOST REV. ARCHBISHOP DIXON, R.C. Primate (three copies), ...	1	10	0
PATRICK JAMES BYRNE, Esq., Clerk of the Crown, Co. Louth,	5	0	0
REV. SIR CAVENDISH FOSTER, Bart., . . .	3	0	0

Allan, Mr.
Arthur, Mr. Nicholas.

BELLEW, RIGHT HON. LORD, Barmeath.
Backhouse, Mr.
Baillie, Robert, Esq.
Barton, James, Esq., C.E.
Bell, Mr.
——, Mr. H.
Bigger, J. J., Esq, J.P.
Black, Rev. Robert.
Boyd, Alexander, Esq.
Boylan, George, Esq.
Brabazon, Burton, Esq.
Brenan, M.
Browne, John, Esq., M.D.
———, Samuel, Esq., M.D., R.N.
———, William, Esq.
Brown, M.
Brunker, E. G., Esq., M.D.

CREMORNE, RIGHT HON. LORD.
Cahill, Mr. J.
Callan, J. M., Esq., M.D.
———, Mr. D.
Campbell, Mr. F.
Cartan, Joseph, Esq.
Carolan, Mr. N.
Caraher, John, Esq.
Carroll, The Misses.
———, Mr. P. J.
———, Mr. James.
Chesterton, Miss.
Clarke, Rev. John, P.P.
Coddington, J. J., Esq.
Coleman, Thomas, Esq.
————, Thomas K., Esq.
Collie, Mrs. (London).
Comyn, Michael, Esq.
Connick, Mr. J.
Coulter, Lancelot, Esq.
Crowe, Mrs.

Daley, Mr. James.
Denvir, C. M'H., Esq.
———, P., Mr.
Devlin, O., Mr.
Dickie, Joseph, Esq.
——— Robert, Esq.
Dowdall, Patrick, Esq.
Duncan, G., Esq.
Dunne, Rev. Dr., O.S.D.

Farquharson, Mr.
Farrell, T., Esq.,
Finegan, P., Mr.
FitzWygram, Col.
Fortescue, Col.
Foster, F., Esq., J.P.

Gartlan, John, Esq., M.D.
Giffney, Mr.
Gilmer, Mr. F.
————, Mr. James.
Graham, Andrew L., Esq.
————, Mr. J.
Gubbins, Miss.

Haggerty, Mr.
Haig, Robert, Esq, J.P.
——, John, Esq.
Hale, John, Esq.

Hamilton, Capt.
Harbour Board, Dundalk.
Hayes, Mr.
Henry, Mr. G.
Hesse, Mr.
Hughes, Mr. D.
———, Mr. T.

Jennings, Mr.
Johnston, Arthur, Esq.

Kearney, Rev. J., P.P.
——— M., M.D.
Kelly, Michael, Esq., J.P.
Kieran, Very Rev. Dean, P.P. (Dundalk).
Kirtland, Mr.
Kidd, W. F., Esq.
Knowles, John, Esq.

Lamb, Mr.
Lang, W., Esq.
Lawless, Mr. R.
Leary, William, Esq.
Lennon, Rev. M., P.P.
Lindesay, John, Esq.
Loyd, Mr.

Macalister, J., Esq.
———, Mr. J.
MacNeill, Sir John, M.R.I.A.
Marmion, Rev John, P.P.
M'Ardle, E. H., Esq., J.P.
M'Cann, Mr.
M'Clintock, John, Esq., D.L.
M'Coy, Mrs.
M'Crackin, N., Esq.
M'Cullagh, Mr. T.
M'Donald, Mr.
M'Dowell, Mr. T.
M'Guinness, Mr.
M'Keever, Capt.
M'Lean, Alexander, Esq.
M'Loughlin, Mr. J.
M'Mahon, Charles, Esq.
———, Mr. M.
———, Mr. Thomas.
M'Master, Mr.
M'Nally, Mr. W.
Meehan, Mr. J.
Miller, J., Esq.
Mouritz, Mr. S.
Moley, Mr.

Murphy, Mr. L.
———, James, Esq.
Murray, Mr.
Murtagh, Mr. J.

Neville, John, Esq., C.E., M.R.I.A.
Nugent, Mr. J. M.

O'Hagan, Mr.
O'Hare, Mr. J.
———, Mr. P.

Patterson, Mr. B.
———, Messrs.
Parks, Miss.
Percivall, Charles, Esq.
Pigot, David R., Esq., Chairman of Quarter Sessions for Co. Louth.
Pooler, Mr.
Porter, Capt., County Inspector
Price, Newton, Esq.

Reburn, Mr.
Rice, Mr.
Robson, William, Esq.
Rogers, W. R., Esq , sen.
———, W. R., Esq., jun.
Rush, Dr.
Russell, Patrick, Esq.
———, Messrs.
Ruxton, William, Esq., J.P.

Sandys, Mr.
Scott, F., Esq.
Shekleton, Alexander, Esq.
———, James, Esq.
Smyth, Mr.
———, Mr. C.
Stokes, Mr.
Stubbs, Rev. J. H.
Studdert, Rev. George.
Supple, E. K., Esq., S.I.

Tarleton, Thomas, Esq.
Tempest, Mr.
Townley, John, Esq., J.P.
Townsend, Rev. Dr.
Turner, John, Esq.

Verdon, Mr. R.

Watters, Mr.
Williamson, Mr.
Woods, Mr. Robert.
Wynne, P., Esq., J.P.

GENERAL SUBSCRIBERS' NAMES.

His Excellency the Earl of Carlisle, K.G., Lord Lieutenant of Ireland.

Academy, Royal Irish, Very Rev. Dean Graves, President.
Allen, W., Esq., Divisional Magistrate, Dublin.
Attorney-General, Right Hon. T. O'Hagan, M.P.

Ball, Right Hon. Judge, Dublin.
Barry, James, Esq., D.L., Ballyclough, Co. Cork.
——, John, Esq., Fermoy
Beardwood, Rev. H., St. Michan's, Dublin.
Blackburne, Rt. Hon. F., M.R.I.A., Lord Justice of Appeal, Dublin.
Briscoe, F. H., Esq., Dublin.
Browne, Right Rev. Dr., R.C. Bishop of Kilmore, Cavan.
——, S., Esq., LL.D., Bandon.
Burke, Sir Bernard, M.R.I.A., Ulster King-of-Arms, Dublin Castle (two copies).

Campbell, Alderman, J.P., Mountjoy-square, Dublin.
Caraher, Edward, Esq., 76, Talbot-street, Dublin.
Carroll, R., Esq., J.P., Fermoy.
Christian, Hon. Judge, Merrion-square, Dublin.
Compton, Francis, Esq., Cavendish-row, Dublin.
Connell, Francis J., Esq., J.P., Betteville, Wexford.
Cooke, James, Esq., Dublin.
Coppinger, Francis, Esq., Monkstown Castle, Co. Dublin.
Corballis, J. R., Esq., Q.C., Rosemount, Roebuck.
Corrigan, Dominick J., Esq., M.D., President College of Physicians, Dublin.

D'Arcy, M. S., Esq., M.R.I.A., Raheny.
Darley, Rev. J. R., Cootehill.
Deasy, Rt. Hon. Baron, M.R.I.A.
Denvir, Rt. Rev. Dr., R.C. Bishop of Down and Connor, Belfast.
Devonshire, His Grace the Duke of.
Dix, Edward Spenser, Esq., Dublin.
Donnelly, Thomas, Esq., Dublin.
Downing, J., Esq., Ashfield, Fermoy.
——, Denis P., Esq., Dublin.
Dowse, Richard, Esq., Q.C., Dublin.
Doyle, Hugh, Esq., Dalkey.
Dublin, Rt. Hon. P. P. M'Swiney, Lord Mayor of.

Falvey, Rev. J., P.P., Glanmire.
Ferguson, Samuel, Esq., Q.C., M.R.I.A., Dublin.
Fingall, Right Hon. Earl of, Killeen Castle.
Fitzgerald, Right Hon. Judge.
——, Hon. Baron (two copies).
——, Thomas, Esq., J.P.
——, Percy, Esq., M.R.I.A.
Fitzgibbon, Gerald, Esq., M.R.I.A., Master in Chancery.
Fitzpatrick, P. V., Esq., Dublin.
Flanagan, S. W., Esq., Q.C., Dublin.
Foster, Sir George, Bart., M.P., Coolderry.
Fyffe, John, Esq., Mountjoy-square, Dublin.

Gernon, William, Esq., Dublin.
Gibson, Rev. C. B., M.R.I.A., Monkstown, Cork.
——, James, Esq., M.R.I.A., Mountjoy-square, Dublin.
Gosford, Right Hon. the Earl of, Gosford Castle.
Guinness, Benj. Lee, Esq., M.R.I.A. (two copies).

Hancock, W. N., Esq., M.R.I.A.
Harkan, John, Esq., Dublin.
Hayman, Rev. S., Rector, Ardnageehy.
Headley, Rt. Hon. Lord, Aghadoe House, Killarney.
Henn, Jonathan, Esq., Q.C.
——, T. Rice, Esq., Q.C.
Heron, D. C., Esq., Q.C.
Howard, Philip H., Esq., Corby Castle, Carlisle.
Hughes, Hon. Baron.

Inchiquin, Rt. Hon. Lord, Dromoland, Co. Clare.

Kavanagh, W. J., Esq., Professor, Catholic University, Stephen's-green.
Keane, Rt. Rev. Dr., R.C. Bishop of Cloyne, Queenstown (two copies).
Kelly, Right Rev. Francis, D.D,, Coadjutor R.C. Bishop of Derry.
Kennedy, Tristram, Esq., Dublin.
Keogh, Right Hon. Judge.
Kildare, The Most Noble the Marquess of, M.R.I.A.
Kilkenny Archæological Society.

Larcom, Major-General Sir Thomas A., M.R.I.A., Under-Secretary of State, Dublin Castle.
Lawson, J. A., M.R.I.A., Solicitor-General.
Leahy, His Grace the Most Rev. Dr., R.C. Archbishop of Cashel, Thurles.
———, Right Rev. John P., D.D., R.C. Bishop of Dromore, Newry.
———, John, Esq., Chairman West Riding, Co. Cork.
Lefroy, Right Hon. Lord Chief Justice.
Leinster, His Grace the Duke of, M.R.I.A.
Lentaigne, J., Esq., D.L., M.R.I.A., Dublin.
Library, Hon. Society King's Inns.
Litton, Edward, Esq., Master in Chancery.

Madden, R. R., Esq., M.R.I.A.
Marley, Charles B., Esq., High Sheriff, Co. Louth.
Maxwell, Patrick, Esq., Dublin.
M'Clintock, Sir Leopold, Capt., R.N.
———, Alfred H., Esq., M.D., Dublin.
MacDonnell, Rev. Richard, D.D., M.R.I.A., Provost, Trinity College, Dublin.
M'Gettigan, Right Rev. Dr., R.C. Bishop of Raphoe, Letterkenny.
Morphy, Alex., Esq., Killarney.

Nagle, James, Esq., Clerk of the Crown, Dublin.
Napier, Right Hon. J., M.R.I.A.
Nelson, Wellington, Esq.
Neilson, James H., Esq., Dublin.

O'Driscoll, William Justin, Esq., M. R. I. A., Mountjoy-square, Dublin (two copies).
O'Hanlon, Rev. John, Dublin.
O'Reilly, Major Myles, M.P.

Palles, A. C., Esq., Dublin.
Peart, J. H., Esq., J.P. (two copies).
Pyne, Mrs., Belgrave-square, Monkstown.

Robinson, Sir John, Bart., Rokeby.
Russell, Rev. Charles W., D.D., President, Maynooth College.
———, Very Rev. Bartholomew T., D.D., O.P., President, Esker College.
Ryan, Thomas, Esq., Dublin.

Shaw, Right Hon. F., Recorder of Dublin.
Shirley, Evelyn P., Esq., M.P., Warwickshire.

Talbot de Malahide, Right Hon. Lord, M.R.I.A., Malahide Castle.
Thom, Alexander, Esq., Dublin.

Wilde, W. R., Esq., M.R.I.A., Dublin.
Windele, John, Esq., Blair Castle, Cork.
Woodhouse, J. O., Esq., J.P., Newry.
Woodlock, Very Rev. Monsignore, D.D., Rector, Catholic University.
Woodrooffe, C. H., Esq., Dublin.
————, William, Esq., Dublin.

THE AUTHORS' ADDRESS.

A WORD TO THE SELECT SECTION OF THE PUBLIC, WHOM WE HAIL AS THE READERS OF OUR "DUNDALK."

WHEN a new production has been brought out before a respectable audience, and the green curtain has dropped upon its performance, it is ever permitted to the Author, or Authors, as the division of labour may have necessitated an increase of their staff, to appear at the foot-lights, with a hope of eliciting from kind auditors that portion of applause which is, at all times, cheerfully conceded by Irishmen to an Irish undertaking. In the present compilation two have been engaged—the one a veteran, "myself at home," popularly known as "*Old Mortality*," now literally worn off his legs by historic travels; the other, a fresh junior, who, although not so deeply dyed by intercourse with antiquarian lore, has been for some time back studying the language of his country, in which his partner is lamentably deficient; while his agreeable style as an author has been evinced on the pages of some of our best periodicals, and more especially in his very graphic *History of the Blackwater in Munster*. But, as he must speak for himself, I shall say no more here in reference to him. However, lest posterity might be puzzled to ascertain the extent of our respective shares in the labour, or that any unfair elevation of the one might be effected by stealing a feather from the other's wing, I do hereby, on my own behalf, confess, premise, declare, and solemnly enunciate, that all the antique portions of the History, from its commencement—which, if I remember rightly, was at an early day after the subsiding of the Flood, to the time of the Virgin Queen—has been perpetrated by myself alone; and for whatever faults may be found therein I own the soft impeachment—*In me convertite ferrum;* while it is but justice to my junior to admit that, as the proof-sheets passed before me, the original rough materials, which my manuscripts supplied, appeared to have been rounded and smoothed off by him—I would almost say to a polish. His own task has been a far more difficult one, in a country so religiously and politically divided as is Ireland. To gather in unadulterated *facts*—a rare commodity here; to select traditional lore where trustworthy, and register it on these pages; to photograph such relics of other days as yet remain within or in the vicinity of our locality; to exhibit the respective statistics, the trade, the manufactures, railways, schools, charitable institutions, religious establishments of Dundalk, has been his task. It has also occurred to him that an opportunity was here opened for preserving the fame of those eminent men who, from time to time, flourished in Dundalk, or have been connected with it; and withal, while neither sacrificing truth nor pampering patronage, to clothe the several details "thereunto belonging" in such a dress, neither orange nor green, as could not justly offend the impartial supporters of this work, which I feel proud to think shall take its place in an Irish library, beside the only other illustration that I have been encouraged to publish for Louth—my DROGHEDA.

And here, before I make my farewell bow, I cannot retire without alluding to the many manuscript collections which, during my long life, it has been my secret patriotism to compile, for illustrating every part of my country alike. They extend over 200 octavo volumes, and are arranged and classified on the preliminary pages of my *Annals of Boyle*. In the limited space which I here take leave to occupy I shall only appeal for those volumes that are illustrative of the Histories of Antrim, Louth, Meath, Tipperary, Waterford, Wicklow, the Course of the Shannon, &c., &c. These, if placed in proper hands, to complete from the materials which I have accumulated, must, especially if accompanied with plates, interest many who are yet strangers to the historic and intellectual associations of our lovely scenery.

That they may not be long so is the prayer of

Yours, faithfully,

JOHN D'ALTON.

My Lords and Gentlemen,—My veteran colleague has so kindly referred to my labours in this work that I shall not weaken his language by any addition of my own. It would, however, be most ungrateful in me if I did not thus publicly convey to him my grateful acknowledgements for the valuable aid his experience afforded me while the work was passing through the press. I must also acknowledge the encouragement I received from you, my Lords and Gentlemen, and particularly the extensive local information carefully procured for me in Dundalk by my zealous friends, Dr. Browne, Mr. Neville, and Mr. P. J. Byrne, who, from first to last, were untiring in their exertions to assist me in the completion of this book. I also beg to acknowledge the zeal and efficiency of the Printer and his intelligent Staff.

With sincere gratitude,

Believe me, faithfully yours,

J. RODERICK O'FLANAGAN, M.R.I.A.

7, Russell-place, Mountjoy-square,
Dublin.

CONTENTS.

GENERAL AND CORPORATE HISTORY.

GENERAL AND CORPORATE
HISTORY OF DUNDALK.

CHAPTER I.

FROM THE EARLY AGES TO THE TIME OF ST. PATRICK.

THE traditions of the early annalists of our country, as adopted by the Four Masters, and confirmed by Nennius, the British historian, relate that in the year of the world 2859, before pestilence destroyed the adventurers whom Nemedius had led to invade Ireland, the forests were cut down which covered the tract of country whose vicissitudes it is the object of this history to record, and which was thereupon denominated Magh-Muirthemne—*i. e.*, the Plain of the Sea. According to custom a fortress was erected upon the clearance; and, in the credence which, in the seventeenth century, those pious historians conceded to the vast mass of native manuscripts then before them, but which, like the chivalry and spirit of the nation, perished soon after in desolating civil wars, it may be admissible to identify the earthwork of Nemedius with the remarkable fort which yet stands at the place now known as Castletown. This mound lies about a mile from Dundalk, in a position that eminently fitted it for overlooking and commanding the bay and the surrounding country, to the mountains of Carlingford. Examination of the work shows it to have been throughout artificial, and surrounded with a formidable ditch.* The height of the terrace work from the plane of the trench is in some places fifty feet, and the circumference of the top is upwards of 560. At its east and west sides are two other forts or redoubts, adjoining to the outward vallum of the ditch, which are again themselves surrounded by a ditch; and these together with the main mount cover a considerable surface; indeed the whole summit of the hill, and seen for several miles to the north and south, present a very formidable appearance.†

The Four Masters, at this period of their Annals, record the erection of many other forts or raths by the same colonists throughout Ireland, as well as the cutting down of forests and the opening of (tochars) roads through the various spaces so prepared for occupation.

Soon after the more successful invasion of Milesius, which occurred, according to the chronology of the same historians, in A.M. 3500, his followers encountered the natives in battle at Slieve Mis, and in the progress of subsequent engagements the fall of Cuailgne, one of the Milesian leaders, gave his

---

* On the summit of one of the highest of the Malvern ridge of hills is a noble and commanding rath, termed "the Herefordshire Beacon," to which this of Castletown is considered closely to assimilate. It is thus described:—"In area an irregular oblong, 175 feet in its longest diameter, and 110 in its shortest, surrounded by a high steep vallum, or bank of stones, and earth, now covered with turf, and by a very deep ditch on the outside. A large but lower outwork grows from it, like a bastion at one end, as does a second at another end, each being surrounded by a high bank and ditch. That great work of ancient times, like this of Castletown, commanded the pass of the country around it for centuries after its erection."—*King's Munimenta Antiqua*, vol. vi., p. 20.

† *Wright's Louthiana*, part i.

name to the mountains of Cooley, between this town and Carlingford, a district which it will be seen was afterwards more strikingly associated with bardic history.

At this time, also, the erection of raths or forts by Heremon, and his younger brother, Amergin, are recorded. Tradition says these earth-works, as seems obvious, were all crowned with buildings, and that the very fosses were arched over in covered ways; but there seems no doubt that all such structures must have been of wood or wicker-work, possibly covered with the ready heath or fern. Those spoken of in the *Leges Wallicæ*, as erected for the use of the Welch kings, suggest the adoption of these materials. They comprised halls, refectories, kitchens and dormitories, with out houses for stabling horses and dogs, workshops, granaries, and forges; and fines for injuries thereto, "by hewing or burning," were rated according to the number of pillars and beams that contributed to sustain the particular edifice.*

The most remarkable of the royal raths of Ireland was that of Eamania, erected within this province by Cimbaeth, the fifty-sixth monarch in the succession of the Milesian dynasty, in A.M. 4484 (according to the chronology of the Four Masters); from which period it continued to be the seat of the Ulster kings, down to the time of its destruction, in the beginning of the fourth century.

The annotators of Geraghty's *Annals of the Four Masters* calculate that there are upwards of 30,000 raths yet existing over Ireland, although many more have been levelled for the uses of agriculture, notwithstanding the popular superstition which long protected them.

---

* *Leges Wallicæ*, pp. 167, 263, &c.

There is no direct evidence extant of agricultural pursuits during this pagan era of Ireland, at least so far as any system of tillage or farm cultivation. The habits of the people were like those of other countries at the day—pastoral and patriarchal. Forests, lakes, and rivers afforded abundance for the hunter and the fisherman, while a partial domestication of herds of oxen, sheep, and pigs, is indicated in the payments of animal currency as tributes to the kings and chiefs, for ransoms of prisoners, fines of malefactors, and such traffic as was then practised—while the mention of mills and the frequent discoveries of rude querns must suggest some agricultural manufactures at this pagan era. The years which immediately preceded the birth of Christ are spoken of as influenced, in the language of the annalists, by that coming event,—"the sea gave up abundance of fish; the woods were pressed down by the weight of their fruits; the nuts overhanging the rivers impeded their current; the herds of cattle wandered safe without the necessity of a shepherd, by reason of the prevalence of peace and order, and no rough wind affected the herds."

In the second year of what may be here termed the Christian era—although Christianity had not been revealed to Ireland for many years after—died the hero of bardic commemoration —Cuchullin, "chief of Erin's wars." Tigernach, the most candid and learned historian of Northern Europe, and who himself died in 1018 (four years after the memorable Battle of Clontarf), records the death of this warrior. He calls him "fortissimus heros Scotorum," and mentions that he had been knighted (as was the early native custom), at the age of seven; that he was engaged in that fierce foray which alone disturbed the halcyon times of Conary the Great, and which is popularly entitled the "Tain-bo-Cuailgne"—"the spoiling of the cattle at Cuailgne;"* and lastly, that he was slain in the above year, being the twenty-seventh of his age. Long tradition, religiously preserved, suggests that the Nemedian fort, before alluded to, then called *Dun-Dalgan*, was the palace of Cuchullin. Here he lived, surrounded by those Knights of the Red Branch whose achievements, in the seven years of feudal hostilities through which the Tain-bo-Cuailgne extended, are the subject of a native poem of considerable length, and yet extant,† recently translated by the lamented Eugene O'Curry.

The Danish historians record invasions of Ulster at this time by their sea-kings, which afforded Cuchullin a more natural and meritorious mode of evincing his courage and patriotism, and which MacPherson has gladly adopted in his *Ossian's Poems*, as more suited to the poetical machinery of that interesting imposition:—"Swaran wasted Erin . . . He advanced as a stream that burst from the desert; the hills are rolled in its course, and the rocks have sunk by its side, but Cuchullin stood before him like a hill that catches the clouds of heaven. The winds contend on its head of pines, and the hail rattles on its rocks, but firm in its strength it stands and shades the silent vale of Cona."‡

Were the narrative of the Scottish editor of these poems to be relied on as trustworthy, the country around Castletown would have been associated with the military appearance of this hero of the North. "The car of war comes on like the

---

* A locality which Dr. O'Donovan identifies with Slieve Cooley, between this town and Carlingford.

† See *D'Alton's History of Drogheda*, vol ii., p. 12, and *Professor O'Curry's Lectures*, p. 14.

‡ *Fingal*, book ii.

flame of death—the rapid car of Cuchullin. It bends behind like a wave near a rock, like the sun-streaked mist of the heath. Its sides are embossed with stones, and sparkle like the sea round the boat of night. Of polished yew is its beam, its seat is of the smoothest bone; the sides are replenished with spears; the bottom is the footstool of heroes. Before the right side of the car is seen the snorting horse, the high-maned, broad-breasted, proud, wide-leaping, strong steed of the hill. Loud and resounding is his hoof; the spreading of his mane above is like a stream of smoke on a ridge of rocks. Bright are the sides of the steed; his name is Suleen-Sifadda. Before the left side of the car is seen the snorting horse, the thin-maned, high-headed, strong-hoofed, fleet-bounding son of the hill. His name is Duo-ronnal among the stormy sons of the sword. Hard polished bits shine in a wreath of foam; thin thongs, bright studded with gems, bend on the stately necks of the steeds, that like wreaths of mist fly over the streamy vales; the wildness of deer is in their course, the strength of eagles descending on their prey. Their noise is like the blast of winter in the sides of the snow-headed Gormal. Within the car is seen the chief, the strong-armed son of the sword; the hero's name is Cuchullin."*

Apochryphal as the description of this chariot of the ruler of "Dundalgan" may appear, it must not be denied that the arts had, even previous to his time, made no inconsiderable progress in our island. The Four Masters record, from far more ancient chronicles, the manufacture of corslets and bracelets, in A.M. 3656; the classifying of dresses and robes, by colours, with sumptuary regulations, in A.M. 3664; the working of collars and necklaces of gold, in A.M. 3872; and,

---

* *Fingal*, book i.

yet more to the illustration of the present inquiry, the introduction of chariots for four horses into Ireland, upwards of ten centuries previous to the era of Cuchullin: while in the ninth year of the Christian era, being seven years after the death of this warrior, the same annalists, narrating the memorable expedition of Crimthain, King of Ireland, into Britain, give a note of the precious spoils he brought home, and amongst them a valuable car, ornamented with gold; arms, adorned with gold, and inlaid with gems; cloaks and housings of wool, with fringes of gold; a war sword, with figures of serpents laid in gold upon it; a shield, with silver bosses; a lance, a sling, and two hunting dogs, with a silver chain worth 300 heifers; and many other precious articles. All *these* articles, however, it must be admitted, were imports. But at a later period, the chariot of St. Patrick, and those of other saints, are made mention of, and this not as novelties. Numerous ornaments, crowns, bracelets, gorgets, clasps, and vessels for civil and religious uses, which could not have been manufactured without great insight into the art of smelting, refining, and working metals, have been discovered throughout the country, and are abundantly displayed in the Museum of the Royal Irish Academy.

Dun-dalgan gave its name to the town, which, as will be seen, grew up along the shore, and a portion is still described as Ballynatraga—*i.e.*, the town on the strand, or Seatown. The appellation Dundalgan, corrupted to Dundalk, was extended over that vicinage now known as the Baronies of Upper and Lower Dundalk; but previously the former was denominated Hy Mac Uais, and ruled by the MacScanlons, the latter as Fera-lerg, or Lurgan,* the whole country being

---

* *Gough's Camden.*

still chronicled as Magh-Muirthemne, or sometimes Conall-Muirthemne, from Conall Carnach, chief of the Red Branch Knights of Ulster; and the Four Masters record, at A.D. 248, a battle fought at Faughart, as within Muirthemne, by Cormac Ulfada, that illustrious King of Ireland, who, although he could not be said to have believed in Christ, yet professed during his life such utter abhorrence of the pagan rites of the day as greatly facilitated the subsequent reception of St. Patrick.* His son-in-law, Finn-Mac-Coul, was, according to bardic legends, the dynast of Dundalk at the close of this century, or the commencement of the fourth, and is the person whom, under the more euphonious appellation of Fingal, MacPherson, regardless of chronology, makes the contemporary of Cuchullin. "Fingal, thou man of battles, early were thy deeds in arms; Lochlin was consumed in thy wrath; when thy youth strove with the beauties of maids, they smiled at the fair blooming face of the hero, but death was in his hand. He was strong as the waters of Lorra; his followers were like the roar of a thousand streams. They took the King of Lochlin in battle, but restored him to his ships. His big heart swelled with pride, and the death of the youth was dark in his soul, for none ever but Fingal overcame the strength of the mighty Storno."

Thus far, perhaps, may be pardoned quotations from this poetic production, as illustrative of characters undoubtedly connected with Dundalk. Whitaker actually relied upon MacPherson's *Ossian* as historical authority; and certainly it should be a source of great satisfaction to Irishmen and Scotchmen if, on such an inference, Whitaker's judgment were sound,

---

* See *D'Alton's History of Drogheda*, vol. ii., p. 13, &c.

and MacPherson's veracity unimpeachable. The poems of the latter are certainly a beautiful mirage—at first too much extolled, and now, by an equality of reaction, too much neglected.

CHAPTER II.

FROM THE TIME OF ST. PATRICK TO THE INVASION OF STRONGBOW.

WHEN early in the fifth century, and before his apostolic mission, St. Patrick was carried captive from Armoric Britanny to Ireland,* according to one of the early biographers of the apostle, as published by Colgan, Lupita, his sister, was the sharer of his destiny. She was sold on this shore of Connal-Muirthemne, while her brother was carried northward to Dalaradia, where, in the service of Milca, his employment was the care of pigs through the trees and forests that surrounded Slieve-Mis. In fifteen years after his subsequent triumphant arrival as bishop from Rome to Ireland, St. Brigid, the future Patroness of Leinster, and foundress of female religious communities in the land, was born at Faughart, near this town.

At the Kalends of May, A.D. 664, according to the Annals of Tigernach, an eclipse occurred, which was succeeded, in the summer, by appearances as if the firmament were on fire; and, in the Kalends of August, of the same year, a great mortality fell upon Ireland. This pestilence had previously ravaged England, from whence, passing over, it made its first appearance on the plain of May Ith of Faughard.

---

* See *D'Alton's Annals of Boyle*, vol. ii., p. 60, &c.

The Four Masters record, at the year 686, a battle was fought at Imle-phich, between Neal, son of Carnach, and Conall, son of Conory, in which the former was victorious, and Ureraidhe O *Osene*, chief of Connal Muirthemne, was slain. In nine years after they relate that Magh-Muirthemne was devastated by the "Britons,"* and the people of Ulster. This hostile incursion furnished materials for an Irish romantic tale, copies of which are said to be yet extant.

In 732 another battle was fought at Faughart, in Connal Muirthemne, by Hugh Allain, then King of Ireland, aided by the sept of the Northern Nials, against the people of Ulidia, whose ruler, say the "Masters," was beheaded at the gate of the church at Faughart, on the stone of decapitation.† Many other victims of that day's field are mentioned by the annalists, who attribute the contest to the desecration of a church by the vanquished Ulidian ruler.‡

In 751, say the Four Masters, an army of the men of Leinster, was led up by Donald MacMurrough, joined by the sept of the Nials, into Magh-Muirthemne, but the historians do not suggest the object or the result of the expedition.

So early as the year 833, a Danish incursion was made upon this coast, in which, as Ledwich§ gives the tradition, Mac-Scanlan, a remarkable chieftain of this vicinage, was engaged. About thirty yards from the rath of Bally-mac-Scanlan, is the entrance into a cave which runs under it, and the work is

---

* The appellation of Scots was not then yet popularly attributed to the Irish colony of North Britain.

† The scene of this avenging death is still distinguishable, and the stone is still pointed out at the door of the Church of Faughart.—O'Donovan's *Four Masters*, note at p. 330, vol. i.

‡ *Colgan's Trias Thaumaturga.*

§ *Antiq.*, p. 47.

regarded as MacScanlan's tomb; while at a short distance from it is a cromlech called "the Giant's load," presenting a stone of enormous size, and incumbent on three supports. Near it is seen an erection of stones, curiously bounding a space thirty feet long by five broad, and covered at the head by a large oblong stone, incumbent on others. It is called the Giant's Grave, and might well suit the carrier of the cromlech.

In 877, during the existence of a war of reprisals between some Irish and the natives of Galloway, Gregory, King of Scotland, as Buchanan relates, in order to reimburse his subjects for injuries alleged to have been done to them, passed with an army into Ireland, took Dundalk and Drogheda, and afterwards laid siege to Dublin. Holinshed, adopting the Scottish legend, says:—"that King Gregory, pretending a title to Ireland, as belonging to him by right of lawful succession, made this journey thither, and within a small time made a conquest of the country. This Gregory (he adds) lies buried in one of the out isles, called Iona, or Columbkill, where they speak, naturally, Irish, and therefore some of the Scots would seem to make the conquest of Henry the Second in Ireland a revolting from the right inheritors."

A record in the Four Masters of the death of Gibhlecan, son of Maolbrigidian, tanist of Connal Muirthemne in the year 886, is succeeded by notices that indicate sanguinary hostilities between the natives of that territory and those of Meath. In 887 Maolmordh, son of Garbeth, tanist of Connal Muirthemne, was beheaded by Ceallach, the son of Flanagan. In 904 Amalgaid, son of Connal, tanist of Bregia, and Flan, his brother, were slain by the people of Conal-Muirthemne. In four years afterwards Murdoch, abbot of Drominisclan, and Garbeth, son of Maolmordth, tanist of Conal-Muirthemne, were slain in the refectory of Drominisclan by Conal, the son of Garbeth. This Murdoch is commemorated by the annalists as "the great denouncer of homicides, a light to the heaven of saints, a shining beacon of harmony." His death was immediately after avenged by the people of Muirthemne, who slew Conal his murderer. In 910, say the annalists, Nial, King of Alichia, led an army into Meath, and having reached Grellach Elte, he proceeded to make spoil over the country, until O'Melaghlin raised a force to oppose him; and a skirmish ensuing, Donald and the son of the before-mentioned Garbeth, and who was then himself ruler of Conal-Muirthemne, was slain.

In 939 was made the memorable political visitation of all parts of Ireland by Murtough, son of that Nial who had been monarch of Ireland some years previously, but was succeeded in his authority by Donough, son of Flan Sionna. In this military movement by Murtough, he gathered to his cause, after plundering the Ebudes, the septs of Conal and Eogan, and all the warriors of the North, and, at the head of 1200 chosen heroes, marched to Alichia, and thence with a hostile army to Dublin, where he seized Sitric, the Danish Prince of that city, and carried him off as a hostage. He afterwards desolated Leinster and Munster, taking prisoner Callaghan, ruler of that province. Conor, son of Thady, King of Connaught, came to the encampment of Murtough, who took no hostages or prisoners from him. He then returned to Alichia with his troops, hostages, and prisoners, and there sojourned nine months in feasting and triumph, after which he honourably transmitted the hostages he had gained to Donough, the reigning king.*

---

* *Annals of the Four Masters.* This circuit was the subject of an Irish poem, recently published in the *Tracts of the Irish Archæological Society.*

The Danes of Ireland, at this period, were ruled by Sitric, son of Turgesius, whose name was sufficient to inspire the Irish with terror. Through policy he professed willingness to enter into a treaty of peace with Callaghan, King of Munster; and, as proof of his sincerity, offered him his sister, the Princess Royal of Denmark, in marriage. The Irish King had fallen in love with this amiable and beautiful princess, and he readily consented to the fair and liberal measures proposed. He sent word to Sitric he would visit him; and, attended by a royal retinue, to be followed in a little time by his guards, as escort for his future queen, proceeded to meet his royal bride.

Sitric's project of inveigling the King of Munster into his district, in order to make him prisoner, under the expectation of being married to the Princess of Denmark, having been disclosed to his wife, who was of Irish birth, she determined to warn the intended victim of the meditated treachery, and accordingly she disguised herself, and placed herself in a pass which Callaghan should traverse, and met him. Here she informed him who she was, the design of Sitric against him, and warned him to return as fast as possible. This was not practicable. Sitric had barred the way with armed men; and Callaghan and his escort, little prepared for an encounter, found themselves hemmed in by an overwhelming Danish force. To submit without a struggle was never the way with the Momonians. They formed a rampart round the person of their King, and cut through the Danish ranks. Fresh foes met them on every side; and, after a bloody struggle, the men of Munster were conquered. Callaghan the King, and Prince Duncan, son of Kennedy, were brought captives to Dublin. Then the royal prisoners were removed to Armagh, and their safe keeping entrusted to nine Danish earls, who had a strong military force at their orders to guard them.

The news of this insidious act rapidly fanned the ardour of the Munster troops to be revenged for the imprisonment of their beloved King. Kennedy, the Prince of Munster, father of Duncan, was appointed regent, with ample powers to govern the country in the King's absence. The first step was to collect an army to cope with the Danes. To assemble a sufficient body of troops on land was easy; but the great strength of the northern rovers lay in their swift-sailing ships. "It must strike the humblest comprehension with astonishment," says Marmion,* "that the Irish, although possessed of an island abounding with forests of the finest oak, and other suitable material for ship-building—enjoying also the most splendid rivers, loughs, and harbours, so admirably adapted to the accommodation of extensive fleets, should, notwithstanding, for so many centuries, allow the piratical ravages of the Danes, and subsequently the more dangerous subversion of their independence by the Anglo-Normans, without an effort to build a navy that could cope with those invaders on that element from which they could alone expect invasion from a foreign foe." This neglect has also been noticed by the distinguished Irish writer—Wilde—who, in his admirably executed *Catalogue of the Antiquities in the Royal Irish Academy*,† observes:—"Little attention has been paid to the subject of the early naval architecture of this country. So far as we yet know, two kinds of boats appear to have been in use in very early times in the British Isles—the canoe and the corragh; the one formed of a single piece of wood, the other composed of wicker-work, covered with hides." Larger

---

* *Maritime Ports of Ireland*, p. 272, a most valuable and instructive work.

† Part i., p. 202.

vessels there must have been; though, from the length of time which has since elapsed, we have no traces of them now. Kennedy not only collected a formidable army by land, but "he fitted out a fleet of ships, and manned it with able seamen, that he might make sure of his revenge, and attack the enemy by sea and land."* The command of the fleet was conferred on an admiral perfectly skilled in maritime affairs, Failbhe Fion, King of Desmond.†

When the army of Munster arrived near Armagh, they learnt the prisoners had been removed thence by Sitric, and placed on board ship. Enraged at this disappointment, they gave no quarter to the Danes, and advanced rapidly to Dundalk, where the fleet lay, with the King and young Prince on board. Sitric, unable to withstand the opposing army on shore, ordered his troops to embark, and resolved to avoid the encounter through means of his ships. While the baffled Irish army were chafing at this unexpected delay to their hoped for vengeance, they espied, from the shore of Dundalk, where they encamped, a sail of ships, in regular order, steering with a favourable gale towards the Danish fleet moored in Dundalk bay. Joy instantly filled their hearts; for they recognised the fleet of Munster, with the admiral's vessel in the van, and the rest ranged in line of battle. The Danes were taken by surprise; they beheld an enemy approach from a side where they rather expected the raven flag of their country floating on the ships. The Munster admiral gave them no time to form. He steered straight to Sitric's vessel, and, with his hardy crew, sprang on board. Here a sight met his gaze which filled his heart with rage—he saw his beloved Monarch, Callaghan, and the young prince, tied with cords to

* *Keating's History of Ireland*, vol. ii., p. 232. † *Id.*, p. 233.

the main-mast. Having, with his men, fought through the Danish troops to the side of the King and Prince, he cut the cords and set them free. He then put a sword into the hands of the rescued king, and they fought side by side. Meanwhile Sitric, and his brothers, Tor and Magnus, did all they could to retrieve the fortunes of the day. At the head of a chosen band they attacked the Irish admiral, and he fell, covered with wounds. His head, exposed by Sitric on a pole, fired the Danes with hope—the Irish with ten-fold rage. Fingal, next in rank to Failbhe Fion, took the command, and determined to avenge his admiral. Meeting the Danish ruler in the combat, he seized Sitric round the neck, and flung himself with his foe, into the sea, where both perished. Seagdor and Connall, two captains of Irish ships, imitated this example—threw themselves upon Tor and Magnus, Sitric's brothers, and jumped with them overboard, when all were drowned. These desperate deeds paralysed the energy of the Danes, and the Irish gained a complete victory in Dundalk bay.

The Irish fleet having thus expelled the pirates from their coast, came into harbour, where they were received with acclamations of joy by all who witnessed their bravery. Such is a summary of Keating's poetic account of this day's achievements; and there are extant fuller accounts in various pieces of native poetry, especially one entitled "The Pursuit after Callaghan, of Cashel, by the Chief of Munster, after he had been entrapped by the Danes."

In 1029, Donogh O'Donovan, Lord of Farney, and Cinaedh-mac-Angeree, Lord of *Conaille*, fell by each other's hands on Killslieve (now Killevy, County Armagh).

In 1032 another Sitric, son of Anlaff, and who, it would appear, was grandson of the former, obtained a victory, at the river Boyne, over the inhabitants of this vicinity, in which three hundred were slain or taken prisoners; while, in more strict connexion with Dundalk, the Four Masters relate, that in 1104, Murtagh O'Brien led an army to Magh Muirthemne, and destroyed the *crops* of the country; at which time also Cuolad O'Condelan, ruler of "Traighbaile" (Dundalk), was thrown from his horse, and died within a month.

In 1101, Donagh O'Melaghlen, Lord of Meath, made predatory incursion into Farney and Conaille, and carried away a great spoil of cows. They were met, however, by Cu-cashel O'Carroll, Lord of Farney and Oriel, at Arget-Glynn, (Moneyglen, in the Barony of Farney), where he killed a great many, and amongst them Eichtegen O'Brian, Lord of Breaghmaine (Brawney, County Westmeath); and the son of Cairthen O'Maolruan and O'Henrichtair, chief of O'Melaghlen's household, and two hundred besides.

Tiernan O'Rourke, and the men of Brefney (County Leitrim), made a predatory excursion into Cuailgne, and plundered Hy-Meth. They were met on their return by the Ulidians, and the men of South Oriel, who were then returning from a similar expedition into Connaught. After the latter had passed Athlone, at Magh Conaille a battle ensued between them, in which Randal O'Heochadha, King of Ulidia, Cumidhe O'Criochan, Lord of Farney, and his son, and Dunslave O'Henrachty, Lord of Hy-Meth, with many others, were killed.

On the death of Turlough O'Conor, in 1156, the supreme sovereignty of Ireland was disputed by Murtough, son of O'Niall O'Loughlin, to the expulsion of Roderic, the son of Turlough; and the latter having, with the forces of Connaught, and the co-operation of those of Thomond, under O'Brien, advanced to Ardee, with the avowed object of despoiling Louth, Murtough led out his forces, and the allied clans of Conal-Eogan, and others of the North of Ireland, to oppose the invaders. A battle ensued at Ardee, in which they were beaten with great slaughter. The Chief of Moylurg (M'Dermott), O'Monnachan, Prince of the O'Briens, O'Fallon, of Clan-Uadach,* and various other leaders of that party fell; while the victor, following up his success, led his forces against Connaught and Thomond, committing great desolation over each.

CHAPTER III.

FROM THE INVASION OF STRONGBOW TO THE REIGN OF RICHARD I.

The while in a distant county of England a Norman family was springing into power and fame, that was destined soon materially to influence the future fortunes of Dundalk. Of that illustrious race, Bertram de Verdon having been settled by the Conqueror in Leicestershire, was succeeded by his son, Norman de Verdon, who, intermarrying with the daughter of Geoffrey de Clinton, the founder of Kenilworth Castle, had issue by her Bertram de Verdon, junior, who was sheriff of Warwick and Leicester-shires from 1170 to 1184, during the most of which time he resided at Alton Castle,† in Staffordshire, whose massive walls and commanding situation still invite attention.

---

* The O'Fallons are recognised by this territorial designation from the ninth century.

† Alton Towers, with the lordship of Alton, passed by marriage to the Talbot family; Joan, daughter of Theobald de Verdon, the lineal descen-

During the time of this Bertram de Verdon occurred the invasion of Ireland by the Earl of Pembroke, popularly styled Strongbow, and the subsequent entry of King Henry the Second into the island. The latter, soon after his arrival, granted the country of Ulster to the celebrated chieftain, John de Courcy, with the impressive monition that he should first reduce that territory by the force of his arms. The native annalists, indeed, detail such existing disunions then over this territory as facilitated, if not invited, its subjugation. In 1172, say the Four Masters, the people of Tyr-connel attacked those of Kinel-Owen, "committing great slaughter among them by the miracles of God, through the intervention of St. Patrick and St. Columbkill, whose churches they (of Kinel-Owen) had plundered." The Trian More of Armagh was subsequently despoliated, and a great prey taken by Hugh Magennis and the Clan-Hugh. The Kinel-Enda—*i. e.*, the O'Gormleys of Raphoe—were "defeated in battle with much slaughter by Eachmarach O'Caher and Neill O'Gormley." Cumaighe O'Flynn, lord of sundry districts in Down, was slain by the people of Firlee (a territory contiguous to Lough Neagh), &c., &c.

Encouraged by this distracted state of Ulster, and sanctioned by the royal authority, De Courcy, in 1177 and 1178, advanced into the fens and mountains of the North, "riding," relates Holinshed, "on a white horse, bearing three eagles

---

dant of the above Bertram, having intermarried with the Lord Furnival, who had issue by her a daughter, married to Thomas Nevil, brother to the first Earl of Westmoreland; who had issue by her, another daughter, Maud, who, marrying John Talbot, first Earl of Shrewsbury, brought with her into his inheritance the said lands and lordship. It was the favourite residence of the late Earl of Shrewsbury, whose magnificent seat preserved the name in "Altón Towers."

painted on his standards, with the artful object of seeming to verify a prophecy—popularly attributed to Merlin—that a knight, riding on a white horse, and bearing birds on his shield, should be the first of the English who would enter and conquer Ulster." At his first onset, however, he was impeded by that devotion of the natives, in burning all before him, which in late years has immortalised Russia, until at length, having encamped at Glanee (the vale of the Newry river), he was confronted, say the Four Masters, by Morogh O'Carrol, Lord of Orgiel (Louth), and by Cu-Ulladh, a gallant chief, the son of Dunslieve,* King of Ulidia (Down), by whom De Courcy was defeated, with the loss of four hundred and fifty men. He was a second time repulsed "with great slaughter, through the interposition of St. Patrick, of Columbkill, and St. Brendan, and with difficulty escaped to Dublin, covered with wounds." Subsequently, however, he succeeded in marching by this town to Downpatrick, where he established his quarters.

The Irish—chiefly the sept of O'Hanlon—according to Hanmer, "camped by south of Dundalk, and by north of the river Dundugan, when De Courcy, having marched to a place within a mile and a-half of the Irish camp, made a stand, with his brother (in law) Sir Armoricus Tristram (ancestor of the noble family of St. Laurence, of Howth), Sir Roger Poer, and others, and consulted what course was best to be held." On that council of war Sir Armoricus advised that "when the enemy hath descried us, we shall perceive by his array what he means to do. If they turn face to us, and offer to fight, our foot shall recover Dundalk afore them; and with

* This cognomen was derived from the circumstance of the chief of the sept having his fortress "dun" at the mountains "Slieve" of Mourne.

our horses we will so handle the matter, that we shall sustain no great loss. If they fly, and take the river, the sea comes in, & we shall overtake them afore half pass. All were well pleased with his advice, & followed the direction. Nicholas St. Laurence, with his company, wheels before; Sir John de Courcy, at once followeth after, & Roger Poer takes the rere-ward. The enemy, having descried them, takes the river. Sir Nicholas gives the sign, whereupon the English army gave a great shout, and followeth on their heels; the Irish break their array; they tumble one upon another in the water; the current drowns some; the sea and the swiftness of the tide take others away. Such as would not venture the water, were overtaken by the English. O'Hanlon, and his company, that had passed the water, seeing the carnage of his men, could not come to the rescue by reason of the salt water. The English horsemen overtook the foot of the Irish, and skirmished with them, until Sir John de Courcy came; by that time the sea, likewise, had stopped the Irish from flying, at a great water, a mile from the Lurgan, on the south side of Dundalk. The Irish, seeing themselves in this strait, turning their faces, choose rather to die with the sword, like men, than to be drowned in the seas like beasts." A desperate engagement ensued, in which Sir John de Courcy was again "sore wounded."—"The slaughter on both sides was great; few of the Irish, and fewer of the English, were left alive. The Irish got them to the Fews, and the English to Dundalk; but who got the best, there is no boast made." The year 1178 is commemorated by the Four Masters for the prevalence of "a great wind, by which many trees were uprooted, and many churches laid prostrate; one hundred and twenty trees fell in Derry Columbkill;" while they mention a no less extraordinary drought prevailing in other parts of the island. "The river of Galway was dried up for several days, so that all things lost in it from time immemorial were recovered, and great quantities of fish were taken by the inhabitants." The same annalists expressively deplore the social state of Ulster in 1180. "All the churches of Tyr-owen, from the mountains southwards, were abandoned on account of the wars, commotions, and famine."

About the same time that Henry the Second confirmed the grant to De Courcy, he originated another in this district to the aforesaid Bertram de Verdon,* Lord of Alveton, in Alton, who thereupon constituted a borough here. Bertram was, about the same time, appointed Seneschal of Ireland, and had a patent of the lordship of Clonmore, with other estates in Louth.†

In 1158, Philip of Worcester, one of the most rapacious of of the Lords Deputy of Ireland, led a predatory expedition by Dundalk to Armagh, where, by force of arms, he wrung from the clergy there a great amount of money and treasure. "From thence," admits Hanmer, "he went to Down, and from Down to Dublin, laden with gold and silver money, & moneys worth, the which he extorted in every place where he came, and other good did he none." When Dundalk and its vicinage recovered from the infliction of this visitation, Bertram de Verdon founded a friary here for the Cross-bearers, following the rule of St. Augustine, which he dedicated to St. Leonard. It was afterwards an hospital for both sexes, and admitted the sick, the aged, and the infirm—supplying the place of poorhouse and infirmary without the modern appliances of rates and taxes.

---

* *Inquis.* 6 Edw. 2 in Offic., Ch. Rememb.

† *Rot. Pat. Exempl.*, 11 Edw. 3, in Tur, Lond.

It is pleasing to reflect upon the origin of many of these monastic institutions. They were emanations from the better part of man's nature, and tell of the heart, engaged in the affairs of this world, yearning for the blessed land. They were, for the most part, offerings from men of the sword to the God of Peace; and we cannot, whatever our creed or opinions may be, but be sensible of the benefits they conferred upon mankind. Without them, where would religion or learning, in the dark ages, find an abiding place? "Had not these retreats," says Lord Macaulay, "been scattered through the huts of a miserable peasantry, or the castles of a ferocious aristocracy, European society would have consisted merely of beasts of burden and beasts of prey." It was in the monasteries of Europe, and no where more zealously than in those of Ireland, the lamp of charity and knowledge was kept alight. When the world was ruled by mailed chiefs and warrior kings, the monks were the unwearied watchers by the pure fire which burned on the altar of knowledge. What a contrast their peaceful lives, passed in prayer and self-denial—feeding the hungry—clothing the naked—tending the sick—copying, with taste and genius which defies rivalry, the works of classic authors; and beyond all—and above all—that Holy Bible which, but for their care, we should never have possessed. What a contrast with the lives of some whose swords were red with the blood of their fellows, whose pride and lust of power constantly led to strifes and conflicts; whose greatest triumphs consisted in defeating a friend in the tournament, or an enemy in the field; whose ferocity and ignorance equally despised learning, yet who possessed sufficient religion to teach them the importance of prayer, and bade them endow churches and monasteries, in hope of securing salvation in the next world, and often a resting place in this.

The time of the monks, being wholly devoted to the service of religion and learning, was passed in prayer and study. We cannot be surprised at the number and variety of beautiful buildings, ornamental missals, and illuminated manuscripts, which remain as evidence of the love and reverence they entertained for all that was sacred and holy. Hence the lofty fanes—the high embowered roofs—the pillared aisles—the gemmed altars in their churches; the gorgeous procession—the combined melody of voice and instrument—the perfumed incense—the number of lights—in their ceremonies. The gold and silver cases in which were inshrined the Holy Gospels—the manuscripts—and relics of those whose virtues and holiness caused them to be regarded as saints on earth. Visible beauty was to them the fitting offering to adorn all that appertained to God; and, in the beautiful memorials which the architects of our day select as their best models, we trace the piety and genius of the monks of old.

About the same time Hugh de Lacy, the great Palatine of Meath (who was soon afterwards assassinated at Durrow), for the good of his soul, and the souls of his predecessors and successors, granted and confirmed "to God, the Blessed Virgin Mary, and the Monks of the Cistercian order, of Mellefont," in this county, Ballymacscanlan, near Dundalk, "with all the land between the water of Adbui and the river Awneure, as each water falls into the sea, and as the Adbui extends from the sea to Algarchan, and the river Awneure extends from the sea to a bog or ditch, which extends from the river beyond Munardnebrach, until it returns to the said river again, where was the mill of Huckinhocled, & so by that river to Inesmorllicher, and so directly to Auvanavela, and so to Kilsaggart, and so by the high road to Crosmoy, and so by the mountains to Algarchan again." The deed of this endowment is exemplified in a patent of the twelfth year of James the First, in the Chancery Rolls of Ireland, and it is stated to have been witnessed by Walter and Robert de Lacy, Roger Peppard, Geoffry de Cosketin, And. Dardis, Philip de Nugent, Nicholas de Netreville, Robert de Mandeville, Henry Fitz-Hay, Henry Begg, Richard Fitz-Humphrey, Thomas and Philip Sacerdote, William Noell, and many others.

This great Palatine, Hugh de Lacy, as the Four Masters record, confiscated and transferred the possession of many churches in Meath, Brefney, and Oriel, to the English. In the division of Connaught its rents were all paid to him. He reduced and seized the greater portion of Ireland for the English, and erected castles in all parts of Meath, from the Shannon to the sea; yet when John, son of Henry the Second, visited Ireland, he being the King's representative then, neither sent him tribute nor hostages from the Irish princes, which, as the endowed Lord of Ireland he claimed, and the omission was, the Four Masters allege, a cause of complaint to Henry on the return of the Prince.

The Four Masters, at 1190, draw an affecting picture of the fallen dynast of Ireland, in connexion with Ulster and its population. "In that year Roderic O'Connor went from Connaught into Tyrconnell, the seat of Flaherty O'Maold-eruidh, and from thence into Tyrone, requesting forces from the North of Ireland to enable him to recover his kingdom of Connaught." It had been assured to him by treaty at Oxford, in 1175, and was all he then sought, disheartened as he was by the disobedience and disunion of his sons.* "But

* His grandson, Cathal Carrach, six years previously, invited the English to his assistance in rebellion. "They marched with him to Roscommon, where he gave them 3,000 cows for their serviees." This example of

the people of Ulster would give him no support. He then proceeded to the English of Meath, for the same purpose, but neither would they assist him. From them he went into Munster, whence he was recalled by the Siol-Muoras, who inhabited a district nearly conterminous with the ancient diocese of Elphin, and who granted to him certain lands in Tyr-Fiachra," &c. A more affecting instance of individual humiliation, or an earlier of the national degradation and passive despair of the Irish people throughout the whole circuit of the land, even in the time of its first English king, could not be adduced. The plains of Leinster, the churches of Kildare and Louth, had been desolated by Strongbow down to the time of his decease in 1176, "by a visitation attributed to Saints Brigid, Columbkille, and other saints, whose churches he had destroyed; and it is said that he thought he saw St. Brigid killing him." One of the lineal descendants of the old *régime*, the most legitimate of Ireland's rulers, "Manus O'Melaghlin, Lord of Munster, was taken treacherously by the English, and hanged by them at Trim."* Connaught was laid waste successively by De Cogan and De Courcy; Meath was plundered to Clonmacnois; Munster was consumed by the hostilities of Prince John's followers; Thomond and Desmond were covered with blood, but the desecration of the country could not in any quarter arouse

---

apostacy was too frequent of adoption. Rory, another son of Mac Dunsleve, whose brother, Cu-Ulladh, was so active in opposing De Courcy, obtained a willing aid from the English, in 1196, for the desolation of Armagh; and in 1199, "joined with a party of the English of Meath, he marched his forces and plundered the monastery of SS. Paul and Peter, at Armagh, and left only one cow in the place."—*Ann. F. M.*

* *Annals of the Four Masters.*

reaction. Reckless and licentious adventurers rioted with impunity over the island. In vain did the feeble and disheartened Roderic endow religious establishments; the clergy were indifferent in his cause. In vain did Cardinal Vivian, when De Courcy refused his mediation and the acceptance of tribute from Dunslevy for the abandonment of his Ulster invasion, exhort the latter to arm in his own defence. Disgusted with the want of union at such a moment, the Cardinal retired to Dublin; held a synod there of the bishops and abbots of Ireland, in which King Henry's right of dominion was relied on as under the Pope's authority, and the necessity of obedience to his authority was inculcated under pain of excommunication.*

In 1196, Roderic MacDunsleve, of the sept who at first gave such spirited opposition to De Courcy, "joined by the English, and the sons of some chieftains of Connaught, marched his forces into the territories of Kenel-Owen, and of Owen MacKenel Owen, of Tulloghogree; and the men of Owen marched to the plain of Armagh to oppose them, and gave them battle. MacDunsleve was defeated, with a dreadful slaughter of his forces. In this battle were slain twelve sons of the nobles and chiefs of Connaught, with a great number of the common soldiery. Among the nobles slain were Brian Buidhe O'Flaherty, the son of Maolisa; O'Conor, of Connaught, the son of O'Conor Faily; and the son of O'Faelain of the Desies."†

---

* *Annals of the Four Masters.*

† *Lanigan's Eccl. Hist.*, vol. iv., p. 233.

CHAPTER IV.

FROM THE REIGN OF RICHARD I. TO THE SUCCESSION OF EDWARD I.

When Cœur de Lion inspired the chivalry of the Crusade, Bertram de Verdon was one of the knights who enthusiastically followed the royal standard to Palestine, where he died, in 1192, at Jaffa, whereupon his possessions here, and elsewhere, passed to Thomas de Verdon; who also dying in 1199, his brother, Nicholas de Verdon, succeeded thereto and, in 1204, obtained from King John a royal order and licence for entering thereupon; when, in conformity with a resolution and vow, very frequent in those days, he forthwith dedicated to the Abbey of Thomas à Becket, in Dublin, the tithes of two knights' fees within the precint of the first castle he should erect on the lands of his inheritance in the County of Louth. Having afterwards, however, taken part against his sovereign in the barons' war, those lands were seized by the royal order, nor was it until the accession of Henry the Third, in 1216, that they were restored to him—the patent including expressly by name the castles and estates of Dundalk and Clonmore. Consequent upon the temporary occupation of the Crown's escheator, disputes arose, on this restoration, as to the rightful boundaries of De Verdon's inheritance as distinguished from the lands of the Crown; when, in the *nisi prius* language, the decision was directed to be deferred to St. John's Day, *unless* a decision shall sooner be awarded by judgment of court.*

* *Rot. Lit. Claus.*, 5 Henry 3, in Tur. Lond.

In the August of 1210, King John, in his second visit to Ireland, passed through this town. His progress is minutely described by the Four Masters; who, however, in their peculiar system of chronology, refer the event to 1209. "John, King of England, sailed for Ireland with a fleet of 700 ships, and landed at Dublin, where he rested for some time after his voyage. He then proceeded to Tipraid Ultain, in Meath, where Cathal Crovdearg O'Conor came to meet him. Walter de Lacy was expelled from Meath into England. The King, accompanied by his nobles, proceeded to Carrickfergus, and expelled Hugh de Lacy from Ulidia into England. Hugh O'Neill attended the King's summons, but he returned without making any submission. The King afterwards besieged Carrickfergus, which surrendered; whereupon he garrisoned it with his own forces. . . . He demanded from O'Conor his son as a hostage. O'Conor would not, however, consent to give his son, but gave four of his chiefs in his stead; namely, Conor Godh O'Hara, Lord of Leney; Dermod, son of Conor O'Mulrooney, Lord of Moylurg; Fionn O'Carmacain, and Aireachtach Mac Donogh, a young prince of O'Conor's friends. The King returned to England, and brought the hostages with him." They were, however, sent back to their own country in the ensuing year.

In 1213, Hugh O'Neill defeated the English with dreadful slaughter; and on the same day burned Carlingford, sparing neither person nor property.*

Dundalk was soon a royal borough, with commons of pasture and rights of fishing. The grant to Bertram de Verdon, by John, while Earl of Morton, gave to this borough the ancient privileges of sik and soch, toll, &c.; and thereon, consequent

---

* *Annals of the Four Masters.*

on this, was the enclosing the town by walls and towers, to protect it from the raids of the O'Neill's, as it stood on the frontiers of the Pale.

In 1221, say the Four Masters, the son of Hugh de Lacy having joined Hugh O'Neill against the English, they proceeded in concert first to Colerain; and, having dismantled its castle, marched thence to Meath and Leinster, reducing the resources of the country through which they passed. The Anglo-Irish collected twenty-four battalions at Dundalk, but Hugh O'Neill and De Lacy attacked them with five large battalions, and they were compelled "to submit to O'Neill* upon his own terms." The harvest of 1224 is recorded to have remained unreaped till the festival of St. Brigid, "by reason of war and the inclemency of the weather."

In 1225, King Henry directed his special letter to Rosia, the only daughter and heiress of the aforesaid Nicholas de Verdon, whose alliance was considered of high political importance, recommending her to marry Theobald le Botiller, of the family of the house of Ormond. His majesty addressed another letter to her father, Nicholas, requesting him to use his influence with his daughter on this occasion.† The marriage

---

* The death of this Hugh O'Neill, who is so often noticed in this work, occurred in 1230, and is thus significantly recorded by the Four Masters:—"Hugh O'Neill, Lord of Tyr-Eeogan, heir presumptive to the throne of Ireland, the defender of Leath-Conn (the northern half of Ireland) against the English and the people of Leath-Mogha (the southern half), a man who had given neither hostages nor tributes to either English or Irish; who had gained many victories over the English, and defeated them with great slaughter, and who had levied tributes both on English and Irish enemies, and contemplated the conquest of all Ireland, died, though it was rather expected that he would have fallen in battle with the English."

† *Rot.*, *Claus.* 9, Henry 3, in Tur. Lond.

took place accordingly; but the issue, John, adopted his mother's name, and is so described in all records that refer to him.

In 1226, Nicholas de Verdon had license for holding fairs in his said manors of Dundalk and Clonmore, with free warren over Ferrard, together with the advowsons of all those churches which were originally annexed to their castellains by Bertram de Verdon and himself. In right of all which possessions his male descendants have since had writs of summons as barons, and possessed high authority and influence during the 14th, 15th, and 16th centuries. The fairs, granted by the patent of 1226, for Dundalk, were prescribed to be held on the eve of St. Martin, and for the seven following days, with all liberties, &c.* Nicholas de Verdon had, besides his old inheritance in Louth, extensive estates in Leicester, Stafford, and Warwick-shires, of which he died seised in 1230, leaving the before-mentioned Rosia, his only daughter and heiress. Her chief residence was at *Alton*, in the neighbourhood of which she had founded the abbey of Crocksden, in which the heart of King John was buried; and in 1243 she established and endowed the nunnery of Grace-Dieu, in Leicestershire. "On the north side of the altar at Belton, in Leicestershire," writes Gough in his *Sepulchral Monuments*,† "is a beautiful alabaster figure of a lady in a close veil, head dress, wimple, close plaited gown; round her waist and over it an elegantly folded mantle, gathered up below in graceful folds by her left hand; her right is laid on her breast, and at her feet is a griffin; her head is on a cushion. On the spandrils of the arch-clustered columns, round her head, three elegant figures kneel, and another at her feet. At the head two angels carry

* *Plea Roll* in Berm. Tower.

† Vol. ii., pp. cxxi., cxxii.

up, in a sheet, a figure, whose ribs are expressed. On the left spandril a kind of scroll on a round charged with a *rose*. This figure, placed at present in a clumsy altar tomb of coarse workmanship, is supposed to represent the Lady Rosia de Verdon—the foundress of Grace-Dieu Abbey, and to have been removed from its chapel at the time of the dissolution." Nichols, in his *Leicestershire*, gives, at the parish of Belton, a drawing of this monument.

This great lady died in 1247, not leaving any trace of her name in connexion with Dundalk. Her son, the aforesaid John de Verdon, however, a few years before his mother's death, erected the Grey Friary here.* The east window of which was "singularly admired for its curious and elegant workmanship."† In 1246, Pope Innocent the Fourth ordered the warden of this house, together with the prior of the Dominicans of Drogheda, to cite to Rome a certain person who had been elected irregularly to the Archdeaconry of Armagh, and also to summon those who had so elected him.‡ The *Annals of the Four Masters*, at 1250, notice the death of a very remarkable character:—"Donogh MacGilPatrick, grandson of Donogh of the Ossorians, was slain by the English in retaliation for the burnings, plunders, and slaughters he had perpetrated on them." This Donogh was one of the three Irishmen who committed the greatest number of depredations on the English, and these three were Conor O'Melaghlin, Conor MacCoghlan, of the Castles, and the before-mentioned Donogh, who was in the habit of reconnoitering

---

* *Rot.* in Tur. London.

† Grose, in his *Antiquities of Ireland*, gives a drawing of the only tower of this house, as it existed in 1770.

‡ *De Burgo Hib. Dom.*, p. 200.

the market towns of the English, by visiting them in the different characters of a beggar, a carpenter, a turner, an artist, or a pedlar, as recorded in the following verse:—

> "He is now a carpenter or turner,
> Now a man of books or learned poet;
> In good wines and hides a dealer sometimes;
> Everything by turns, as suits his purpose."

From the chronicled habits of this singular person, who might well be the hero of an historic romance, it may be permitted to assume that in his wanderings he did not overlook the then great market town and seaport of Dundalk. In 1252, the English interest in Ulster was sought to be strengthened by the erection of castles at Caol-uisge (Narrow-water, near Newry), and at Moy-coba, near Downpatrick. The County of Louth—then ecclesiastically consisting of the church of Louth, and the three deaneries, Dundalk, Drogheda, and Ardee—was disunited from the Diocese of Clogher, and annexed to that of Armagh; while, at the same period, the Four Masters record that "the Lord Justice of Ireland marched with a great force to Armagh, and thence to Iveagh; he then returned back to Cluain-Feachna (probably Clonfeacle), where Bryan O'Neill submitted to him, and gave his brother, Rory O'Neill, to him as a hostage. It was on this occasion that a dispute arose in the camp of the English at Dundalk, between the men of Meath and Munster, in which many of the latter were slain." The annalists go on to remark that "great heat and drought prevailed this summer (1252), so that the people passed with dry feet over the principal rivers of Ireland. The harvest commenced twenty days before Lammas (1st August), and the trees became ignited by the heat of the sun. New money was ordered by the King of England to be coined in Ireland, and the old money hitherto

D

in circulation was discontinued." In the following year the same Bryan O'Neill, Prince of Tyrone, was engaged "in war against the English, and having gone to the before-mentioned Moy-Coba (Downpatrick), he demolished its new castle, and many others, burned Tradbhaile (Dundalk), and cleared from the English the entire plain of Ulidia."

In 1260, Milo or Malachy O'Conor was here consecrated Bishop of Elphin, by Abraham O'Conellan, Archbishop of Armagh, at which time a severe battle was fought at Downpatrick "by the said Bryan O'Neill and Hugh O'Conor against the English of the North of Ireland, in which many of the Irish chiefs were slain. Bryan O'Neill, the chief ruler of Ireland, Donal O'Cairre, Dermod MacLoughlin, Manus O'Cahan, Cahan O'Hennesy, Dunslevy MacCann, Conor O'Dowdiorma, and his son, Hugh O'Cahan; Murtogh O'Cahan, Aulaff O'Gormley, Cu-ulla O'Hanlon, and Neal O'Hanlon; and, in the whole, fifteen chiefs of the O'Cahans were slain there. A number of the chiefs of Connaught were also killed there; namely, Gilcreest, son of Conor, son of Cormac, son of Tumultach MacDermott, Lord of Moylurg; Cathal, son of Tiernan O'Conor; Maolromey MacDonagh; Cathal, the son of Donagh, son of Murtogh; Hugh, son of Murtogh; Fionn Teague, son of Cathal, son of Bryan O'Mulrooney; Dermod, son of Teague, son of Murrogh, son of Tumultach O'Mulrooney; Conor MacGillaruith; Teague, son of Cian O'Gara; Gillbaraigh O'Cuinn, Carolus MacAnaspeg O'Murrey, with many others of the chiefs and common soldiers of the Irish."*

In 1262, John de Verdon, the Lord of Dundalk, was distinguished in an invasion of Connaught. "The English of

* Stephen Longespé, *alias* Longsword, Earl of Salisbury, then Viceroy of Ireland, commanded the English forces at this battle.

Ireland marched with an immense force to attack Felim, son of Cathal Crovdearg (O'Conor), and his son Hugh; upon which O'Conor sent the greater part of the cattle of Connaught into Tyrconnel, to secure them from the English, while he himself remained at Inis-Saimer (Ballyshannon), to defend his property and people. MacWilliam Burke proceeded, with his forces, from the west, across Tocher-Mona (Toomona, County Roscommon), and arrived at Elphin. The Lord Justice of Ireland and John de Verdon came by Athlone to Roscommon. They sent out scouting parties into Kinel-dobtha MacAongusa (the present Barony of Ballintober), and plundered all that remained in Connaught after O'Conor, and they also marked out the place for a castle in Roscommon. Hugh O'Connor, at the same time, collected his forces, marched into the west of Connaught, and plundered all the country, eastward from Mayo, of the Saxons and Bulla; burned the towns in the English interest, and the corn as far as Slieve Lugha (in Mayo), and slew many people between those places. He sent his chiefs and young officers into South Connaught, and they burned and plundered the country, from Tuam to Athlone, and slew all the fighting men whom they met between those places. After this the English sent messengers to O'Conor, and his son, offering them terms of peace. Hugh O'Conor went to Ath-doire-chuiri, to hold a conference, in which they made peace, neither party yielding to the other hostages or securities on the occasion. Hugh O'Conor and MacWilliam Burke slept together that night, after the peace, in the same bed, cheerfully and amicably; and on the following day the English departed, after taking leave of O'Conor." What a significant illustration this annal affords of the amnesty of a native prince amid all his sufferings. About the same time the before-mentioned John de Verdon obtained a royal charter of free warren to himself and his heirs in all his demesne lands of Leicestershire. Clynne relates that in 1270 "the King of Connaught, by force of arms, in the plain field, overthrew Walter Burke, Earl of Ulster, who hardly escaped with life, yet died the year following; and slew a great number of nobles and knights that held with the Burkes, and amongst others, by especial name, the Lord Richard Verdon, and the Lord John de Verdon; and that there ensued over all Ireland great famine and pestilence, as the sequel of wars."

In 1270, a very eminent ecclesiastic resigned his soul to the hands of his Maker, in the Abbey of St. Leonard's, at Dundalk. This was Patrick O'Scanlan, Archbishop of Armagh. He had belonged to the illustrious order of Dominicans, or Friars Preachers, which has given so many distinguished bishops to the Church, and martyrs to heaven. As has been well said of them by the present Attorney-General for Ireland,* "for 800 years the fathers of this order have been most eminent in the prosecution of those arts which adorn the life of man, and exalt our humanity itself. They set themselves to breast the torrent with which barbarian hordes were sweeping civilization from the world, and succeeded in maintaining art when art seemed about to be extinguished. They produced not only wise theologians and profound thinkers, but able men, engineers, architects, sculptors, and painters, in long illustrious array, whose glory is memorable in the world." This eminent Archbishop was promoted from the bishopric of Raphoe to the higher dignity of Archbishop of Armagh, under a licence granted by the King, 27th February, 1261. Henry confirmed his election, which was ratified by Pope Urban the same year.

---

* Right Hon. Thomas O'Hagan, M.P.

The Archbishop had held a provincial synod at Drogheda, 18th January, 1262; and was assisted at this synod not only by the suffragan bishops of his own see, but by some from the archdiocese of Tuam, as subject to Armagh by primatial right.* In these days it was not irregular, it appears, for lay persons to be present at these conclaves; for, it is recorded, the Lord Justice, the privy council, and several of the principal men of the kingdom dignified this synod by their presence †

In 1263, it is stated Pope Urban issued a bull by which the Primacy of all Ireland was confirmed to the see of Armagh.

It 1275, the earliest perpetual grant of customs payable in wool-skins, &c., was made to the Crown, by the Parliament of England, many of whose Lords were likewise Magnates or Barons of Ireland, to whom belonged the principal sea-ports of the latter country, where such customs would become payable. In consequence of the grant therefore from his English Parliament, the King thought right to obtain the written sealed certificates of these certain Magnates, amongst whom was Theobald de Verdon—then, as hereafter shown, Lord of Dundalk—certifying that they confirmed to the Crown the same customs in Ireland as had been established in England.

In 1275, say the Masters, "the English sustained a great defeat in Ulster, in which they lost two hundred of their cavalry, both men and horse, beside what were slain of common soldiers."

---

* *Ware's Bishops*, p. 68.

† Lodge—quoted in *Stuart's Hist. Armagh*, p. 173.

CHAPTER V.

FROM THE SUCCESSION OF EDWARD I. TO THE INVASION OF EDWARD BRUCE.

On the death of Lord John de Verdon, his son and heir, Theobald de Verdon, then aged twenty-two, succeeded; and to him, in favour of this town, was granted the remarkable charter of the staple in 1275.

This Theobald had married Margaret, the daughter and co-heiress of Walter de Lacy, Lord of Meath; and, accordingly, in 1277, he proffered the service of one knight's fee for the inheritance of his father, and two knights' fees and a-half for his property of the inheritance of Walter de Lacy, for the expedition against Llewellyn, Prince of Wales. In the Parliamentary writs are to be found various other summonses of him to do military services; and in 1283 he was required to attend a Parliament at Shrewsbury.

In 1282, a chapter of the order was held in the Grey Friary here; and in two years after Edward the First confirmed to said Theobald de Verdon one weekly market, on Mondays, at his manor of Dundalk, and a fair there every year, for fifteen days together, with several fairs and markets at other places, and all liberties and free customs thereto appertaining.*

In 1285, the Lord Theobald de Verdon, then styled Constable of Ireland, in the prosecution of military service at Offaley, and with the object of avenging the capture of the Castle of Lea, by the Irishry of that country, was himself afflicted, writes Marleburgh, by a severe loss of men and

---

* *Rot. Pat.* in *Canc. Hib.*

horses. In two years after this lord granted to Richard, Prior of the House of Crossbearers of Dundalk, the advowson of the churches of Dundalk, Old-Castle, and Keen, with three burgesses, half a corucate, and twenty-three acres of land in Dundalk and Ballybabriel, to hold at the yearly rent of seventeen marks and an half. In consideration of which grant the said Prior gave to Theobald a sum of £100 in silver.* About this time, it appears on record, that a judgment was obtained against this Theobald, for waste by him committed on the lands of Simon de Phepoe, during an interval for which they were possessed by him. This Irish judgment was, however, subsequently reversed in England.† In 1288, he was besieged in the Castle of Athlone, by Richard de Burgo, Earl of Ulster, commonly called the Red Earl, who asserted title to the Lordship of Meath. In 1290, attending the Parliament of Westminster, he gave his sanction for an aid towards portioning the King's eldest daughter, and had subsequent summonses for military service in Scotland and Guernsey. Of one of these expeditions, in 1296, the Four Masters write:—" The King of England marched with an army into Scotland, and gained great power over that country. The nobles of the English of Ireland were in that army, namely—Richard Burke, Earl of Ulster, Gerald FitzGerald, and John FitzThomas (FitzGerald); and they plundered Scotland, both churches and people. A monastery of friars in that country was plundered by them, and they levelled it to the ground, so as not to leave one stone upon another on its site, after they had slain a number of its clergy, besides many of its people, both male and female, which acts were, indeed, disgraceful." In 1295, Theobald was twice summoned to

* *Archdall's Mon. Hib.*, p. 462. † *Plea Roll* in Dom. Cup. Westm.

Parliaments held in Westminster, and had also a Royal mandate, as one of the "Fideles" of Ireland, to levy forces and do military service in support of its Justiciary, John Wogan, and even to hold himself in readiness to accompany the King in parts beyond the seas. Frequent service was afterwards required from him against the Scots. In 1300, he attended a Parliament at Westminster, and in the following year was one of those who addressed the memorable letter from Lincoln to the Pope in behalf of the Commons of England. In this latter year he incurred the serious displeasure of the Crown by confining in his own prison, instead of sending to the King's gaol, his own chamberlain and an accomplice, who were accused by their fellow-servants of purloining a red carbuncle, which had been set in their lord's ring, and was valued at 1,000 marks. The Lord Theobald, though his high office gave him cognizance of the most serious crimes, was impeached for this, and mulcted in a heavy fine.* It is very probable that had he not been able to pay the fine the charge against him would not be made

In the meantime, in 1296, Richard, the prior of the house of Cross-bearers, before alluded to, was attached to answer the complaint of Robert le Mercer, for proceeding against him in the Court Christian, contrary to the King's prohibition. The prior appeared, and maintained his plea, and gave for answer that the said Robert was an excommunicated person. [This Robert le Mercer had, in six years after, a lease for three years of the Church of St. Nicholas of Carrickfergus, subject to a payment of 45 marks yearly therefor, and of all ordinary and extraordinary charges, and of all "Papal tithes," and that

---

* *Roll* in Ch. Rememb. Off., 28 Edw. 1.

he should, likewise, perfect the chancel of said church as he had begun it.*]

In 1298, a writ issued to the Archbishop of Armagh, directing him to levy, out of the goods of the Prior of the Cross-bearers of Dundalk, the sum of £100, due by him to Theobald de Verdon. The Primate, however, made his return, that there was not effects to answer such demand, for that the full value of the goods in the priory was insufficient to support the fraternity, and the sick and poor belonging to the hospital; and, further, that the said prior was indebted to him (the Primate) in a certain sum, which, being his own debt, he would levy before the demand of any other. Another writ hereupon issued, directing him forthwith to levy the sum of £51, and have the same before the justices, in Dublin, on the Octave of St. John the Baptist, the same to pay over to said Theobald, and there to receive the judgment of the court on his proceedings. On the 28th August following, the said Theobald, styling himself Constable of Ireland, came into court, and acknowledged that he had received from the prior the sum of £40 sterling, as in full of his demand.†

In 1301, at the Parliament of Lincoln, Theobald supported the memorable remonstrance of the Peers of England to Pope Boniface the Eighth, denying rights claimed by his Holiness over Scotland as the fee of the Church, alleging that, from the first institution of the kingdom of England, as well in the time of the Britons as in that of the Angles, the rulers of that country had the preëminent command of Scotland, and that never at any time did it pertain in temporals to the Church, nor did they answer for it to any ecclesiastical tribunal. "Wherefore, on diligent deliberation of the letter of your

---

* *Rot. Pat.*, 31 Edw. 1., in *Canc. Hib.* † *King's MSS.*, Dub. Soc., p. 64.

Holiness advancing such claim, the common, concurrent, and unanimous consent of all and each of us is, and shall be, with the will of God, unchangeable—that our said King should in no manner concerning the rights of Scotland or other his temporalities, make claim before you, or subject his rights, or suffer them to be brought into question. Neither should he send proxies or envoys to you, as such proceedings would operate to the dishonour of the Crown of England, the subversion of his state, and the prejudice of those liberties and customs which we have sworn to maintain, and which, with the assistance of God, we shall maintain with all our strength," &c. What a contrast does this bold assertion of independence exhibit to the prompt submission in which, little more than a century previous, Pope Adrian's letter was received in Ireland by kings and chiefs. The letter from Lincoln has, amongst others, the signature of "Theobald de Verdon;" and on his seal appended thereto he is represented on horseback, while the reverse contains a plain shield of his arms between two lions passant guardant, and a small bird on each of the upper corners of the escutcheon, which appears to be suspended from a tree.

In 1303, say the Four Masters, "the King of England (Edward the First) led a great army into Scotland, and the Earl of Ulster, and many of the English and Irish went with a large fleet from Ireland to assist him. They took many cities, and gained full power over Scotland in that expedition; and Theobald Burke, the Earl's brother, after his return from that army, died, on Christmas night, in Carrickfergus." The Lord Theobald de Verdon was doubtless engaged in this expedition, but he died in 1308, leaving Theobald de Verdon, junior, his son and heir, who had previous frequent summonses to the Parliament of England. In 1310, he had livery of his father's various estates here and elsewhere, with a royal mandate for the future payment to him of an ancient annuity which his father and early ancestors had theretofore received out of the town of Drogheda. The sergeantship of the county of Meath was even found, on inquisition, to belong to him, with many other rights within that Liberty, which he had acquired by marrying one of the co-heiresses of Hugh de Lacy, an alliance which made him obnoxious to the jealousy and hostility of his compeers of the Pale. "The English lords and settlers in every part of Ireland," remarks Leland (*Hist. of Ireland*, vol. i., p. 256) "in the lust of power and possessions, were become the bitterest and most implacable enemies to each other. . . . . . The power Lord Theobald de Verdon possessed of a considerable demesne in Meath, by right of his marriage with a daughter of Walter de Lacy, excited the enmity of Gerald FitzMaurice, Baron of Offaley, who attacked his castle, defeated his forces, but was himself defeated in turn and made a prisoner."

In 1312, Nicholas de Verdon, who appears to have been the nephew of Theobald, was arraigned at Drogheda, for resisting the King's authority in the county of Louth; and overt acts were charged against his brother, Robert de Verdon, of despoiling the lands of the Abbot of Mellefont, those of the King at Ardee, and those of the Lord Louth, which he held of the King, with the countenance and aid of the said Nicholas. The whole proceedings are given fully in the *History of Drogheda* (vol. ii., p. 60, &c.) Nicholas de Verdon defended himself on the grounds that after he had received a Royal Commission to subdue the insurgents, he proceeded with the *posse comitatus* to Dundalk, to parley with them, and that, while he was engaged in inducing them to surrender, he saw the town of Louth, and other towns and villages thereabout, on fire, which, finding to have been done by some of these rebellious persons, he attacked them, and slew several, and that, in a word, he did so to resist incendiarism and robbery. In the prosecution of forfeitures against the offenders it was found, on inquisition, that this Nicholas was seised of Calliaghtown in this county, with the manor of Duleek, and other lands in trust for the prior and fraternity of Lanthony, near Gloucester.

In 1312, King Edward directed that an inquiry should be held, by jury, to ascertain whether any prejudice would arise to the Crown's rights in confirming to the prior of St. Leonard's of Dundalk four acres of pasturage, with the appurtenances, in "New Dundalk," which said prior had obtained from the Corporation of said town, in frank almoigne, without Royal license previously obtained therefor. An inquest was thereupon taken at Drogheda, when the jury found that it was not to the King's prejudice to confirm said grant, but rather for his advantage, because thereby more chaplains can be maintained in said priory of St. Leonard than have been maintained heretofore; and they thereto annexed a finding of the high antiquity of the borough of Dundalk, as incorporated by the ancestors of Theobald de Verdon, "soon after the acquisition of Ireland, who enfeoffed divers burgesses with burgages and bounds, with commons of pasture, of which the said four acres were a part; and that they were granted to the said prior with the unanimous assent of said Corporation.* "And be it known that the said inquisition, together with the writ, was delivered to Adam Goodman, attorney of said prior, to be carried to the King into England."† In the same year a Royal mandate issued for purveyance from this town in aid of the war in Scotland.

* *Inquis.* 6 Edw. 2, in Offic. Ch. Rememb. † *Harris' Hibernica*, v. 2, p. 79.

In 1313, the Lord Theobald de Verdon was appointed Justiciary of Ireland,* with a fee of £50 *per annum*, on which occasion he left England, having empowered the Bishop of Bath and Wells to present to all his advowsons in that kingdom. In 1314, he was summoned back to attend, with others, the English Parliament, and treat (as is expressed in the writ) with the King, his prelates, and nobles, about the affairs of Ireland, and other the King's arduous and urgent concerns. About this time it appears he intermarried a second time with Elizabeth, one of the daughters of William, Earl Marshal. She had been first married to De Burgo, Earl of Ulster, and afterwards to the Baron of Fermoy. This connexion was secretly entered into, and induced some Royal jealousy, as appears by a Roll of the English Parliament of 1314. It states that the said Elizabeth de Burgo, one of the sisters of Gilbert de Clare, late Earl of Gloucester, having been summoned over from Ireland on the Royal mandate, and lodged, by the King's order, in the Castle of Bristol, the said Theobald caused her to be carried off from said Castle, and received her outside it, without the Royal licence and in contempt of the King of £1,000. And the said Theobald, in his defence, relied that the said Elizabeth had previously espoused him in Ireland, and that, at his command, she came out of the castle a league's distance, and that he there married her, adding, "that he did not, in any manner, enter the castle, nor believed that he was doing any contempt to the King," but submitted himself to the Royal discretion. Thereupon Roger de Mortimer, of Chirk, and others became securities for his abiding the Royal decision, and he was accordingly released. He appears to have returned, with his co-commissioners, to

---

* *Rot. Pat.* 6 Edw. 2, in Tur. Lond.

Ireland in the spring of that year; and "we find," writes Leland, "Lord Edmund Butler, the Chancellor, and the Treasurer of Ireland, instructed to deliver the result of their deliberation, not only to the prelates, nobles, and magnates, but to the principal chieftains of the Irish race, whom the King directed to give due credence to his commissioners, and assist them in promoting the general interest."

Theobald died at the close of the same year, leaving two daughters—Margery and Isabella—but no issue male.* Whereupon his portion of the de Lacy estate, vested in said daughters that were married to noblemen, who, as Baron Finglas, remarks in his "Breviate," (*temp.* Henry the Eighth) "dwelled in England, and took such profit as they could get for autrell, and sent small defence for their lands in Ireland, so as within few years after all their portions were lost, except certain manors within the English Pale, which Thomas, Baron of Slane, Sir Robert Hollywood, Sir John Cruis, and Sir John Bellew purchased in King Richard the Second's time; and this hath been the decay of half of Meath, which did not obey the King's laws this hundred years and more."

CHAPTER VI.

FROM THE INVASION OF EDWARD BRUCE TO THE TIME OF ARCHBISHOP FITZRALPH.

"In the ninth year of King Edward's reign," writes Hollinshed, "Edward Bruce, brother to Robert Bruce, King of Scots, entered the north part of Ireland, with 6,000 men.

---

* *Rot. Pat.* 2 Edw. 2, in Tur Lond.

There were with him divers captains of high renown among the Scottish nation, of whom were these:—The Earls of Murray* and Monteith, the Lord John Stewart, the Lord John Campbell, the Lord Thomas Randolf, Fergus of Ardrossan, John Wood, and John Bisset. They landed near to Cragfergus, in Ulster, and joining with the Irish (a large force of whom was led out by Fellim, son of Hugh O'Conor). Thus assisted, he conquered the Earldom of Ulster, and gave the English there divers great overthrows, took the town of Dundalk, spoiled and burned it, with a great part of Orgiel. They burned churches and abbeys, with the people whom they found in the same, sparing neither man, woman, nor child. Then was the Lord Butler chosen Lord Justice, who made the Earl of Ulster and the Geraldines friends, and reconciled himself with Sir John Mandeville, thus seeking to preserve the residue of the realm which Edward Bruce meant wholly to conquer, having caused himself to be crowned King of Ireland."

Dundalk was heretofore the stronghold of the English power, and the head-quarters of the army for the defence of the Pale. At the north, as Barbour preserves in his metrical history of Robert Bruce:—

> "At Kilsaggart Sir Edward lay,
> And wellsom he has heard say
> That at Dundalk was assembly
> Made of the lords of that country."

It was not, however, within this town that the ceremony of Bruce's coronation took place, but, according to the best avouched tradition, on the hill of Knock-na-Melin, at half a mile's distance.

* One of the Scottish leaders who commanded at Bannockburn.

Connaught the while was torn with dissensions and family feuds, of which availing himself, "the Lord Justice" (to resume the narrative of Hollinshed) "assembled a great power out of Munster and Leinster, and other parts thereabouts; and the Earl of Ulster, with another army, came in unto him near unto Dundalk. There they consulted together how to deal in defending the country against the enemies; but, hearing the Scots were withdrawn back, the Earl of Ulster followed them, and, fighting with them at 'Coiners,' he lost the field. There were many slain on both parts; and William de Burgh, the earl's brother, Sir John Mandeville, and Sir Alan FitzAlan were taken prisoners." Bruce's adherents afterwards ravaged other parts of the Pale, Meath, Kildare, &c., but met with much resistance. At length "Robert le Bruce, King of Scots, came over himself, landed at Cragfergus, to the aid of his brother, whose soldiers most wickedly entered into churches, spoiling and defacing the same of all such tombs, monuments, plate, copes, and other ornaments which they found and might lay hands on." Ultimately "the Lord John Birmingham, being general of the field, and having with him divers captains of worthy fame, namely—Sir Richard Tuiyte,* Sir Miles Verdon,† Sir John Cusack,‡

---

* Of this renowned Palatine knight, ancestor of the ancient family of Sonnagh, County Westmeath, see *History of Drogheda*, vol. i., p. 92, &c.

† He was another brother of the last-mentioned Nicholas de Verdon, and had, in 1335, a Royal liberate for ten marks on account of his good services in storming the O'Geoghegans and O'Ferrals, felons and enemies, as well as for his loss of horses therein. He was afterwards Governor of the Castle of Trim.

‡ He was of the Cusacks of Gerardstown, and was summoned by the King to attend a great council in Dublin, in 1359, after which he enjoyed other official honours.

Sirs Edmund, and William,* and Walter† Bermingham, the Primate of Armagh, Sir Walter de la Pulle,‡ and John Maupas (with some choice soldiers from Drogheda), led forth the King's power to the number of 1,324 able men, against Edward Bruce, who had, with his adherents (the Lord Philip Moubray, the Lord Walter Soulis, the Lord Allan Stuart, with three brothers, Sir Walter Lacy, Sir Robert and Aumar Lacy, John Kermerelyn, Walter White, and about 3,000 others, writes Pembridge), encamped, not two miles from Dundalk, with 3,000 men, there abiding the Englishmen to fight with them if they came forward, which they did with all convenient speed, being as desirous to give battle as the Scots were to receive it. The Primate of Armagh,§ personally accompanying the English power, and blessing the enterprise, gave them such comfortable exhortation

* This William Bermingham was appointed, in 1325, Constable of the Castle of Roscommon.

† In 1346, King Edward the Third empowered this Walter de Bermingham, being then Lord Justice, to remove such sheriffs, bailiffs, constables, and other Ministers of the Crown whom he found inefficient, and to appoint others in their places; and, likewise, himself to parley and make peace with English and Irish rebels. He also had the custody of all the Crown lands, and of all such estates as had been theretofore forfeited, or might be so, during his Viceroyalty. He had also an allowance for upholding ten men at arms and fifty archers, same to be paid over and above his regular salary.

‡ In a few years after, *he* was constituted the King's escheater, and, in 1346, had a Treasury order for the payment of £20 in aid of his expenses in going to Connaught to take up the lands which had there lately belonged to Richard de Burgo, Earl of Ulster, viz., in the counties of Limerick, Connaught, Tipperary, and Kildare.

§ This prelate, Roland Jorse, affected by the desolation of his province on this incursion of Bruce and his Scots, resigned the Archbishopric in 1321.

as he thought served the time ere they began to encounter, and herewith buckling together, at length the Scots fully and wholly were vanquished, and 2,000 of them slain, together with the Captain, Edward Bruce. Maupas, that pressed into the throng to encounter with Bruce hand to hand, was found, in the search, dead, aloft upon the slain body of Bruce. The victory thus obtained, upon St. Calixtus' day, made an end of the Scottish kingdom in Ireland; and Lord Bermingham, sending the head of Bruce into England, presented it to King Edward, who, in recompense, gave him and his heirs male the Earldom of Louth, and the Baronies of Ardee and Athenry to him and his heirs general for ever," as hereafter noticed.

"Edward Bruce," say the Four Masters, "a man who spoiled Ireland generally, both English and Irish, was slain by the English, by force of battle and bravery, at Dundalk; and MacRory, Lord of the Hebrides, MacDonell, Lord of the Eastern Gael (in Antrim), and many others of the Albanian or Scottish chiefs were also slain; and no event occurred in Ireland for a long period from which so much benefit was derived as that, for a general famine prevailed in the country during the three years and a half he had been in it, and the people were almost reduced to the necessity of eating each other." Edward Bruce was, however, unquestionably a man of great spirit, ambition, and bravery, but fiery, rash, and impetuous, wanting that rare combination of wisdom and valour which so conspicuously marked the character of his illustrious brother.

During the sojourn of Edward Bruce in this kingdom he did much to retard the spread of English rule. Having for allies many of the northern Irish, whose chieftain, O'Neill, invited him to be King over the Gael in Ireland, and whose neighbourhood to the Scottish coast made them regard his followers as their fellow-countrymen, he courted them on all occasions, and thus the Irish customs of gossipred and fostering—preferring the Brehon laws to statute law, whether enacted at Westminster or by the Parliaments of the Pale—destroyed all traces of the rule which the English wished to impose upon the province of Ulster. Many of the English settlers—Hugh de Lacy, John Lord Bissett, Sir Hugh Bissett, and others—openly took part with Bruce.

The eastern shores of Ulster, Spenser informs us, previous to Bruce's arrival, bounded a well-inhabited and prosperous English district, having therein the good towns of Knockfergus, Belfast, Armagh, and Carlingford; but in process of time became "out-bounds and abandoned places in the English Pale." According to the metrical history of Barbour, Edward Bruce was by no means disposed to continue a subject, while his brother reigned King; and, though Robert conferred his hereditary Earldom of Carrick upon him, it by no means satisfied his ambitious projects:—

"The Erle of Carrick, Schyr Eduward,
That stouter was than a libbard,
And had na will to be in pess,
Thoucht that Scotland to litill was
Till his brother and hym alsua,
Therefor to purpose he gav ta
That he of Irland wold be king."

Shortly after his landing at Carrickfergus he proceeded towards the Pale. Dundalk, then the principal garrison within the Pale, had all the Englishry of the country assembled in force to defend it, when the Scots proceeded to the attack, "with banners all displayit." The English sent out a reconnoitering party, who brought back the cheering news, the Scots would be but "half a dinner" to them. This dinner, however, was never eaten. The town was stormed with such vigour that the streets flowed with the blood of the defenders; and such as could escape fled with the utmost precipitancy, leaving their foes profusion of victuals and great abundance of wine. This assault took place 29th June, 1315.* It was upon this success the Scots crowned Edward Bruce King of Ireland, on the hill of Knocknamelan, near Dundalk, in the same simple national manner in which his brother had been inaugurated at Scone.†

The new monarch, however, was not disposed to rest inactive, and his troops had many skirmishes with Richard de Burgh, called the Red Earl of Ulster, who drove them as far as Coleraine. There they were in great distress; and they would have suffered much from hunger and want had not a famous pirate, Thomas of Down, or Thomas Don, sailed up the Bann and set them free. De Burgh's army were supplied with provisions from a distance; and one of Bruce's famous leaders, named Randolph, Earl of Murray, who commanded the left wing at Bannockburn, having surprised the convoy on its way to De Burgh's camp, equipped his men in the clothes of the escort, advanced at dusk with his cavalry, and the banner of the English flaunting in the night wind. A large party of De Burgh's force, perceiving, as they thought, the approach of the expected provisions, advanced unguardedly to drive off the cattle, when they were vigorously assailed by the Scots, shouting their war-cry, and they were chased back with the loss of a thousand slain.‡ De Burgh's army included all the chivalry of Ireland—that is, the English

* Grace's *Annals*. † *Ulster Jour. of Arch.*, vol. v., p. 8.

‡ *Vide* the valuable papers on "The Bruces in Ireland," *Ulster Arch. Jour.*, vol. v. p. 10.

portion, viz.:—"The Butlers, earls two, of Kildare and Desmond; Byrnhame (Bermingham), Widdan (Verdon), and FitzWaryne, and Schyr Paschall off Florentyne, a Knight of Lombardy; with the Mandvillas, Bissetts, Logans, Savages, and Schyr Nycholl off Kilkenave." *The Ulster Journal* thinks this list of Barbour's incorrect; certainly Sir Edmond Butler was not among them, nor probably either of the Geraldine lords. Some lords of Munster, however, were present—Power, Baron of Donisle; Sir George Lord Roche, and Sir Roger Hollywood, of county Meath.

On the 10th September, A.D. 1315, De Burgh, being reinforced, marched to attack Bruce's position; but the Scots, leaving their banners flying to deceive the Anglo-Irish, fell upon their flank and gained the victory. This gave them Coleraine; and next day they bore off a great store of corn, flour, wax, and wine, to Carrickfergus.

This success gave to the Gael of the north an opportunity of declaring their exultation. Bruce, whose royal authority was previously confined to his Scottish troops, was proclaimed King of Ireland, and addressed as such.

He then sent the Earl of Murray to Edinburgh, where the King of Scotland kept his court, entreating him to join him in Ireland.

> "For war thai both in to that land
> Thai suld find nane culd thaim withstand."

Robert gladly promised compliance, but was for some time prevented by the exigencies of his own kingdom. Murray*

---

*The title seems diversely written—Murrray and Moray. *Vide* the *Ulster Arch. Journal*, vol. v., "The Bruces in Ireland," from which these details are extracted.

returned with a small reinforcement, but 500 men, and landed at Dundalk, where Edward Bruce met him. This was in the December of 1315.

In January, 1316, Edward Bruce led his forces into the county of Kildare, and was stoutly opposed by the Lord Justiciary, or Viceroy, Sir Edward Butler, who, backed by the Geraldines, under John Fitzgerald, first Earl of Kildare, bravely repulsed the invaders. They retreated with the loss of Sir Walter Murray and Sir Fergus of Ardrossan, with seventy men, as Clyn records. A new ally for the Palesmen arrived at this juncture—Mortimer, Lord of Meath, in right of his wife, Joan de Joinville. He assembled a large force, and endeavoured to intercept the Scots at Kells, but, on the eve of the onset, was deserted by the Lacys and others, who left him almost defenceless. The season and scarcity made war against the Scots, and vast numbers perished from hunger. Bruce was forced to retreat once more northward, where his chief adherents lay. The citadel of Carrickfergus resisted the attacks of Bruce's army for a year. It was in this town that (probably in September, 1316*) Robert, King of Scotland, with a strong force, came to his brother's help. Barbour gives the number who accompanied Robert at 5,000. This was enough to make the Viceroy take heed for his government. He hasted, Barbour says:—

"To Dewellyne, in full gret hy,
With othyr lordis that fled him by,
And warnysit both castyls and towness
That war in their possessionnys."

The stout defence of Dublin is already mentioned; and, as on the fate of this metropolis the duration of English rule

* Grace's *Annals*.

depended in Ireland, the public spirit and intrepidity of the citizens of Dublin ought, according to Lord Hailes, be held in perpetual remembrance.* The citizens took the defence of the city into their own hands. The chief civic dignity was at that time most worthily borne by Robert Nottingham, who seems to have distanced the celebrated Sir Richard Whittington considerably, being *seventeen times* Mayor of Dublin.† Knowing the close connexion between the Earl of Ulster and the Bruces (he was father of the Queen of Scots), the Mayor headed a strong band of citizens, and resolved to make him a hostage for the safety of the city. This was not effected without loss of life. The Mayor succeeded, and announced "he would put the earl to death if the city was attacked." This prompt step had the desired effect. Robert Bruce feared to risk his father-in-law's life, and, instead of entering the city, turned aside and encamped. Time was gained, of which the citizens promptly availed themselves. That night the blazing suburbs told they were ready to anticipate the fire of Moscow, rather than allow their invaders to possess their capital. They also worked so hard to strengthen the walls that the Scots, seeing such determination, broke up their camp and retired. The value set upon the earl as a hostage was so great that, although the King of England instantly wrote for his liberation, he was detained until the Scots left the kingdom.

Disappointed in their efforts on Dublin, the Scots ravaged the Pale, burned Naas, plundered Castledermot, passed on to Gowran, and advanced to Callan; thence they went to Limerick. Sir Edmond Butler followed with an army of

---

* *Hist. of Scotland*, by Lord Hailes.

† Grace's *Annals*, edited by Dean Butler, p. 78.

30,000 well-armed men; but, at the express desire of Roger Mortimer, Earl of March, the Lord Deputy, who was himself desirous of having the command against the King of Scots, delayed the encounter.

Mortimer did not accomplish this; for, shortly after, Robert hastened to his own kingdom, leaving a great number of his bravest knights to carry on the war for his brother. Edward continued in the north for several months, and once more proceeded south.

> "For he had not then in that land
> Of all men, I trow, two thousand,
> Owtane (except) the Kings of Irischery
> That in great route raid him by,
> Towart Dundalk he tuk the way."

When the Viceroy was aware of the advance of the Scots towards the Pale he assembled a great army, said to amount to "20,000 trappit horse," and an equal number of foot.

The approach of this immensely superior force did not dishearten the brother of the lion-hearted King of Scotland. He declared he would fight were they sixfold more numerous.

In vain his officers and allies counselled caution; in vain the Irish chiefs recommended him to avoid a pitched battle, and harass the enemy by skirmishing. Edward indignantly bade them "draw aside, and look on," which Barbour declares they did. A very interesting account of the battle on St. Callistus' day is given in the *Ulster Archæological Journal.** The battle was on Sunday, 14th October, 1318. According to Barbour, Edward Bruce had a presentiment of his death, and would not use his usual coat-armour. The legend is, that having the idea the fall of King Edward Bruce would decide

* Vol. vi, p. 69.

the battle, Sir John Bermingham, leader of the Anglo-Irish army, disguised himself as a friar, passed into the Scottish camp, and, being shown the king, who was hearing Mass, craved alms, so as to induce Bruce to look up from his prayer-book. This gave Bermingham the opportunity of marking well his face, in order to single him out in the fray. The king ordered relief to be given to the importunate friar; but the eager glance of the intrusive applicant so disquieted him—agitated, doubtless, from the idea of his small force being about to engage at such desperate odds—that he presently caused the attendants to look for the friar, but he was nowhere to be found. This caused him to array one Gib Harper in his armour, and appoint Lord Alan Stewart general of the field. The fight commenced with a rapid charge on the Scots by the Anglo-Irish under Bermingham. With him were divers lords and a great army. The force was chiefly composed, however, of yeomanry, or, as an ancient record says, "the common people, with a powerful auxiliary *dextram Dei*." Bermingham, believing Lord Stewart was Bruce, singled him out, and, after a terrible combat, slew him, whereon the Scots fled. According to the *Howth Chronicle*, few escaped, their loss being 1,230 men. Bruce's death is generally ascribed to John Mapas, one of the Drogheda contingent. The *Ulster Journal* states:—"There can be little doubt that the ancient Anglo-Irish family of 'Mape,' of Maperath, in the shire of Meath, was descended from this distinguished slayer of Edward Bruce." The heiress of John Mapas, Esq., of Rochestown, county of Dublin, was married to the late Richard Wogan Talbot, Esq., of Malahide. After the defeat at Dundalk, the small remnant of the Scottish invaders yet alive fled northward, where they met a body of troops sent by King Robert as a reinforcement to his brother. They could not make head against the victorious troops of Bermingham, so they made their way to the coast, burning and destroying the country through which they passed.

The note to the interesting series from which we have so largely quoted, mentions that several branches of a family lineally descended from King Robert Bruce still exist in the north of Ireland; and that the Rev. William Bruce, of Belfast, is the present representative of the family.

Amongst those whose services on this occasion were rewarded by Royal patents were John Gernon, ancestor of a most distinguished family in Louth, to whom the King granted the whole fishery from Gernonstown to the sea, for the term of his life, at the annual rent of one mark.* Roger Gernon, who had a grant in fee of the castle and manor of Taghobrecock, which, as the writ recites, had been the estate of Hugh de Lacy, but escheated to the Crown by reason of his adherence to Bruce.† Richard le Waleys, who, for "his services in leading an armed band against the Scots, at Louth, Skerries, &c., and against the Irish in sundry parts, had an order for £255, in which the Abbot and Convent of Inchelaunagh were indebted to the merchants of the Society of the Ricordi of Lucca, and which had come to the Crown in right of debts due to the King by said merchants;"‡ while Winton de Rosponte had a liberate for certain quantities of "wine supplied by him for the armies engaged to oppose Bruce."§ The Royal Letters Patent for John de Bermingham bear date the 12th July, 1319; and therein, after reciting that the King

---

* *Rot. Pat.*, 14 Edw. 2, in *Canc. Hib.*

† *Rot. Pat.*, 13 Edw. 2, in *Canc. Hib.*

‡ *Rot. Pat.*, 11 Edw. 2, in *Canc. Hib.*

§ *Rot Claus.*, 18 Edw. 2, in *Canc. Hib.*

had, in his Parliament of York, granted to him, on account of his achievements against Edward Bruce, and to his heirs male, the annual sum of £20, out of the issues of the County Louth, under the name and honour of Earl of Louth; and that he had promoted said John to the said Earldom of Louth; these letters further witnessed that his Majesty further granted him the residue of the issues of said county, with the whole county itself, and the office of sheriff of the same, and all things thereto appertaining, and the liberty of said county, to have and to hold for the term of his life, with the knight's fees, advowsons of churches, chapels, abbeys, priories, hospitals, and other religious houses in said counties, and all liberties thereto appertaining in as full a manner as Thomas, Earl of Kildare, holds said County of Kildare, excepting only pleas of rape, offences on the highway, arson, and treasure-trove; and the town of Drogheda, with its appurtenances, and excepting the homage and services of the King's nephews and nieces, and excepting all cross-lands, as in other counties, with reversion to the Crown on the decease of said John de Bermingham.*

In 1320, Nicholas de Verdon succeeded to the honours and possessions of his brother Theobald; and in 1324 he sat in right thereof in a Parliament at Dublin.† About this time Niall O'Hanlon, Lord of Orier, came to levy a tribute at Dundalk, but he was warmly opposed by Robert de Verdon, then Governor of that town. Two hundred of his followers were left dead on the field, and himself, of whom the Four Masters give no favourable account, was, as they express it, "treacherously slain by the English of Dundalk." The

* *Rot. Pat.*, 12 Edw. 2, in Tur. Lond.

† *Roll* Ch. Rememb. Off., 18 Edw. 2.

Masters relate that in 1327 "the small-pox raged through Ireland, of which great numbers died." The annals of this county are, in 1329, stained by the massacre of the aforesaid Earl of Louth. He was, as Sir John Davis remarks, "so extremely envied by the Gernons, Verdons, and others of the ancient colony planted in the County of Louth, as that in this year they did most wickedly betray and murder that earl, with divers principal gentlemen of that name and family, using the same speech that the rebellious Jews are said to use in the Gospel:—"Nolumus hunc regnare super nos."* This atrocious treachery took place at Ballybragan, in this county, on the vigil of St. Barnaby. Sir Richard Talbot, of Malahide, was then in the suite of de Bermingham, and was slain with him. The Four Masters record the event with sympathy:—"Sir John Bermingham, Earl of Louth, the most valiant, powerful, and hospitable baron of the English of Ireland, was treacherously slain by his own people, the English of Oriel (Louth). Many of the English and Irish along with him were also slain, among whom was the blind O'Carrol, that is Mulrooney, who was the chief minstrel of Ireland and Scotland in his time. . . . Awful thunder and lightning," they add, "occurred in the summer of this year, by which the vegetation and fruit of Ireland were extensively destroyed, and the corn blighted, and an epidemic disease prevailed throughout the country, called 'Ilasdan' (a cough or influenza), which continued in every person seized by it for three or four days, and proved almost fatal to them."

In 1333, at a place called the "Fords," near Carrickfergus, another barbarous murder was perpetrated on the young Earl of Ulster, then aged but twenty-one years. It was the result

---

* *Davis's Hist. Rel.*, p. 66.

of some family feuds, and was perpetrated by his own people, headed by Sir John Mandeville, who was married to a relative of the Earl. De Burgo was married to Maud, daughter of Henry Plantagenet, Earl of Lancaster, grandson of Henry the Third, and by her he had a daughter, Elizabeth, who was married to Lionel, Duke of Clarence, son of King Edward the Third, who, in right of his wife, was created Earl of Ulster and Lord of Connaught, and hence the title of Earl of Ulster has been since that time retained in the Royal family of England. "The English who perpetrated that deed," say the Masters, "were put to death in an extraordinary manner by the people of the King of England. Some of them were hanged, others were slain, and some were torn asunder to avenge his death."

In 1333, the Lord de Verdon was one of those who engaged himself and his estate as surety for the future fealty of the Earl of Desmond. In five years after the King commissioned Roger Gernon, junior, William Dowdall, and others, to hold an inquiry, on oath, as to who had been guilty of violating a treaty of peace which had been theretofore agreed upon between the King and his lieges of Louth of the one part, and Donald O'Hanlon and those of his name and sept of the other.* This necessity, probably, arising from the event before alluded to.

In 1338 the Lord Theobald de Verdon obtained a license for holding a Monday market and an annual fair at Dundalk; the latter to continue for fifteen days, viz.:—the eve, day, and morrow of St. Martin the Bishop, and twelve succeeding days.

In 1343 the Provost and Bailiffs of this town were commanded by ordinance of the English Privy Council to make

* *Rot. Pat.*, 11 Edw. 3, in *Canc. Hib.*

proclamation that none of the King's Ministers, nor any prelate, or earl, or any other person, regular or secular, save merchants and their servants, should go out of their port without the King's special mandate, and that the ships and mariners of any offending therein should be forthwith arrested.

In 1345 the King appointed James de Audeley, Dowdall, and others Commissioners for inquiring on oath whether it was advantageous for the King and the people of Dundalk that Awley and Peter O'Rogan, Irishmen, should, with their *suite*, be taken into the King's peace, and permitted to sojourn amongst the Englishmen there; and, if so, to take sufficient security from said Awley and Peter, and then to cause proclamation to be made that none should injure or molest them while they continued liege and faithful.* Four years after, "a great plague raged in Ireland." About this time Richard FitzRalph, a native of this town, and hence frequently styled Richard of Dundalk, succeeded to the Primacy of Armagh. He was strenuously opposed to the Order of Mendicant Friars, whom his predecessor, Maolpatrick O'Scannail, first introduced in Armagh, "surrounding their church with a broad and deep ditch." FitzRalph's animosity, Wadding, in his *Annals of the Franciscans*, attributes to his having been defeated in an attempt which he made to convert the ornaments of a friary in Drogheda to his own use in his own palace. A long controversy ensued; and, in its support, he preached many sermons here and at Drogheda, copies of which are said, by Ware, to be extant in his day. He was ultimately silenced by the Pope, who authoritatively maintained the rights of the friars in relation to preaching, confession, and sepulture. Immediately after—and, it would seem, affected by this

* *Rot. Pat.*, 19 and 20 Edw. 3, in *Canc. Hib.*

denunciation of his conduct—he died on the Continent, whence, according to Ware, his bones were, in 1370, translated by Stephen de Valle, Bishop of Meath, to Dundalk. Camden, nevertheless, says he was originally buried in this town, and that his monument was effaced about his time.

By an entry in Birmingham Tower, 1350, the Provost, Bailiffs, and Commonalty of this town were entitled to have murage and paveage, tolls of things coming for sale thereto, provided always that the moneys thence arising should be expended on the enclosing and paving of this town, and not to any other purpose; and the Chancellor was directed to cause letters patent to be made out for the same, to endure for six years; and, in some years later, the bailiffs of the town were ordered to make proclamation that no one (knights and their squires excepted) should presume to carry swords, lances, or other arms within said town.

In 1355, in consequence, it would seem, of existing scarcity, the wisdom of King Edward's Irish Government prohibited the exportation of corn or fish out of any of the harbours of Ireland, from Dundalk to Holmpatrick inclusive,* an interdict which was enforced within six weeks after by the seizure of three vessels loaded for exportation within the harbour of Drogheda.† In the following year, intimation having been received that Hugh O'Neill of Ulster was about to come to Dundalk or Louth (the Four Masters represent him at this time engaged in feuds with the inhabitants of Monaghan, Armagh, and Fermanagh), with a great army of Irishmen, on the professed object of parleying with the English; and it being apprehended that, as the Deputy was engaged in defending the Southern Marches against the O'Byrnes, O'Neill

---

* *Rot. Pat.*, 29 Edw. 3, in *Canc. Hib.* † *Id*

might act hostilely if he was not opportunely met, Richard, Archbishop of Armagh (the aforesaid FitzRalph), then engaged on a visitation of his province, was directed to meet him here and parley with him regarding his designs; and the Bishop of Meath and his clergy were ordered, under pain of forfeiture, to admit the said Archbishop to resume his visitation where he had left off.*

The first formal charter of this town—that of Richard the Second—was granted about this time. It is enrolled on the Rolls of Parliament, 8 and 9 Henry the Eighth, 7 James the First, and 2 Charles the First, but its own date does not appear. By it, however, the King confirmed to the burgesses of Dundalk that their town should be a free borough for ever—the burgesses to have a guild merchant, with house and other liberties pertaining to such guild; no one not of the guild to be a merchant unless with the consent of the burgesses. He granted them to have sak, soch, toll, theam, and infangthef; to be free from toll, lastage, passage, pontage, and tollage, through all the King's dominions; to be tried for murder only within the franchises; to be free from duel on any appeal; to clear themselves from pleas of the Crown according to the custom of Dublin; no one to hold a lodging there by force; to hold lands, &c., according to the custom of the borough or of Dublin; to plead in Dundalk for all debts contracted there; to have free ingress and egress to and from the port of Dundalk with their merchandize; to hold a hundred at Dundalk once every fortnight; and no burgess should be fined in the hundred beyond twelve pence; to elect whomsoever they pleased provosts annually; the common council of the borough to elect two of the more lawful and discreet men thereof

* *Rot. Claus.*, 29 and 30 Edw. 3, in *Canc. Hib.*

to hold the assizes in the presence of the King's justices when they came to Dundalk, and to keep the pleas of the Crown, and to see that the provosts do justice to rich and poor; that no one take anything of them by loan or force without the consent of the burgesses; to bestow in marriage their daughters and widows according to their own pleasure; that King's justices, bailiffs, or officers, should not act in the town; to elect a seneschal from among themselves, who should see that the provost and other bailiffs of the town do justice to the poor as well as to the rich; that no foreign merchant should remain in the town more than forty days; that no burgess be compelled to replevin unless with his own consent; that no burgess within the borough answer for any plea unless for writ of right for any tenements within the franchises; that no merchandize be prevented from being brought into the town; that prise of wine be not taken except for that brought to sale; that if a burgess be attached beyond the franchises the seneschal and burgesses are to hold their court on him, and to administer justice as any lord of Ireland holds his court over his own men; also, to hold an annual fair for fifteen days from the Monday next after the Feast of Saints Philip and James, and fourteen days following.

CHAPTER VII.

FROM THE TIME OF ARCHBISHOP FITZRALPH TO THE REIGN OF HENRY VI.

BY inquisition of 1359, Elizabeth, wife of Bartholomew de Burgersh, was found seised of Dundugan, Ballybalrick, the manor of Dundalk, &c.;* and, about the same time, another

* *Inquis.*, 34 Edw. 3, in Tur. Lond.

more powerful Elizabeth, she whose marriage at Bristol, to Theobald de Verdon, has been before alluded to (*ante* p. 45), was found to have been seised of divers manors in Lincoln, Dorset, Warwick, Leicester, Hertford, Essex, Norfolk, Suffolk, Wilts, Bucks, and Shrop-shires, and on the Marches of Wales.*

In 1372, the King conveyed, in manner of a pledge, to Stephen Fleming the manor of Duleek, &c., and a certain portion of the customs and services, as well of the free tenants, as of the Irish, to the said manor appertaining; likewise, a portion of the manor of Lough Suidy, two hundred acres in "le Rothe," and the customs and free services of the free tenants and Irish of the towns of Dunboyne, Kene, Gormanston, Ballygarth, &c.; and seven marks' rent in Dundalk, together with the lordship and service of all the King's tenants there, and also the advowsons of the vicarages of Dundalk and Cooley, to secure a debt due by the Crown to him. In 1374, King Edward directed a special summons to Richard de Verdon to attend a Parliament in Dublin, on which occasion were also summoned the Primate and prelates of Ireland, the mitred abbots, various earls, Robert de la Freigne (French), knight; Richard de Burgo, knight; Thomas Tuit, knight; Thomas Talbot, knight; Roger Gernon, Richard and John Taaffe, Richard Plunket, John Hussie, Baron of Galtrim; John Bedlowe (Bellew), William Wellesley, Robert de Preston, knight, and the sheriffs of the then recognised counties. And the seneschals of liberties were directed to cause two persons within their respective districts to be elected to attend said Parliament.† In the following year, in conse-

* *Inquis.*, 34 Edw. 3, in Tur. Lond.

† *Rot. Claus.*, 48 Edw 3, in *Canc. Hib.*

quence of existing scarcity, overseers were specially nominated to prevent the exportation of grain from the harbour of Dundalk, and to seize upon any ships and their cargoes that should be freighted contrary thereto.* Some special dispensations to this interdict are preserved in the Chancery Rolls, while John Keppock was appointed to enquire into certain extortions and grievances affecting said restraint on commerce within this county.†

In the same year (1375) the King granted to James Bellew one carucate and a-half of land in the County of Louth, which had been the property of the Abbot and Convent of "Nynore"—and likewise one carucate on the Curragh, near Dundalk, which had been the property of the Abbot and Convent of Armagh, and which had come to the King's hands by reason that the said abbots and their fraternities were mere Irish, and of Irish intercourse; the said James Bellew to hold same for the term of his life, if they should be so long in the King's hands, at the yearly rent of forty shillings.‡ William Spalding was further ordered at this time to watch over the harbours and maritime places in the County Louth, lest any merchants or sailors should go out of Ireland, or export wool or hides without paying custom, and to arrest any offenders therein, with their ships; and likewise to arrest and punish any persons selling or supplying horses, armour, iron, gold, silver, corn, or other provisions to the King's enemies.§

In this year King Edward issued the remarkable summons by which he hoped to assemble an Irish Parliament at

---

* *Rot. Claus.*, 49 Edw. 3.

† *Rot. Pat.*, 49 Edw. 3, in *Canc. Hib.*

‡ *Id.* § *Id.*

Westminster. The sheriff of this county was, amongst others, commanded to return two members to meet the King in his Parliament of England; and thereupon the Magnates and Commons of Louth being assembled, "with their common consent and with one voice alleged, that according to the right, privileges, liberties, laws, and customs of the land of Ireland, used since the conquest of the same and before, they are not obliged to choose or send any persons from the same land to the Parliaments or Councils to be held in England, to treat, advise, and agree, as said writ requires; nevertheless, out of reverence to our Lord the King of England, and on account of the very pressing necessity of said land, their said rights, privileges, &c., being saved, they grant unto Roger Gernon and Richard Verdon, chosen by themselves, full power to transport themselves to the parts of England, there to appear before our Lord the King, to treat, advise, and agree about the safety, defence, and good government of said land, excepting, nevertheless, that they do not give unto the aforesaid Roger and Richard, power of granting any other burdens or subsidies, to be imposed on them for the present, on account of the poverty of said community, and the great and daily expenses they are at in feeding men-at-arms, light horse, &c., for the defence of the Marches of said county, against the more potent Irish, enemies to Ireland, and rebels to our Lord the King.

In 1377 William Fowler, being Prior of the House of St. Leonard, of Dundalk, was joint obligor in a recognizance to the Bishop of Meath with John and Richard Dovedale (Dowdall), of a family early settled in this county. In 1380 the Sheriff of Louth was ordered to enlarge Richard de Verdon, who had been committed to gaol on a plea of debt, at the suit of Thomas, the Abbot of St. Thomas the Martyr, near

Dublin.* In the same year Peter de Howth, who had married Matilda, daughter and co-heiress of Sir Thomas de Verdon, and for whose lands he then did homage and fealty to the King, was ordered to be put in possession thereof, same having been theretofore held of the Crown *in capite* by her father.† In 1380 Edmund Mortimer, Earl of March and Ulster, who was married to Philippa, daughter of Lionel Duke of Clarence, one of the sons of Edward the Third, "came to Ireland, with sovereign power, as Lord Justice; and the Irish nobility, with the heir-presumptive to the throne of Ireland," write the Four Masters, "waited on him—namely, Niall O'Neill (of Tyrone); O'Hanlon (of Armagh); O'Ferrall (of Longford); O'Reilly (of Cavan); MacGeoghegan, and the Sionach (Fox of Westmeath), with other chiefs." Such was the loyalty and ardour of the whole country for an immediate scion of their legitimate King. Yet, soon after his arrival, this representative of Edward the Third "marched with an army into Ulster, where he destroyed many fortresses and towns on his expedition, together with the churches and country," soon after which he died. In two years afterwards Niall O'Neill, exasperated by the conduct of the English in the north, gathered around him his sons and the chiefs of Tyrone, "marched with a great force into Trian-Congail to attack the English, and they completely plundered and burned many of their towns. The English of the district collected together to oppose them; and Hugh O'Neill and Raibelin Savage having encountered each other in a charge of their cavalry, they pierced each other's bodies with two violent thrusts of their spears. Raibelin returned to his horse desperately wounded, where he was

---

* *Rot. Claus.*, 4 Ric. 2, in *Canc. Hib.*

† *D'Alton's Hist. Co Dublin*, p. 160.

again attacked and killed by the son of John Bisset; and Hugh O'Neill died on the third day from the effects of his wounds; and the son of John Bisset was slain by Raibelin's people three days after Raibelin himself was killed."* Carrickfergus was immediately after "burnt by Niall O'Neill, who gained great power over the English."† He was at this time the liberal founder of "a house of general entertainment and support, at Armagh, for the learned men of Ireland."‡

In 1352 license was granted to Henry Tikill to buy certain quantities of corn and meal in the counties of Dublin, Louth, &c., and to transport same to certain ports of Ulster.§ Thomas Chambre had also, at the same time, leave to export flour, meal, and corn, from this county to Ulster or to Carlingford.‖

In 1383 proceedings were taken against the Bailiffs of Dundalk, for that John Druming and other alien merchants who visited the town were disturbed by them, and prevented from selling or cutting their cloth, &c., to the great damage of the people adjacent. The defendants pleaded, amongst other things, that, from time immemorial, no strange merchant nor any other, except the burgesses of said town, in said town dwelling—"præter mercatores qui fuerunt burgeses dictæ villæ et in eâdem villâ commorantes"—could buy or sell by retail there any cloths, wines, salt, or other merchandize, without licence of the Bailiffs; and that those offending therein were attached by the Bailiffs. Whereupon a jury being summoned, verdict was found according to the plea, and judgment given for the defendants.¶

---

* *Annals Four Masters.* † *Id.* ‡ *Id.*

§ *Rot. Pat.*, 5 Ric. 2, *C. H.* ‖ *Id.*

¶ *Roll* in Ch. Rem. Office.

In 1386, William Spalding, then Admiral in certain harbours of Ireland, was commanded to proclaim in those of Uriel, Meath, &c., that none should export grain or fish to foreign parts without the King's licence.* William Byfeild had, in the following year, a similar mandate;† while William De Everdon was authorised to transport certain quantities of corn to Waterford, from the harbours of this county;‡ and purveyors were appointed to provide for the Viceroy, who, with some of his Privy Council, was desirous, in the performance of official duties, to visit Dundalk and Carlingford—at which period Cônor, son of Bryan Carach O'Neill, was slain by the English of this town. The law of Sanctuary was curiously illustrated in connexion with Dundalk in this year. One Nicholas Burgess having sued out a pardon from the Crown for sundry felonies, conspiracies, and combinations by him committed; and likewise for this, that, having previously fled for sanctuary to the Carmelite friary of Drogheda, he there, before the Coroner of said town, made confession of his having feloniously slain Thomas Melaghlin, at Ardee; and having abjured the realm, he was directed to depart therefrom at the harbour of Dundalk; but had not done so. This, his pardon, however, extended to a remission of the last offence also; and he was restored as a liege man to the liberty of the law of the land. It may well be suspected from the name of the victim that, as *he* was but an Irishman, the offender obtained more indulgence from the English law as then administered.

In 1392 the chieftain beforementioned—"Niall O'Neill, King of Tyrone—accompanied by the chiefs of the province,

---

* *Rot. Pat.*, 9 Ric. 2.

† *Rot. Pat.*, 10 Ric. 2, *C. H.* ‡ *Id.*

marched with a great force against the English at Traghbally and Dundalk, whom he brought under subjection on that occasion; and Seffin White fell by him in the conflict." Afterwards (add the Masters) with the sons of Henry O'Neill and all the Ultenians, he marched with a great force into Tyrconnell, against Turlough O'Donnell, whose people fled with their cattle before him into the fastnesses and inaccessible parts. Niall died in five years after, and the feuds of these two great septs was soon after determined.

In 1394 John Clifford, Deputy Constable of the Castle of Dublin, had a Treasury Order for £11 12s. by reason of his expense, in keeping and maintaining Bernard O'Neill, a hostage of The O'Neill, whom he had for some time in his charge in said castle; and for the conducting of said Bernard and others of his suite at Trim, Drogheda, Ardee, and Dundalk; and likewise for conveying seven other hostages of The O'Neill and their guards for safe conduct from Dundalk to the Castle of Dublin.*

Here the great chieftain of the North was received by no less a personage than the King of England, Richard the Second, who came into Ireland determined to win over the native princes by his gifts and honours. The account of the visit by Froissart† relates, with all his picturesque details, how this Monarch, in 1394, endeavoured to put an end to the war which lasted, between the Irish and English, for two centuries, and entertained and knighted the four native Irish kings; but makes such grotesque changes in the names, that it is not easy to discover who they were. For instance:—1st. "Le Grand Anel (O'Neal), Roy de Methe;" this clearly is a

---

* *Rot. Claus.*, 17 Ric. 11, in *Canc. Hib.*

† *Livre* iv., chap. 42.

GIANTS LOAD, CROMLECH

mistake—should be, *Ultonæ* or Ulster; 2nd. "Brin (O'Brien), Roy de Thomond;" 3rd. "Artus Maquemaire, Roy de Linstre," for Arthur MacMurrough, King of Leinster; and 4th. "Connor, Roy de Chenour (Connaught) et d'Erpe"—doubtless Eyre-Connaught.

The good offices of the King were not productive of much result. The presence of the Sovereign was no sooner removed than matters returned to their former footing.

This unhappy English Monarch visited Ireland a second time in 1399.* He did not remain long absent; his subjects in England evincing dispositions of rebellion. Had he been aware of the cruel fate in store for him, he would, doubtless, have been in no hurry to leave the Irish coast. He had scarcely landed in England before he was made prisoner by his traitorous subjects, confined in Pomfret Castle, and brutally murdered in February, 1400.

A branch of the White family, settled in this locality, had been seised of considerable estates, including the spacious and boldly situated Castle of Roch; but having remained faithful to Richard II., they were deprived of their possessions; and, in 1403, the manor of Roch was granted, by Henry the Fourth to John Bellew, *Chivaler*, from whom the present Lord Bellew, of Barmeath, is descended.†

In 1395 a royal mandate directed the Sheriff of Louth and the Guardians of the Peace (the Magistrates) throughout that country to attend to enforcing an existing ordinance against selling grain to any Irishman not dwelling amongst English liege subjects.‡ Four years after, "the sons of

* For an account of this visit, *vid. Harris's Hib.*

† See the elaborate account of this family in *D'Alton's Hist. Drogheda*, vol. ii., p. 162.

‡ *Rot. Claus.*, 18 Ric. 2.

Henry O'Neill having gone to attack the English of Traghbally (Dundalk), the English collected their forces to oppose them; and Donal, the son of Henry was taken prisoner, and a great many of his people were slain. Donal was sent to England the year following, after his release had been refused."* Henry the Fourth appointed Adam Herward; Thomas Gernon, of Dunmaghan; Roger Ball; John Ellis, of Dundalk; Reginald Taylour; Henry White; and Walter Alger, to collect over the barony of Dundalk its proportion of a subsidy which the Commons of the county of Uriel had made, to the extent of 10s. off every carucate of land within said county, in aid of resisting Nelan O'Neill, Captain of the Irish, and in maintaining horse and foot in the marches of said county.† Soon afterwards, John Ellis, of Reynoldston, and John White, of Renagh, were commissioned to purvey flour and oats within this barony; while the clergy of the diocese of Armagh having granted to Thomas de Lancaster, the Deputy, an assessment on their benefices in aid of the Irish wars, Thomas Hadser, Vicar of Stabannon, and John Galgan, Vicar of Dromyn, were appointed to assess same within the Deanery of Dundalk.

The commencement of the fifteenth century was disgraced by another act of atrocious murder amongst the English party. In 1402, writes Marleburgh, "While a Parliament was being held in Dublin, Sir Bartholomew Verdon, Knight, James White, Stephen Gernon, and their 'complices, slew John Dowdall, Sheriff of Louth."

By patent of 1403, the King granted to John More, then Constable of Carlingford and Greencastle, the manor of

---

* *Annals of the Four Masters.*

† *Rot. Pat.* 1 Henry 4, in *Canc. Hib.*

Raskeagh, in the marches of Dundalk, near O'Neill, Magennis, and O'Hanlon, Irish enemies, and entirely wasted; but which had vested in the Crown by reason of the forfeiture of Reginald Hudson; to hold same, subject to the render of one sparrow-hawk in each year in full of all services.* A more extensive royal grant was at the same time made to John D'Arcy, in tail male, of the manors of Mandevelleston and Staunton, one messuage and sixty acres in Reynoldston, and six messuages and fifty acres in the town of Louth, which had belonged to Bartholomew de Verdon, Knight, but were likewise forfeited to the King; the manor of Philipstown, in said county, formerly belonging to Christopher White, attainted; and six burgages and forty acres of land in Dundalk, which had belonged to the aforesaid Christopher, and were in like manner forfeited; to hold of the King for ever by services and customs.† Henry Houth, Prior of the House of St. Leonard's, here obtained a license in this year to pass over into England without incurring the statutable forfeiture of the revenue of his benefice during the interval.‡

In 1407, Thomas Stanyhurst, "on account of his immense labours," had a grant from the Crown of one messuage and sixty acres of land in the Curragh, near Dundalk, and of other premises in Dundalk, which had come to the Crown by forfeiture;§ and the King at the same time confirmed to John Bellew, Knight, six messuages, four carucates of land in Baronstown and Verdonstown, near the Roche, and one-fourth of the manor of Dundalk and of the manor of Roche.‖

* *Rot. Pat.*, 1 Henry 4, in *Canc. Hib.*

† *Rot. Pat.*, 4 Henry 4, in *Canc. Hib.*

‡ *Id.* § *Id.* 8 Henry 4. ‖ *Id.*

This Sir John Bellew claimed to be also entitled, in right of his wife, to the advowson of the vicarage of Dundalk.*

The year 1412 was a sad year for the whole province of Ulster. The wars and insurrectionary movement of the sons of Henry O'Neill have been before alluded to. One of these, Hugh, had been held in custody in the Castle of Dublin for ten years, whence in this he "made his escape, and brought several other prisoners along with him; among whom were the son of Maguire (of Fermanagh) and the son of O'Neill—namely, his own brother's son; and it was on O'Neill's account he became a hostage. After his escape the entire province was much disturbed, the English demanding O'Neill to he delivered to them by Owen O'Neill, O'Donnell, Maguire, and the Orgiallians.†

In 1412, King Henry the Fourth assigned to Philip Kylberry, in consideration of his services, an annuity of ten marks, which the bailiffs and burgesses of this town were bound to pay to the Crown, to hold same for two years without rent‡ (a grant which Henry the Fifth assigned as for the payment of a royal debt to John Kirkham). And in the same year (1412), by patent, reciting that the bailiffs and commons of Dundalk, which is situated on the north border of the marches, near the Irish enemy, intended to enclose it with a stone wall, granted to them and their successors, in aid of such work, and for repairing and paving said town, a license, to enure for eighteen years, to take certain tolls and customs—subsequently extended to fifty-five years.

In 1413, Thomas, the son of John Cruys, was found seised

---

* *D'Alton's Drogheda*, vol. ii., 164.

† *Roll* in Ch. Rememb. Offic.

‡ *Rot. Pat.*, 13 Hen. 4, *C. H.*

of a fourth part of the several manors of Dundalk, Duleek, Kells, &c.* The second year of the then reigning Monarch (Henry the Fifth) is marked by peculiarly vigilant measures for the settlement of the entire County of Louth. John Saunder and John Hanley were appointed guardians of the harbours, with the accustomed fees.† The latter had more particularly the office of searcher of said harbours during pleasure.‡ Thomas Talbot and others were commissioned to inquire on oath as to certain offences committed in this and the adjacent counties of the Pale, and their Crosses, as well in the times of Edward the Third, Richard the Second, and Henry the Fourth, as in that of the then King. Similar commissions were ordered to inquire concerning treasures, felonies, goods, cattle, &c., belonging to the King and concealed; all escheats, and matters connected with the clerks of the market; offences concerning workmen, servants, mechanics, and all sales of provisions contrary to the statutes; to inquire as to persons unfit to be retained in office; to decide civil pleas, and to levy fines and amerciaments. In the same year Bartholomew de Verdon, Knight; John Clynton, of Keppok; Roger Gernon, of Gernonston; and Nicholas Taaffe, were nominated conservators of the peace for the County Louth, with authority to assess the men of said county according to their lands and goods; to contribute horses, arms, archers, hobillers, horsemen, and infantry; and for arraying and mustering these, and putting them in rank and file. And the said officials were directed to lead out these forces, when so arrayed, against the enemies and rebels at such part of the marches as necessity might most

---

* *Rot. Pat.* 1 Henry 5, *C. H.*

† *Rot. Pat*, 2 Henry 5, *Canc. Hib.* ‡ *Id.*

require, with powers to parley, treat, and make truces with said enemies and rebels; to give safe conduct, and to amerce all offenders against any matters so within their cognizance.*

In 1419, William Cashell had a grant from the Crown of seven messuages and forty acres in Dundalk, as had John Abbot, at the same time, of two messuages and twenty-eight acres in the County Louth, which had been the estate of John Cashell; and of a messuage and one garden in Dundalk, which had been the estate of William Lack, to hold while the King had title thereto.†

In 1421, Owen O'Neill was apprehended by the son of O'Neill, of Claneboy, while on his journey to hold a conference with the Earl of Ormonde, Lord Justice, at this town. He was in the following year released by his wife and sons.‡

In the first year of the reign of Henry the Sixth, on the security, or mainprise, of Walter Field and Thomas Cashell, of the County Louth, the custody of "one messuage, with an orchard, in the New Town of Dundalk," was committed to Richard Field and Matilda, his wife. In the same year the Commons of this County having granted a subsidy of forty pounds for the defence thereof, under the assessment of Bartholomew de Verdon, Knight, and others, the portion chargeable upon this Barony was directed to be collected by William Cashell and Thomas Serene. §

---

* *Rot. Pat.*, 2 Henry 5, in *Canc. Hib.*

† *Rot. Pat.*, 6 Hen. 5, in *Arch. Dom. Cap. Westm.*

‡ *Annals of the Four Masters.*

§ *Rot. Pat.*, 1 Henry 6, *C. H.*

CHAPTER VIII.

FROM THE REIGN OF HENRY VI. TO THE SUCCESSION OF HENRY VII.

In 1423, very active proceedings were taken for the defence so projected. The Sheriff of Louth, according to the *Patent Rolls*, was directed to interdict the exporting of any wheat, oats, or other grain, from this county to foreign parts, under penalty of forfeiture, as the Deputy was meditating an immediate excursion thither; while the Mayor and Corporation of Dublin had a grant of £19 7s. 4½d. towards their expenses in proceeding, at his request, with a great force of men-at-arms and archers, to Louth, to resist Donal O'Neill and MacMahon.* The result is collected from the Four Masters:—"Donal O'Neill and Nial O'Donnell, and Owen, the son of Nial, marched with the Irish of Ulster to attack the English. They first proceeded to Traghbally (Dundalk), to the plain of Oriel, to Louth, and from thence to Meath, where they engaged in battle with the King of England's Viceroy (the Earl of Ormonde), in which the commanding knight of the English battalions, with many more of their people, were slain; and the Irish obtained immense booty on that expedition. They then made peace with the English, and put Dundalk and all the English of the surrounding country under tribute."

The year 1425 was one of a severe visitation of plague in Ireland, of which, amongst others, died the Earl of March, the King's Viceroy The before-mentioned right of Thomas Cruys to one-fourth of the manor of Dundalk is attested by

* *Rot. Claus.*, 2 Henry 6, in *Canc. Hib.*

a Patent Roll, whereby, after reciting that he had in his life-time granted an annuity of forty shillings to William de Preston, merchant and burgess of Drogheda, issues out of said fourth of the manor of Dundalk, with clause of distress, and after reciting that said fourth was then in the King's hands by reason of the death of said Thomas, who held it *in capite;* said William had thereby license to distrain therefor, according to his agreement.* At the same time Bartholomew de Verdon was, with John, Prior of Louth, Nicholas Taaffe, John Haddeson, Jenico Dartas, &c., appointed Justices and Guardians of the Peace in Louth, with commission of array and other powers.† In the following year the King directed a payment of £11 5s. 0d. to be made to the aforesaid Nicholas Taaffe, for that he having been burdened with £45, for military service at Dundalk, £11 5s. 0d. thereof had been levied off him as a portion of same, though he was prevented from rendering the service in consequence of being engaged in other parts of Ulster, in the King's service, at that time.‡

In 1427, Philip Norreys was, on the presentation of —— Bellew,§ admitted by the Archbishop of Armagh to the Vicarage of Dundalk, and had shortly after license from this Prelate to go abroad for seven years, in order to pursue his studies. During his sojourn in England he studied at University College, Oxford, and, after the example of Primate FitzRalph, he spoke many sarcastic speeches against the Mendicant Friars, which drew much odium upon him, and made many enemies; after sundry promotions, however, he died in 1465.‖

---

* *Rot. Pat.*, 3 Henry 6, in *Canc. Hib.*

† *Id.* ‡ *Id.*

§ *Visitation Book of* 1622.

‖ *Mason's St. Patrick's*, p. 139, &c.

In 1430, "Owen, the son of Niall Oge O'Neill, marched a great force against the English of the plain of Oriel (Louth), and plundered, burned, and laid waste all belonging to the English of the entire plain. He also burned the fortress of Dundalk; and having compelled the inhabitants to submit, and pay him tribute, he returned home with triumph and victory.* In the same year Thomas Hanly and Thomas Bathe were appointed to take the prisage of wines to the use of the King in the harbours of Dublin, Meath, and Louth; while William Hudson, Bishop of Meath, and a native of the County Louth, was appointed by the King a conservator of the peace therefor during pleasure.†

In 1432, say the Four Masters, "great and frequent depredations were committed on the English, and numbers of them were slain, by Manus MacMahon (of Monaghan), who raised their heads on the spear-poles of the guards of the town of Lurgan (Lurgan-Green, near Dundalk), Manus's own fortified residence, a disgusting and hateful sight to those who beheld their putrefaction. . . . In the summer of 1433 a famine occurred, which was designated, for a long time afterwards 'the summer of slight acquaintance,' for no one could recognise a relative on account of the greatness of the famine." In 1434, "Owen O'Neill and Niall O'Donnell marched, with the whole forces of the Province of Ulster, to spoil and plunder the English of Meath. The English of Dundalk came to O'Neill and paid him his tribute, and gave him much valuable articles besides. O'Neill and O'Donnell afterwards proceeded and burned the plain of Oriel; and the sons of O'Neill went to burn some of the fortresses belonging to the English, and, while

* *Annals Four Masters.*

† *Rot. Pat.*, 9 Hen. 6, in *Canc. Hib.*

engaged in the burning, they did not perceive them until the King's Viceroy with his forces came up to them. Henry and Hugh, the sons of O'Neill, sent their party before them, while they themselves covered the retreat, and made their escape without losing a man. . . . In the following year occurred an extraordinary frost and ice, which was so intense that the people were enabled to travel over all the lakes and rivers of Ireland on the ice."

The *Patent Rolls* of the last year (1435) record the endowment of the widow of the late Baron of Slane of the third part (amongst the property assigned to her) of the services of all the burgesses of the Corporation of Dundalk, while the custody of two messuages and twenty-seven acres of land in the town, which had been the estate of John Cashell, were on the mainprise of Richard Bathe and Thomas White, clerks, committed by the King to John Blakton, clerk.

The years 1439, 1440, 1447, and 1448, were saddened by the visitation of the plague; and in 1444, "O'Neill," says Dudley Firbiss, "marched with a great army to and on the English of Orgial, and ransacked the 'Stradvally' (*i.e.* the uncastellated town) of Dundalgan, when he received sixty marks and two tuns of wine for not burning the town, after he had already preyed and burned a great part of the County." The Irish Parliament interposed in 1450, and, by an act of that year (unprinted), ordered O'Neill to evacuate a position which he endeavoured to maintain in this vicinity, and to remove with his men from certain lands of Bellew of the Rock (Roche near this), called the Fews, into which he had forcibly entered.

In 1452, the aforesaid "Owen O'Neill, with his forces, joined by Maguire, marched into the Fews to war with the English of the plain of Oriel. The son of O'Neill—namely,

Owen Oge O'Neill—and Maguire's people, proceeded to Clogh-an-Bhodaigh* to plunder the English, from whom they carried off prey to their camp. The English and the people of MacMahon, with their friends, pursued them to recover the prey, until they came to the camp. O'Neill and Maguire, with their forces, prepared to oppose them, and a conflict ensued in which MacDonnell, of the Gallowglasses—namely, Sorley More, and many besides, were slain, and others of their (O'Neill's and Maguire's) forces were taken prisoners. O'Neill returned to his fortress that night in great wrath; and Henry, his son, on receiving intelligence of this, came to his father's place; and after that MacMahon went to O'Neill and his son, and they made peace with each other, and an eric was given to O'Neill as a reparation for the dishonour done to him, and also a fine for the death of MacDonnell.† In the same year occurred the death of the celebrated Lord Furnival, first Earl of Shrewsbury, whose name and achievements the historian and the poet have alike concurred in commemorating. The monument to his memory in the chancel of Whitchurch, Shropshire, maintains, amongst his titles, that which associated him with the Verdon Lordships of Dundalk and Clonmore. It runs—" Orate pro animâ prænobilis Domini Johannis Talbot, quondam Comitis Salopiæ, Domini Furnival, DOMINI VERDON, Domini Strange de Blackmere, and Marischalli Franciæ, qui obiit in bello apud Burdeux, 7 July, 1452."

In 1454, on the occasion of a Parliament in Dublin, the clergy of Armagh appointed the Prior of Ardee to be their proxy at that meeting, and voted, as an allowance for this said representation, an assessment of eighteen pence out of every

---

* The Giant's Stone, situated in the parish of Ballymaescanlon.

† *Annals of the Four Masters.*

pound in the valuation of all the benefices within the Deanery of Dundalk, as well as within those of Drogheda and Ardee.* In the following year "Owen O'Neill (so frequently before alluded to) was deposed from his Lordship by his son, Henry; and the coarb of St. Patrick (the Primate), together with Maguire, MacMahon, O'Cahan, and all the O'Neills, accompanied Henry, son of Owen, the son of Niall Oge, to Tullaghoge,† to inaugurate him; and he was nominated 'The O'Neill,' according to the usual custom." The ex-chieftain, Owen, died in the following year. The death of another son of his, a brother of the above Henry, is thus singularly commemorated by the Four Masters, *ad. ann.*, 1461:—"Felim, son of Owen, son of Niall Oge O'Neill, died of a sudden fit; and he was a man distinguished for hospitality and feats of arms; an entertainer of learned men and strangers; a man who purchased more poems and possessed a greater collection of poetry than any other man in his time. He died after having gained a victory over the world and the devil."

In an assembly held about this time, in St. Peter's Church, Drogheda, the clergy of Armagh elected, as a person to represent them in the Parliament to be held before the Earl of Kildare, Justitiary, Alan Ashe, Prior of the House of St. John the Baptist, of Ardee, and assigned him, for his expenses in so attending Parliament, 8d. out of every mark of the annual value and taxation of the benefices in the Deaneries of Drogheda, Dundalk, and Ardee. At that Parliament Thomas Bathe, of the family heretofore alluded to, having

---

* D'Alton's *Drogheda*, vol. i., p. 18.

† This place is situated near Dungannon, in the County Tyrone, and the inauguration chair of the O'Neill dynasty existed there until broken up by order of the Lord Deputy Mountjoy in the time of Elizabeth.

pretended to be Lord of Louth, was, by special ordinance, summoned to appear in Court on a certain day, or be out of the King's protection; and it was further ordained thereby that he never should take place in the Parliaments of this land, nor be eligible to any office therein of the King's grant. At the same time the Vicarage of Dundalk was put under sequestration by the Primate, in consequence of the non-repair of the Chapel of Castletown, and other causes.

In 1458, an Irish stat. (unprinted) provided that two men should be sent from each ploughland in the county to aid in carrying the sea-water round this town, to protect it from the Irish, on penalty for non-attendance of 4d. per day for each man.

In 1465, on inspeximus, the grant of Richard the Second to this borough, and the grants of customs of Henry's the Fourth, Fifth, and Sixth, were confirmed by the authority of a Parliament, held at Trim and Dublin by Thomas, Earl of Desmond, then Lord Deputy, and whose removal from the Government soon after the Masters emphatically deplore:— "A Saxon Lord Justice arrived; Thomas, Earl of Desmond, was removed, which caused the ruin of Ireland."

In the year 1461, Thomas, son of Robert Pilkington, had a grant from the King of the manor of Keppock, in the County of Uriel, and of all the lands, tenements, and hereditaments, &c., in Dundalk, Ardee, Barnemouth, Tullaghallen, and Tullagh-downhill, in said county, theretofore the property of John Hadsor, attainted; to hold same, together with the knights' fees, courts, warrens, &c., to said Thomas and his heirs male for ever, without rent.*

In 1464 was passed the remarkable Irish Act, "that

* *Rot. Pat.*, 1 Edw. 4, in *Canc. Hib.*

Irishmen dwelling in the Counties of Dublin, Uriel, Meath, and Kildare, should go apparelled like Englishmen, wear their beards after the English manner, swear allegiance, and take English surnames, as of a town, colour, or office; and that they and their issue should continue thenceforth to use such names." Another statute of 1471 (unprinted) exempted Richard Verdon, styled of Termonfeckin, for a certain time to come, from all subsidies and state charges.

In 1468, a Parliament was held at the latter town, and afterwards adjourned to Dublin, wherein a very extensive Act of Resumption was passed, which, among many savings, contained one of the rights of this Corporation; and on the 16th of June, 1515, an inspeximus of that of 1465, and of the charters of the Henrys, above-mentioned, was enrolled, granting and confirming to the burgesses of Dundalk that their said town should be a free borough for ever, have a guild merchant, with soc, sac, and other privileges; a Provost, to be chosen by their Common Council; the fishing of the water of Dundalk as amply as ever they had enjoyed the same; a fair, to continue for 15 days from Monday next after the first of May.

Amongst the measures which Baron Finglas promulgated about the year 1534, as calculated to advance the common weal, was a recommendation " that the city of Dublin, and the town of Drogheda, and the town of Dundalk, do go with the King's Deputy when required to hostings, and that, in consideration thereof, their customs and poundage be forgiven, which was soon after carried into effect.

In 1472, a Parliament of Dublin granted an aid to Richard Bellew, Esq., on account of his building his Castle at Castletown for the defence of the marches of Dundalk and Louth. May of the latter year is commemorated by the Four Masters for "a fall of showers of hailstones, accompanied with lightning and thunder, which destroyed the blossoms and fruit, and each stone measured from two to three inches, and they inflicted great wounds and sores on those who were struck by them." The following annal of those historians records a singular zoological importation at this early period:—"An extraordinary animal (a camel or dromedary) was sent by the King of England to Ireland, of a form resembling a mare, of a yellow colour, having the hoofs of a cow, a long neck, a very large head, an ugly trailing tail, scarce of hair, having a saddle of its own (the hump); wheat and salt were its food, and it would draw a sliding car, with the greatest burden, by the tail, and go on its knees when entering a door and in taking a rider on its back." Another unprinted statute of 1473 restored Richard de Verdon, the younger, to certain lands usurped from him by James Gernon, Sir Laurence Taaffe, and others; while a third, of the same session, granted to Nicholas Verdon an aid towards building a Castle at Lowaryngeston. Among the unprinted Acts of 36 Henry the Sixth is one to provide for the defences of Dundalk.

On the night of the festival of St. John the Baptist, in 1477, "a great wind happened, which destroyed an immense deal of stone and wooden buildings of cranoges and corn stacks." In the following year a great plague was imported by a ship which entered the port of Ballyshannon; and this pestilence spread through Fermanagh, Tyrconnell, and throughout the Province of Ulster in general. Its ravages were subsequently not less violent over Leinster; while, on Christmas night of the next year (1478), "occurred an awful wind, which proved a destructive night to many, from the number of persons and cattle that perished, and the trees, and buildings, and ships that were destroyed, both by land and water, throughout Ireland."

In 1483, say the Four Masters, "a great contest arose between O'Donnell (*i.e.* Hugh Roe) and O'Neill. Con O'Donnell collected the forces of Tyrconnell and of North Connaught, and Hugh Oge, the son of Hugh Buighe O'Neill, marched with all his forces and joined them. They then proceeded along in battle array, in defiance of all enemies, on their way, until they arrived at 'Traghbally-of-Dundalk,' which they plundered and burned, and also the surrounding county. The Lord Justice (*i.e.* Gerald FitzGerald), son of Thomas, Earl of Kildare, went in pursuit of them with a great army of the English, and overtook them; but, however, they bravely opposed that great pursuing force, and defeated them, and a great many of the English were slain. On their own side MacQuillan and the son of Torlogh Carragh O'Conor were killed. O'Donnell, after that, marched with his forces to the town of Louth, which he burned, and he received presents and payment from the inhabitants for protecting and sparing their town. O'Donnell returned back, and parted from Hugh Oge, tho son of Hugh Buighe, who proceeded to Glenree (near Newry), to attack Trian Congail (in Down). He himself (O'Donnell), on his return through Tyrone, spoiled and burned the country in every direction through which he passed until he arrived at Avonmore (*i.e.* the 'great river,' probably the Blackwater). His forces cut and cleared the way through very dense and impassable woods, which were along the banks of Avonmore, so as to make a free and easy pass for his forces through the woods. He then commanded his men to construct strong wooden hedges, or wicker-work, across the river, by which the whole of his forces, both foot and horse, crossed the stream without either a man or horse being drowned; after which they let the bridge down the stream, and their enemies could do nothing but behold them from the opposite side; and O'Donnell then returned home with triumph and victory."

CHAPTER IX.

FROM THE SUCCESSION OF HENRY VII. TO THE REIGN OF QUEEN ELIZABETH.

In the Parliament held at Trim in 1485, a chantry was confirmed in the Church of St. Nicholas, in this town, in honour of God, the Blessed Virgin, St. Nicholas, and *St. Richard* of Dundalk.* In the following year "a general Synod of the Province of Ulster was held, in the beginning of July, at Drogheda, by the Archbishop of Armagh, Octavian de Palatio, which was attended by all the bishops and clergy of the North of Ireland. Twenty-eight towns belonging to the English of the plain of Oriel (Louth) were in this year burned by MacMahon—namely, Hugh Oge, son of Hugh Roe, son of Roderick."† "Very wet, stormy weather happened in the Summer and following harvest of the year 1491, which resembled a deluge, and all the corn crops of Ireland failed." In 1492, "John, son of Carbry O'Neill, was killed by the sons of O'Hanlon and the sons of Redmond O'Hanlon, at 'Traghbally' of Dundalk."‡ By an Act of Poyning's Parliament of 1495, it was provided that the *shores* (oras) of the four Counties—Dublin, Meath, *Kildare*, and Uriel, should be surrounded with a rampart and foss, whereupon the King appointed certain commissioners to execute the said works,

---

* *Ware's Bishops*, p. 508.

† *Annals of the Four Masters*. ‡ *Id.*

and to levy the expenses off the respective counties benefited thereby. During the following two years Ireland was afflicted by such "an awful famine, that the people ate food which is not fit to be mentioned, such as was never served in dishes for human beings." *

In 1514, "the Earl of Kildare (*i.e.* Gerald FitzGerald) gained great sway with his forces; for he overran the Province of Ulster as far as Carrickfergus, and Munster as far as the palace of MacCarthy." † In 1521, the Lord Lieutenant, the Earl of Surrey, writing to Cardinal Wolsey, besought his Grace "to be favourable unto Sir William D'Arcy, of Platten, that, by his good favour he may obtain the King's grant, for the term of his life, of the office of the customship of the towns of Drogheda and Dundalk, which undoubtedly he hath right well deserved." ‡ In this latter year, "Roderic, the son of Eigneachan O'Donnell, was killed by the English at Dundalk, while in company with O'Neill—namely, Con, the son of Con." § On the Friday before Christmas, in 1528, say the Masters, "a great wind arose, which prostrated a great number of trees throughout Ireland, levelled many stone and wooden buildings, and also swept away, sunk, and destroyed many vessels." ‖ In four years after James de Verdon, of that still recognised influential lineage, was summoned to render scutage at the great hosting in Owenstown. A sad visitation of "diseases and distempers raged in the year 1536, viz:—A general plague, the 'galar-bræac' (small-pox), the flux, and fever, of which many died." ¶

In the following year Robert Casy was appointed gauger

---

* *Annals of the Four Masters.* † *Id.*

‡ *D'Alton's Drogheda*, vol. ii., p. 103.

§ *Annals of the Four Masters.* ‖ *Id.* ¶ *Id.*

and searcher of the ports of Dublin, Dundalk, and Drogheda, for life.—(*Patent Roll* in Chancery, 28 Henry the Eighth.)

In 1538, the Deputy, Lord Leonard Gray, in a letter to the Secretary Cromwell, alluding to some hostile position taken by O'Neill, "for that he was not paid his wages" (black mail), acknowledged the assistance he received, as required, from Dundalk, Drogheda, and Ardee (see fully *History of Drogheda*, vol. ii., 191). The vengeance of the Irish Prince was not long averted. In the following year, "O'Neill (Con) and O'Donnell (Manus) marched, with mutual accord and consent, with their forces into Meath; and such territories as did not pay them tribute they devastated and burned before them as far as Tara. They seized an immense booty on that expedition; and the Irish had not mustered an army to attack the English in the latter times, that spoiled so much of the property of Meath, than did these predatory forces. Great, indeed, was the booty; consisting of gold, silver, brass, iron, treasure, and every kind of property and goods in general, they took from the town of Ath-fiardach (Ardee), Nua-Chongbhail (Navan), having completely plundered them on that expedition. On the return of these forces there was exultation, boasting, vain glory, and pride, about the immense booty they obtained without any opposition. When the Saxon Lord Justice, Lord Leonard (Gray), received intelligence of this he collected all the English forces in Ireland, with those of many of the great towns of Meath, both lay and ecclesiastic, and all the fleets on the neighbouring coasts, and particularly an immense fleet which lay in Cuan-Cairlinne (the Bay of Carlingford). After all these forces were brought together by the Lord Justice he marched in pursuit of the Irish army, through Oriel, to a place called Bellathahoa (Bellahoe), in Fearnmaegh (Farney). The Irish forces were not able to form into proper order, as they should, neither did they obey the commands of their leaders to keep and defend the field of battle, but rather dispersed in a scattered and disorderly manner, and left a great deal of their own property, as well as the booty they had taken from the English, in the hands of their enemies at that place. After they were defeated many of their common soldiers were slain, and not a few of their chiefs besides; and of the Tyrconnellians Maolmurry Meirgeach, son of John Roe MacSweeny, fell on the field of battle. Magennis (*i.e.* Murtagh) was taken prisoner by a party of the people of Oriel, after having been separated, with a few from his own forces, in that defeat of Bellahoe. He was kept privately in imprisonment for a considerable time; and they afterwards treacherously slew him, at the instigation of some of his own tribe, who gave a bribe to those who had him in confinement for putting him to death."

In the latter year (1539) King Henry the Eighth presented John Wylley, late Prior of Dundalk, to the Priory of the House of the Blessed Virgin Mary of Louth, in the same diocese (*Roll*, 30 Henry the Eighth); and about the same time the Chantry of St. Mary's, of this town, was valued to the First Fruits at £5 6s. 8d.; that of St. Catherine, there, at £2 13s. 4d.; and that of the Holy Trinity, also there, at £5 6s. 8d.; while the Vicarage was more anciently assessed at £7 10s. 3½d. About this time a branch of the illustrious family of De Verdon having been established in the County Limerick, Gillyduff O'Grady married Eleanor, daughter of William Verdon, styled of Kilmallock, County Limerick, in whose venerable abbey monuments of this family, erected at early periods of the seventeenth century, are still traceable. While, on the 18th of October, in this year, Lord Leonard Gray being encamped before Dundalk, wrote, with the authority and signatures of his Council, a letter to Henry the Eighth, acquainting the King with the death of the Bishop of Kildare:—" And if it may stand with your Grace's determinate pleasure that this bearer, William Meagh, Dean of the Cathedral of the same, may supply his room, I, your Grace's Archbishop of Dublin, who have examined the said William, what for his learning and other virtuous qualities, think him able thereunto. Most humbly desiring your Excellency the rather to prefer him thereunto at this our humble petition unto your Grace; and thus the Holy Ghost send your Highness many good and prosperous years to your Grace's high contentation. Written in the camp beside your Grace's town of Dundalk, the 18th of October." * Donald O'Behan, a Franciscan friar, was, however, in a few months after, by the Pope's provision, declared Bishop of that See; but soon after his nomination he died, when Thady Reynolds, Doctor of the Civil and Canon Law, was, by the like provision, appointed. The King however, being now declared Supreme Head of the Church in Ireland, rejected the election, and raised the above William Meagh to it, and afterwards called him into his Privy Council. On the last day of October in this year the same Deputy reported to Secretary Cromwell, by letter from Maynooth, that, after a successful hosting against O'Reilly, he had gone with his forces to Dundalk. " And being at Dundalk, I sent to O'Neill to have communication with him, who appointed to have met with me at a certain place beside Dundalk, called Carrick-Bredagh. The said O'Neill brake appointment with me, and sent me word that he could not at that time have kept promise. And to Dundalk came Mr. Treasurer (Sir Wm. Brabazon), with his

* *State Papers*, Temp. Henry 8.

company, to me; and seeing that my purpose was settled as touching O'Neill, and for so much as Mr. Treasurer was farmer of the King's country of Lecale, and that Savage, chief captain of his nation, would not pay his farm unto the Treasurer, and, besides, the said Savage brought into the said country divers sects, which had much of the said country in their subjection, then it was concluded between the said Mr. Treasurer and me that we should have gone towards the said Lecale; and so, with the host, we set forward and entered into the said country, and took all the castles there, and delivered them to Mr. Treasurer, who hath warded the same."*

In the following year (1540) John Alen, Chancellor, and Sir William Brabazon, acquainted Lord Essex that, on the 11th of May in that year, O'Neill, as they alleged, "under colour to parley with my Lord Justice, proposes to come with a great company to the borders of Dundalk, for whose meeting my said Lord Justice, with the most power he can conveniently make, repaireth to the North. And for that, after his departure, secret knowledge hath come unto us that O'Connor, on one side, and MacMurrough on the other part, and the Tooles on this side, have determined, in his absence, to invade the country, for the safe-guard whereof we will rear all the power we can, and lie for defence till he return, doing what should lie in us to make some stay ere we depart. Howbeit, if we had been secretly advised beforehand of your conclusions, peradventure these broils had not happened, the default whereof, as your said servant can show your Lordship, is commonly here ascribed to the late Deputy."† In a few days after, the then Lord Justice, Sir William Brereton, made his

* *State Papers*, Temp. Henry 8. † *Id.*

report to the said Lord Essex:—"Pleaseth your Right Honourable good Lordship, as we advertised that this country is in very ill ease, being assured of none Irishman's peace, as the bearers hereof can inform the King's Highness, to whose Majesty I beseech your Lordship to take their excuse for their abode so long from his presence, and to give them his most gracious thanks for their service done unto this time, in defending the country from the invasion of O'Connor, while I was in the North parts to meet with O'Neill; assuring your Lordship that albeit the said O'Connor, accompanied with a great number of men of war, hath done great hurt in mine absence, yet, if they had not tarried for stay of the country, he and his confederates, the Tooles and others, had made such invasion to the King's dishonour, and losses of his lands, as I think was not done by no man's remembrance. And touching O'Neill, I came to Dundalk the 14th day of May to parley with him at the Carrick-Bredagh, a place appointed by us of the King's Council to meet with him; and when I and the Chief Justice came to Dundalk, the said O'Neill sent to me that he durst not come to parley to the said place appointed, fearing to be betrayed, mistrusting to come to any Englishman after the deceit of the Lord Deputy (Lord Leonard Gray), saying openly, in presence of divers, that he deceived so many with untrue promises, as well made unto him as to others, so that he durst not come to Carrick-Bredagh, and desired that I and the said Justice might come to the Narrow Water, beside MacGennis's Castle; and so we determined to do, and concluded a peace with him. . . . Whether he will perform his sayings therein or not I cannot well tell; but, by the plainness of his communication, and also by his sending of his servant to the King, I hope that he will perform all that he hath promised. And, as the bearers can tell your Lordship, if this way had not been taken, the country was at immediate destruction and danger." *

We can see very plainly, from the language of these *State Papers*, that there was little confidence in either of the high contracting parties to this truce. O'Neill openly avowed that his countrymen had been so unblushingly betrayed, and so often deceived by the late Deputy, Lord Leonard Gray, he would place no confidence in any Englishman; and therefore declined going to the neighbourhood of the Pale to parley with the Lord Justice, Sir William Brereton, and urging that the Lord Justice should go to the Narrow Water, where O'Neill was in his native country. This he did; but we find he placed small hopes in O'Neill keeping his promises.

There was at this period one of the race of Hy-Nial destined to become a stubborn foe to English rule. This was Shane, who had "grown to believe, with all his soul, that the Kinel-Eoghain was the hero-race most favoured by heaven; that Tyr-owen was the eye of Erin and the very pride of the earth; and that of all titles of honours and sovereignty by far the most dread and illustrious was THE O'NEILL."† The great source from which the English fed their hopes of the conquest of Ulster lay in the constant warfare carried on by the native chieftains against each other. O'Reilly, of Cavan, had dared to deny the power of O'Neill, and a heavy chastisement fell upon him. Thus the haughty chiefs of Tyrconnell rivalled the Chiefs of Tyr-owen; and, as the latter claimed tribute from the O'Donnells, frequent wars ensued. The correspondence usually was of the laconic style, reminding the classic reader of the reply which the Spartan chief sent to the

---

* *State Papers*, Temp. Hen 8.

† *Life of Hugh O'Neill*, by Mitchell.

envoy of the King who demanded tribute:—"Let your master come and take it." The Irish, who were of a highly imaginative temperament, sent their letters only half expressed, but perfectly intelligible. "Send me my tribute, or else——." "I owe you none; and if——." Shane's blood was up, and he resolved to make the O'Donnells find he was not to be trifled with. At the head of a large army, he fell upon the Country of Tyrconnell, and heedlessly suffered his forces to disperse, in pursuit of plunder, through the defiles. This was what O'Donnell wished. He attacked O'Neill's camp, and easily became master of great spoil, Shane O Neill narrowly escaping with his life. A vast quantity of arms, clothing, and horses, fell to the share of the victors; no less than eighty horses, besides O'Neill's own horse, fell to the share of Con O'Donnell. Not long, however, did the O'Donnells enjoy their victory. Shane O'Neill soon turned their triumph into a defeat; and, more cautious than before, he took sore revenge, and carried off the Chief of the O'Donnells and his wife. The former he allowed to depart, but his wife remained. She, we regret to say, became the concubine of the conqueror, and bore him many children in the hall of Benburb. It was those desperate conflicts between the native Irish Lords that enabled the English to make head against them; but we shall see the difficulty experienced in reducing the Ulster Chiefs to obedience.

In 1535, a grant was made to the bailiffs, burgesses, and commons of Dundalk of the offices of customs, and collector of the customs and subsidies within the port and creeks of Dundalk, by land and sea; also, of the custody of the seal of the cocket and the office of searcher, to hold for twelve years at a certain rent; while, at the same time, the office of searcher in this port, as well as in those of Dublin and Drogheda, was granted by the King to Robert ap Howell, otherwise called Robert Powell, an office which, in the year afterwards, was conferred upon Robert Carey. In 1540, Patrick Galtrym, then Prior of St. Leonard's of Dundalk, surrendered its possession to the Crown.

In 1543, a report was made to Parliament of the condition of the harbours. It, of course, included those at this side of the Channel, and represented Carlingford as a good haven; Dundalk, a creek; Drogheda, a bad haven, &c. In two years after James Brandon, the patentee of the Franciscan Friary in this town, was found seised also of one large mansion-house, sixteen messuages, one mill, and one hundred acres of land, in said town, which he held of the Corporation.*

In 1543, James Dowedall, of Ballyscanlan, having intended to build a castle in the Upper Castletown, in Cooley, on the borders and marches of the Irish, it was enacted that, in consideration thereof, said Sir James Dowedall shall have freedom of a plow-land in Upper Castletown, of and from all manner of exactions and charges; and also have off the County of Louth £10, for the building of said castle; said James finding sufficient security, before two justices, for the building of said castle.†

In 1547, Dundalk, Dublin, and Drogheda, were charged with 300 marks, as an addition to the salary of Sir Richard Rede, Chancellor of Ireland,‡ which charge was continued for the benefit of his successors on the woolsack—Sir John Allen, Sir Thomas Cusacke, and Hugh, Archbishop of Dublin. At this period Henry the Eighth commenced that rapacious

---

* *Harleian MSS.*, No. xxxv., p. 119.

† *Roll in Chancery*, 19 June, 34 Henry 8.

‡ *Id.*, 1st of Edw. 6.

course of confiscation which transferred the estates which former piety had consecrated for religious uses to the aggrandizement of state flatterers and favourites. In this town, on the 23rd of November, 1540, Patrick Galtrym, the last Prior of the Hospital of St. Leonard, executed a deed of surrender of its possessions, in which he was (as requisite) joined by the community of his house; * while, in order to secure the fullest value thereof, it was thereupon enacted in Parliament, that any leases by the governors or governesses thereof of parsonages appropriate thereto, or of tithes appertaining to said houses within two years before the dissolution, should be void, provided such parsonages or tithes had not been let to farm within five years previous. Said Patrick Galtrym was at this time found seised of a church and chapter-house here, a dormitory, hall, and other buildings, within the precincts, which contained two acres; also of one hundred and twenty acres of arable land, part of the demesne of the Priory, called the Prior's Land, annual value, besides reprises, 10s. 8d.; twelve messuages, seven cottages, a horse-mill, a close of four acres of pasture, with two of meadow; another park, containing three acres; another close, with eighty-two acres of arable, and three roods; two acres of arable in Dundalk, and in le "Lurgyn," near Dundalk; annual value, besides reprises, £6 13s., &c. There were also appropriated to the said Prior the Rectory of Dundalk, annual value, besides reprises, £22 13s. 4d.; and the tithes of the parish of Haggardstown.† By inquisition, held at the same time, the House of the Grey Friars here was found seised of a church, belfry, and dormitory; a park, an orchard, two gardens; one messuage; a park, called Brandon's Park, and a rood of land; all of the annual

* *Rot. Pat.*, 31st Henry 8.

† *Arch. Mon.*

value of 10s., besides reprises. The Prior of Louth was then found seised of (*inter alia*) four messuages, four acres of arable and two of meadow, in Dundalk—annual value, besides reprises, 6s. 8d; as was also the Prior of St. Mary's, of Drogheda, of two messuages in this town—annual value, besides reprises, 6s.; as also of thirty acres of arable land, with the tithes thereof, in the townland of Carlingford—like annual value, 13s. 4d.

In 1542, the possession of the Grey Friary, including various messuages, three stangs of land, with a wind-mill, within the franchises of this town, were granted, *in capite*, to James Brandon, at a fine of £9 10s. 0d., and an annual rent of 6d. This Brandon was at same time seised of a messuage in Carlingford under that Corporation, and of other premises in this town, which he held under its Corporation; also of two-messuages and twenty-four acres in Painston, fifteen acres in Labanston, which he held under James Clinton, and twenty-eight acres in Stephentonsay, held from Christopher Bellew. In 1544, Henry Draycot, of Mornington, in the County Meath, an especial recipient of Royal bounty, at this time had a lease of the Rectory of Roche, with the alterages and appurtenances thereunto belonging; also the tithes of Ballyhurgan and the tithe-corn of Jenkinstown, as parcel of the possessions of St. Leonard's of Dundalk, to hold same for twenty-one years at the annual rent of £2 6s. 8d. Irish, an interest which was renewed to him in 1553 for other twenty-one years.* The College of Nyven, it may be here mentioned, had, at this time, rights in certain lands within the Barony of Dundalk; but all were seized upon, and passed into lay hands. "The English," say the Four Masters, "in every place

* *Inq.* in Offic. Ch. Rememb.

throughout Ireland, where they established their power, pursued and banished the nine religious orders, and particularly they destroyed the Monastery of Monaghan, and beheaded the Guardian and a number of the friars."

"The year 1541 is mentioned by the Annalists as having commenced with such "boisterous and excessively stormy weather as prevented the tillage and ploughing from being properly performed throughout Ireland;" and in 1546 so great a famine is recorded to have occurred that "six pence of the old money were paid for the loaf in Connaught and six silver pennies in Meath." The scarcity of money was, indeed, then so great as necessitated a new coinage to maintain the charges of Government in Ireland. "New coin," say the Four Masters, "was introduced into Ireland made of copper, and the Irish were compelled to use it instead of silver money. The English power," they add, "was very great at this time in Ireland; and it is doubtful if the people of the south of Ireland were ever in such bondage before that time." In 1547, "a great wind arose on the night before the festival of St. Bridgid; and it is doubtful if so great occurred since the birth of Christ. It destroyed churches, monasteries, and castles, and particularly the two western wings of the CHURCH of Clonmacnois.*

In 1549, King Edward the Sixth demised to John Wakeley, of Navan, Gent., for thirty-one years in reversion, a great portion of the many rectories and tithes with which the Priory of Louth had been endowed previous to its dissolution; and amongst those the rectory and tithes of Faughart, Anisis, Ballybrian, Doongoole, Rathgiagh, Ballybeney, Urney, *alias* Norney, Ballynacleske, Lurgankeele, Lislery, and Carrick-

* *Annals of the Four Masters.*

brannane; the tithes of Dundalk, Maine, Kilclogher, Philipstown, Dromyn, &c. In 1553, Queen Mary renewed to Henry Draycot the lease which he had obtained in 1544 of the Rectory of Roche, and the tithes demised thereby; and also granted to him, for twenty-one years, the site of the House of Crossbearers of Dundalk, containing two acres; sixty acres of arable, called the Prior's Land; sixty acres of arable in the Rath; some land and three parks, with their appurtenances, in the Maudlins; part of the demesne of the Hospital, and sundry other premises, with a water-mill in Dundalk; a messuage, with thirty acres of arable land, in Dromisken; to hold same at £11 annual rent.

1549—Writ of Entry (Common Pleas) by Anthony Howth, otherwise St. Lawrence, and Nicholas White concerning the Castle and lands of Dundalk (obliterated).—Morrin's *Patent, &c., Rolls*, v. 2, p. 139.

During this period, 1549–1550, an attempt was made by Henry the Second, then King of France, to enter into alliance with the Northern Irish Chiefs, to the detriment of the English rule in Ireland. Two envoys of France, Raimond de Beccarie, Baron de Fourquevaux, and Jean de Montesquiou, Protonotaire de Montluc, proceeded on this mission. The Baron wrote an account of the embassy, intituled—"Discours jour par jour du voyage et exploit que firent Messieurs de Montluc et de Fourquevaux au Royaume d'Hirlande, par commandement du feu Roy Henry, en l'année, 1549, selon que le dict Fourquevaux s'en peut souvenir." The reception of the ambassadors by O'Neill and O'Donnell speaks well for the manners of that age, when rudeness was the rule and decorum the exception:—"Et le reçurent le dit Hirois (O'Donnell) et pareillement sa femme, le moins mal civilement qu'ils scurent." It appears the Scotch Lords and Highland Chieftains, or, as the manuscript rather impolitely calls them (Eccossais Saulvages), endeavoured to frighten the ambassadors by exaggerating the dangers of visiting Ireland; and even the captain of the vessel hired for the voyage from Scotland, on learning they were bound for Ireland, refused to proceed:— " Disant qu'il aimoit autant perdre tout son bien comme de passer en Hirlande, où il n'y-avoit que trahitres et meurtres."

It is amusing to find the Scotch of that day described in terms equally complimentary.* The envoys of France found no difficulty in effecting the object of their mission. The Ulster chiefs were ready to transfer all their allegiance (they never pretended to much) from Edward the Sixth, of England, to Henry the Second, of France, who was to unite the crowns of France and Ireland; but, in proof of the small reliance to be placed on the treaties of Kings, in one month from the date of this treaty, 23rd February, 1550, a peace was concluded between England and France on the 21st March, wherein the Irish Chiefs were abandoned by the King of France.

In 1552, " a great war arose between the English on one side, and the Ultonians, excepting a few, and the Scots on the other; and many evils were committed between them. In consequence, the Lord Justice marched, in harvest, with an army into Ulster, and only succeeded in destroying the crops. Some of his people were slain, and he returned without gaining submission or peace." † In six years after, the Lord Deputy, Sir Henry Sidney, made a similar attempt on this province, marching from Dublin to Dundalk to fortify and strengthen the English Pale in that direction. On his arrival

* *Hume*, 5, p. 38.

† *Annals of the Four Masters.*

here he despatched messengers to Shane O'Neill, requiring his presence; but that chieftain declined coming, unless Sidney gave earnest of his good intentions by entering into the tie of gossipred with him; to which proposition the necessity of the times obliged the Deputy to consent. In this year patents for pardon were sued out by Patrick Stanley, of Dundalk, and by Walter Stanley, of same, merchants.*

In 1553, occurred a case of manslaughter in this town, which has been thought worthy of record in a special Roll of Chancery. In that year Bernard, of Balregan, labourer, assaulted Patrick Stanley, of Dundalk, gentleman, at Lisnedaghow, within the franchises of said borough of Dundalk; whereupon the said Patrick, in his own defence, and to avoid the peril of death, struck the said Bernard in his belly, of which wound he died within eleven days after. This entry is to record that said Patrick slew said Bernard in self-defence. In this year Sir Thomas Cusacke, knight, having been appointed Lord Chancellor, the usual fees were assigned to him, payable out of the customs, tonnage and poundage of the ports of Dublin, Drogheda, and *Dundalk;* or, if these be insufficient, out of the funds in the hands of the Treasurer.†

About this time Archibald Laughlin, otherwise Lill, and Edward Larkin, of Skerries, had licence to pass and trade freely with their goods to Scotland, and to purchase there sundry articles for importation in Scottish vessels, and by Scottish mariners, to the havens of Carlingford, DUNDALK, Drogheda, Dublin, Wexford, Waterford, or Ross.—Morrin's *Calendary of Patent Rolls, &c.*, Vol. I., p. 374.

In 1556, Henry Draycot surrendered to the Crown the

---

* *Rot. Pat.*, 6 Edw. 6, in *Canc. Hib.*

† *Rot. Pat.*, 1 Mary, in *Canc. Hib.*

site and possessions of the Monastery of Saint Leonard's, "near Dundalk," comprising two acres; sixty acres arable, called the Prior's Land; eleven messuages; six cottages; one garden; one hundred and two acres arable; two-and-a-half acres and three stangs of meadow; three closes; one park, containing twelve and a-half acres; a water-mill, in the town of Dundalk; two acres in Lurgan, near Dundalk; sixty acres arable in le Rath; parcel of the demesne of the Hospital; certain lands and three closes, called parks, in the Maudlins; and a messuage and thirty acres in Dromeskin. All these premises were, with many others, re-granted, in the first year of the reign of Queen Elizabeth, to said Henry Draycot in tail.*

In 1556, John Challoner, Thady Duffe, John Nagle, and John Ussher, citizens and merchants of Dublin, had licence to import, by themselves or their factors, in their ships or galleys, 1,000 hogsheads of wine, 400 weys (25 quarters) of salt, and 400 tons of iron, before the feast of the Purification of the Blessed Virgin, into the ports of Wexford, Dublin, Drogheda, and DUNDALK, with protection to the merchants engaged therein, whether French or other.† Walter Peppard, of Dublin, and James Doven, of Waterford, had a similar licence for importing into said four ports, with the addition of Waterford and Carlingford.‡

---

* *Roll*, 1 Eliz., in *Canc. Hib.*

† *Rot. Pat.* 4 and 5 Phill. and Mary. ‡ *Id.*

CHAPTER X.

FROM THE COMMENCEMENT OF THE REIGN OF QUEEN ELIZABETH TO THE YEAR 1575.

A MANUSCRIPT account of the journey of the Earl of Sussex, in 1556, says he left Kilmainham on the first of July, "and came that night to Holm Patrick, by Skerries, and there lay that night, and on Thursday came to Drogheda, and there was honourably received by the Mayor and Aldermen in their scarlet robes, and so to the High Church, where was the Most Reverend the Primate in his pontificals; and they afterwards removed to the Tholsel House; and that night his Lordship came to Dundalk, and there remained Friday all the day, and in like manner on Friday his Lordship was received, and afterwards departed to his lodging. Saturday my Lord Deputy departed Dundalk, and camped that night at Belloclara, by Mahera, Rathkay, by a little inn and a grove of small woods," and so through Ulster. On the 7th of August, on his return, he "came to Dundalk, and there lay that night; and soon after his arriving was raised a sudden alarm by reason of a boy that brought news that the Scots had set on part of the rereward. Friday, the 7th of August, the Lord Deputy removed from Dundalk, and came to Drogheda, and there lay that night. Saturday, the 8th, he removed from Drogheda and came to Kilmainham, and dined by the way at Gormanstown."

In May, 1559, the Lord Deputy got instructions from England to have an Act passed prohibiting the discharge of wines, salt, iron, or other merchandise, from any other ports than those of Carrickfergus, Strangford, Carlingford, Dundalk, Drogheda, Dublin, Wicklow, Arklow, Wexford, Waterford, Dungarvan, Youghal, Cork, Kinsale, Kildengin, Limerick, Galway, and in one certain haven, under the Burkes, in Connaught, and another under the O'Donnells. The order states the number of tuns of wine that are to be allowed for discharge at each port, and directs that any breach shall be attended with forfeiture of ship and cargo.*

In 1560, Henry Draycot, that favourite of successive monarchs, obtained from Queen Elizabeth a grant in fee of those premises, which a political timidity made only determinable, in the first year after the dissolution. The premises, which, in point of fact, he had surrendered to Queen Mary in 1556,† are, in his instance, described as the churches and rectories of Dundalk and the Maudlins, with their appurtenances; the tithes of the parish of Ballybalruk; the tithes of the lands beyond the bridge of Dundalk; the tithes of the land of Lurgan, with the appurtenances; the tithes, altarages, and appurtenances of the land of Haggard, being parcel of the possessions of St. Leonard's Hospital.‡ In the Irish Parliament of this year Christopher More and Patrick Stanley were the sitting members for Dundalk.§ At this time The O'Neill made two unsuccessful attempts on Dundalk; but in the following year "he went to England, about the 1st of November, to visit the Queen. He proceeded in great state, with a train of guards, and showed little respect for the Statutes of Kilkenny—his attendants wearing their glibs in curling tresses. They wore the *lein croich*, or saffron doublets, and, armed with bright battle-axes, were looked on with surprise by the sober citizens of East Chepe and the St. Paul's.

---

* *Harleian MSS.*, No. 35, p. 119.

† *Rot. Pat.*, 4 & 5 Phill. and Mary, in *Canc. Hib.*

‡ *Chancery Roll*, Feb. 13, 2 Eliz.

§ *Chancery Roll.*

"Elizabeth received The O'Neill with the honours due to his rank, and conversed with him upon Irish affairs. She inquired by what right he excluded Hugh from his inheritance; and, as Camden informs us, he answered fiercely, "By my good right." He explained at much length to the Queen the Brehon customs and laws of succession; and that, so far from exercising any undue authority over his tributaries in Ulster, he did no more than his forefathers were wont to do; and appears to have impressed the Queen very favourably, so that he was sent home again with honour. He returned back in the May of the following year." *

Amongst the Cottonian Manuscripts in the British Museum are various remonstrances and memorials, referring to this date, from the bailiffs, magistrates, and townspeople of Dundalk to the Lord Lieutenant; some complaining of oppressive proceedings of Shane O'Neill, whereby their traffic with Tyrone was prohibited; others stating that said O'Neill had refused to restore certain preys which he had made upon them; and again, that he had agreed to a mutual restoration of cattle with them: one advising the Lord Lieutenant of a plot concocted by said Shane; another representing the depredations committed by him and his "rebels;" and yet another denouncing Cowley MacCormick, who had robbed the inhabitants of this town of some cattle. The differences between the parties seem to have been compromised by a mutual restitution of plunder. About this time it may be curious to notice that there were only 138 houses and 690 inhabitants in Liverpool.

"In 1563, on the first of April," writes Harris, "the Earl of Sussex, Lord Lieutenant, advanced his standard against

---

* *Annals of the Four Masters.*

Shane O'Neill, who was then in rebellion, and Edward Baron, one of the sheriffs of the City of Dublin, attended his Lordship on this expedition to Dundalk, at the head of eighty archers and gunners, for twelve days; and, on the 8th of May, Walter Clinton, colleague of Baron, came to the camp with sixty fresh men, and continued there eight days. On the 1st of July the same sheriff again marched out with sixty men, and continued six weeks with the Lord Lieutenant, who, during these expeditions, had the better of the enemy in several encounters; and returned to Drogheda, and thence to Dublin, with great booty."* The Four Masters are wholly silent of Shane O'Neill at this year, but at that of 1565 they relate:—"O'Neill, *i.e.* John, the son of Con, son of Con, son of Henry, gave the sons of MacDonnell, of Scotland, *i.e.* of Alexander, the son of John Cathanah—namely, James, Angus, and Sorlay, a great overthrow, in which Angus was slain, and James wounded and taken prisoner; and he died in a year after of a mortification of his wounds. His death was very much lamented. He was a man distinguished for hospitality, feats of arms, liberality, conviviality, generosity, and bestowing of gifts, and there was not his equal among the Clan Donnell of Ireland or of Scotland; and his own people would not hesitate to give his weight in gold, and he be thereby ransomed. Many others were also slain in that battle of Glen-Taisi (Glen-Task, County Antrim) who are not recorded."† Holinshed, at 1566, gives a more explicit annal:—"Likewise the arch-traitor, O'Neill, knowing that preparation was made against him, he doth the like also on his part against her Majesty, and at a lordship or manor of his, about six miles out

* *Harris's Dublin*, p. 314.

† *Annals of the Four Masters.*

of Dundalk, he musters all his whole army, which was of 4,000 footmen and 700 horsemen, and glorying much in himself of such his great force and puissance, which he thought to have sufficed to conquer all Ireland withal, and that no man durst to adventure upon him, he marched to the town of Dundalk, where he encamped himself and besieged the same. He made sundry attempts of invasion and to enter the town, but the soldiers within were as valiant to resist and defend, which, in the end, turned to his reproach; and he had the repulse, being with shame driven to raise his siege and to depart with the loss." Harris, in his *History of Dublin*, alluding to this siege, writes:—" Shane O'Neill having made his submission to the Queen, after the last chastisement given him by the Earl of Sussex, broke out again this year into rebellion, and invaded Fermanagh, expelled from thence Maguire, at that time a peaceable subject, burned the Cathedral of Armagh, and at length laid siege to Dundalk; but the valour of the garrison preserved the place until William Sarsfield, Mayor of Dublin, marched out with a chosen body of citizens, and, without any other assistance, raised the siege, and delivered the Lady Sydney, who was then enclosed in it; for which service, as well as for an expedition he made this year against O'Reilly, he was, upon his return to Dublin, knighted, by the Lord Lieutenant."

In the following year " O'Neill," says Hollinshed, " again entered the English Pale with sword and fire, wasted the country, and slew many of her Majesty's subjects, and, in the end, besieged her town of Dundalk, where his pride and treason were justly scourged, who came out with so much glory to besiege it as he did, return with shame to leave and lose it."

In the August of this latter year, Sir Henry Sydney, Lord

Deputy, thus fully reported to Robert, Earl of Leicester:—"I have long forborne to send my advertisements into England, because, since the first day of this month, I have been hourly in expectation of news from thence, and especially for the supplies of men and money necessary for the extirpation of the tyrant and traitor, Shane O'Neill; and albeit this bearer, my Lord Primate, having seen, and I suppose noted, the actions of the rebel, can sufficiently report and testify the insolency of him, yet have I thought good to advertise to your Lordship thus much of his doings. About the 26th of the last month I was certainly informed that he would forthwith repair to the borders with his whole force to invade the English Pale; whither he came indeed, and therein confirmed my opinion in my former letters to the Queen's Majesty, wherein I judged that, after the beginning of August, he would break out into war. His coming known, it was thought meet that I likewise, with a convenient force, should repair to Dundalk; which force I gathered, through the willingness of the people, within two days. I repaired thither with the garrison and the country people, to the number, as I suppose, of 1,500 foot and 600 horsemen, and, in the mean season, received letters of him of divers effect—some humbly urging a Parliament, and others full of insolency, refusing to be any subject to those that should keep or assist his servant, Maguire, as he termed him. Notwithstanding being advertised that he had taken an oath to give us battle, if we issued out of Dundalk, I marched forth to the hill foot, where he encamped, and there continued till the evening without any matter offered saving small skirmishes. The next day likewise we went again to the mouth of his parts, and through the greatest; all which time he kept himself in his fastness, without offering any fight, save with a few horsemen and certain kearns, whereof part were slain. On our part none hurt save one of the Earl of Kildare's gentlemen, wounded with a Scottish arrow, and the Earl himself, with desperate following of a horseman into a pace, shot through a slop of his nose with a culliver, but not hurt. At our return to Dundalk it was thought meet that necessary force should be left to defend the towns, and that the rest should repair, some being thereunto constrained through the want of victuals. Within two days after my departure thence O'Neill made a rade into the Pale. and, for lack of due observation of my former commandments, wherein the people were willed to 'stripe' their houses, he burned certain villages on the border, whereof the chief was the Haggard (Haggardstown). The next day he repaired to Dundalk and besieged that town, where I had left the soldiers under the leading of Captain Bryan Fitz-Williams. The town was of itself so ruinous as it was scarce guardable, and, besides, of so great circuit that it offered no small disadvantage to the defendants. The Irish entered the town, but had such a welcome as the traitor lost there of his gentlemen so many, as I was credibly informed, there were seventeen of their country horse-litters filled with dead corses, and sent to be buried at Armagh, besides those that he buried near the town, which, as some of them have confessed, were about the number of a hundred. Those that were slain within the walls do now garnish the gate with their heads; but such was the repulse as he could not procure any more of his men to follow the enterprise; and sure, my Lord, it was manfully and honorably defended. From there he departed towards Carlingford, where he made a shew as though he would have attempted that town; nevertheless he did nothing, but departed with speed to the farthest part of Ulster, to treat with the Scots to have assistance from them. I am certainly informed that he offered to them of Cantyre all Clandeboy, all the 'geld kine' of his country, to deliver Sorleboy, and to give them pledge and assurance of his fidelity towards them. But I, fearing this beforehand, have temporized with the Captain of Cantyre, Sorley, his brother, that they have utterly refused his requests, as I am certainly advised. Without hope of aid and relief from them, he has now again returned to the borders." * The character and result of this temporizing is denounced by the Four Masters at 1567.

"O'Neill, *i.e.* John, the son of Con Bacagh, son of Con, son of Henry, son of Owen, having mustered a very large force for the purpose of marching into Tyrconnell against O'Donnell, namely Hugh, his sister's son, the son of Manus, son of Hugh Oge, son of Hugh Roe, and to prey and plunder the country as he had formerly done when O'Donnell was not able to defend or protect his principality or country through infirmity and sickness, and the quarrels and conflicts of his own sons with each other. The place where O'Donnell happened to have been with his few forces along with Hugh, the son of Hugh Oge, *i.e.* Hugh Dubh, the son of Hugh Roe, and his relative, was at Ard-an-Ghaire, on the north side of the bay of Swilly; and having received intelligence that O'Neill had marched with his forces to the country, he sent messages calling on these chiefs in his neighbourhood, while he himself remained in expectation of them; but, however, they did not all come at his call, as it was very early in the day. Such, however, as were there along with him, unexpectedly beheld at a distance, on the opposite side of the 'fearsad' (pass) of Swilly, a mighty force advancing towards them, in troops and companies; they did not halt, but marched on in battle array,

---

* *Sydney's State Letters*, v. i., 15–6.

and, without stopping, crossed the pass, as the tide was out at the time. O'Donnell having perceived that, at once drew up in order and array his small select force, and sent a troop of his cavalry, commanded by the son of O'Donnell, namely, Hugh, the son of Hugh, to attack the front of the enemy, in order that he himself might bring his foot forces across the open plains to some secure place where his foes could not circumvent or surround them."

Although the narrative is not of strict connexion with Dundalk, it yet has so much of national interest, and ultimately so develops the destiny of O'Neill, that its full particulars seem worthy of insertion.

"O'Donnell's horsemen having engaged with the advanced cavalry of O'Neill, Nial, the son of Donough Cairbreagh, son of Hugh Oge, son of Hugh Roe; Donal Ultach MacDunlevy, the son of the doctor, chief physician to O'Donnell; and MacRafferty, the keeper of the Cathach* of Columbkill, were slain by O'Neill's forces; some, however, state that it was by his own people, Nial O'Donnell. On the side of the Tyronian, the son of MacMahon, and several others were

---

* This "Cathach" is still existing. It is a brass box, nine and a-half inches long, eight broad, and two in thickness, and originally contained a copy of the Psalms in MS. from the Latin Vulgate, and was called the Psalter of Columbkille, as having been supposed transcribed by that celebrated saint in the sixth century. The top consists of a plate of silver, richly gilt and chased, riveted to one of brass, and on it are figures of St. Columbkille, the crucifixion, &c. This reliquary took its name of "Cathach" from being carried as a military ensign before the forces of the O'Donnells in battle, and was carefully preserved in the family of that sept. It has latterly been deposited in the Museum of the Royal Irish Academy, the fitting repository for all the national antiquities of Ireland.

slain. When the son of O'Donnell, *i.e.* Hugh, the son of Hugh, perceived the great numbers opposed to him, and that his Lord had retired to a place of security, he followed him and halted there in expectation of receiving re-inforcements from his people to overtake him. He had not been long in that great suspense when he beheld companies of his faithful friends advancing towards him, and was overjoyed at their arrival. Those who came to his aid were, in the first place, MacSweeney of the districts, namely, Murrough, Mael, the son of Owen, son of Owen; the sons of MacSweeny of Fanat, Turlogh Oge, and Hugh Buighe, and MacSweeney Banagh, *i.e.* Maolmurry, the son of Hugh, son of Niall; and when these forces had come together they formed no great force, for they did not number more than four hundred. O'Donnell then complained to these chiefs of his wrongs and injuries, and said to them that it would be better and more agreeable for him to die in the field rather than suffer all the disgrace and ignominious treatment exercised by the people of Tyrone against himself, his kindred, and relations, such as none of his ancestors had ever endured or submitted to before; but particularly the insult and ignominy which they had then exercised against him, viz., by forcibly expelling and banishing him from his fortress. All these chiefs coincided in the sentiments delivered by the noble Prince, and said that the complaints and opinions he had expressed were true, and that they were willing to attack O'Neill and his forces. Intrepidly bold, and bravely determined was the resolution they came to, viz., to encounter so great a hazard and danger as awaited them; but, however, they regarded more their honour and their inheritance than they valued their lives and bodies. With elated unanimity they then returned back in a well arranged small body, and amicably united force, to attack O'Neill's camp. When O'Neill beheld them advancing directly towards him he was greatly excited in his mind with compassion for them, and said:—'I am very much surprised and astonished that those people should not find it easier to submit to us and acquiesce in our terms than come before us to fight, and be forthwith annihilated.' While engaged with these observations, the troops of Tyrconnell rushed forward with boldness and impetuosity in front of O'Neill's forces; that seemed to be no startling sight to O'Neill's soldiers, for they were accoutring themselves as fast as possible, until they had marched up to them. When they came in close view fierce and ill-favoured were the threatening and grim looks they exchanged with each other from their piercing eye-balls, and they raised aloud their united war-cry, which was sufficient to put to flight unwarlike and faint-hearted soldiers on their rushing together. . . . Thirteen hundred of O'Neill's forces were either slain or drowned in that battle; and it is stated in other books that upwards of three thousand of O'Neill's forces were lost on that day. As to O'Neill he escaped from the battle, and he would have preferred that he had not, for his mind and faculties were affected ever after it; he privately fled, unnoticed by any one, southward along the river until he passed Ath-Tairsi, in the neighbourhood of Sgariff-Sholais, by the guidance of a party of the O'Gallaghers, who were of O'Donnell's own clan and people, and he did not stop, but proceeded through every private uninhabited place until he arrived in Tyrone. Few houses or residences, from Carlingford to the river Finn, were without copious weeping and general lamentation; immense and incalculable was the booty, consisting of horses, arms, and accoutrements left in possession of the Tyrconnallians on that occasion. It was on the 8th of May that battle of the Pass of Swilly was fought.

"After O'Neill had gone to Tyrone, as we have before stated, he took no rest or recreation, nor did he sleep a wink until he sent despatches, inviting the sons of James, the son of Alexander, son of John Cathanach, of the race of MacDonnell from Scotland. That was the cause of shortness of life and of death, for him to invite the sons of the man who had fallen by his hands on a former occasion. They accordingly came, with a large fleet, and landed at Bun-Avon-Dune (Cushendun Bay, County Antrim), where they constructed a strong camp, with numerous entrenchments. When O'Neill received intelligence of that large force having come to his aid, without taking into consideration his former enmity towards them, he incautiously committed himself to the protection of that fierce and revengeful clan, without pledge or security, in order that he might avenge his enmity and hatred against the Tyrconnallians. The reception he got from them, after being in their company for some time, and after they had detailed their former animosity and injuries, was suddenly to attack him, and instantly cleave him with their swords, so that they left him dead on the spot.* The race of Eogan, son of Nial, much lamented the death of him who was there slain; for that O'Neill—namely, John, was their Concevar, as a Provincial King; their Lughaidh of the Long Hand in valour; their Champion in chivalry and bravery."

---

* William Piers, an officer and agent of the Court, is stated, by Stuart, in his *Armagh*, to have excited the Scots to assassinate O'Neill; and he and Ware allege that, after O'Neill had been buried four days, Piers raised the body, cut off the head, and presented it to the above Lord Deputy, Sir Henry Sydney, who directed it to be put up on the gate of Dublin Castle, while Piers received a reward of 1,000 marks, for the part he had taken in stimulating the Scots to this act of atrocity.

In two years after an Act of Attainder was passed against this chieftain; and thereupon all his extensive estates, together with the greater part of the County Tyrone, were confiscated, and seized by the Crown. A yet more extensive massacre of this devoted sept was perpetrated in 1574, when, according to the Four Masters, "an amicable treaty having been concluded between Bryan, the son of Felim Bacach O'Neill and the Earl of Essex, then residing at Carrickfergus,* the former gave invitations to a feast to the Lord Justice and the nobles of his suite, where they enjoyed themselves together in mirth and cheerfulness for the space of three days and three nights. At the termination of that time, while drinking and carousing agreeably together, Bryan, with his brother and wife, were taken prisoners by the Earl, and all his people, without reserve—men, women, sons and daughters—were put to the sword in his presence. Bryan, with his wife and brother, were sent to Dublin, where they were cut into quarters; and this was the result of their entertainment. That monstrous massacre and detestable and treacherous misdeed which was perpetrated on the Lord of Clandeboy, O'Neill, Chief and senior of the race of Eogan, the son of Niall of the Nine Hostages, and of the greater portion of the Gael of Ireland, excepting a few, was a sufficient cause of abomination and disgust to the Irish people." The same annalists record that in the Kalends of May, in this year, "a shower of hailstones fell, which was so

---

* "Within these few years there were some vestiges of the house in which he dwelt, at the south end east side of Essex-street. The walk adjoining the house was also called, from him, Governor's Walk, lately changed to Governor's Place. A double row of elm trees remained in the walk till 1820. At the west end was an embattled bastion, called Essex-Mount."—*M'Skimmin's Carrickfergus*, p. 29, n.

extraordinary and uncommon that there were many persons in Ireland who never witnessed such a shower; and there were many others whose strong-built family residences were swept away by it. The corn crops, which had been sown three months or half-a-year previous to that time, were left without stalk or blade; and the same shower left soft, blue lumps, as large as the hailstones that fell, on the legs of those who were struck by them.

CHAPTER XI.

FROM THE YEAR 1575 TO THE BATTLE OF BEAL-AN-ATH-BUIDHE.

In 1575, Sir Henry Sydney was a second time deputed for the Government of Ireland. On account of the prevalence of plague in Dublin he landed at Skerries, whence he proceeded to Drogheda, where he took the oaths, and afterwards kept his Court for some time. The Four Masters, speaking of his arrival, say, he "found all Ireland in one wave of war and commotion. He established peace, union, and friendship, between the Tyrconnallians and Tyroneans, and throughout the Province of Ulster; and he expelled to England the Earl of Essex, who had invaded Ulster, and acted treacherously towards Con, the son of Calvach O'Donnell, and Bryan, the son of Phelim Bacagh O'Neill." It was at this time that the new Deputy made a report that "the good towns of Carlingford, Dundalk, and Ardee, are extremely impoverished; and only the town of Drogheda in better state, which was more amended and increased in wealth through the great expenses of the Earl of Essex, who lay and continued there much; and during his abode very bountifully and honorably spent in the same." The efforts of Sir Henry Sydney to establish peace in Munster and Connaught are no less extolled by the Four Masters at the year 1576.

In 1577 John Bellew, of Bellewstown, was seised in fee of fifteen messuages, fifteen gardens, and eighty acres in this town, of a chief rent issuing thereout, and of the presentation to the vicarage of Dundalk. He was also seised by like title of the manor of the Roche, adjacent, containing one castle, twenty cottages and gardens, and three hundred acres of arable land; Killaglie, one castle, fifteen cottages and gardens, and one hundred and eighty acres; Castleton, two castles, thirty houses and gardens, and three hundred acres; also of one castle, fifteen cottages and gardens, and one hundred and eighty acres in Donamore, certain chief rents issuing out of Tullaghodonnell, &c.*

The years 1581 and 1582, are commemorated by the Irish annalists as years of great wind, constant rain, stormy weather, and excessive dearth then prevalent, while the former year was remarkable for an abundance of large nuts.†

In a letter dated 24th March, 1582, Sir Nicholas Malby, by a despatch to Lord Burghley, preserved in the State Papers' Office, thus represents the condition of the Pale at that time:—" Touching the northern borders, adjoining the English Pale, it may please your Lordship to understand that lately I was appointed by the Lords Justices, amongst other Commissioners, to repair to Dundalk, where were found such disorders of spoiling, robbing, and murdering of Her Majesty's good subjects by the men of the Fews, Farney, MacMahon's country, the Dartreys, and O'Reilly's country, as pitiful as is

---

* *Inquis.* of 1614, in *Canc. Hib.*

† *Annals Four Masters.*

to be heard; we passed many orders against them, but no restitution could be had from them; and to take it by force that may not be done for fear of stirring the Irishry to rebellion, which will breed charges to Her Majesty; which the Irish perceiving, do not only scorn the orders, but hold on their wicked doings against the subjects, which be made thralles to the Irishry." Soon after this, at another meeting held in Dundalk, Hugh O'Neill, then styled Baron of Dungannon, offered to defend the Pale if a force of two hundred footmen were provided and maintained for him. Ultimately, however, this responsible trust was deputed to the Baron of Dunsany, who, by warrant of July 30, 1583, was constituted Guardian of the Borders of the Breney (Cavan), the Fews, Farney, and MacMahon's country (Monaghan), where his ancestors, the Plunketts, have most continued, with a small band of twenty horsemen to attend him."* "All that part of the country to the north, beyond the mouth of the river Boyne, makes the fifth part of Ireland, and is a large province watered with many considerable loughs, and sheltered with huge woods. It is fruitful in some places and barren in others, yet very green and sightly in all parts, and well stocked with cattle; but as the soil, for want of culture, is rough and barren, as the inhabitants, for want of education and learning, are very wild and barbarous—to keep them in subjection and order (for neither the bonds of justice, modesty, nor duty could restrain them) the hither part was divided into three counties—Louth, Down, and Antrim; and, since, the rest was divided into these seven counties—Cavan, Fermanagh, Monaghan, Armagh, Coleraine, Tyroen, and Donegal or TyrConnell, by the wise contrivance of John Perrott, Lord Deputy, a person

* State Papers' Office.

truly great and famous, and thoroughly acquainted with the temper of this province; for being sensible that nothing would more effectually appease the tumult of Ireland than the regulation and settlement of these parts of Ulster, he went thither in person, in that troublesome and dangerous juncture, when a Spanish descent was daily expected there and in England, and by his gravity and authority, while he took care to punish oppressions (the great causes of rebellion), he gained so much upon the petty Kings here, that they willingly suffered their seignories to be divided into counties, and admitted sheriffs to govern them. But being quickly recalled, and aspiring to greater honours, some envious persons, who were too powerful for him, together with the licentiousness of his own tongue (for he had thrown out some words against his Sovereign, whose majesty may not be violated by word or thought), brought him unawares to ruin. But when we speak of the wildness and barbarity of the inhabitants of Ulster, this is to be understood of the Irish inhabitants only, who are now so routed out and destroyed by their many rebellions, and by the accession of Scots, who for the most part inherit this province, that there are not supposed to be left ten thousand Irish able and fit to bear arms in Ulster." So writes Camden of this province, at the close of the sixteenth century, when it was the interest of his royal mistress that the condition of this noble territory, and its tanists and occupants, should be decried.

In the Harleian MSS. is preserved a copy of a letter written in this year by Sir Henry Wallop, then residing in Dundalk, to Queen Elizabeth, in which he entreats to know—"wherein he hath offended Her Majesty, since report said she had conceived some hard opinion of him, whereof he could not find the reason."

In the memorable Parliament which commenced in 1585, Richard, son of Sir John Bellew, of Verdonstown, represented, together with Thomas Bathe, the borough of Dundalk, while, of the more ancient family of the founder of this town, John Verdon was the member for the distant borough of Kilmallock. The assembling of this first great coalition Council was preceded by a Royal proclamation to "the men of Ireland," commanding their chiefs to attend in Dublin precisely in May; for most of the men of Ireland were obedient to their Sovereign, so that they all came to meet each other at that command. Thither came the Chiefs of Tyrconnell, and Tyrone—namely, O'Neill, Prince of Tyrone, *i.e.* Turlogh Luineach, the son of Nial Conallach, son of Art, son of Conn, son of Henry, son of Owen—namely, the young Baron O'Neill, who was nominated Earl of Tyrone at that Parliament; and O'Donnell, Prince of Tyrconnell, *i.e.* Hugh, the son of Manus, son of Hugh Dubh, son of Hugh Roe, son of Nial Garv, son of Turlogh of the Wine; Maguire, Prince of Fermanagh, *i.e.* Cuchonaght, the son of Cuchonaght, son of Bryan, son of Philip, son of Thomas. . . . MacMahon, Prince of Orgiel—namely, Rossa, son of Art, son of Bryan-na-Moicherge, son of Redmond, son of Glaisne," &c., &c., &c.*

It was the most independent and respectable Parliament that hitherto met in Ireland—Sir John Perrott being the Lord Deputy—yet were its Acts, as printed, but few. The attainders of the Earl of Desmond, of the Viscount Baltinglas, of John Browne of the County Limerick, and their adherents, with a confiscation of their extensive estates, together with statutes against wilful perjury; against witchcraft and sorcery; against forging and publishing false and untrue charters and

---

* See *Annals of the Four Masters, ad annum.*

deeds; against counterfeiting foreign coin; an act of imposts and customs of wines; and another concerning the avoiding of fraudulent conveyances made by the late rebels in Ireland to defraud the Queen of forfeiture, were the chief enactments.

The year 1586 is represented by the Four Masters as one of "wet weather, unproductive corn, and a great deal of nuts;" while they also state that "five hundred Irishmen left their country to aid the Queen in the war of Flanders; and although the most of them were lost in that country, their fame and renown spread throughout Europe, as being distinguished for valour and bravery." An inquisition of 1587 finds that all the possessions of the Cross-Bearers of Dundalk, all their rents, services, rectories, tithes, &c., in the County of Meath, and which are therein enumerated, had been some years previously granted to Henry Draycot and his assigns.*

In 1589, a suit was instituted in Chancery, by Lord Delvin and Thomas FitzSymons against Patrick Sharane and Nicholas Corbet, late Bailiffs of Dundalk; Richard Horton, Henry Dowdall, and others. The plaintiffs alleged that they and their ancestors, and those whose estate they have, in the manor of Haggard, County of Dublin, were, from time immemorial, quietly seised of a common of pasture, called the "Messes," between the Haggard and Dundalk, for themselves, their tenants, and the inhabitants of the manor, for all manner of cattle, and so continued seised until said bailiffs, in July, 1585, came to the "Messes," and wrongfully and forcibly drove thereoff the cattle of the petitioner and his tenants. An answer to this bill affirmed that the Bailiffs and Commons of Dundalk were seised, time out of mind, of the place and soil of the "Messes," discharged of any such common of pasture

---

* *Inquis.* in *Canc. Hib.*

as sought by the complainants. The Lord Chancellor (assisted by Master Robert Gardiner, Chief Justice of the Common Pleas) decreed, that the Bailiffs and Commons of Dundalk had been seised in their demesne of the "Messes" in right of their Corporation, and took the profits thereof as of their several soil, discharged of any common except from Knocktully to the lake, or river, adjoining to Carrick Denrake, on which piece of ground only, of all the "Messes," the complainants had and do enjoy a common for all their beasts without interruption.

In 1594 Hugh O'Donnell, Prince of Tyrconnell, made his escape from the Castle of Dublin. This renowned chieftain was called *Bal Dearg O'Donnell*, or *Red Hugh*, from a red spot on his skin. His capture, during the Viceroyalty of Sir John Perrott, was one of those pieces of treachery which retarded the growth of any confidence between the native Irish and their English rulers—one of those instances of mistaken policy which defeated itself, and invariably produced a fertile crop of disasters. Perrott, dreading the power of Manus O'Donnell, and other Ulster chiefs, proposed they should give him hostages of their fidelity, and, on their refusal, bethought himself of a notable stratagem to gain his object. He employed a merchant of Dublin, named Bingham, to freight a vessel with wine, and manned her with fifty armed men. The captain of the vessel had instructions to touch at the ports of Tyrconnell, under pretence of selling the cargo, the real object being to decoy the young Prince, Hugh O'Donnell, and his companions on board, and bring them to Dublin. The vessel arrived in Lough Swilly, and Hugh O'Donnell, with Eugene MacSweeney, Lord of Tuath, MacSweeney of Fanid, Sir Eugene O'Gallagher, and others, went on board to examine the wines. The captain received them with respect, but, true to his base instructions, bore off his prey; and the young Prince and nobles, finding themselves outnumbered by the armed band on board the ship, were powerless to resist. The nobles of O'Donnell's suite were exchanged for hostages, but the young Prince was kept in captivity in Dublin Castle, which all honourable men regarded as a gross breach of faith.

Perrott met his just reward. On his return to England he was himself placed in confinement, and died in the Tower of London.

For seven dreary winters, and while seven summers shed bloom over the rich plains of Tyrconnell, Red Hugh pined in the fortress of Athcliath. He had, for fellow captives, Henry and Art, sons of Shane O'Neill, Philip O'Reilly, Fiach O'Byrne, the implacable enemy of the English,* and Edward Eustace of the noble house of Baltinglas. These gallant spirits planned a mode of escape which proved successful. Procuring a supply of linen for shirts, they united their stock, and cut it into strips, which formed a rope sufficiently strong to sustain a man's weight, and, by means of this, all, save Art O'Neill, descended in safety from their prison under the cover of night, and, crossing the outer wall, got clear of the city. Art O'Neill had the misfortune to be struck by a stone that got displaced from the wall, as he descended, and his death, shortly after, terminated his captivity. Supplies of horses, and every means that was needed to ensure their safe return, were readily placed at the service of the Irish chieftains by their countrymen, and, unquestioned, they passed Dundalk, the frontier of the Pale, and soon the glad shout of *O'Donnell aboo! Bal Dearg aboo!* rang through the glens of Tyrconnell. On his

* *MacGeoghegan*, vol. iii., p. 206.

arrival, his father, who was advanced in years, yielded him the chieftainship with the consent of the clan. He was unanimously elected and acknowledged "The O'Donnell," Prince of Tyrconnell, by O'Phile, who was minister of that ceremony in the family of O'Donnell. He soon commenced hostilities against those he regarded as the invaders of his country.

In the commencement of the year 1595, Red Hugh O'Donnell, crossing the river Erne, and passing over Leitrim, invaded Connaught, and subsequently burned the town of Longford, while the O'Neill's were plundering the country round Kells and Slane. "When the English were convinced that the Earl O'Neill rose in alliance with O'Donnell in the war, the Lord Justice, Sir William Russell,* and the Council sent 1,000 warriors to Newry, to fight against the Tyroneans; and the Lord Justice promised to follow them with his forces to plunder and spoil the country. O'Neill sent messages to O'Donnell requesting him to come to his aid against the oppressors who had come to his country, which was not negligently heard by O'Donnell, for he mustered his forces, proceeded through Tyrone to the place where O'Neill was, and then both marched to Foghart of Muirthemne, near Dundalk, in the month of May. When the Lord Justice received intelligence that they were both at that place prepared for him he remained in Dublin on that occasion."†

In 1596, "when the Lord Justice and the Council of Ireland perceived the strength and power of the Irish against them, and that all those whom they had brought under subjection to themselves before that time were joining in alliance with the forementioned Irish in opposition to them, the resolution they

* Youngest son of the Earl of Bedford.

† *Annals of the Four Masters.*

came to was, to send ambassadors to O'Neill and O'Donnell to sue for peace and truce from them. The persons chosen for negotiating affairs between them were Thomas, Earl of Ormonde, and the Archbishop of Cashel, Meyler Magrath. The Earl of Ormonde proceeded to Dundalk, where he remained, and sent despatches to O'Neill, informing him of the object of his arrival there. O'Neill sent the same messenger to O'Donnell; and O'Donnell, with a large body of cavalry, having gone to where O'Neill was, they both proceeded to Foghart Muirthemne. The Earl and Archbishop having come to them, they related to the chiefs the object which had brought them, viz.:—That it was to treat for peace they were sent; and they related the terms which the Lord Justice proposed—the confirmation of the Province of Ulster to them, except the country from Dundalk to the Boyne, which was inhabited by the English for a long period before that time; and along with that, they promised that the English should not encroach on them beyond that boundary, except the English that were in Carrickfergus, in Carlingford, and in Newry, who were always permitted to deal and traffic; that no stewards or collectors of rents or tributes should be sent among them, but that the rents which had been some time before upon their ancestors should be forwarded by them to Dublin; that beyond this no hostages or pledges would be required; and that the Irish in the Province of Connaught, who had risen up in alliance with O'Donnell, should have privileges similar to those. O'Neill, O'Donnell, and all the Chiefs of the Province who were there along with them, went into council upon these conditions which were brought to them; and, having reflected for a long time upon the many that had been ruined by the English since their arrival in Ireland, by specious promises, which they had not performed, and the numbers of Irish high-born princes, gentlemen, and chieftains, who came to premature deaths without any reason at all, except to rob them of their patrimonies, they feared very much that what was then promised would not be fulfilled to them; so that they finally resolved on rejecting the peace. They communicated their decision to the Earl, who proceeded to Dublin to the Lord Justice and the Council, and related to them his having been refused the peace, and the answer he received from the Irish. The Lord Justice and the Council sent despatches to England to the Queen, informing her of those affairs; so that she then sent an immense number of men to Ireland, with a supply of military stores; and their number was not less than twenty thousand of paid forces and common soldiers, for the purpose of carrying on war against the Irish. A very great army was afterwards mustered by the Queen's war general in Ireland—namely, Sir John Norris—to march into the Province of Connaught, for the purpose of subduing all those who had risen in alliance in the war of the Irish. The Earl of Clanrickard—namely, Ulick, the son of Rickard Sassenach, son of Ulick of the Heads, with all his forces, joined the army. The Earl of Thomond—namely, Donogh, the son of Conor, son of Donogh O'Brien, also joined them with his forces, and numerous other forces besides, which are not recorded; but, however, some have stated that such an army belonging to the Sovereign had not been collected for a long period of time in Ireland as that, for the greatness of its full muster, its foreign forces, and their extraordinary equipment and superior power.*

"In 1597, a new Lord Justice—namely, Thomas, Lord Burrough, came to Ireland in the beginning of the month of

* *Annals of the Four Masters.*

June, with a great deal of arms and soldiers, and having received the sword from the Lord Justice, who had been in the Government for three years till then—namely, Sir William Russell, he deprived Sir John Norris of the office which he held from his Sovereign, viz., the generalship of the war, and he himself assumed that office. He afterwards issued a proclamation to the men of Leinster and Meath, and to all those who were obedient to the Queen, from the Meeting of the Three Waters (at Waterford) to Dundalk, to meet him, with all their forces fully mustered, at Drogheda on the 20th day of July. Those orders were attended to by the Earl of Kildare and by the English of Meath and Leinster. The Lord Justice, with all the force he could muster, arrived at the same place; and, after the forces had met together, they marched to Tyrone, and proceeded to Avonmore (the Blackwater) without opposition or halting; and, what was unusual with O'Neill, an advantage was obtained of his watching until the Lord Justice had crossed the river, without battle or opposition, and had arrived on the other side of it. The Lord Justice broke up and demolished the guarding fort which O'Neill had on the banks of the river, and he raised a new fort for himself on the opposite side of the same river (the fort of Blackwater, in Armagh); and, although that opportunity was gained of O'Neill through the information and instruction of Turlough, the son of Henry, son of Phelim Roe O'Neill, the Lord Justice or any of his forces did not attempt to proceed the distance of a mile beyond that into Tyrone; and they were not allowed rest or quiet, sleep or peace, from a continued skirmishing and firing carried on against them by O'Neill's people, both by day and night. It was impossible to enumerate or relate the immense numbers of the Lord Justice's people that were slain and destroyed, and all the horses and booty that were taken from them. On a certain day the Lord Justice went to a hill in the neighbourhood of the camp to reconnoitre and view the surrounding country; and truly it were better for him he had not gone, for a great number of his officers were slain by O'Neill and his men. Amongst these were the brother of the Lord Justice's wife, the chief officer of his forces, together with a great number of captains and gentlemen, besides some of the Earl of Kildare's people, were also slain there; and were it not that the camp was so near the Lord Justice those who escaped would not have survived that conflict. It happened to the Earl of Kildare—namely, Henry, the son of Gerald—that, either by cause of some wound or fever, he was obliged to set out for his home; and, having arrived at Drogheda, he died in that town. His body was conveyed to Kildare, and buried with honour and solemnity in the tomb of his ancestors; and his brother, William, was appointed his successor. After the Lord Justice had completed that new fort on the banks of the Blackwater, and having considered all he lost of his men, and that he was not suffered to advance into the country farther than that place, he put provisions and guards into the fort, and he prepared to return back himself. He first proceeded to Newry, and from thence to Dublin, and his forces returned to their homes. . . . On the Lord Justice leaving Tyrone, as we have before stated, and having left provisions and guards in that new fort (Portmore), which he himself raised on the banks of the Avonmore, he proceeded to Dublin. As to O'Neill, he and his people did not cease after that, either by day or by night, endeavouring to take, by stratagem or assault, that fort, and be avenged on the guards who were in it. One day that they attacked that place thirty of their people were slain, and they effected nothing against the fortress. When the Lord Justice learned that his guards were harassed in that manner, and that they were in want of stores, he collected a very great force, for the purpose of proceeding to put provisions and all other sorts of stores into the fort. The Lord Justice having arrived at Armagh with his forces, he proceeded, with all the cavalry of the army about him, some distance before his soldiers and companies, in the hope of taking by surprise some of O'Neill's people. When he came near the Blackwater, he fell in with a troop of cavalry and a company of soldiers of O'Neill's people; a fierce conflict and violent engagement ensued between them, and many men were slain and horses lost, on the side of the Lord Justice, in that battle. When his soldiers came up to the Lord Justice he proceeded to the fort; and some have stated that he was not well from that day forth. Having left provisions and guards in the fort, on the following day they prepared to return back, and they did not go beyond Armagh that night; it was in a carriage the Lord Justice was conveyed, or he was carried in a litter by his people, *i.e.* either by his relatives or friends, without the knowledge of the greater portion of the forces. O'Neill carried on firing and skirmishing on the Lord Justice's camp that night, by which the chief commander of the forces, and many others besides, were slain. They marched from thence to Newry, and the Lord Justice died in that town from the effects of the wounds which were inflicted on him while coming from Armagh to the new fort. The keeping of the sword of state was entrusted to the Chancellor (Adam Loftus) and to the Chief Justice of the King's Bench—namely, Sir Robert Gardiner—until a new Lord Justice should come from England."*

Dundalk was the scene of an important conference shortly

---

* *Annals of the Four Masters.*

after this. The Earl of Ormonde, who always maintained a friendly front towards O'Neill, was made Commander-in-Chief of the Queen's army, with the title of Lord Lieutenant of Ireland, instead of that of Lord Deputy, heretofore used. He had instructions to come to terms with O'Neill, and make a peace, if possible. A truce of two months was agreed upon, and O'Neill met the Lord Lieutenant at Dundalk to arrange the terms upon which peace would prevail.

The conditions of the Irish chieftain were:—

First.—Religious freedom throughout Ireland.

Secondly.—Reparation for the spoil and ravages by the English garrisons in the north.

Thirdly.—Entire control over their native territories and clansmen by the Irish chiefs.

These claims were to be submitted to the English Council; and during the truce O'Neill was to hold no communication with Spain, to recall his troops from Leinster, to allow safe conduct to the English officers going to and from their castles, and allow his people to supply victuals to the garrison at Portmore. On the 11th April, 1598, authority arrived from the Queen giving Ormonde power to grant O'Neill her pardon, on his engaging to break up the northern confederacy, disband his forces, repair the Blackwater fort and bridge, renounce the title of *O'Neill*, and all jurisdiction thereto belonging, deliver up all traitors, surrender into the hands of Ormonde Shane O'Neill's two sons, and finally, give up his own son as a hostage for the due performance of his engagements.*

These terms were instantly rejected. Ormonde had the pardon made out, with the great seal attached, and pressed its acceptance upon the Irish chieftain.

---

* *Moryson.*

Dundalk was to be the limit of English rule, and the Irish were to possess all the country north of this town. It was in vain. The haughty Irish chieftain's pride was hurt at the conditions sought to be imposed, and, as Moryson states—"Continuing his disloyal courses he never pleaded the same pardon, so upon his indictment you shall find him outlawed in 1600." These negotiations for peace were regarded but as pretexts, on the part of O'Neill, to prolong the truce until the arrival of succour from Spain; but it failing to arrive, he organized his allies in the north for a resolute stand against the English. Moryson computes the Ulster troops at 1,702 horse, and 7,220 infantry, a large army considering the state of the north of Ireland at the time, and the difficulty attending an invading force from the want of roads and the means of support, while engaged with the Irish in their fastnesses.

Hugh O'Neill and Red Hugh O'Donnell commanded the Ulster troops. Though equal in rank and authority they seem to have worked harmoniously. It must have been an anxious time for the English garrison in the Pale when these renowned commanders took the field. In July, 1598, O'Neill sent word to the chief of the O'Byrnes that he might fall upon the Pale, while he himself assaulted Portmore, the stout fortress on the Blackwater that frowned over the fertile valleys of Tyrone.

O'Neill led his forces to the assault; but if there were strong arms without, there were brave hearts within. The fort had been entrusted to the command of Captain Thomas Williams, and well he deserved the trust. Undismayed by the numbers or appearance of the besiegers, the English commander kept alive the courage of his men, and they met the foe hand to hand. In vain, with wild shouts and daring courage, O'Neill's troops sought to drive the strangers from Kinel-Eoghain. In vain the Red Hand* was pointed against the hated fortress, bristling with English spears. In vain the gallowglasses and light armed kernes clambered to the parapets, or strove to creep through the embrasures; they were hurled down by sheer force, and heavy stones crushed them when they fell. Devoid of ordnance or engineering skill, the Irish chiefs were baffled; they could do nothing save wait, so O'Neill turned the siege into a blockade, and, encompassing the walls to prevent food reaching the garrison, sought to starve them into submission. Meanwhile the sufferings of the brave men within may be imagined; the food stored in their vaults was gone; they then slaughtered their horses until there were none left; the grass that grew in wild luxuriance adown the sides of their ramparts, or on the borders of the ditches, was seized on with eagerness. Day by day many a wistful eye was turned southward to see the glinting of spears, or the waving of St. George's flag, announcing that succour was at hand. At last the wished for relief drew nigh, and Marshal Sir Henry Bagnal, at the head of the best appointed army that ever fought in Ireland, advanced to the relief of Portmore.

O'Neill, acting in concert with O'Donnell and MacWilliam Burke, determined to meet the Marshal before he reached the Blackwater. The clans of Connaught and Tyrconnell stood side by side with the ranks of O'Neill. Turlough O'Hanlon attended as Standard-bearer of Ulster. The ground selected by the Ulster chiefs for giving battle was about a mile from Portmore, on the route to Armagh, where the level ground was terminated by a narrow pass, bordered on one side by a wood, on the other by a low swamp. The place was called

* The symbol of the O'Neills.

Beal-an-Ath-Buidhe—"The Mouth of the Yellow Ford." The sun, on the tenth of August, rose over the spot, and all was calm and quiet; but, as the day advanced, it shone on many a well armed gallowglass, lurking among the thick wood bordering the approach. O'Neill posted under this covert five hundred light troops to guard the defiles. With the early dawn the English Marshal led his host from the city of Armagh, and proudly waved their banners in the morning air, as with trumpet peal, and glittering armour, they advanced to the relief of Portmore. They were men to raise that siege! In the full confidence which superior skill and numbers inspired, the English troops entered the narrow pass, little thinking of the conflict so close at hand. Outpoured a deadly volley that emptied the saddles of the foremost rank; another, and another succeeded, and created confusion; but Bagnal, in person, led on the first division, and by a vigorous charge carried the pass, and dislodged the troops defending it. The centre division under Cosby and Wingfield, was then advanced, and the rear-guard, with the supports of cavalry, pushed forward and quickly formed on the open ground, where the Irish main body was already drawn up in heavy columns, a well disciplined force. O'Neill, however, had prepared his ground with defences the English general knew not of. In front he caused deep pits to be dug, and covered over with wattles and brushwood, so as to resemble solid earth. With loud cheers the English horse advanced; but, as the cavalry charged, the horses sinking into the concealed pits, fell heavily, pitching their riders head-foremost on the Irish spears, while the Irish shouting "*Lamb dearg aboo*," and "*O'Donnell aboo*," taking advantage of the confusion, fell upon them and committed great slaughter. In vain the brave Marshal brought his veterans again and again to the charge; they could not resist the deadly onslaught of the Irish, led on by their chosen chiefs. The Marshal well sustained his fame as a gallant soldier, and probably met the death he desired when he beheld his noble army thoroughly beaten. He was shot through the brain, as a waggon of gunpowder, exploding in the midst of the English ranks, spread death on every side. The cannon were all taken, the cavalry of Tyrone bore down the columns of Wingfield and Cosby, and the banner of St. George was lowered before the flag of O'Neill.

The retreat of the English was a rout. They were pursued with hideous slaughter; and to this day a pass in which numbers fell, is called the "Bloody Loaning." Moryson gives the English loss at 1,500, but it is supposed to have been much greater. Immense was the spoil abandoned to the victors; twelve thousand pieces of gold, thirty-four standards, besides arms, and waggons laden with provisions, fell into the hands of the conquerors; and it was the most signal victory ever achieved by the Irish over the forces of England.

The effect of this triumph was soon felt throughout the north. The fort of Portmore at once yielded, and the brave garrison were generously allowed to join the English settlement in the Pale. Armagh, to which the fugitives fled, was invested, and, after holding out for four days, surrendered. Some of the Irish chieftains would have shown small mercy to the enemy, but the humane counsels of O'Neill prevailed. They were merely disarmed, and permitted to retire within the Pale.

CHAPTER XII.

FROM THE BATTLE OF BEAL-AN-ATH-BUIDHE, A.D. 1598, TO THE BREAKING OUT OF THE CIVIL WAR IN 1641.

THE importance of Dundalk as a garrison, to which the English forces might resort for security, was never more apparent than after the defeat of the English at the battle of Beal-an-ath-Buidhe. The Irish, flushed with victory, arose everywhere in arms. Throughout each province, from the Giant's Causeway to Cape Clear—from the Isles of Arran very nearly to the Hill of Howth, the long pent vengeance of the natives now burst forth, rousing them to active warfare. There was no safety for the English colonists but behind the ramparts of walled towns, and Dundalk, the nearest fortified garrison within the Marches of the Pale, was eagerly resorted to.

In 1599, Robert Devereux, Earl of Essex, arrived in Dublin, determined to crush O'Neill. His reputation as a soldier was high, and he had won great favour as a courtier. "He had an army," says Moryson, "as great as himself required, and for such number and strength as Ireland had never yet seen." Instead, however, of employing this well-disciplined force against the Ulster troops, he preferred going southward to Leix, the country of the O'Mores. Here a terrible defeat awaited him. Five hundred of the clansmen of Leix took advantage of a narrow defile through which the English cavalry were passing, and fell upon them so unexpectedly, they slaughtered so many, that the place has since been called "*Bearna-na-Cleite*," the Pass of Plumes, in remembrance of the gay feathers rudely shorn from the crests of the mailed warriors of England. Having been thus weakened, Lord Essex lost considerable time besieging Cahir Castle, and suffering discomfiture in Munster, where the gallant President, Sir Thomas Norris, was slain,* he then returned to Dublin, pursued by the Irish. He attempted to keep the O'Byrnes in check, but these Wicklow mountaineers defeated his troops so signally, that he attributed it to misconduct in the officers and soldiers. He had the survivors of the former tried by court-martial, and decimated the latter. Again he led his forces against the O'Mores, with more success than before; and, as the Queen expected he would measure swords with O'Neill and O'Donnell, sent orders to Sir Conyers Clifford to attack Belleek, while he advanced into Ulster by Dundalk. Sir Conyers obeyed, having with him fourteen hundred infantry, a strong body of cavalry, under Lord Southampton, and some auxiliary cavalry from Connaught, under Lord Dunkellin. The meditated invasion reached the ears of O'Donnell, and calling to his aid O'Rorke, Prince of Breffny, they mustered their clans for battle.

Aware of the superior discipline and arms of the English, the Irish leaders thought it far more prudent to avoid meeting them on the plain, where the cavalry and artillery could act, and determined to see what could be achieved while the troops of Clifford were passing over the *Corsliabh*† Mountains. O'Donnell posted a strong body of marksmen along the wooded defiles, while O'Rorke, with the Breffny kernes and gallowglasses, were close at hand, ready and willing to fall upon the foe at the fitting time.

Clifford was too prudent a general to trust the main

---

* *Gibson's History of Cork*, vol. i., p. 317.

† Commonly called the Curlew Mountains.

body of his army into a defile without exploring it; so, leaving his artillery, cavalry, and baggage, on the plain, he led the infantry up the mountain to clear the way. The Irish kept concealed beneath their covert, and gave no sign of their presence until the main body of the English troops had fully entered the gorge, and retreat was impossible. Then the cry of death arose—the shout of *O'Donnell aboo!* rang from rock to rock. Before many had time to see where were the foes, they felt their weapons pierce their breasts. Sir Conyers Clifford was slain, other officers of rank fell with him, and the men perished in scores. They fought with desperation, but the odds were against them. When the cavalry could act they did so gallantly, but the Irish were too wary to give them the power to do much. They, too, had to retreat, having expended their ammunition.*

These defeats having proved the utter incapacity of Essex as a general, he was replaced by Charles Blount, Lord Mountjoy, who landed at Howth 24th April, 1600. He determined to show O'Neill the little truth of the prediction, that "he was a commander who would lose the season of action while his breakfast was preparing;" for he took prompt measures to protect the settlers on the Pale. The better to effect this, he stationed at Dundalk the very considerable force of one hundred horse and six hundred and fifty foot; in Ardee, fifty horse and seven hundred foot; in Kells, fifty horse and four hundred foot; in Newry, fifty horse and a thousand foot; and in Carlingford, a hundred foot. He also placed a garrison at Lough Foyle, and formed a plan for fortifying and securing Derry.† These active measures

* *Camden*, p. 736.

† *Stuart's Armagh*, p. 291.

soon informed the great Irish general he had a soldier to encounter, instead of a pedantic courtier to amuse; and those wavering Irish chiefs, who watched the scales in order to cast their strength with the stronger side, hastened to make submission to the new Lord Deputy. In a short time Mountjoy, in person, took the field, and forming a junction with the Earl of Southampton, almost under the walls of Dundalk, at Faughart, advanced towards Newry, and about the 20th May defeated the Irish at the Pass of Moyry; but the restlessness of O'Neill allowed the Lord Deputy short respite. Hardly had he returned to Dublin before he was again summoned to the field, and obliged to take the same route through Dundalk, northwards. He again mustered his troops in the vicinity, at Faughart,* and they numbered three hundred cavalry, with two thousand four hundred foot.† They were detained here by the inclemency of the season until the 9th October, when the order to march was given. Strangely enough, O'Neill selected as his battle-ground the Pass of Moyry, which witnessed his defeat in May. In the meantime he had fortified it with strong fences and wooden stakes, pitched,‡ and driven firmly into the ground. These were connected with hurdles, and strengthened with stones. Mounds were thrown across the hills, and the Pass well manned with the Ulster troops. When the weather permitted Mountjoy stormed these lines; the memory of their late success urged the English to desperate efforts, and the Irish were driven from their entrenchments at the point of the bayonet. Mountjoy, again crowned with victory, returned to Dundalk, cutting down the dense woods that rendered the country almost impenetrable.

---

* *Moryson*, p. 185. † *Cox*, 188.

‡ *Camden*, 134.

The presence of Mountjoy, at the head of a powerful army, was the only means of preventing the Prince of Tyrone from possessing the sovereignty of the North. O'Neill quickly made himself master of Armagh and Portmore, and would have overrun the entire country if not checked; so again, on the 22nd May, 1601, Mountjoy left Dublin, for the third time, to restore portions of Ulster to the English rule.

On the 25th he again passed through Dundalk, on his way to Moyry Pass, where, towards the close of the year, in order not only to secure the ground he had won, but to keep this dangerous Pass open to the English on their way to the North, he built a fort, to which he gave the name of Mount Norris, after the late President of Munster, Sir John Norris, from whom he learned the art of war. This fort still presents a massive tower, though much decayed; a portion of the rampart is also standing, on the verge of the rocks, showing a strong wall. Having left a garrison of 400 men in this fort, Lord Mountjoy returned to Dundalk.

On the death of Queen Elizabeth, A.D. 1603, James the Sixth of Scotland succeeded her, as descendant of Margaret, eldest daughter of Henry the Seventh. By his accession the rival nations of England and Scotland were united under one Sovereign, while the descendants of the ancient Irish revered the Milesian blood which filled the veins of the young King, and, therefore, considered him their natural ruler. Another claim existed, which must not be forgotten by the historian of Dundalk. The Irish knew that Edward Bruce, brother to Robert, King of Scotland, ancestor of James, had actually been crowned King of Ireland at Dundalk; and thus, by a happy combination of circumstances, the crowns of the three kingdoms devolved on him, with equal satisfaction to the people of each.

In Ireland there appeared every prospect of peace. The great Chieftain of the North, Hugh O'Neill, after long years of protracted war, seemed disposed to lay down his arms. He consented to exchange his Irish title of "The O'Neill," with the state and jurisdiction appurtenant thereunto, and be henceforth known amongst men as Earl of Tyrone, wearing the coronet of his rank, and suffering the broad lands of his ancestors to become shire-ground, subject to the laws and customs of the realm of England. The expense of this Ulster war may be estimated from the fact that, in A.D. 1599, Queen Elizabeth spent twelve hundred thousand pounds in six months' service in Ireland; and Sir Robert Cecil stated that, in ten years, Ireland cost three millions four hundred thousand pounds.* When we consider the difference in currency then as compared with the present time, we may form an idea of the enormous sum then spent. The terms on which O'Neill yielded his submission were most honourable. He was to have full pardon for himself and his allies, and he and his people were to have free exercise of their religion and estates on condition they would lay down their arms. The Chief of Tyrone and his friends, having accepted the terms, entered again formally into possession of their inheritance, and peace was thus restored.† The new King seemed disposed to conciliate the native Irish. The Catholic religion, banned and proscribed during the Queen's reign, was openly professed, and "Popish ecclesiastics," as Dr. Leland calls the Catholic clergy, "practised, with their votaries, without any decent caution or restraint." The abbeys and Catholic churches were again thronged with devout worshippers, and the country beginning to recover from the paralysing effects of the dreadful struggle so recently endured.

---

* *Hume.* † *MacGeoghegan*, vol. iii., p. 330.

This happy state of things was not destined to last long. The English party in Ireland, the *undertakers*, as they were not unaptly called, found that, instead of having a dead body to dismember, and divide as spoil amongst themselves, there was vitality in every part, and a prospect of longevity, which, if not cut short, would defeat their greedy longings. Accordingly, there was loud preaching in State chapels against the "backsliding of the times" and the "guilt incurred by any compromise with Jezebel." The religious element is always ready to ignite in Ireland. We have abundance, at all times, of

> Fire-eyed disputants, who believe their swords,
> On points of faith, more eloquent than words;

and these ardent spirits, clerical and lay, yearned for action, and chafed at the time they were restrained from proving themselves—

> Orthodox
> By apostolic blows and knocks.

But their wished-for day was close at hand. The Irish Executive, located at that time in Dublin Castle, discovered the Act of Uniformity, which prohibited the attendance of persons at Catholic worship. A proclamation, issued on the 4th July, 1605, which dispelled all hopes that persons professing the Catholic faith could continue to enjoy that liberty of conscience they were led to expect. "It commanded all priests, by a certain day, to depart the realm." * Cecil, the English Secretary of State, and the steady enemy of the Catholics, is said to have employed an agent to originate a conspiracy in Ireland, which involved the Earls of Tyrone and Tyrconnell, the Baron of Delvin, and other leading

* Dr. Mant allows the *severity* of this proclamation, p. 350.

Catholics.* The designs attributed to them are supposed to be fictitious, but suspicion was all that was wanted. They were at once proclaimed rebels; and not only their individual estates declared forfeited, but six counties of Ulster afforded King James and his "undertakers" a wide field for the settlement of that province. Dundalk did not escape being implicated, for, among those attainted on this occasion, appears the names of several inhabitants.

A new progress was now made to the North, which took Dundalk in its route. Instead of the army of horse, foot, and dragoons which, of late years, escorted the Viceroy in his progress to encounter the Ulster chiefs, who fought beneath the Red Hand of O'Neill, the Lord Deputy, in 1607, Sir Arthur Chichester, accompanied by the Lord Chancellor, the Lord Chief Justice, Sir Oliver Lambert, Sir Garrett Moore, and the Attorney-General, Sir John Davies, proceeded to hold inquisitions into both ecclesiastical and civil affairs. "Albeit" (writes Sir John Davies, in a letter to Robert Cecil, Earl of Salisbury) "we were to pass through the wastest and wildest parts of all the North, yet had we only for our guard six or seven score of foot and fifty or three score horse, which is a good argument of a good time, and a confident Deputy; for in former times, when the State enjoyed the best peace and security, no Lord Deputy ever did venture himself into those parts without an army of eight hundred or a thousand men."

The confiscations, which then took place, comprised upwards of half-a-million of Irish acres, which were seized upon by the King, and granted to various bodies,† many of them London

---

* *MacGeoghegan's Hist. of Ireland; vide* also *Curry's Review.*

† Among the Irish then deprived of all they possessed were the O'Neills, O'Donnells, Maguires, O'Flanagans of Tura, MacMahons, O'Reillys, O'Dohertys, O'Hanlons, and many other ancient nobles of Ulster.

Corporations. Dundalk, at this period, appears to have been the property of the Barons of Slane, Sir John Bellew, of Roch, knight; and Sir John Draycot, knight.

In 1626, Sir John Bellew, of Roch, died, seised of (*inter alia*) five messuages and 160 tenements in this town, and certain chief rents, leaving Christopher Bellew, his son, heir-at-law, then aged twenty-five, and married. The Lady Amynett was his widow. In 1639, Sir John Draycot, knight, died, seised in fee-tail, reversion expectant to the Crown, of the site, &c., of the lately dissolved Priory of St. Leonard, of Dundalk, and of twenty messuages and 240 acres of land in Dundalk; also, of the Rath, near Ballybalricke, called the Maudlins, Little Lurgan, and Prior's Land, of Dundalk; also, of the Rectory of the Church of St. Nicholas, of Dundalk, and of the tithes and altarages of the parish of Haggardstown; also, of the tithes of the Lurgan and land beyond the bridge of Dundalk, and of divers closes, and one messuage and thirty acres of land in Dromeskin; all which were parcels of the possessions of the lately dissolved Priory of Dundalk, and held of the King *in capite* by knight service, leaving John Draycot, his cousin and heir, aged twenty-eight, and married.*

By the Civil Survey of Dundalk, remaining in the Surveyor-General's Office, the following persons were proprietors in 1640, whose lands formed grants for Cromwell's partizans:—

Patrick Cashell; Oliver Cashell; Stephen Dowdall; William Sharkey; Thomas Brandon; Bartholomew Moor; Bartholomew Thunder; Nicholas Cashell; Michael Skoyne; Alexander Mapass; James Brandon; John Mortimer; Isaac Doo; Patrick Dardiss; Sir Christopher Bellew, of Castletown-Bellew; Bartholomew Cashell; John Draycot, of Mornan-

* *Inquis.*, A.D. 1640, in *Canc. Hib.*

town; Patrick Bellew, of Verdonstown; John Stanley, of Morlistown; Patrick Levan, of Desart; Bartholomew White, of Carlingford; and Nicholas Gosling, of Dundalk.

Besides the above-named proprietors there were also returned chantry lands, in various parts of the town; rood lands, held for pious uses; and corporate lands. The Corporation town and fields of Dundalk were therein stated to contain 1,640 acres of arable land, with 150 acres of meadow, and a common of pasture, containing about 840 acres. The said lands were bounded on the east by the sea; on the south, by the lands of Haggardstown; on the west, by Ballnamony, Killaly, Donaghmore, Balrigan, Castletown-Bellew, and the Rath; on the north, by the lands of Armagh, in the parish of Faughart, and by the parish of Ballymaskanlan. Oliver Cromwell subsequently granted the greater portion of these lands to one of his followers, Sir Robert Reynolds, in recompense of services during his Irish campaign. This led to further gifts to the same favoured knight. Some years subsequently, in 1667, Sir Robert Reynolds obtained a grant of various lands in the barony and liberties of Dundalk; part of Lisdonagh, forty-six acres and three perches; Carnbeg, and Lurgankeele, 334 acres.*

* *Roll*, 19 Chas. 2, in *Canc. Hib.*

CHAPTER XIII.

FROM THE COMMENCEMENT OF THE CIVIL WAR, IN 1641, TO THE ARRIVAL OF CROMWELL, A.D. 1649.

In order to understand the motives which influenced the Catholics to take the field in 1641, we must examine the declaration agreed to in the council of the confederates:—"Whereas we, the Roman Catholics of the Kingdom of Ireland, have been continually loving and faithful subjects to his sacred Majesty; and, notwithstanding the general and heavy oppressions suffered by subordinate Governors to the ruin of our lives, honours, and estates, yet, having some liberty of religion from his Majesty, out of the affluence of his princely love to us, we, weighing not corporal loss in respect of the great immunity of the soul, are inviolably resolved to infix ourselves in an immutable and pure allegiance for ever to his Royal Majesty and his successors. Now it is that the Parliament of England, maligning and envying any graces received from his Majesty by our nation, and knowing none so desired of us as that of religion, and likewise perceiving his Majesty to be inclined to give us the liberty of the same, drew his Majesty's prerogative out of his hands—thereby largely pretending the general good of his Majesty's kingdoms. But we, the said Catholics and loyal subjects of his Majesty, do probably find, as well by some Acts passed by them the said Parliament, touching our religion, in which the Catholics of England and Scotland did suffer, as also by threats to send over the Scottish army, with the sword and Bible, against us, that their whole and studied plot was, and is, not only to extinguish religion (by which only we live happily), but also likewise to supplant us, and rase the name of Catholics and Irish out of the whole kingdom; and seeing this surprise so dangerous, tending absolutely to the overthrow of the liberty of our consciences and country, and also our gracious King's power forced from him, in which and in whose prudent care of us our sole quiet and comfort consisted, and without which the fear of our present ruin did prescribe opinion, and premonish us to save ourselves. We, therefore, as well to regain his Majesty's said prerogative, being only due to him and his successors, and being the essence and life of monarchy, hoping thereby to continue a strong and invincible unity between his royal and ever happy love to us and our faithful duty and loyalty to his incomparable Majesty, have taken arms, and possessed ourselves of the best and strongest forts of the kingdom, to enable us to serve his Majesty, and preserve us from the tyrannous resolution of our enemies. This in our consciences, as we wish the peace of the same to ourselves and our posterity, is the pretence and true cause of our present rising in arms, by which we are resolved to perfect the advancement of truth and safety of our King and country. Thus much we thought fit in general to publish to the world, to set forth our innocent and just cause, the particulars whereof shall be speedily declared. God save the King."*

We may well imagine the dismay with which the news of this formidable rising was received by the English throughout Ireland. Affrighted messengers came thick as Job's comforters, one upon another, informing the garrisons of the Pale that the sons of those who struck down the banner of St. George at Clontibret, Beal-an-ath-Buidhe, and other battle fields, were preparing to emulate the deeds of their sires. At

---

* *D'Alton's History of Drogheda*, p. 222.

first the English and Scotch, who had obtained grants of the erenach and termon lands, which Catholic piety devoted to religious houses, and which had been declared by inquisitions, forfeited, and at the King's disposal, could scarcely credit the fact that the race which they had driven from their pleasant homes beside lake and river—the outcasts whom they had hunted to the mountains, and left to perish in the bogs and fens, without a rood of the ground over which they once held sway, could suddenly start up as a formidable army, with noblemen and well-trained officers to command; yet so it was. The fact was indisputable, and the Drapers, Hollow-Sword Blades, and other guilds of tradesmen, in famous London town, felt that their "Irish plantations" were already slipping from their grasp.

Then ensued one of the most fearful struggles ever recorded in history. It was a life or death conflict of race against race, of creed against creed. The different elements into which Protestants were divided—Lutherans—Calvanists—Baptists—Anabaptists—Zuinglians—merged all distinctions of sect, and combined for the uprooting of Popery. The Puritan element was exceedingly strong at this period, and impelled these zealots to tear down the crucifixions, the pictures, and statues of the Virgin, the shrines of the saints, and whatever they regarded as savouring of Catholicism. This conduct towards all that was regarded with reverence by Catholics, lashed them into fury; they saw in the march of the Puritans legions of infernal spirits doing their master's work; while iconoclastic hands were levelling the Gothic abbeys, the Irish remembered how often they listened to the hymns of praise rolling through the pillared aisles, and, with indignation, beheld the shattered windows, once rich with sacred blazonry; the defaced cherubs sculptured over arch and mullion, and felt that angels and saints were no more respected than themselves. This formed the Catholic confederation, and loyalty to Charles was strengthened by loyalty to God. Twelve centuries had elapsed since St. Patrick preached the Gospel and rescued the Irish from heathenism, and the memory of the fidelity with which their fathers clung to the doctrines of Rome, was a powerful motive to incite their descendants to smite the persecutor of race, and the enemy of creed.

With these strong influences at work on both sides, we cannot be surprised that fearful atrocities stained the progress of this war. Of all the strifes calculated to arouse the worst passions of man's nature the war of retaliation is the worst. No one who studies Irish history can shut their eyes to the fact, that such was the war on which the most violent partizans of both sides now entered.* Most of the towns of Ulster fell at once into the possession of the confederates. Sir Phelim O'Neill carried the Red Hand, the emblem of his race, into Charlemont, Newry, and other forts. Dundalk and Dromisken were also taken, and Drogheda alone held out against the Irish. Lord Moore, in this emergency, took the direction of affairs in Drogheda, and resolved to defend the town. He was quickly joined by Sir Henry Tichburne, at the head of a thousand foot, and a hundred horse. Sir Henry was appointed governor, and, by his skill and courage, justified the appointment. The protracted siege of Drogheda is detailed in several works,† so we pass on to the town with which we are more immediately concerned. Suffice it to say, the garrison under

---

* The barbarous order of Coote to his troops, when pursuing the Catholics, was—"To give no quarter, to spare neither age or sex, not even a child, were it but a hand high."—*Memoirs of Lord Castlehaven*, p. 29.

† *D'Alton's Hist. Drogheda*, vol. ii., p. 227 to 246. *Dean Bernard's Siege of Drogheda.*

Sir Henry Tichburne made a valiant defence, until, at last, the besiegers under Sir Phelim O'Neill, despairing to reduce it, retired to Dundalk, then in the possession of the confederate Catholics. Sir Henry was not disposed to remain inactive long. Finding his strength sufficient to enable him to take the field, he burned Slane, and defeated a considerable party of the Irish at Ardee. Emboldened by these successes, and, as he was not trammelled by restrictions with regard to his operations, which seems to have been the case with the Earl of Ormonde, who had no authority to march north of the Boyne, Sir Henry directed his army towards Dundalk, and resolved to besiege that town. Upon the 26th March, 1642, the assault of Dundalk was made. It contained a large garrison, as far as numbers went; and, in addition, the inhabitants of the country round, retired before the English forces, and drove their cattle into the town. There must then have been good store of provisions to maintain the Irish during a siege. The town was well defended by nature and art; there were double walls, a double ditch, low marshy ground on the one side, and the sea on the other.

"We approached the town," writes Dean Bernard,* "about nine o'clock in the morning, planted our ordnance upon a little hill, not far from the gate, which five hundred of them within defended; a forlorn hope of an hundred of ours drew up, and gave fire at such as were in the gatehouse, and, for a while, there was hot work on both sides. At length they within finding some of them to drop, run away, whom ours perceiving, increased their fears by shouting, but their commander beat them back to their guards, and so the same peal was rung again by each. At length a division, under the command of

* *Siege of Drogheda*, p. 89.

Lieutenant-Colonel Waineman, of about three hundred, resolutely approached the gate also, and some with pick-axes began to beat down the walls, while the rest replyed to the tower with their shot. Abundance of great stones were poured down from a castle, yet, by God's goodness, no great hurt to any. By the sight of our men's continued undauntness, with one consent they all ran away, upon which that division entered, and the horse pursued them a full gallop to the killing of many of them. But upon their turning towards the next gate, seeing two or three brass guns planted, and five hundred men ready to receive them, they fairly retreated; but a castle placed at the head of that out street, manned with their best musketeers, which ours minded not, and for fear of endangering their own men (at whose heels our men), had yet stood dumb, now, in our return, played very hot upon us, whereby ten of ours were slain, an ensign, one sergeant, and one that carried the colours for another; a horseman with another's horse was killed also. Lieutenant Francis Moore was shot upon the shoulder-piece of his armour, which from thence rebounded upon his head, broke the skin, and stuck within his hair, doing no further hurt. The loss of these men, especially of Ensign Fortescue, the first officer we yet lost in fight, enraged Lord Moore and the Governor, the rather upon a resolution of present revenge, who else had contented themselves with the taking of the out town for that night, and to have lodged themselves there till morning." This castle, standing so advantageously, and so well provided with shot, was the only "*Remora*" to the success of Lord Moore and Sir Henry Tichburne, so they set fire to some houses near it, and, concealed by the smoke, soldiers got beneath the walls, blew up the door, and Captain Owens, with five men, put the garrison to flight. Upon this success all felt their hopes revive. They manned it with thirty musketeers, who, being within half musket shot of the streets, played so thick that no one could venture to stir without being marked down. They then drew cannon against the inward gate, and finding ten woolpacks opportunely in the castle just taken, turned them to their own purposes, and advanced against the garrison, who retired without even discharging their guns. Sir Phelim O'Neill seeing the town encompassed, and himself like to be taken in the net, stole away over the river, accompanied by divers others; and the approach of night, together with full tide, secured his safe flight. Pillage was found in abundance, as being of late the Treasury of the County of Louth, for the share of which each captain took the fortune of his quarter. Nor did the soldiers fare worse; there were all sorts of provisions ready dressed. The consumption of fowl was immense; turkeys, and birds of less magnitude in such quantities that the Dean of Ardagh mentions—four thousand were eaten in four days. It was an ordinary event at one time to see ten or twenty couples of them, in rank and file, cut off in an instant.* The numbers engaged in this siege are stated by the Dean as follows:—On their side, seven hundred and fifty foot, and two hundred horse; and there were, he says, "three thousand rebels in the town." If this was the case, with the store of provisions, and means of defence at the disposal of the Irish, they certainly afforded their assailants every reason to plume themselves upon their rapid and decisive victory. The excuse offered for the Irish is, that the town was taken by surprise.

The "great rebellion," as this rising of the confederate Catholics has commonly been called, having been at length crushed, the State authorities were soon engaged in punishing those who

---

* *Bernard's Siege of Drogheda*, p. 92.

had taken part therein. Some notion of the inability of the Ulster Irish to protract the war may be formed from the circumstance that, in April, 1642, Sir Phelim O'Neill had but one firkin and a-half of powder left.* He continued, however, to live in hostility to the English for ten years after this, when he was taken and tried. Although he would have received pardon if he could prove he acted in this war under a regular commission from King Charles the First, he refused to save himself by doing so, and was executed.

In September of the year 1643, a truce being proclaimed, it was agreed on, that "the County of Dublin, the County of the City of Dublin, the County of the Town of Drogheda, and the County of Louth, and as much of the County of Meath as lies on the east and south side of the Boyne, from Drogheda to Trim, and thence to Moylagh, and thence to Moyclare, &c., should remain and be, during the cessation, in the possession of his Majesty's Protestant subjects, and of such as adhere unto them respectively, save and excepting unto the said Roman Catholic subjects now in arms, &c., and their party, all such castles, towns, lands, territories, and the lands and hereditaments thereunto belonging, which then were possessed in the said counties, or any of them, by any of the said party." On the part of the Government, for the encouragement of persons who would bring provisions and other commodities to Drogheda, Dundalk, Carlingford, &c., for the relief of his Majesty's army and good subjects, it was ordered, in Council, that *they* should be free from all customs and impositions whatsoever.†

It would appear that this attempt of the Irish Roman Catholics

* *Carte*, vol. i., p. 307

† *Borlase's Irish Rebellion*, p. 264.

to defend the prerogatives of the Crown (invaded by the Puritan faction, then in rebellion in England), as likewise their own religion, lives, liberties, and estates, threatened with extinction in Ireland, was abetted by most, if not all, the leading Catholics of the kingdom. Lords—Fingal, Gormanstown, Netterville, Trimleston, and others, also many Members of the House of Commons, participated in this war; which ought not to be termed rebellion, as the confederate forces fought for the King, against whom his disloyal subjects were in arms in England and Ireland. On the 22nd June, 1643, Oliver Cashell, one of the representatives for the Borough of Dundalk, was expelled the Irish House of Commons for the share he had taken in these warlike proceedings. He appears to have escaped forfeiture, as we shall find hereafter; but this shows the feeling of the House was strong against the Catholics, and entirely opposed to the war they carried on. A cessation from the din of arms soon blessed the land; and, in 1646, the Lord Lieutenant and Council instructed Sir Gerard Lowther, Sir James Willoughby, and Sir Paul Davis, to proclaim perfect freedom of trade to Dublin, Drogheda, Dundalk, and Carlingford, the merchants having been much impeded by the restrictions theretofore imposed.

CHAPTER XIV.

FROM THE ARRIVAL OF CROMWELL TO THE LANDING OF SCHOMBERG, 1689.

THE state of Ireland since the commencement of the civil war, according to English views, had been "a series of distracted controversies, pleadings, excommunications, treacheries, conflagrations, of universal misery, of blood, and bluster, such as the world, before or since, had never seen."* It is true much division existed in the confederate councils; several who professed the same religion, distrusted others, because they were not of the same race. Then the Milesian-Irish Catholics were, if not hostile, certainly not over friendly, with the Catholics of the Pale. The Royalists, who followed Ormonde as their leader, were for the King, and against the Covenant. The Presbyterians of Ulster, a united, and, therefore, important body, were determined for upholding King and Covenant; while the partisans of Cromwell and the Commonwealth of England were for neither King or Covenant. On the arrival of Cromwell these discordant elements—the Catholics, the Royalists, and the Presbyterians true to the King—formed a kind of alliance, and were determined to resist the future Protector of the Commonwealth. It was a formidable coalition. apparently, and demanded strong measures to break it up. Oliver Cromwell felt his courage equal to the occasion. He came like Attilla, the scourge of God, and his fiery track has left traces in the land which time can never efface.

The slaughter of the garrison of Drogheda, showed at once

---

* *Carlyle's Cromwell.*

what manner of man he was. Ormonde had sent orders to the Governor of Dundalk, the next town which held out for the King, commanding him to burn the town before quitting it. The atrocious massacre of 2,000 men, in Drogheda, by Cromwell's orders, on the 10th September, 1649, was not calculated to give courage to the defenders of smaller towns. From "Tredah" there came to Dundalk, on the 12th September, the following very explicit cartel, directed:—

"For the Chief Officer commanding in Dundalk, these:

"Tredah, 12th September, 1649.

"SIR,—I offered mercy to the garrison of Tredah in sending the Governor a summons before I attempted the taking of it, which, being refused, brought the evil upon them.

"If you, being warned thereby, shall surrender your garrison to the use of the Parliament of England, which by this I summon you to do, you may thereby prevent the effusion of blood. If, upon refusing this offer, that which you like not befalls you, you will know whom to blame.

"I rest your Servant,

"OLIVER CROMWELL."

The garrison thought it more prudent not to wait Cromwell's approach. They were in too much haste to be able to comply with Ormonde's directions about firing the town, and Cromwell got possession of it unburnt. He left a garrison therein; and, after sending Colonel Venables to Derry, proceeded on his conquering way to the South of Ireland.

When Cromwell's ambitious designs in England induced him to try and get rid of those he feared would thwart his aims, he caused the Parliament to nominate Ludlow, Lieutenant General, and Commander-in-Chief of the Horse in Ireland.

This stern Republican resolved to emulate his rival in deeds of savage atrocity upon the unfortunate Irish. Having garrisoned Carrickmacross, he gives the following account of his exploits in this neighbourhood:—"From thence I went to visit the garrison of Dundalk; and being on my return, I found a party of the enemy retired within a hollow rock, which was discovered by one of ours, who saw five or six of them standing before a narrow passage at the mouth of a cave. The rock was so thick that we thought it impossible to dig it down, and therefore we resolved to try and reduce them by smoke. After some of our men had spent most part of the day in endeavouring to smother those within, by fire placed at the mouth of the cave, they withdrew the fire; and the next morning, supposing the Irish to be made incapable of resistance by the smoke, some of them, with a candle before them, crawled into the rock. One of the enemy, who lay in the middle of the entrance, fired his pistol, and shot the first of our men into the head, by whose loss we found that the smoke had not taken the designed effect. But, seeing no other way to reduce them, I caused the trial to be repeated, and, upon examination, found that, though a great smoke went into the cavity of the rock, yet it came out again at other crevices; upon which I ordered those places to be closely stopped and another smother made. About an hour-and-a half after this one of them was heard to groan very strongly, and afterwards more weakly, whereby we presumed that the work was done; yet the fire was continued till about midnight, and then taken away, that the place might be cool enough for ours to enter the next morning; at which time some went in, armed with back, breast, and head piece, to prevent such another accident as fell out at their first attempt. But they had not gone above six yards before they found the man that had been heard to groan, who was the same that had killed one of our men with his pistol, and who, resolving not to quit his post, had been, upon stopping the holes in the rock, choaked by the smoke. Our soldiers put a rope about his neck and drew him out. The passage being cleared, they entered, and, having put about fifteen to the sword, brought four or five out alive, with the priest's robes, a crucifix, chalice, and other furniture of that kind. Those within preserved themselves by laying their heads close to a water that ran through the rock. We found two rooms in the place, one of which was large enough to turn a pike; and having filled the mouth with large stones, we quitted it and marched to Castle-Blaney, where I left a party of foot and some horse."*

The cruelties practised by Ludlow recoiled on his own head. He had taken such an active part in the death of King Charles the First, that he was one of those excepted from the Act of Indemnity at the Restoration, and withdrew to Switzerland. While beneath the shadow of the Alps he wrote his Memoirs, and, after the Revolution of 1688, had the hardihood to return to England; but his presence in London gave such offence that an address was immediately presented to King William the Third, by the House of Commons, praying his Majesty to issue a proclamation for his apprehension. Upon this significant hint, Ludlow fled from the land he disgraced by his inhumanity, and returned to Switzerland, where he died in 1693.

The command of the garrison of Dundalk was entrusted by the Parliament of England to Colonel Monk. The town was again exposed to the horrors of a siege, and invested by the Irish army, commanded by Lord Inchiquin. The lines were

* *Memoirs of Edmund Ludlow*, p. 181.

drawn so effectively by the besiegers that all supplies of provisions were cut off, and the garrison threatened with famine. It would appear as if a necessary ingredient in carryiug on the siege, was wanting in the camp of Lord Inchiquin, and a rather strange bargain was entered into by the commanders on both sides. Monk undertook to supply the besiegers with the powder they needed to reduce the town, and, in return, the Irish were to furnish the garrison with provisions, to enable them stoutly to defend it. The troops of Lord Inchiquin, however, refused to be parties to this accommodation; for, when Monk's ammunition waggons left the town, the Irish troops seized them, and refused to give any food; on which Monk, finding he could no longer hold Dundalk, consented to yield the town, requesting permission for his own safe conduct into England; this was granted, but the *ci-devant* commander of Dundalk found a cold reception from the Parliament, who suspected him of betraying his trust.

We have little historic notices to record for some years. The Protector, having surrendered the reins of power on his death, the days of the Commonwealth ceased, and Charles the Second was restored to the throne of England. He confirmed the grants of Cromwell, and treated the Irish Catholics with base ingratitude.

In 1667, Marcus Trevor, Viscount Dungannon, obtained a grant of various houses, tenements, gardens, castles, and abbeys, in Dundalk. Amongst these, one castle in North-street; three castles in High-street; one castle in said street, without Warr's Gate; two ruined abbeys and a castle in Seatown, with other tenements, with all bogs and commons formerly belonging to the Corporation of Dundalk, saving the rights of Henry Draycot and Sir John Bellew, knight. It would appear as if the Royal family were not above having a share in the good things going in Dundalk. In the Rolls of Charles the Second, in *Cancellaria Hiberniæ*, we find James, Duke of York, afterwards King James the Second, granted the Mill of Grange and one acre of land, situated in the Barony of Dundalk. The next entry seems more reasonable and natural. Thomas Veazy, Clerk, Vicar of Dundalk, obtained a grant of a house, with a garden and the appurtenances, on the south side of the church in Dundalk, to hold to the minister of the town of Dundalk. Those bogs and commons granted to Lord Dungannon were afterwards assigned to Viscount Limerick, created Earl of Clanbrassil, and now form part of the estate of the Earl of Roden, as representative of the Earl of Clanbrassil.

By deed of 10th May, 1667, made between Marcus, Viscount Dungannon, on the one part; Henry Bellingham, of Gernonstown, in the County Louth, Esq., and William Foxteth, of Drogheda, Esq., of the other part, reciting. Whereas, at an assizes held at Dundalk, 18th March last, the Grand Jury judged that it was necessary to erect his Majesty's gaol for securing malefactors in Dundalk, in regard it was the Shire town where gaol delivery had been constantly held; and accordingly found that the castle called Castlenyrooty, otherwise Hyndes Castle, in the said town, being his lordship's property, might be conveniently converted to the use of a gaol, purchased the same for £70; his lordship conveying same to said Bellingham and Foxteth, and their heirs, for ever, in trust for the county. Inrolled 18th May, 1667.*

During the reign of Charles the Second, there was no favour shown to the great majority of the people in Ireland. When the Parliament sat in Dublin, 8th May, 1661, the holders of the

* Birmingham Tower, Dublin Castle.

confiscated estates viewed with alarm the great preponderance which the Catholics presented in numbers, and both houses expressed a desire—"to purge the towns of the Papists."* The same spirit of intolerance abhorred the Solemn League and Covenant, and determined to crush the Presbyterians. This influential body had few friends in the Commons, and but one in the Lords, who bore an honoured name—Lord Massareené. The Catholics had but one member of their creed in the Commons. In this Parliament severe laws were passed both against the Catholics and Presbyterians. In the year 1661 not less than sixty-one Presbyterian ministers in Ulster, nearly the whole body of the clergy, were deposed from their ministry; and although conformity met rich rewards, only *seven* joined the Established Church.†

The Corporation of Dundalk was specially mentioned in the New Rules of 25 Charles the Second, A.D. 1672, and the persons elected to serve in the offices of Chief Magistrate, Recorder, and Town Clerk, were required to be approved of by the Lord Lieutenant and Privy Council of Ireland. The governing charter was granted by King Charles the Second; it bears date 4th March, A.D., 1673.‡

This charter recited that—"The towne and borough of Dundalk, in our County of Louth, in our Kingdom of Ireland, is an Antient Borough, and the Bailiffs, Burgesses, and Commonalty of the said town, have heretofore had, used, and enjoyed divers liberties, franchises, and privileges, as well by virtue of the Charter of our Royal Predecessor, King Henry the Eighth, and several other charters to them and their

* Earl of Orrery's Letters.

† *Cassell's History of Ireland*, p. 108

‡ *Rot. Pat.* 26 Car. 2.

Predecessors heretofore granted and confirmed by several of our noble progenitors, Kings and Queens of England, as also by reason of several prescriptions, customs, and uses in the said Borough, time out of mind, used and enjoyed." It then recites the confirmation of same, and ordains that Dundalk shall be a free Borough of itself, with a body politic, by the name of the Bailiff, Burgesses, and Commonalty of the Borough of Dundalk, and that there may be for ever thereafter persons able and capable in the law, to have and hold the lands, &c., and dispose of same, plead and be impleaded, and have a common seal, and a Bailiff, and sixteen Burgesses; and that all and every person and persons, which now are freemen of the said Borough, or that hereafter shall be made free, shall be called the Commonalty of said Borough, with a Guild-hall, where the said Bailiff, Burgesses, and Commonalty, and the Recorder, or the major part of them, shall meet, and have power to make such reasonable laws and ordinances whatsoever, as they, or the major part of them, shall consider necessary for governing said Borough, with power of disposing, setting, &c., all or any lands, tenements, &c., by these presents or otherways assigned to said Corporation. The Bailiff and Recorder to be present in making such laws as aforesaid. The Charter constituted Walter Cox, Esq., first Bailiff, and he was to continue such from the date of these presents to the 29th September next following, and from thence until one other of the Burgesses shall be elected, and sworn into the office. The charter then named Richard Bolton, Henry Bellingham, Arthur Ward, Walter Cox, George Lambert, Arthur Bucklay, Robert Mason, James Smallwood, Henry Baker, John Wilshire, George Blyke, John Mortimer, Thomas Percevall, junior, Walter Eglestone, Josias Hogg, and William Beckardike, first and present Burgesses during life, or removal for just and reasonable cause. With powers to the said Bailiff, Burgesses, and Commonalty, and their successors, or the major part of them, the said Bailiff being always one, to assemble yearly on the 29th June; or if that day was Sunday, the next day, in the Guild-hall, or other fit place, and proceed to elect one of the Burgesses to be Bailiff for one whole year, from 29th September then next following; who, after election, shall take his oath for the due execution of his office, and thereupon execute the office from 29th September until his successor shall be duly elected, with provision in case of the Bailiff's death, or removal for reasonable cause, to appoint a new Bailiff, and also to fill up any vacancies among the sixteen Burgesses by election from the Commonalty. Liberty was given for the Bailiff to appoint a deputy from the list of Burgesses; and that the Corporation may and shall have within the said Borough, one discreet and learned man in the law of our Kingdom of Ireland, to be elected as therein described, as Recorder of said Borough. Abraham Wood, Esq., was named first Recorder, and it empowered said Corporation, on death or removal of said A. Wood, within a month after such vacancy, to assemble in the Guild-hall, and there elect his successor. It provided for the office of Town Clerk, and named Thomas Long, gentleman, first Town Clerk. The Bailiff and Recorder were to be Justices of the Peace within said Borough. The said first Bailiff, before acting as Bailiff and Justice of the Peace, or Clerk of the Market, Weights and Measures, Scale Master, or Coroner, was required to go before Sir John Bellew, Knight, Robert Moore, Esq., and Nicholas Gernon, Gent., or any one or more of them, and take his oath for the due execution of the said offices, and also the oaths to be taken by Justices of the Peace. The Borough Court was to be held weekly, on every Thursday, before the Bailiff or his Deputy, and Recorder, to take cognizance of all pleas, and actions on the case, deceits, debts, accounts, covenants, detriments, and trespasses, taking and detaining goods and chattels, and other contracts whatsoever, for any causes arising within the Borough, &c. Cause of action was limited to £50, with power of process by execution against goods or person. The Charter granted to the said Corporation all fines, issues, redemptions, amercements, penalties, forfeitures of recognizance, and all perquisites arising from said Court of Record of the Borough. And empowered the said Corporation, or the major part of them, to have authority upon reasonable cause to disfranchise any of the Members, Officers, or Commonalty of the said Borough, and to nominate, elect, and enfranchise persons willing to be of the Commonalty, in the place of these removed or disfranchised, or in the place of any deceased Member, Officer, or other person of the Commonalty of the said Borough. It gave and confirmed to said Corporation the fishing and fishery in the waters of Dundalk, and all tenements, &c., on the 22nd October, 1641, held by the said Corporation in their politic capacity, lying and being in the Town and Borough of Dundalk, and the liberties and precincts thereof, and in the town and fields of Haynstown, Dromgooter, and Stonehouse, and elsewhere in the County of Louth. Excepting and reserving unto Lewis, Viscount Dungannon, his heirs and assigns, and to Sir John Bellew, of Roch, Knight, and all other persons, all such title and interest as they have in any of the manors, tenements, as aforesaid. Provided that if, on any trial between the said Corporation of Dundalk and Lewis, Viscount Dungannon, the said Corporation should obtain a verdict by virtue of these presents, for the recovery of any lands hereby granted, which were grantable to Lewis, Viscount Dungannon, then the

Corporation, within six months after such verdict, should surrender to the Crown the said lands.

The death of Charles the Second, placed his brother James on the throne. He was proclaimed King in Dublin, 11th February, 1685, and the early measures adopted in his reign were calculated to fill the Irish Protestants, as well as the members of that church in England, with great alarm. He seized the charters of most of the towns, Dundalk amongst the rest, but the judgments of the Court of Exchequer relating thereto, being declared void, subsequently, the Charter of Charles the Second became the governing charter of Dundalk. Here we may notice the corporate officers, and glance at their respective duties and privileges.

The Recorder had considerable powers. He was constituted by the Charter, with the Bailiff, a Judge of the Borough Court of Record, and had authority as Justice of the Peace, within the Borough, its liberties and precincts. It was not necessary to choose him out of any class of the Corporation. He was to be "honest, discreet, and learned in the laws of Ireland." He, as well as the Bailiff, was a necessary party to the making of any bye-laws. The Borough Court, over which he presided, was to be held weekly, on Thursdays; and had jurisdiction in personal actions, arising within the Borough, to the extent of £50, with power of attaching goods, and arresting the person. Although it might be supposed highly advantageous to preserve such a tribunal, especially in a maritime port, where questions were likely to arise involving legal lore, and requiring prompt decision, this Court has long ceased to exist. No process seems to have issued from it since 1779. The Assizes for the County Louth are held in this town every Spring and Summer, and the Quarter Sessions, before the learned Chairman, David R. Pigot, Esq., disposes of all civil and criminal business. The Petty Sessions are held on Thursday in every week.

The Bailiff was Returning Officer of the Borough, and either he or his deputy attended all Corporate meetings. The Charter appointed him Coroner within the Borough; and, in conjunction with the Recorder, as we have seen, he presided in the Borough Court of Record. He was likewise a Justice of the Peace within the Borough, and held what was termed "The Bailiff's Court" each morning. He also sat on Thursdays at Petty Sessions. The Bailiff was, by Charter, Clerk of the Market, Weights and Measures, with custody of the Borough Seal. The fee of 10s. 6d. was demandable for affixing the Town Seal on documents, and this appears to have been the only emolument which accrued to the Bailiff. Neither his office, or that of the Recorder, had any salary attached to their possession.

The power of the Corporation was considerable:—

*1st. The power of disposing of the Corporate property.

2nd. The power of making bye-laws

3rd. The power of electing the Bailiff and Burgesses, the Recorder, Town Clerk, and other officers; of admitting Freemen, and also removing them for misbehaviour.

4th. The Burgesses were considered exempt from Toll. A bye-law, dated 20th October, 1707, enacted that no persons, though made free, not inhabitants of the Corporation, or its liberties, should be exempt from paying toll or customs for any goods or merchandise, bought or sold within the market of the Corporation, except the Recorder or Burgesses.

5th The children of Freemen were considered entitled to

---

* *Report of Commissioners of Municipal Corporations in Ireland*, p. 895.

be admitted as day scholars to the endowed school, for teaching Latin and English, at the rate of two guineas a year.

The state of the country, during these times, kept the officers of justice in full work. The Justices of Assize had few presents of white gloves from the High Sheriff, as appears from the following:—

1686.—In a letter from the Earl of Clarendon to the Earl of Sunderland, his lordship thus refers to this part of the locality:—"Mr. Justice Nugent went to Dundalk, where he found a very full prison. He tried near three score persons; some were condemned, and most discharged after having been whipt or burnt in the hand, and some were turned over to other prisons. But this commission has been a great relief to the County of Louth."* Matters were greatly changed since the days when no circuits could be traversed without a guard of soldiers to protect the judges; and it is probable the javelin men, who still grace the arrival of the judges at the assize towns, now more for ornament than need, are relics of those olden times, when they formed a guard to protect the King's Justices in Eyre.† Under James the Second the penal laws against the Catholics were inoperative. Indeed Tyrconnell, the Lord Lieutenant, was suspected of aiming at promoting the ascendancy of the Church of Rome; the Corporations of towns became changed from exclusively Protestant to exclusively Catholic. Of the High Sheriffs for 1687, only one was a Protestant, and the anxiety of the High Church party every day increased.

---

* *Singer's Correspondence of Clarendon*, vol. ii., p. 121.

† A witty judge, on being asked the pertinent question, "Of what use are these javelin men?" promptly replied, "I suppose to help me to *charge* the Grand Jury."

The Irish Protestant discontent was the echo of the English. The Prince of Orange, James's son-in-law, was invited to be the "Deliverer" of these kingdoms from the bigotry of the King; and the Earl of Mount-Alexander proclaimed William and Mary, in Ulster, where the Protestants took up arms. The King's troops were sent against them in March, 1689, and having gained some victories, drove the Protestants to seek refuge within the walls of Londonderry.

CHAPTER XV.

FROM THE LANDING OF SCHOMBERG TO THE BATTLE OF THE BOYNE.

THE heroic defence of Derry, and the ineffectual attempt on Enniskillen, cheered the prospects of the Protestants. On the 13th August, 1689, an army of 10,000 men, on board a fleet of nearly 100 sail, commanded by the brave old Marshal the Duke of Schomberg, landed in Antrim. Notwithstanding his high repute as a general, he found great difficulty in maintaining order and authority amongst those who flocked to his camp, and were supposed to be under his command. Having made terms with the troops forming the garrison of Carrickfergus, that, on his obtaining possession of the town, they should depart unharmed, no sooner were the Irish at the mercy of the descendants of the Scottish settlers, who were hostile to their creed, than these bigots declared the terms of capitulation were nothing to them; and the disarmed soldiers of James would have been slaughtered, without mercy, had not Schomberg, pistol in hand, rushed among the infuriated Ulstermen, and, by his personal intrepidity, and at the imminent risk of his life, prevented the massacre.* In his progress towards Dundalk this brave old man witnessed, at every step, the desolating track of war—the labours of the husbandman everywhere neglected, and the crops rotting on the ground. The Irish troops, beaten out of Ulster, retreated southwards, destroying wherever they went. Newry was burnt, Carlingford laid prostrate; and the country people, leaving their harvests uncut, drove their cattle before them, and flocked to the standard of James, which floated over the walls of Drogheda.

Towards the middle of September, 1689, the army of Schomberg arrived close to Dundalk. Here he resolved to fix his winter quarters. The site of Schomberg's camp is thus described:—† "We encamped on this side (north) of the town of Dundalk, in a low, moist ground, having the town, with the river towards the west, between us and the enemy; the sea towards the south, the Newry mountains to the east, and towards the north were hills and bogs intermixt. The Protestants that were left there told us, the Irish boasted when they went away, that they would drive us all back into the sea again, or else *we would die of ourselves*, the English not being used to the field, especially in a strange country, and at that time of the year." (Prophecy more truly fulfilled than most prophecies.) "At our coming hither we got about 2,000 of my Lord Bedloe's (Bellew's) sheep, which came in very good time to the army, for it had gone hard with us before for want of provisions; however, bread was so scarce that the General gave orders that what there was should be for the men, and not for the officers (because he judged they

---

* *Macaulay's History of England*, v. iii.

† *Story's Impartial History*, pt. i., p. 15.

could shift better). It was also ordered, the first night we came there, that an officer, with a party of men out of every regiment, should go back and take up what men they met withal upon the road sick; for several were beginning to faint already, by reason of the bad weather, and constant marchings, and want of provisions."

The English occupied the town, and made a storehouse of the "Popish chapel." Entrenchments were thrown up at the west end of Dundalk, and mounted with several field-pieces. The Irish army displayed their standard Royal, and drew out both horse and foot, bringing along a very handsome field train. The English officers were anxious to engage them, and wished the Duke would send for their cavalry; and the artillery asked leave to open fire; but the Duke was resolved not to fight; and his answer to his officers always was—"*Let them alone.*"*

The reasons Schomberg assigned for conduct which produced such disastrous results to his army were chiefly these:—The great bulk of his soldiers were so only in name, fresh from their cottages in England. Not one in four knew how to load a gun; and whoever succeeded in discharging it, no matter in what direction, thought he performed a great feat.† The Enniskilleners and other Ulster troops, who had joined him, were full of eagerness to fight the soldiers of James, but were not very submissive to his command; while, among the Dutch and French troops, there were many he could not trust. In fact, it afterwards appeared that, if Schomberg had yielded to the importunity of those who wished him to give battle at that time, several French companies would, in the heat of the

---

* *Story's Impartial History*, p. 22.

† *Macaulay's Hist.*, vol. iii., p. 426.

action, have fired on the English, and gone over to the enemy.* Besides these grave reasons, he had another, which seems to follow the footsteps of an army, as the vulture hovers over his bleeding prey—the prevalence of peculation. Commissaries, ravenous as sharks, and numerous as wolves, plundered whenever they had the opportunity. Of these, one Henry Thales, obtained unenviable notoriety. The beef and brandy he furnished for food was rejected by the troops in their sorest need. Their tents fell into rags through rottenness; muskets broke in pieces when handled. Unfed, badly armed, shoeless, and almost unclad, Schomberg's forces suffered fearfully at Dundalk. Here he entrenched himself on the ground extending towards the Castletown river; and traces of the lines exist on the new Fair-green.

James, emboldened by the apparent timidity of his veteran adversary, advanced towards Ardee, and drew up his troops in battle array before the English lines, on Kilbarrack Hill. He did not press the fight, it is said, through compassion for his English subjects; and Schomberg would not risk a battle until his men were better prepared. While the work of drill was progressing in Schomberg's camp, the conspiracy among the French allies of the English was discovered. Such a defection might well have produced a general panic in a better army than that encamped before Dundalk. It was necessary to be severe. Six of the conspirators were hanged; two hundred of their accomplices were sent, in irons, to England. Even after this winnowing the rest of the refugees were regarded with unjust, but not unnatural, suspicion. For some days there was great reason to fear the enemy would be entertained with a conflict between the English soldiers and

* *Macaulay's Hist.*, vol. iii., p. 426.

their French allies.* But though no sword, or shot, perilled the entrenched camp of Schomberg, at Dundalk, he was fated to meet a foe that neither his indomitable courage or military skill could conquer. The autumnal rains had been heavier than usual, in 1689; and the low swampy ground of the camp, retaining the moisture, soon converted the site into a quagmire. The Dutch, accustomed to inundations at home, provided against this state of ground; and the Irish troops were inured to the climate; but the English suffered terribly. The bad food supplied by the Commissariat aggravated the prevailing mortality. There were few surgeons, or medical men of any kind, with the army. The medicine chests were only prepared against the cut of a sword, or the wounds of fire-arms; and bandage or sticking-plaster was useless in fever, scurvy, and ague. Death mowed down the ranks in hundreds; and his progress would have been more rapid but for the humanity of the Irishwomen, whose medicated drinks—prepared from anti-scorbutic herbs—were found most efficacious. It is recorded that there died in the camp at Dundalk, in the hospital at Belfast, or on the sea, returning to England, above six thousand men.†

James's remissness in taking advantage of an enemy thus weakened and powerless, induced one of the French officers—Marshal Rosin—to exclaim:—"If you possessed a hundred kingdoms you would lose them all." He returned to Drogheda; and, finding that Schomberg, shortly afterwards, evacuated Dundalk, he sent a detachment of his army to occupy the town.

In June, 1690, James being apprised that the Prince of Orange was expected in Ireland, left Dublin, and advanced

---

* *Macaulay's Hist.*, vol. iii., p. 427. † *Id.*, 430.

towards Dundalk. In the manuscripts of Trinity College, Dublin, we read:—"King James has 20,000 men encamped about Bedloe's Castle, and this night they expect 10,000 French. Their artillery is not yet come up to them, but expected in one day or two. Their King is at Dundalk, and soon designs to remove thence to Armagh." *

William arrived at Carrickfergus on the 14th June, and was preparing to march forthwith to Dundalk, at the head of a powerful army, when James, thinking his present position not tenable, retired to Ardee, and, on the 28th of June, crossed the Boyne. He encamped on the south side of this river, with his right wing extending towards Drogheda, and his left towards the river. Here he resolved to make his stand, though his forces were, for the most part, ill-disciplined, and but half armed; while William's army of between 40,000 and 50,000 men were more numerous, with far greater odds on the score of discipline and arms. They had, moreover, the signal advantage of being led by a soldier, while the Irish were led by one who proved the very reverse.

The progress of William towards the Boyne is given in a number of publications, many of which have recently been collected, in that ably conducted periodical the *Ulster Journal of Archæology*. In one of these talented contributions to this Journal, entitled "King William's Progress to the Boyne," the following passage is given, from a French work, *Histoire de la Revolution d'Irlande, arrive sous Guillaume III.*† After fixing the order of march, the work states:—"Les choses estant ainsi disposées il fust résolu de faire marcher l'Armée

* *D'Alton's History of Drogheda*, vol. ii., p. 316.

† *Ulster Journal of Arch.*, vol. i., p. 132. This work was obtained from the library of Herbert J. Hore, Esq., Co. Wexford.

vers Market-hill, et dentrer ensuite dans le grand chemin qui conduit d'Armagh à Dundalke. Le Roy, au mesme temps, commandu Monsieur de Scravemoer, Major-General, pour aller avec trois cens cavaliers, et deux cens dragoons reconnoistre les ennemis, voir ou l'on pourroit camper, et 's approcher aussi près de Dundalke qu'il luy seroit possible, afin d observer la countenance des ennemis, qui estoient en cét endroit-là, au nomtre de neuf ou dix mille hommes; le reste de l'Armée du Roy Jaques estant du coté de la rivière de Boine."

The Diary of Rev. Dr. Davis gives the following account:*—"June 24th, King James, baving quitted the strong pass at Moyra Castle, we staid in camp until all the forces were come up. In the afternoon a deserter from Colonel Sheddon's Regiment came over to us, and gave the King a good account of the state and proceedings of the army; that they were 43,000 men, and all drawing together in order to oppose us; and that Captain Torlow was taken prisoner, and amongst them. We were this day much affected with apprehension that our fleet at Carlingford are surprised, and destroyed by the enemy, having heard very many cannon that way, much after the method of an engagement at sea. The evening all our detachment returned, and brought news the foe had quitted Dundalk and Ardee.

"25th.—We still lay encamped, our way being now clear before us; only the left wing and all the foot marched before us. We had an account, also, that the cannon we heard was from our own ships, entering the bay of Carlingford, and that Major-General Kirke was entered into Dundalk.

"26th.—In the morning we decamped, and, going over Poins Pass, we came to Newry, and, passing the bridge,

---

* *Ulster Journal*, vol. iv., p. 39.

pitched our tents on a hill beyond the town. The King lay in a small tent by us, being well assured that our way was open to Dundalk.

"27th.—We marched from Newry over the pass at Moyra, where the enemy, if they had any spirit, might easy have stopped us for some time. About ten of the clock we saw Dundalk, and passing the river near Bedlow Castle, and going over the ground of the last encampment, we pitched, a mile beyond the town, on the same ground where King James lay last year."

Even now, with the great advantage derived from the clear state of the country, Moyra Pass might be stiffly contested. The ground, at both sides, slopes gradually leaving the pass narrow, and in the centre stands the abrupt crag, bearing the broken tower erected by Lord Mountjoy, as a stronghold against the Ulster Irish, in 1600.

We now proceed to give a few extracts from another Diary, kept by Colonel Bellingham, ancestor of Sir Alan Bellingham, who served under King William:—*

"June 27th, 1690.—Very hot. About two this morning I moved towards Dundalk, and entered it about six, with Lieutenant-General Holmes and Major-General Kirke. The town was wholly desolate, but strongly fortified; no inhabitant left but Captain Bolton and his wife, who are both stript. Our army encamped about a mile south of Dundalk, being now entire, Doyle's party having joined ours. J. White and I went as far as Lurgan-race, and sate there some time, eating bread and cheese. The King resolved to attack the enemy this night in their quarters at Ardee; but hearing by some dragoons, who were at the very gate, and killed two of their

---

* *D'Alton's Hist. Drogheda*, p. 341.

men there, that the enemy was retired, he put off his resolution. I waited on the King at supper, when he discoursed me most of the time, and was extremely pleasant and cheerful."

From this narrative it is, we think, clear that William was then at Dundalk; and, Lord Roden informed us, occupied the house which afterwards came into his Lordship's possession in that town. The greater portion, however, has been rebuilt, but several old rooms yet remain. We continue Colonel Bellingham's Diary:—

"28th.—Very hot. I waited on the King to Ardee; from thence was ordered by him to go with Generals Ginkle and Gamboon to view all the river for encamping. We went as far as Cappock-bridge, and so returned to our camp near Dundalk. I staid by the way some time at Gernonstown,* and found several of the tenants, with their cattle, had stayed at home at my instance. The enemy are retired beyond the Boyne.

"30th.—Very hot. I called at Mr. Townleys on our march towards the Boyne. I was some time with the King on the hill of Tullaghesker, from which he viewed Drogheda, and then went towards Oldbridge. On the south side of the Boyne lay the enemy's camp, which the King going to view, he was hit by a cannon-shot on the shoulder, which put us into the greatest consternation imaginable. The cannon fired at each other all the afternoon. We drew a great body of our horse up on the hill, in sight of the enemy. We fired several bombs, some of which did execution, and our cannon dismantled two of the enemy's batteries."

This interesting diary then describes, how, on—

---

* Now Castle Bellingham.

"July the first in Oldbridgetown
There was a grievous battle—"

But as this has already been fully mentioned in the *History of Drogheda*,* to which it properly appertains, there is no necessity for repeating it here. The brave old Marshal Schomberg was killed while crossing the river. William, who charged in person at the head of the Enniskilleners, remained master of the field, while James fled to Dublin, and it is said rested for the night at a house still standing near Dunsink.

CHAPTER XVI.

FROM THE BATTLE OF THE BOYNE TO THE DAYS OF THE IRISH VOLUNTEERS.

The struggle which had wasted the country for so many years was over at last. The cause of the Stuarts was lost—their adherents lay beneath the walls of Limerick and Athlone, under the turf at Aughrim, or the rippling current of the Boyne water.

It is time that Irishmen of all denominations—whether tracing their descent from the Celt or the Saxon; from Milesius of Spain, or Chepstow's stalwart Earl, hight Strongbow; from the planter of the first James, or the trooper of Cromwell—should consider themselves as best serving the land of their birth by living in harmony, thus promoting her prosperity, and the advancement of her general good. We have had more than enough of discord and dissension, let us now begin to forget our past differences. By doing so we shall implant

* *D'Alton's Hist. Drogheda*, vol. ii., p. 320.

in each others breast mutual respect and toleration, and rejoice at finding our beautiful country rescued from these blighting influences which division has engendered and perpetuated, and realizing the words of the poet in becoming—

> "Great, glorious, and free,
> First flower of the earth, and first gem of the sea."

According to Hutchinson's work on the *Commercial Restraints of Ireland*, there was then considerable commerce and industry in the kingdom, and at this period of our history trade flourished. Dundalk possessed its share of these advantages; for, by the privileges granted by Charles the Second, free export was allowed of all commodities, except those the exportation of which was forbidden by the colonial laws. But a deplorable change was at hand; and it is to be lamented that King William the Third should have listened to the interested addresses of the traders in one part of his dominions, jealous of the rivalry of those of another. However, it was so; the English woollen manufacturers, annoyed at the success of this branch of manufacturing industry in Ireland, presented petitions to the King, representing the Irish trade detrimental to the English staple, and praying its prohibition. There was no spirit then alive in Ireland, to resist, or resent the impending blow. The Irish Houses of Parliament (if the assemblage of Lords and Commons in Dublin, which bore that name, deserved to be so called) made no effort to save the free trade of their country. Ready to carry out the policy dictated by English interest, they acquiesced in the destruction of the great woollen trade hitherto carried on in Ireland. The bill to prevent the exportation of woollens, passed the English Houses, and became law in 1699. At once the baneful effects of that measure were felt throughout this country—no less than twenty thousand skilled artisans, deprived of employment, and without prospect of means of subsistence at home, carried to France, and other countries, the skill which hitherto found employment in Ireland. Soon obtaining work in these more favoured lands, they established a trade far more dangerous to that of England than she experienced from this country. The disastrous condition of affairs here grew from bad to worse. The right of this country to be governed by laws made by the King, Lords, and Commons of Ireland, instead of England, was denied. The Act of 6th George the First, chap. 5, enacted that the House of Lords of Ireland had no appellate jurisdiction. In a short time the nation, though blessed by Divine Providence with all which ordinarily contributes to make a country rich and flourishing—possessing a fruitful soil, a patient, laborious population, safe ports, havens for commerce, and a mild climate—was in so wretched a condition as to cause the Protestant Dean of St. Patrick's to declare—"A stranger would be apt to think himself travelling in Lapland or Iceland, rather than in a country so favoured by nature as ours, both in fruitfulness of soil and temperature of climate. The miserable dress, and diet, and dwellings of the people—the old seats of the nobility and gentry all in ruins, and no new ones in their stead—the families of farmers, who pay great rents, living, in filth and nastiness, upon butter-milk and potatoes, without a shoe or stocking to their feet, or a house so convenient as an English hog-stye to receive them. These, indeed, may be comfortable sights to an English spectator, who comes for a short time only to *learn the language*, and returns back to his own country, whither he finds all our wealth transmitted—

"Nostra miseria magna est." *

---

* Swift's Works, vol. iii. p. 169, Hawksworth's Edition.

This is a sad picture of a country wherein considerable efforts had been made to encourage trade and promote industry. The Earl of Ossory at Charleville, Baron Harstongue at Bruff, Dutch merchants at Cork, and Limerick, promoted trade and manufacture. Lord Dungannon, the chief proprietor of Dundalk, established the linen trade here in the time of Charles the Second; and the Scotch settlers in Ulster applied themselves to weaving linen, and, by the attention paid to this branch of industry, so improved the quality of the fabric, that, from thence to this day, it cannot be excelled. The jealousy of England, in seeking the monopoly of woollens, and procuring the enactment by the Irish Parliament of 10 William the Third, c. 3, gave the greatest check and discouragement to Irish trade. Every effort was then made to encourage the linen manufacture. A Linen Board started into existence, with powers to grant bounties on linen exported abroad and on flax-seed imported; which, however, was soon withdrawn, it being found more fitting to encourage the growth of seed at home. Ulster was occupied by the industrious race, who lost nothing of Scotch prudence by breathing Irish air, and they soon settled themselves steadily to make the best of the existing state of things. Instead of losing their time in vain regrets for the departed woollen trade, they sedulously sought to employ themselves in the linen; and, as there was no steam machinery then invented for the spinning of yarn, the hum of the spinning-wheel was heard in every house, and the female population—young, old, and middle-aged—fed the flying shuttle. The farmers cultivated flax to a great extent; and thus full and remunerative employment made the northern peasants happy and contented. Agriculture, far from looking on commerce as a rival, became a partner in trade: and the Ulster farmers, instead of having only the precarious result of their crops to depend upon, had the produce of their looms besides, and, from the union, grew wealthy and prosperous. Belfast rapidly expanded. The small town, in a cove on Carrickfergus bay, swelled into the entrepôt for this important linen traffic; and, from the year 1713 to 1787, the export of linen from Ireland, or rather from Belfast and Dublin, increased, from less than two millions of yards in the former year, to close on thirty-one millions of yards in the latter.

We must follow more closely the fortunes of Dundalk. The great question of Irish manufactures occupied the time and thoughts of a very distinguished Englishman, the Most Rev. Hugh Boulter, D.D., who had been translated from the See of Bristol to the primatial chair of Armagh, in August, 1724. He was not long in Ireland before the unfortunate state of the people, having no resource but agriculture, suggested to his active mind the necessity of removing this evil by the introduction of manufactures. Knowing the importance of water carriage, as the means of transporting the produce of native industry to the sea-board, through his exertions was opened a communication with Lough Neagh, by the formation of a canal from Newry to the river Bann. He was an active member of the Linen Board. He assisted at the formation of a company, by which a cambric manufactory was established, in 1737, at Dundalk, on the estate of Lord Limerick, afterwards Earl of Clanbrassil. The following letters of the Primate* show his zeal in this good work:—

"TO THE DUKE OF DORSET.

"Dublin, April 28th, 1737.

"MY LORD—I have the honour of your Grace's of the 25th

---

* *Boulter's Letters*, vol. ii., p. 166.

post, by M. De Ioncourt; and since his arrival we have had a Linnen Board, and have furnished him and his brother with money to go with their workmen to Dundalk, where we have fixed this new manufacture, which I hope will turn to good account of this nation, and deserve our further encouragement. I shall still be ready to give them what further support may be necessary upon your Grace's recommendation, and shall always be proud to receive your Grace's commands.

"I am, my Lord, &c."

By another letter, addressed to Horace Walpole, who, it appears, recommended M. De Ioncourt to the Primate, as qualified to conduct this cambric manufactory, it appears every exertion was made to have the work properly executed:—"We agreed with M. De Ioncourt and his brother on the terms for which they are to carry on the cambrick manufactory, and gave one of the brothers money to go to France and bring over skilful workmen. Before his return we had fixed on Dundalk for the place to settle that manufacture in, with the approbation of the brother; and since his return we have advanced money to send the workmen thither to begin their business." The place where the manufactory was located is now occupied by the cavalry barracks, and few traces exist of what must, at one time, have been a very extensive establishment.

CHAPTER XVII.

THE IRISH VOLUNTEERS.

The Irish Volunteers, those champions of freedom, are ever remembered with pride. Their career, though short, exerted a powerful influence upon the destinies of their country, and the lesson they taught English statesmen will never forget. They rose to protect their country when she had no other defence; and, before they laid down their arms, they placed her in a position which, but for them, she never would have reached. Their history is briefly told. In 1760, Thurot, with a French force, sailed into the bay of Carrickfergus, and speedily became master of the town. The news, "the French are in the bay," rapidly spread, and the neighbouring loyal peasantry of Belfast assembled to give them battle. "Their appearance," said Lord Charlemont,* "was singular and formidable. They were drawn up in regular bodies, each with his own chosen officers, and formed in martial array; some few with old firelocks, but the greater number armed with what is called in Scotland the Lochaber axe—a scythe fixed longitudinally to the end of a long pole—a desperate weapon, and which they would have made a desperate use of. Thousands assembled in a small circuit; but these thousands were so thoroughly impressed with the necessity of regularity that the town was perfectly undisturbed by tumult, by riot, or drunkenness." The French rapidly re-embarked, and avoided the encounter. The danger, however, of leaving the coast undefended by regular troops suggested to the leading authorities of Belfast

* *Stuart's History of Armagh.*

the propriety of applying to the Lord Lieutenant for sufficient force to repel invasion. The following letter from Sir Richard Heron to Stewart Burke, Sovereign of Belfast, shows how powerless was the Irish Executive to send any formidable number of soldiers:—

"Dublin Castle, August 14th, 1778.

"SIR—My Lord Lieutenant having received information that there is reason to apprehend that three or four privateers, in company, may, in a few days, make attempts on the northern coasts of this kingdom, by his Excellency's command I give you the earliest account thereof, in order that there may be a careful watch, and immediate intelligence given to the inhabitants of Belfast in case any party from such ships should attempt to land.

"The greater part of the troops being encamped near Clonmel and Kinsale, his Excellency can, at present, send no further military aid to Belfast *than a troop or two of horse, and part of a company of invalids;* and his Excellency desires you will acquaint me by express whether a troop or two of horse can be properly accommodated in Belfast, so long as it may be proper to continue them in that town, in addition to the two troops now there.

"I have, &c.,

"RICHARD HERON."

This communication at once showed the people they must not expect protection from the Government. *A troop or two of horse, and part of a company of invalids*, was all the force available when the ships of France were floating on the seas, and a large army of Britain taken captive across the Atlantic. But if the crisis was imminent, Irish courage supplied what was needed. The Irish Volunteers arose! Everywhere was heard the tramp of measured footsteps, the stirring sound of the trumpet, the lively roll of the drum. Everywhere was seen the gay, sparkling uniform—scarlet, faced with white; blue, relieved with scarlet; scarlet and deep green; green, faced with white. Every locality, as it enrolled its band of warriors, delighted to give them such distinction as would infuse courage in the hour of strife. There was quickly embodied a noble army, consisting of over a hundred thousand men, as the following return shows:—

Ulster, ...	34,152
Munster, ...	18,056
Connaught, ...	14,336
Leinster, ...	22,283
22 Corps not included in these returns, estimated at . . .	12,000
	100,827 *

They had a fair proportion of cavalry, and 130 pieces of cannon. This patriotic army was composed of the substantial classes of the country, officered by noblemen and gentlemen of the first rank; but loyal, as the institution undoubtedly was, willing, nay desirous, of keeping up that ascendency of creed which is the bane of Ireland, it was looked on with deep suspicion by the British Government. In a letter from Lord Buckinghamshire, then Lord Lieutenant, to Lord Weymouth, in May, 1799, we find him throwing cold water on the movement:—"Discouragement has been given on my part, as far as might be without offence, at a crisis when the arm and

* *History of the Volunteers*, by M'Nevin, p. 222.

good-will of every individual might have been wanting for the defence of the State." * Despite the want of encouragement from the Castle, the work went on. From every barony, from every town throughout the kingdom, Volunteers arose. Every rank aspired to be enrolled. In towns, the professional men, the artizans, the shopkeepers, filled the ranks; throughout the country, the gentry and farmers. They had a variety of uniforms, which rendered their appearance, in large masses, brilliant and picturesque; and they went through their evolutions with the firm port of discipline. In 1780, the Earl of Belvedere reviewed the troops of Westmeath; Lord Kingsborough those of Clare and Limerick; the Londonderry corps were inspected by Lord Erne; the Cork regiments by Lord Shannon; the Dublin Volunteers by Lord Carysfort. The chief command of the Irish Volunteers was entrusted to James Caulfield, Earl of Charlemont. He earned the compliment by a life of consistent virtue and patriotism.

Dundalk was no recreant from the field of glory. The ancient town was well represented in the army of Volunteers. Two troops of cavalry, a corps of infantry, and one of artillery, bespoke at once the respectability, and scientific skill of the patriotic inhabitants. The commander of the Dundalk Independent Light Dragoons was Captain Thomas Read; that of the Dundalk Horse, J. W. Foster, Esq. Scarlet, faced with green, was the uniform; † while other towns of the County of Louth—Ardee, Duleek, and Drogheda—supplied a large contingent. The spirit of nationality was thoroughly roused, and the desire of using Irish manufactures prevalent. Associations to promote native industry sprung up in all directions;

---

* *Grattan's Life*, by his Son, vol. i., p. 348.

† *History of the Irish Volunteers*, Appendix, 227.

and the Volunteers appeared on parade in uniforms which were grown on Irish soil, made by Irish hands, and covered Irish hearts. The ladies, whose influence and example is all-powerful with Irishmen, caught the contagion, and enhanced, by their beauty, the fine textures wrought in the Irish looms, in which fabrics they took pride in being dressed. Much discontent was manifested among the mercantile classes of the country at the unjust restrictions placed upon Irish trade. Regimental meetings were held by the Volunteers for the support of "home manufactures, and no other;" and a resolution to that effect, adopted by the gentry and people of Meath, had the following very proper condition annexed:—"Resolved—That we consider ourselves as solemnly engaged to adhere to the above resolution as long as the traders and manufacturers of this kingdom approve themselves, by their conduct, worthy of liberal encouragement from the public."

The events which followed were of national importance, and affected every town and hamlet throughout the kingdom, more especially the trading ports. The session of the Irish Parliament of 1779–80 opened. The speech from the Lord Lieutenant was considered vague. He alluded to certain kind intentions on the part of the King respecting Irish trade; but there was no actual promise given, such as the distressed state of the country demanded. An address was proposed by Sir Robert Deane, one of the Court party, which was an echo of the speech, when up rose Henry Grattan, well known for his ardent love for Ireland and the Irish. He moved an amendment, embodying:—"That it was the duty of the House to lay the state of the country before his Majesty, and point out the only effectual means for its relief;" and, to the dismay of the Government party, when Grattan resumed his seat, Walter Hussey Burgh, then filling the high office of Prime Sergeant, one of the leading men of his time, addressed the House in support of Mr. Grattan. He concluded an eloquent speech by the words:—"We beg to represent to his Majesty it is not by temporary expedients, but by a *free trade alone*, that this nation is now to be saved from impending ruin." The resolution was carried unanimously. The following day the addresses of Lords and Commons were brought to the Castle. The streets were lined with the Dublin Volunteers, who received their favourites with military honours.

Success quickly followed on success. The political horizon, so long overcast, grew bright, and the confidence of the Volunteers rose with each peaceful triumph. While the fervid eloquence, and statesmanlike views, of Grattan, Flood, and Hussey Burgh, and the other renowned men of '82, were doing good service in the cause of constitutional liberty, in the Irish Parliament, the Volunteers were engaged in holding a series of splendid provincial reviews in every part of Ireland. These repeated displays of strength without, powerfully seconded the speeches within. The review in Belfast lasted three days—sixty thousand spectators were present. Finding the majority of the House of Commons indisposed to respect the constitutional rights of Ireland, a resolution was agreed on, to hold a convention of delegates from the Volunteer regiments of Ulster, at Dungannon, in the County Tyrone, to consider and take action on the state of public affairs.

On the 15th February, 1782, the delegates met. They represented an important constituency—thirty thousand armed men. No insignificant body to trifle with. The Church of Dungannon—the temple of the Most High—was not considered desecrated by the presence of men armed in the cause of their native land. Colonel Irwin, a gentleman of high family and firm loyalty, who united prudence with vigour, presided. Resolutions were passed to the effect—"That a citizen, by learning the use of arms, does not abandon his civil rights." "That a claim by any body of men, other than the King, Lords, and Commons of Ireland, to make laws to bind Ireland is unconstitutional, illegal, and a grievance." "They protested against Poyning's law, requiring the Privy Council's assent to the bills submitted to Parliament." "That trade should be free." "That a perpetual mutiny bill was unconstitutional, and should be limited from session to session." "That judges should be independent." "That private judgment in matters of religion should be sacred." "That as men, and as Irishmen, as Christians, and as Protestants, they rejoiced in the relaxation of the penal laws against the Roman Catholics, and conceived the measure fraught with the happiest consequences to the union and prosperity of Ireland."

This should ever be remembered by Irishmen. Toleration to the Catholics was declared cause of rejoicing by the Protestants of Ulster, on the 15th February, 1782, in the Church of Dungannon; and on the same day Mr Gardiner's Catholic Relief Bill was introduced into Parliament The measure proposed they should have—1st. Enjoyment of property. 2nd. Free exercise of their religion. 3rd. The rights of education. 4th. Of marriage. 5th. The right of bearing arms. After some modification, it passed into law. Other measures, in accordance with the wishes of the Volunteers, quickly followed. The Lord Lieutenant, the Duke of Portland, appeared disposed to concede all the Irish patriots demanded. The Perpetual Mutiny Act was repealed; the independence of the Irish judges secured; the appellate jurisdiction of the House of Lords restored. Fifty thousand pounds were voted to Mr. Grattan, for his services in restoring Ireland to the dignity and independence of a nation.

A proposition being made to consolidate the various corps of the County of Louth, a meeting of delegates, from the Dundalk Independent Troop of Light Dragoons, the Ballymascanlan Rangers, the Ardee Rangers, and the Dundalk Train of Artillery, was convened by notice for the 18th March, 1782. The meeting was held, and Thomas Read, Esq., called on to act as Chairman; when it was resolved, that all these various corps be united, and called "the County of Louth Regiment," and the Earl of Charlemont appointed Colonel. The Lieutenant Colonelcy was then offered to the Chairman, Thomas Read; but that gentleman was obliged to decline the command, owing to the delicate state of his health, which precluded him from taking that active part in the reviews which such a position imposed. The choice then fell upon Thomas Lee, Esq., who was unanimously elected. The following other appointments were made:—

Major—Robert M'Neale, Esq.

Chaplain—Rev. Edward Hudson.

Surgeon—William Lee, Esq.

Adjutant—Mr. Jeremiah Hatch, in room of Pullein Spencer, Esq., who declined acting, as he was already Adjutant of the Dundalk Troop, which still continued a distinct corps.

The meeting then unanimously resolved:—

"1stly.—That we, from our hearts, approve of the resolutions entered into by the Ulster Delegates, at Dungannon, on the 15th ult.—resolutions dictated by that firm, yet temperate spirit, which, if persisted in, must ensure success.

"2ndly.—That, as we shall never be wanting in loyalty to our Sovereign, so we are determined to be equally regardful of that duty which we owe to ourselves and to our posterity; and that, therefore, we shall cheerfully co-operate with our fellow-subjects in such legal and constitutional exertions as shall be deemed most effectual for obtaining a redress of those grievances under which we labour.

"3rdly.—That Lieut.-Colonel Lee and Pullein Spencer, Esq., do wait upon the Earl of Charlemont with the following address, and that the same, with his Lordship's answer, be published in the *Dublin Evening Post*:—

"TO THE RIGHT HONOURABLE THE EARL OF CHARLEMONT.

"MY LORD,—Ambitious of being commanded by a nobleman of your Lordship's exalted reputation, the County of Louth Corps, having formed a regiment, unanimously solicit your Lordship's acceptance of the command.

"Should we be so happy as to succeed, we shall use our best exertions to emulate those truly respectable corps who already enjoy the honour to which we aspire.

"Signed, by order,

"THOMAS READ, Chairman."

The deputation, consisting of Colonel Lee and Mr. Spencer, having presented the address to his Lordship, bore back his reply:—

"TO THE GENTLEMEN OF THE COUNTY OF LOUTH REGIMENT.

"GENTLEMEN,—Though many cogent reasons, drawn more especially from the various avocations in which I am already engaged, and from my consciousness of the want of sufficient ability properly to perform the tasks assigned me, concur to dissuade me from accepting the high and singular honour conferred on me by your address, yet, the preference given to me by a body of gentlemen so truly respectable is too agreeably flattering to every feeling of my heart to allow me calmly to follow the dictates of a diffidence, which is, I fear, but too well grounded. I do, therefore, most gratefully accept of the high office to which you have raised me, hoping and expecting that the same partial goodness which has prompted your choice will induce you to pardon my deficiencies; and, beseeching you to accept my warmest acknowledgments, as the only retribution I can make for so great and so unexpected a favour.

"I have the honour to be, Gentlemen,

"Your most obliged, faithful,

"And obedient, humble Servant,

"CHARLEMONT.*

"Dublin, March 23rd, 1782."

Parliamentary reform then began to be regarded with a hopeful glance, as the sole means of restoring a national spirit to the Irish Parliamant. In England the project met the approval of the Duke of Richmond and Mr. Pitt, and some of the Reform Association entered into correspondence with the Irish Volunteers. In July, 1783, delegates from several corps in Ulster summoned a general meeting of the province; in pursuance of which, on the 8th September, 500 delegates again met in Dungannon. The president on this occasion was Mr. Stewart, afterwards Marquis of Londonderry. It is enough to say he was a valued friend of Lord Charlemont to convince the reader of his love for Ireland; and it is cheering to think his spirit still survives in his accomplished descendant, the present inheritor of his title, and love of country. Among many important resolutions passed at this meeting was the following:—

---

* *Resolutions of the Volunteers*, by Wilson, p. 78.

"That a committee of five persons be appointed to represent Ulster in a grand National Convention, to be held at noon, in the Royal Exchange of Dublin, on the 10th November then next ensuing; to which they hoped that each of the other provinces would send delegates, to digest and publish a plan of Parliamentary Reform; to pursue such measures as may appear most likely to render it effectual; to adjourn from time to time; and to convene provincial meetings, if found necessary."

As truth must be stated, however disagreeable, one glaring anomaly pervaded these proceedings, and presented a striking contrast between professions and practice. Protestant ascendency was to be maintained over the Catholics; yet the Catholics encouraged the Volunteer movement by every means in their power, and deserved better than the sectarian intolerance evinced towards them.

The Congress met. Monday, the 10th November, 1783, was truly a great day for Ireland. One hundred and sixty delegates of the Volunteers, in the Royal Exchange of Dublin, elected Lord Charlemont Chairman; and the Earl of Bristol, Bishop of Derry, was one of the most active members. They adjourned to the Rotunda, and their progress through the streets was attended by all the pomp of military parade. The air resounded with bands playing, colours flying. Thousands of spectators cheered to the echo as the armed representatives of political progress marched, two and two, between the ranks lining the streets along their way to the Round Room, at the top of Sackville-street. Never did this spacious apartment appear to greater advantage. The raised orchestra was crowded with ladies. Circular seats, ranged round the chair, were occupied by the *élite* of the popular party, while every available space in the wide area was densely thronged.

The County of Louth was well represented. Dundalk sent the commanding officers of its various corps. The following officers, among others, took their seats as delegates:—

Lieutenant-Colonel Thomas Lee.
Major William Sheil.
Captain Thomas Read.
Captain Zachariah Maxwell.
Lieutenant J. W. Foster.

Alas for the fatal want of union amongst Irishmen! It was not long before symptoms of dissension showed themselves. Hardy, in his *Life of Lord Charlemont*, gives some idea of the difficulty experienced at this Convention of fixing upon any reasonable plan of reform:—"From every quarter, and from every speculatist, was poured in such a multiplicity of plans of reform—some of them ingenious, some of which bespoke an exercised and rational mind; but, in general, so utterly impracticable, so rugged and so wild in their attire, they looked not like the offspring of inhabitants of the earth, and yet were on it, that language would sink in pourtraying this motley band of incongruous fancies, of mis-shapen theories—valuable only if inefficient, or execrable if efficacious." The plan approved of by Flood and the Earl of Bristol, Bishop of Derry, was selected. It aimed at the destruction of borough influence, and the creation of a sound county franchise. It provided that pensioners of the Crown, receiving their pensions during pleasure, were disqualified from sitting in the House; that members, on receiving a pension or place, should vacate their seats; that members should take an oath they had not used undue influence in procuring their election; and that the duration of Parliament should not exceed three years.

There was, as might have been expected, a stormy debate on this bill being introduced into the Irish House of Commons.

The army of placemen and pensioners were all against it. As they formed the majority, it was almost folly to go to a division. The result was—for the motion, 77; against it, 157. The House then moved a resolution to maintain its "just rights and privileges against all encroachments whatsoever;" which was considered tantamount to a declaration of hostility against the Volunteers and their plans of reform. The indignation of the members of the Convention was very great; and it was dreaded a collision between the rival houses might ensue, in which the peace of the country would be involved. The Volunteers received their delegates, on their return to the country after the Convention broke up, with menacing aspect; but, though they beat their drums, and held stormy meetings, and passed strongly-worded resolutions, so long as they confined themselves to threats, the Government refrained from noticing them. Time diminished their anger, and wore out their hope of effecting reform. A second bill, introduced by Flood in 1784, was read a second time; but, on the motion for its committal, was thrown out by a majority of 74. In a few years the army of Volunteers, uncemented by union, and wanting that solid basis which is found in popular support from persons of every religious denomination, and every rank in the State, rapidly degenerated. Forsaken by the men of rank, this once respected national army became officered by enthusiasts, who caught up the revolutionary spirit which the tyranny of the *ancien regime* evoked in France, and sedition supplanted the language of ineffectual remonstrance. The fate of the Volunteers was sealed on the 16th February, 1785, when the bill for establishing a national militia was passed.

CHAPTER XVIII.

FROM THE DAYS OF THE VOLUNTEERS TO THE UNION.

While these important public events were taking place, an effort, having considerable interest for the townspeople of Dundalk, was being made. We have seen that the chief Anglo-Norman proprietors of the district were originally the De Verdons, to whom succeeded the Bellews; next, Marcus Trevor, Lord Dungannon, who parted with his interest to James Hamilton, of ancient Scottish descent; he was returned for Dundalk in George the First's reign. Being raised to the Peerage, by that monarch, as Baron of Claneboye and Viscount Limerick, in 1719 he took his seat in the Irish House of Peers, having also a seat in the House of Commons of England, as Member for the borough of Wendover. (He also represented Tavistock and Morpeth.) Though absent, he was not unmindful of the interests of Dundalk; for he was chiefly instrumental in procuring the charter of incorporation for carrying on the Dundalk cambric manufactory. In 1746 he was appointed Governor of the County Louth and Earl of Clanbrassil, and died in 1758, leaving his son, James, who succeeded as second Earl of Clanbrassil, and two daughters, Lady Anne and Lady Caroline, him surviving. Lady Anne, in 1750, married the Earl of Roden; and Lady Caroline died unmarried.

James, the second Earl of Clanbrassil, was born in 1729, and in 1742* received a grant in reversion, after the decease of Lord Palmerston, of the office of Chief Remembrancer of his

* *Lodge's Peerage of Ireland*, vol. iii., p. 12.

Majesty's Court of Exchequer, in Ireland. He, likewise, sat in the British House of Commons as Member for Helston, in Cornwall. He was Governor of the County Louth, a Knight of St. Patrick; and, in 1774, married Grace, daughter of Thomas Foley, afterwards Lord Foley, of Stoke-Edith Park, in Herefordshire; but had no issue.

Having become the principal proprietor of the town and commons of Dundalk, by the assignments of the rights of Sir John Bellew and Lord Dungannon, and with the assent of the Corporation, it was natural that the Earl of Clanbrassil should claim the chief management of local municipal affairs. The few Protestants, who formed the portion of the Corporation hostile to his views, were powerless against the more numerous supporters of the Earl. At length a new and unlooked-for opponent to the Clanbrassil interest appeared, and joined those who desired to open the borough, and who, though finally conquered, gave very determined battle. This was Mr. Thomas Read, whose father, Isaac Read, had been agent to the Earl, but had lost the agency. This gentleman, who, as well as his father, was constantly Bailiff of Dundalk, was Bailiff in 1781; and during his year of office he sought to procure the admission of freemen—considering that, unless those already admitted were out-numbered, the representation of the borough could never be taken from the hands into which it had fallen. On going to the Session House—where such meetings were usually held—it was found locked, by order of the Earl of Clanbrassil; whereupon he held the assembly in the Guildhall, and admitted over twenty inhabitants to be freemen, which led to a great deal of confusion and protracted litigation.

An information by *quo warranto* was filed in the King's Bench—successive trials and arguments followed; and the case having gone through various appeals, was finally brought, in 1792, to the Irish House of Lords, where Lord Chancellor Fitzgibbon, Lord Clare, pronounced final judgment. He decided "that, by the charter, the commonalty of Dundalk consisted of the freemen existing when the charter was granted, and such persons as should be substituted for *deceased or disfranchised freemen only;* and that the Corporation, having accepted a charter empowering the body thereafter to elect persons in the room of such members as should die or be disfranchised, could not elect any persons unless there were vacancies by such events."*

The consequence of this decision was to oust all the freemen created by Mr. Read, and restore the Corporation to the power of Lord Clanbrassil.

While these proceedings were slowly progressing from each Court of Appeal to the ultimate tribunal of the Lords, a heavy charge was speedily disposed of affecting Mr. Read. This was nothing short of an indictment for a most heinous crime.

It appears from the informations sworn in the matter, that, upon the removal of Mr. Isaac Read from the agency of the Clanbrassil estates, James Forde, of Dundalk, Esq., was appointed agent; and several papers came into his possession, from the late agent, which Mr. Forde suspected were forged by Mr. Thomas Read, who transacted business for his father, and was aware these documents were in the office in Mr. Forde's house in Dundalk.

While Mr. Forde was absent in Lurgan, County Armagh, about three o'clock in the morning of Wednesday, 8th January, 1783, Mrs. Forde was awakened by a violent knocking at the street door of her house in Dundalk; and,

* *Vide* 2 *Ridgeway's Parl.* (Ir.) *Cases*, p. 445.

on proceeding to inquire into the cause of the disturbance, she heard a man named M'Evoy, one of the servants, ask for the key of the office, which was on fire. He called out to some persons whom he saw standing outside the house:— "Stop, stop; we are ready for you;" but these men, as also two at some distance, ran away. M'Evoy then proceeded to the hall, and perceived a light under the door of the office. He opened the door, and entered. The office was in flames. In endeavouring to ascertain how the fire originated, four flambeaux were found. Three were nearly consumed; the fourth had been lighted, but had gone out. It was placed under the desk where Mr. Forde kept his papers. On examining closely, Mrs. Forde and the servant discovered the window-shutter had been forced open, the sash raised, and a stone placed to keep the window up, as if to fan the flames. Intelligence was at once sent to Mr. Forde, who, on his return, finding what had occurred, suspected Mr. Read; and as the flambeaux appeared to afford some clue to the incendiary, he proceeded to Dublin. Here he traced the purchase of four flambeaux, a blunderbus, and some masks, the day before the fire, by Mr. Thomas Read.

From the information of Mr. May, watchmaker, in Capel-street, Dublin, at whose shop the parcels were left, it appeared Mr. Read was desirous of having the circumstance of those articles being left there kept private; and Henry Gardiner, apprentice to Mr. May, gave evidence to the same effect.

On these informations the Grand Jury of the County of Louth found:—"That Thomas Read, on the 8th January, in the 23rd year of George the Third, at Dundalk, feloniously, wilfully, and maliciously, did set fire to a certain house of one James Forde, there situate, against the peace and statute," &c.; and in a second count of the indictment he was charged with "procuring the setting the same house on fire." This, as may well be supposed, was the great case of the assizes; and great was the excitement in Dundalk, where Mr. Read, from his youth, had always been regarded with respect, and treated with the utmost deference. He, as also his father, were, we are informed, magistrates of the county.

The assizes came on, and, on the 3rd of September, 1783, Thomas Read, Esq., was called on to plead to the above indictment. On the Bench sat the Right Hon. Walter Hussey Burgh, Chief Baron of the Exchequer; while the Crown was ably represented by the Attorney-General, Yelverton,* and the Solicitor-General, Carleton.† The prisoner was successfully defended; and the verdict, "Not Guilty," we make no doubt, caused cheers to rend the air, and bonfires to redden the skies.

The attention of the inhabitants of Dundalk was soon attracted to other important matters. The hopes of the nation rose with the Volunteers, and Catholics equalled their Protestant fellow-subjects in their anxiety to further the movement. We have seen how these hopes were baffled—how the Parliament of Ireland treated the measures introduced for Reform, and dashed these hopes to the ground. The despair which ensued engendered disaffection, and the Rebellion of 1798 was the outburst of the smouldering flame. The country, for some years previously, had been in a disturbed state. The relations of landlord and tenant then, as now, were in an unsatisfactory condition. The reckless extravagance which marked the career of the Irish gentry in those days, and which their descendants have expiated in

* Afterwards Lord Avonmore, Chief Baron of the Exchequer.

† Afterwards Lord Carleton, Chief Justice of the Common Pleas.

the Incumbered Estates Court, could only be supported by grinding the vitals out of their tenantry; and the poor Catholic tenants, not possessed of the lease which enables the lessee to claim legal protection against any illegal act of his landlord, were powerless against imposition. Middlemen fattened on the plunder of the poor under-tenants, and these unhappy men were glad to combine with any who held out the faintest hope of redress from their intolerable misery.

There resided at this time, in the neighbourhood of Dundalk, at Castletown, a highly respectable Catholic family, named Byrne. A member of this family, Patrick Byrne, junior, was possessed of a strong desire to aid his suffering fellow-countrymen; and, knowing the importance of union among all classes of Irishmen, he addressed to the Presbyterians of Ulster a letter on the state of Ireland. This document censured the conduct of various public men in strong terms, and recommended union of Irishmen—that all religious distinctions should be forgotten—all should remember they had a common interest, and success would follow; an end be put to tithes and taxes, under which Presbyterian and Catholic equally groaned. He signed it "Common Sense"—September, 1792.

This letter was distributed in various places, and the writer was traced. The informations of the persons he employed to distribute it were taken, and an indictment for seditious libel preferred against him. The case came on at the Lent Assizes of Dundalk, in 1793, the heaviest ever held in Louth, the calendar of prisoners being the most numerous, three judges presiding. Mr. Byrne was prosecuted by the Attorney-General, for writing and publishing a seditious libel. He was tried before the Hon. Baron Power, Hon. Judge Boyd, and Hon. Judge Downes; convicted, and the sentence of the court passed upon him was:—"To be imprisoned two years, and until he paid a fine to the King of £500, gave security to be of the peace for seven years, himself in £1,000, and two sureties in £500 each, and then to be discharged, paying fees." He underwent this sentence, and complied with its terms, which were enforced to the letter. He died, unmarried, at Berlin, in 1812.

Mr. Byrne's able and impressive appeal in this matter was not without fruits. A coalition took place between many of the Presbyterians and the Catholics. They united for the formation of "a brotherhood of affection, a communion of rights, and a union of power among Irishmen of every religious persuasion, and hoped thereby to obtain a complete reform in the legislation, founded on the principles of civil, political, and religious liberty." This agitation appeared to have relaxed the chains of the Catholics. They were admitted to the Bar; the marriage of Protestants and Roman Catholics was permitted, and the educational restrictions, which hitherto confined the intellect and enslaved the mind of Catholics, to the scandal of mankind and reproach of the civilised world, were removed. These concessions, however, failed to satisfy the views of the extreme party. Annual Parliaments, and universal suffrage by all males aged 21, possessed of sound mind, and resident within an electoral division for six months, was required. No property qualification was to be necessary for membership; but the candidate should be 25 years old, a resident within the kingdom, holding neither place nor pension, and payment of members was part of the plan. The educated and higher class of Catholics considered these propositions most objectionable; the lower orders were for them. Money was subscribed, a National Guard enrolled, orders for a general muster issued; but the Lord Lieutenant put it down by proclamation. A Convention Act was passed; several of the seditious leaders, who were chiefly either Protestant gentlemen, or northern Presbyterians, desirous of establishing a Republic, were prosecuted.

The neighbourhood of Dundalk was occasionally visited by the illegal society called Defenders. James Napper Tandy, Secretary to the Dublin Society of United Irishmen, was deputed by that society to ascertain the views of the Defenders. Accordingly he met a party of Defenders at Castle Bellingham, and took the oath of that body. Informations were shortly afterwards sworn against him, and a bill of indictment was prepared at Dundalk, which was at once found by the Grand Jury of the County of Louth, then impanneled. He was informed of this, at Dundalk, in time to enable him to escape arrest, and soon after he quitted the kingdom.* The meetings of the society of United Irishmen were at first public, but, being proclaimed by the Government, became secret and revolutionary. Imagining the solemnity of an oath was security against detection, treason was hatched and a rebellion projected. The organization, skilfully ramified throughout every part of the kingdom, counted among its adherents no less than four hundred thousand armed men, ready to take the field at the command of their leaders. Wretched dupes! Among those leaders were the spies and paid agents of the British Government. From 1795 a regular system of *espionage* was established, and sustained by reckless expenditure of public money. Protestant and Catholic equally traded upon the credulity of their misguided countrymen, and every *secret meeting* (?) was known at the Castle shortly after the conspirators dispersed.

---

* *Madden's United Irishmen*, vol. iii.

The mind revolts from the consequences which ensued—an Insurrection Act was followed, in 1796, by the suspension of the Habeas Corpus Act. We are, unhappily, too well aware of the effect of such a measure. Secret informations, causing illegal, and often unjustifiable, arrests: suspected persons hurriedly tried, and hastily condemned and punished—districts driven into violence, and then visited by the horrors of military license. These are the sure results of so fearful a state of affairs. Dundalk, unhappily had sad experience of them. The Corporation, exclusively Protestant, had no sympathy with the Catholic population, and considered all members of that creed as objects of suspicion, if not actually disloyal. The town and district was placed under martial law, and the pitch cap and triangle found many victims. It could serve no good purpose to dwell upon this sad state of the town during this time. Severity produced retaliation, and the cruelties inflicted upon the Catholics often caused equal enormities to be perpetrated by them upon unoffending Protestants.

The state of disorganization of the army in Ireland induced the Government to select for the command General Sir Ralph Abercromby, who returned to England, from the West Indies, in 1797. He found the Irish people disaffected and misgoverned, the civil authority subverted, and military power grossly abused. "His estimate of the people," states his son, Lord Dunfermline,* "led him to appreciate justly the liveliness of their parts, and the levity which exposed them to the danger of being misguided by able and artful demagogues; but while he knew their vices, and the origin of them, he knew that there was in their character much of

---

* *Memoir of Sir Ralph Abercromby*, p. 72.

generosity and warmth of feeling, which made them acutely sensitive when they were treated considerately and kindly. His judgment of the upper classes of society, and of the purity and wisdom of the Government, was less favourable. He saw that the gentry were imperfectly educated; that they were devoted to the pursuits of pleasure, and of political intrigue; and that they were ignorant or neglectful of the duties imposed on them as landlords, and as the friends and protectors of those who depended on them for their existence. He saw that the acts of the Government and of the Legislature were not regulated by respect for principle, which was the more to be lamented, as they were not controlled by the influence of an intelligent public opinion." Impressed with these views, Sir Ralph resolved to maintain his own independence, and distinctly informed Mr. Pitt, that "if his measures were disapproved of, he would willingly resign. That if the offices of Commander-in-Chief and Lord Lieutenant were united in the person of Lord Cornwallis, he was ready to serve under him." Lord Camden was, at this period, Lord Lieutenant. There was not much cordiality between these high personages. In a letter to the Duke of York, Commander-in-Chief of the Army, Sir Ralph says:—"I have no reason to say that Lord Camden has refused me his support, but the difficulties and delays I experience will render my situation irksome, and my labour unavailing"*

On the 26th February, 1798, Sir Ralph issued the Order, so often quoted, to show the fearfully demoralized state of the army:—"The very disagreeable frequency of courts-martial, and the many complaints of irregularities in the conduct of

---

* *Memoir of Sir Ralph Abercromby*, p. 85.

the troops in this kingdom, having too unfortunately proved the army to be in a state of licentiousness which must render it formidable to every one but the enemy, the Commander-in-Chief thinks it necessary to demand from all Generals commanding districts and brigades, as well as commanding officers of regiments, that they exert for themselves, and compel from all officers under their command, the strictest and most unremitting attention to the discipline, good order, and conduct of the men, such as may restore the high and distinguished reputation which the British troops have been accustomed to enjoy in every part of the world."

The consequence of such an admission of disorganization was to draw down the wrath of the ascendency party upon the head of General Sir Ralph Abercromby. When he went to the north, in order to inspect the troops, the Government party in Dublin endeavoured to weaken his influence with Lord Camden, and to impress the militia officers with the idea that the order was intended as an insult to them. Lord Moira having, in his place in the House of Lords, described the distracted state of the country, and the excesses committed by the troops, the enemies of Sir Ralph asserted that his order was a stroke of political intrigue, and that he was acting in concert with Lord Moira. He disclaimed this, most distinctly, in a letter to Lord Camden, but referred to a proclamation of the 18th May, 1797, authorising the military to act without waiting the orders of a civil magistrate. This, he thought, highly inconvenient, and even dangerous. Lord Camden, in reply, stated that, "as the necessity for such a proclamation existed, it should be acted upon;" which being entirely opposed to the views of Sir Ralph, led to the earnest wish of this good and brave man that he might be removed from Ireland, so as to give "the least possible interruption to the military business in so distracted a country, and the least handle for speculation."*

For some time the British Government laboured hard to induce Sir Ralph to retain the command in Ireland; and, although he never could act with any cordiality, when his feelings were opposed to the duties he was obliged to execute, in order not to embarrass Lord Camden, he remained for a short time longer. He did all he could to compose the disturbances which were rapidly assuming a serious character, and was of opinion, that, by a judicious distribution and employment of the military, order might be preserved. This soothing course was not suited to the desires of the Irish Government. Coercion was their resolve, and a General who would execute the wishes of the dominant party was appointed Commander-in-Chief.

General Lake has earned unenviable fame by his command in Ireland. On the 17th May, 1798, he issued an order, so severe and unjust, that it is regarded as unparalleled in history, and as Lord Dunfermline observes:—"It can excite no surprise that the same people who, in the preceding year had displayed so much loyalty in resisting the French, were, within three weeks from the date of this order, driven into rebellion."†

It is due to the memory of King George the Third to state, that when Sir Ralph Abercromby went to his levee, immediately on his arrival in London, the King came and addressed these words to him:—"They have used you very ill in Ireland, and you are now going to Scotland, where they will know how to respect you, and to treat you better." When the King retired to his closet, he said to one of his Ministers:—"I

* *Memoirs*, p. 108. † *Id.*, p. 123.

watched my opportunity, when certain Irish politicians were within hearing, and I took good care that they should be in no doubt as to my opinion of Sir Ralph and his conduct." *

The following letter to Sir Ralph Abercromby from General (afterwards Lord) Hutchinson, was written in Dundalk, and gives very frank expressions of the writer's views on the then deplorable state of parties in Ireland:—

"Dundalk, 12th June, 1799.

"MY DEAR ABERCROMBY,

"I was sent down here to command a brigade of English militia a few days after the French left Brest. Two of my regiments have returned to England. One of them, the Warwick, would stay no longer. The King of England has a great number of armed men in his service; but where his army is I am at a great loss to find.

"In my opinion, the rebellion in this country is entirely put down. The rebels seem to be sick of their own machinations, by which they have been themselves the chief sufferers. I suppose you know that I support the Union. After all my patriotism, I have been obliged to vote for the annihilation of the Irish Legislature; but such are the hopes of man, and such the termination of his most proud designs. And yet, I never was so convinced of anything in politics as of the necessity of this measure. If ever there was a nation unfit to govern itself, it is Ireland; a corrupt aristocracy—a ferocious commonalty—a distracted Government—a divided people. I solemnly believe that the great mass of every religious persuasion in this country have no wish so near their hearts as to enjoy the power of persecuting each other. The

---

* *Memoirs*, p. 125.

Catholic would murder the Protestant in the name of God; the Protestant would murder the Catholic in the name of Law. Both sects seem to consider their common country only as an extended field of battle, where each are at full liberty to display their sanguinary dexterity. The bulk of the people, in my opinion, are by no means averse to the Union. The South is, certainly, for it; the North, silent; Dublin, clamorous; the lawyers, outrageous. The chief opposition will, therefore, be in Parliament, where money and influence can do everything. But Lord Castlereagh will be deceived if he thinks that he can pay the needy members of Parliament in sentences, and not in cash. The fact is, people are so used to be bribed in this country that they will not do what is right, or their own business, unless they are paid for it."

No sooner was Lord Castlereagh convinced that cash, and not sentences, would purchase the Union, than he announced his intention to purchase votes under the name of *compensation* for loss of patronage. He bid high, as he was dealing with needy men of expensive habits and lofty titles. He devoted one million five hundred thousand pounds towards his object; and no wonder he succeeded. The most specious views, at the same time, were put forth, to remove, or silence, opposition. Lord Castlereagh stated the Union would cure the evils of religious divisions, the defective nature of the Imperial connexion, and commercial inequalities. Catholic Emancipation, an adjustment of the Tithe system, and endowment of the Roman Catholic and Presbyterian clergymen, were among the inducements held out by the Government; and many Catholics gave the measure their support.

Marquess Cornwallis, the Lord Lieutenant of Ireland at

this period, was the successor of Lord Camden. He was a General Officer who had seen much service, and brought to his official station the honourable and straightforward views of a soldier and a gentleman. He was thoroughly impressed with the notion that Ireland would benefit by the Union, and most anxious to promote the success of the only measure which, in his opinion, would save the country, and amalgamate all classes of the people. No one tried to put an end to the oppression of the Catholic population by the Yeomanry, calling themselves Loyalists, more anxiously than his Excellency; and it was said of him that "if he was less of an honest man, and more of a politician, he might have carried the Union more quickly; for his strenuous efforts to stem the torrent of corruption, and his disgust at the profligate jobbing, then so openly carried on by almost every man who could make anything by the barter of his principles, lost the Government *nineteen* different votes in three families, and the support of many others. It was," as our informant writes, "his wish to introduce a mild government, which would be a happy change from the flogging and torture, so generally resorted to."

When the country was restored to tranquillity, the Viceroy determined on a progress through the north—there being a much better chance of his making his way successfully in that quarter than in the south or west. Although considerable efforts were made to induce the Roman Catholic population to present addresses in favour of the projected union, these efforts were, in general, very fruitless, and after some attempts to get up meetings in the south, they were quickly abandoned. The *Cornwallis Correspondence*, published by Mr. Ross, of Bladensburgh, throws much light upon this dark and troubled time, and several of the interesting letters show how far more successfully these attempts to enlist a popular support for this measure were attended in the north, and especially in Dundalk, than in other parts of the kingdom.

In a letter dated Dublin Castle, October 22, 1799,* we find Lord Cornwallis thus informing the Duke of Portland of the state of feeling in Dundalk towards the then impending Union.

"Dublin Castle, October 22, 1799.

"My Dear Lord,

"Although a change of political circumstances, and the temper of the times, will often affect the general opinions of the multitude—and it is therefore unsafe to trust entirely to appearances—yet, from my reception in the North, there is certainly reason to entertain very sanguine hopes of the good disposition of the people in that part of this kingdom towards the very important measure of a legislative Union with Great Britain.

At Dundalk, which was the first place that I visited, I received, according to my expectations, an address in favour of the Union from the Corporation, which is pretty much under the influence of Lord Roden; but, to my surprise, another address to the same effect was presented by the priest, in the name of, and attended by, several of the Roman Catholic inhabitants. At Armagh, where the Primate† is all-powerful, the Corporation, clergy, &c., came forward, and everything passed smoothly; but the point of difficulty was the management of matters at Belfast."

---

* *The Cornwallis Correspondence*, vol. iii., p. 138.

† Dr. William Newcome, D.D.

In another letter written to Major-General Ross,* the Lord Lieutenant repeats, in nearly the same words, the account of his reception at Dundalk.

"Phœnix Park, October 24, 1799

"Dear Ross,

"My northern tour has answered my most sanguine expectations. At Dundalk—the first place that I visited—exclusive of the address from the Corporation, which is under the influence of Lord Roden, I received an unasked and unsought-for address from the Roman Catholic inhabitants, in favour of the Union. I did not enter the County of Down, lest that proud leviathan, Lord Downshire, should call it a declaration of war; but I was received with open arms at Belfast; and throughout the whole counties of Antrim and Derry the cry for an Union is almost unanimous."

That there was the fullest assurance held out to the Catholics that Emancipation would quickly follow, may be judged from the following:—

Minutes of a conversation between the late Marquess Cornwallis, Lord Lieutenant of Ireland, and Commander of the Forces, and the late Henry Howard, Esq., of Corby, then Captain in the 1st West York Regiment of Militia, serving in Ireland (inserted by permission of his son, Philip H. Howard, Esq., of Corby):—

"My connection and friendship with the present Duke of Norfolk† has given me frequent opportunities of seeing that

---

* *The Cornwallis Correspondence*, vol. iii., p. 140.

† Charles, 11th Duke of Norfolk.

excellent person Lord Cornwallis, his Grace's next neighbour in Suffolk. I was afterwards under his lordship's command at Warley camp; and then, when quartered in Dublin, for ten months, with the 1st West York Militia, I was honoured by his lordship's kindness, and frequent invitations to his table. While at Dublin, I never saw him without his making the pending Union the subject of his conversation, and chiefly as it related to Catholics. He was aware of my early friendship with Lord Fingall, and my intimacy with many Catholics, and that I had a common cause with them; and he more than once desired me to impress on them the advantage the Union would be to them, and the expediency of their placing confidence in him. Of these conversations I took minutes on my return home, and shall transcribe one of the last, word for word, without correction:—

"1799, 11th December.—Dined, Park. After dinner, sat by Lord Cornwallis. Addressing me on the subject of the state of Ireland between Catholic and Protestant, I said 'that I thought, from what I had perceived of the state of men's minds, that the best and most useful part of Government was to hinder the people from cutting each other's throats.' He—'That, unfortunately, was not what the Government had done here.' I said, 'I thought that justice began to be done here on that score, which, when I first came, was by no means the case.' This brought on the subject of Union, which he thought the only remedy and means of doing that which, left to them here, would never be done. Speaking of the inflamed state of mind between sect and sect, I said that 'I thought it was owing to him that it had not come to the full extent of mutual extermination, which I conceived had been daily gaining ground.' 'That,' he said, 'must have been the event.'

I mentioned Dr. Duigenan's work, which he said 'was a wretched work; but such as he thought everybody would pass over as the work of a madman.' I stated that 'it did not fail, from his official situation, to give uneasiness. I trusted, however, with respect to the Catholics, that, as it appeared to be the interest to conciliate them, that they would be an object of the Union; that without this I thought the Union was nothing.' He repeated that 'Certainly the Union, without it, was nothing. That it was, however, impossible to bring anything forward before, because in an Irish Parliament it could not be carried.' I said 'that the mystery and silence created both uneasiness and impatience.' He answered 'he believed it to be so; and he thought that the Catholics had shown a great deal of temper, more than he could have expected, by some joining in it, none appearing actively against it, and not coming forward to distress him with their claims; that he heartily wished they would place confidence in him.' We had some conversation about an establishment for the clergy, which he said he had talked over with Lord Fingall, whom he highly esteemed. 'Depend upon it,' he said, 'the Catholics will be the first object of consideration, when we are able to act free from shackles.' He added, 'he was most fully convinced that an establishment for the clergy would be most amply compensated by loyalty; that now, he knew, priests were not their own masters.' I repeated 'that a loyal priest with a disloyal flock must starve.' He said 'he knew many were driven to silence, inaction, or to take part with their flocks. He inveighed strongly against the Orangemen.'

"Lady Mary Singleton used something of the same language to Mrs. Howard; certainly an echo.

"December 13th.—Mentioned this conversation to Lord

Fingall. He told me that Lord Cornwallis had said to him that he authorised him to call upon him, after the Union was passed, to move, from his seat in the House of Lords, and propose the emancipation of the Catholics; that he promised so to do, and depended on success."

CHAPTER XIX.

FROM THE UNION TO THE YEAR 1817.

By the Act of Union Ireland became an integral part of the British empire. Previously her separate Parliament made her very much a colony, in which the settlers, although they mingled and intermarried with the aborigines, formed, to a great extent, a distinct race. The continual revolts of the Irish chieftains afforded repeated opportunity for confiscations, which, promptly availed of, enabled the Governments of the day to reward active and zealous adherents with the lands of the ancient proprietors. The lower order of Irish, attached to the old families, looked coldly on the strangers, and the new occupants naturally kept aloof from the friends and associates of those whom they had displaced. When to hostility of race was added that bitter ingredient, poisoning the sweet charities of life—religious hate, matters became tenfold worse; and, as the emancipation of the Catholics was expected to follow the Union, men looked eagerly for the promised boon.

For some years after 1800, the historian of Dundalk has little to record. The insurrection of Emmet, in 1803, was confined to the metropolis, and expired with the ill-fated enthusiastic projector on the scaffold. The death of Mr. Pitt, in 1806, caused a change of Ministers; and the accession of the Whigs to power infused fresh hopes into the minds of the Catholic party. Agitation was determined upon—the Catholic Board was formed; but its deliberations were far from being unanimous. A young barrister, a native of Kerry, who possessed great fluency of speech, and ability, which, in after years, made him a power in the State, was soon recognised as the exponent of the popular Catholic feeling, He was firmly and consistently opposed to the members of the Board, who, on the important question of appointment of the Irish Catholic Bishops by the Pope, were for allowing the English Government a *veto*, unless the person appointed had a certificate of his loyalty, and consented to be bound by oath not to hold any communication with Rome tending to involve the British Constitution or the Established Church. Several Catholic peers took part in these discussions. Lord Fingall was one of the noblemen whose virtue increased the respect due to his rank. Ever true to his word, never was his promise known to be broken. His face, beaming with mildness and benevolence, was a sure index to the kindness of his nature. In him a gentle heart was united to a firm and unbending will, and a manly assertion of the claims of his creed and country. Through weal and woe he adhered to his countrymen; and left to his son the proud inheritance of his untarnished name, which the present Earl has maintained unsullied.

Meanwhile Dundalk made little stir in the world. Its inhabitants pursued their various avocations peaceably; and, under the *regime* of the excellent vicar, the Reverend Elias Thackery, all men dwelt without strife or discord. In 1811, a public butter market, stores, &c., was erected by subscription in Dundalk; and the Corporation agreed with the subscribers to erect a weigh-house when the butter stores were completed, which was accordingly done—Lord Roden, who was a subscriber for several shares, giving the necessary ground.

It appears the Corporation formerly possessed a Guildhall. The building now called the Guildhall, or Market-house, is the property of Lord Roden. It was probably in the old Guildhall the Michaelmas dinners to the freemen were given; for in some of the old Corporation accounts, from 1755 to 1759, charges for the "Michaelmas dinner" appear against the Corporation. Not having the books to refer to, we are unable to state more particularly the nature of these banquets; but, from the time corresponding with the date at which the Bailiff entered on his year of office, it is but fair to presume they were analogous to the Lord Mayor's banquet, annually given shortly after each Lord Mayor of Dublin occupies the civic chair. The charge for the dinner against the Corporation would appear rather shabby on the part of the Bailiff, who, of course, presided as the host on these occasions; but we do not find he had any salary, and certainly was entitled to a dinner at the expense of the Corporation, having to discharge the duties of a number and variety of offices, without fee or reward.

CHAPTER XX.

THE BURNING OF WILD GOOSE LODGE.

During the Spring Assizes of 1818, a number of persons were arraigned, in the Court-house of Dundalk, charged with a crime of unusual magnitude. In fact, the crime was so terrible, both as regarded the number who perished by its perpetration, and those who were immolated as victims to the outraged majesty of the law, that it then had no equal, and since has, happily, only one parallel—the burning of the Sheas. The Louth outrage was called the Burning of Wild Goose Lodge.*

The history of this terrible event is shortly this:—There was a small farm-house, built on a grassy knoll, rising from some low marshy bottoms, often flooded after rain, situated in the County of Louth, about four miles from the town of Carrickmacross, in the County of Monaghan, and nine from Dundalk. Here a family of the name of Lynch, or Linchy, resided. They were of the Roman Catholic religion, and peaceable, well-conducted people. One of the sons was solicited by the secret society of Ribbonmen—then spreading their atrocious net to catch the innocent youth of Ireland—to enrol himself a member of their body; and, on his refusal, he became a mark for the displeasure of this lawless and wicked confederacy. Having been assaulted by some of these desperate men, Lynch prosecuted them to conviction, and they were executed in front of Dundalk Gaol; whereupon dire vengeance was sworn against him and his. A ruffian, named Devan, was the chief of the avengers; and he summoned the Ribbon gangs of the counties lying adjacent to Louth, to meet, by night (the 30th October, 1817), in the chapel of Stonetown,† of which he was clerk. The dread summons was obeyed, though the season was winter, and tempests swept the earth, and sleet like hail fell piercingly upon the wayfarers. Through darkness and storm the steps of men tramped on, and, by the appointed hour, about eighty crowded the little chapel. Their aspect and demeanour showed how little they regarded the sacredness of the spot. The altar of God,

---

* For a graphic account, see Carleton's *Stories of the Irish Peasantry*.

† Brett's *Reminiscences of Louth*, p. 6.

usually so reverenced by the lower orders, was polluted by the presence of the most abandoned characters in the country. The house of prayer resounded with oaths and blasphemy; and drink—the bane of so many—was liberally supplied, to stimulate the timid and to sustain the bold.

By the dint of coaxing and libations of whiskey, the leader of this gang induced his comrades to swear they would do his bidding, and keep secret whatever occurred. He then placed a quantity of half-burned turf in a pot, and, having made the men drink more whiskey, they sallied out to do their hellish deed.

On through the darkness—meet hour for such men to be abroad—the ruffians sped. Over roads sloppy with rain, while the cold wind rushed through the ravines of the hills, they advanced on the doomed dwelling. They were nearly baffled: the ordinary approach to the house was flooded, and they were about returning, when the ringleader stumbled on a causeway, raised in order to admit a passage under inundations like the present, and along this the gang passed. Once at the house, the work of destruction began. The fatal arrangements were soon made; the fire, carefully preserved in the pot, was placed to the thatch, and in less than fifteen minutes the dwelling was in flames. "No mercy!" was the order, and no mercy was shown. A fearful sight appeared at one of the windows—a woman's head, with the fire burning like a glory around. She shrieked for mercy; she received the thrust of a pike, and was flung back into the flames.

The whole dwelling soon showed one lurid blaze, and the shrieks of its perishing inmates rose fearfully above the crackling of the rafters. Doors were wrenched open, and windows shattered to atoms, in the efforts of the inmates to escape; but the fiends, who guarded every egress, had their lesson, and *no mercy* was extended to man, woman, or child—even an infant was doomed to perish. The owner of the house—Lynch—made a pathetic appeal on behalf of his daughter. She was yet unhurt, and he begged, in moving terms, for her life; or, if that was not granted, that he might be shot, rather than see her perish by fire.

"You'll prosecute no one now, you bloody informer," was the inhuman response.

The work of destruction was complete. Not one remained alive; about a dozen human beings perished.

But, though the Lynches were no longer able to prosecute the perpetrators of this savage deed, the general feeling of horror throughout the country was too great to admit of justice being baffled. Some of the criminals were immediately made amenable; but the greater number were not tried until the spring of 1818, when their trials took place in Dundalk, before Judges Mayne and Fletcher.

We have been furnished, by Mr. Byrne, Clerk of the Crown for the County of Louth, with abstracts of the indictments, which charged them with murder and arson. They were ably defended by the well-known eminent criminal lawyer, the late Leonard Macnally; but even his skill could not avail. The following were convicted:—Patrick Devan, Hugh M'Cabe, Pat. Waters, James Campbell, Owen Gaynor, Laurence Gaynor, Pat. M'Guillan, James Loughran, Thomas M'Cullagh, Edward M'Quillan, Michael Kieran, Michael Floody, Mat. Clarke, Pat. Craven, John Kieran, George M'Quillan, Pat. Malone, Pat. Meaghan, James M'Alarney, James Morris, James Smith, and Pat. Malone. These wretched men were sentenced to be hanged, and their bodies to be delivered for dissection. In order to inspire terror into the people of the district, the ringleader, Devan, and twelve of his companions in guilt, were directed to be hanged in chains; and their mouldering bones long remained on the gibbets, a source of terror and dread, as they recalled the memory of such atrocious guilt.

During this period (1817) the town and neighbourhood of Dundalk suffered from scarcity of food, consequent upon the failure of the harvest. It was a time to call forth an active spirit of benevolence; and foremost in the cause of charity was the Rev. Elias Thackery, Vicar of Dundalk. No danger appalled—no amount of labour caused him to pause in the service of God's poor. Fever, of a most malignant kind, was fearfully prevalent, and the ministrations of the Catholic clergy were required night and day. Some of these ever-active pastors of their flocks sacrificed their lives at their posts, and fell victims to their faithful discharge of duty. The close proximity of penitent and confessor exposed them to the contagion of typhus; they caught the infection, and died. Nor were the medical men less diligent, or more secure. The proprietors of the Dundalk Distillery had large quantities of oats and barley in stores for malting, but, desirous of assisting the poor, generously had this stock ground into meal, and sold at a rate within the poor man's reach. Conduct like this deserves to be recorded.

CHAPTER XXI.

FROM THE ELECTION OF 1818 TO THE PASSING OF CATHOLIC EMANCIPATION.

THE Parliamentary election of 1818 found a candidate for the representation of Dundalk, whose "career," observes a late gifted writer,* "possesses strong points of interest, as it was very characteristic of the state of society in Ireland during his lifetime" This man was Gerard, third son of Daniel Callaghan, one of the most enterprising and successful of Irish merchants. He was a native of the "beautiful city" watered by the Lee; and in Cork, Gerard, son of Daniel, served mass and said his prayers, as a Roman Catholic child should. But with the increasing wealth of his father there grew ambition in the soul of Gerard. Of what avail the vast stores and profitable contracts, by which the house of "Callaghan and Sons" made immense gains. Here was Gerard, young, handsome, with an English education, and an undeniable English accent, through the solid plating of which no dross of Munster ore ever found its vulgar way; yet the lowest member of the Protestant Church looked down from the pedestal of his ascendency upon the young Papist. This was more than the soul of Gerard, could bear. Freedom from such condition he must have, though he staked his future on the issue. He possessed a ready wit and satirical talents. Too proud to remain under the ban which pressed upon his co-religionists, he went openly to Church, became a Protestant, and

* Daniel Owen Madden in *Revelations of Ireland*, p. 185.

resolved to enter Parliament. To do this in his native County of Cork was impossible. For years the great feudal lords monopolized the political influence of nearly all the counties of Ireland. The Lords of Meath, and Blessington, held Dublin; the Earls of Enniskillen, Fermanagh; the Earl of Roden had great influence in Louth; the Beresfords were supreme in Waterford; while the Lords of Shannon, and Kingston, with the great commoners, Hyde, of Castle Hyde, Hedges Eyre, of Macroom Castle, and the Longfields, left no room for an intruder into Cork. The representation of the city was in the hands of the Boyles, Hutchinsons, and Colthursts. Among these potent chiefs Gerard Callaghan would be reckoned an intruder. They had ancient blood in their veins, and could trace back a pedigree from the ancestor who fought with William at Hastings, or with William at the Boyne, and looked contemptuously on the mushroom who traced his descent from Callaghan, King of Munster, in the year 994, because his immediate progenitors sold pork. In the Province of Munster, then, Gerard had no chance of a seat; so he looked northward, and found that a corporate town, situate, lying, and being in the County of Louth, and the capital of the same, was ready to send to Parliament a staunch Protestant, so Gerard made overtures for the place, and, having shown his competency, was declared duly elected.

Having gone so far in the biography of this representative, it is fair to add, his career, while Member for the Borough of Dundalk, showed the trust reposed in him was well placed. Mr. Madden informs us:—"He was certainly a strange mixture of great talents and vanity, with some absurd and many excellent traits. While he sat for Dundalk he was an active and intelligent Member, and took a strong interest in

Irish subjects. He was one of the first who loudly complained of the inattention then paid to Ireland. He said nothing about Catholic Emancipation, and professed that peculiar kind of political creed which Mr. Flood introduced into Ireland—namely, a system of popular Liberalism, which was not to extend beyond the Protestants." *

His connexion with the borough was not of long duration. In 1820, the aged Monarch, whose reign is the longest yet recorded in the annals of England, George the Third, passed away. Parliament, of course, was dissolved, and Gerard Callaghan ceased to be Member for Dundalk. Those interested in his subsequent career will find it in the pleasant work from which we have quoted.

While Gerard Callaghan sat for the borough, Lords Ferrard and Jocelyn represented the county. On the death of the Earl of Roden, in 1820, his son, the present Earl, having succeeded to the peerage, left a vacancy in the representation of the county, which afforded an opportunity for a contest. Mr. Balfour, of Townlay Hall, was accordingly put in nomination against the Honourable John Jocelyn, uncle to the Earl of Roden, and Mr. Lee Norman, the High Sheriff, fixed the time for holding the election; but Mr. Balfour feared the result, and addressed the electors, thanking those who promised to support him, but declined the contest; on which, the Honourable Mr. Jocelyn was returned unopposed.

During Sir Walter Scott's visit to Ireland, in July, 1825, he passed through Dundalk, *en route* from Belfast to Dublin, His son-in-law, Lockhart, accompanied him; and in the Memoirs of the illustrious novelist we find the following letter, written by the Editor of the *Quarterly* to his wife,

---

* *Revelations of Ireland*, p. 197.

descriptive of this part of the country at the time of the visit:—*

"Erin deserves, undoubtedly, the style of *Green Erin*. We passed through high and low country, rich and poor, but none that was not greener than Scotland ever saw. The husbandry to the North seemed rather careless than bad, I should say *slovenly;* for everything is cultivated, and the crops are fine, though the appearance is quite spoiled by the bad, or, oftener, the *no* fences; and, above all, to unaccustomed eyes, by the human wretchedness everywhere visible. Your papa says, however, that he sees all over the North marks of an improving country; that the new houses are all greatly better than the old, &c. He is, no doubt, right as to the towns, and even villages, on the highway; but I can't imagine the *newest* huts of the peasantry to have been preceded by worse, even in the days of Malachi with the Collar of Gold. They are of clay, without chimneys, and without any opening for light, except the door and the smoke-hole in the roof. Where there is a window it seldom has even one pane of glass; and I take it the aperture is only a Summer luxury, to be closed up with the ready trowel whenever the Winter comes. Yet your father swears he has not seen one face decidedly careworn and unhappy; on the contrary an universal good humour and merriment, and, to us, every sort of civility from the poor people. As yet few beggars. An old man, at Dunleer, having got some pence from Anne while the carriage stopt, an older woman came forward to sell gooseberries, and we declining these, she added that 'we might as well give her an alms too, then, for she was an old

* *Lockhart's Life of Sir Walter Scott*, vol. vi., p. 49.

struggler.' Anne thought she said *smuggler*, and dreamt of potheen; but she meant that she had done her best to resist the 'sea of troubles;' whereas her neighbour, the professed mendicant, had yielded to the stream too easily. The Unknown says he shall recollect the word, which deserves to be classical. We slept at Dundalk—a poor little town by the shore, but with a magnificent Justice Hall—a public building superior, I think, to any in Edinburgh."

From Dundalk the Great Unknown and his companions proceeded to the battle-field of the Boyne. "When we halted at Drogheda, a retired officer of dragoons, discovering that the party was Sir Walter Scott's, sent in his card, with a polite offer to attend him over the field of the battle of the Boyne, about two miles off, which, of course, was accepted; Sir Walter rejoicing the veteran's heart by his vigorous recitation of the famous ballad—*The Crossing of the Water*—as we proceeded to the ground, and by the eager and intelligent curiosity with which he received his explanations of it."*

The year 1826 was a most important year in the history of the County of Louth. At this period, in Dundalk was waged a conflict, equal in desperation and the earnestness of the combatants, with any we have heretofore narrated. True the weapons were somewhat different. No cleaving sword, or quivering spear, of mail-clad knight or half-naked kerne, was wielded; yet the rallying cries were not dissimilar to those heard in days of yore. The proud nobles of the Pale were banded, as of old, against the Irish; and stormy contentions of debate, and vollies of speeches, succeeded to the boom of cannon, or the sharp rattle of musketry.

* *Lockhart's Life of Scott*, vol. vi., p. 51.

The Catholic Association unfurled its standard in the South, and Villiars Stuart, of Dromara, now Lord Stuart de Decies, broke down the power of the Beresfords, and sat in their place as Member for Waterford County. This success, however, was so natural, people hardly regarded it with surprise; but, great indeed was the excitement, when a rumour arose, that a Liberal candidate would contest the representation of the County of Louth with the nominees of the powerful houses of Roden and Oriel. The long acquiescence by the electors of Louth in the selection of the candidates of the Jocelyns and Fosters, had established a sort of prescriptive right, in these distinguished families, to have the County, as well as the Borough of Dundalk, in their hands; and it seemed not only the height of presumption, but something bordering on folly, to hope for success against the coalition thus formed. The attempt, nevertheless, was made. The individual selected as the popular candidate had been a barrister; but retired from the profession, and led the unassuming life of a studious country gentleman. He was called from this tranquil state to have greatness thrust upon him. His name was Alexander Dawson; and, without great wealth to sustain, or connexions to assist his canvass, prepared for the struggle. He possessed many high qualifications for the post he aspired to—considerable eloquence; a high character; devoted love for Ireland, and the people, with whose cause he identified his political career. Sir Edward Bellew, at first, shrunk from the request to support the popular candidate, as he ever experienced the friendship of the Protestant gentry; but feeling it a point of duty, he consented, and entered boldly into the struggle. The day for nominating the candidates was an eventful one in Dundalk. From an early hour in a glorious morning of June, with a bright sun blazing down upon the streets, came thronging in dense multitudes of the forty-shilling freeholders; and when the man of their choice appeared, no conqueror in his hour of triumph, ever received so warm a welcome. Arrived at his committee rooms, Mr. Dawson addressed the assembled thousands. He told them it was for their sakes, and not to gratify any personal ambition, he was determined to contest the county with Mr. Foster and Mr. Fortescue. His speech was received with approbation—it created an extraordinary degree of popular excitement—and he was brought, amid cheers, to the Court-house, where the High Sheriff, John Woolsey, Esq., of Castlebellingham, presided.

Three candidates appeared at the hustings. Mr. Leslie Foster, being first proposed and seconded, addressed the electors in a speech which his supporters loudly cheered. He dwelt upon the natural capacities of the county. Its position, so calculated to promote both commercial and agricultural industry, and his resolve, while in Parliament, to devote his energies to its progressive advancement. Mr. Matthew Fortescue came next; he was a country gentleman of good fortune, fond of field sports, popular with the gentry, but regarded as the nominee of the Earl of Roden, his address was coldly received by the people. Mr. Dawson was proposed by Sir Edward Bellew, Bart., amidst enthusiastic cheers, and seconded by Henry Chester, Esq. On coming forward to address the electors he was received with a perfect tumult of applause, and his energetic harangue produced continuous cheering. Mr. Sheil, who acted as counsel for Mr. Dawson, then spoke on behalf of the Liberal candidate, and his speech was well received. The following morning, when the polling books were opened, crowds of forty-shilling freeholders, in cars, on horseback, or on foot, poured into Dundalk. As a number of the Oriel tenantry came in to vote for Mr. Foster, the women in the crowd reproached them for deserting their country, and asked them "would they submit to continue slaves, driven to vote at the bidding of their master?" on which they leapt from the cars, went in a body, and voted for Mr. Dawson. The contest soon assumed the aspect of a religious war. Though not only was Mr. Dawson a Protestant, but his conducting agents also belonged to the Established Church, the Catholic party rallied round him. His counsel was a host in himself—Richard Lalor Sheil. The exertions made by the conflicting parties were unparalleled—priests and laymen combined to secure the return of the popular candidate, while parsons and landlords used their most strenuous exertions to secure the return of their favourites. Mr. North, one of the ablest members of the Irish bar, brother-in-law of Mr. Foster, threw the weight of his genius into the cause, and worked with more than professional zeal. The assessor, Mr. Chaigneau, had much difficulty to restrain the ardour of the professional men at both sides. The people were very quiet, save in sound, for nothing could be more stentorian than the shouting; while music, not of the kind that gives satisfaction at concerts, continually deafened the ears. Drums thundered, and fiddlers played that lively air, *Nancy Dawson*, in compliment to the people's candidate. A freeholder, named Harry Mills, and a maltster from Drogheda, named Christy May, were distinguished in their efforts to sustain the popular cause. Early on the first day, the tide of popular support having triumphantly borne Mr. Dawson to the head of the poll, the contest lay between Mr. Foster and Mr. Fortescue. The excitement which hitherto prevailed respecting the return of Mr. Dawson, was now directed towards them, and the final result was—Messrs. Dawson and

Leslie Foster were returned. The popular candidate was chaired through the town, and thus terminated the famous election of 1826. From this period to the passing of the Catholic Emancipation Act of 1829, the history of each part of Ireland is the unhappy history of the struggles of the few to restrain the advance of the mass of the Irish people to civil and religious liberty. The energy and perseverance of O'Connell, the great leader of the Catholic party, had worked the Catholic Association from the assemblage of half a score of individuals, to a society numbering millions. The Corn Exchange of Dublin was the arena in which large masses congregated, and the spirited speeches of O'Connell, Sheil, Lawless, and other eloquent Irishmen, delighted the auditory, and kept up the agitation. The return of O'Connell to Parliament, as Member for Clare, in 1828, brought matters to a crisis. The Duke of Wellington and Sir Robert Peel felt they could no longer delay the emancipation of the Catholics without incurring the risk of civil war, and to the mortification of the ascendency party, the Catholic Relief Bill of 1829 passed into law.

CHAPTER XXII.

FROM 1829 TO THE SUCCESSION OF QUEEN VICTORIA.

THE death of King George the Fourth, in 1830, caused, as usual, the dissolution of Parliament, and it was soon rumoured that Dundalk would witness a renewal of the stormy scene of angry contention, and bitter memories—a contested election. The elevation of Mr. Leslie Foster to a seat on the Judicial Bench, as one of the Barons of the Court of Exchequer, prevented his soliciting the renewal of the votes of the county freeholders; but on the same interest stood an extensive landed proprietor of the county—Mr. M'Clintock; while the Liberal Party had three Richmonds in the field. One was Mr. Alexander Dawson, who had fought for the people's right to send their own candidate to Parliament in 1826, and his return was certain. Another was Richard Lalor Sheil, whose reputation as a brilliant and fervid orator entitled him to aspire to a seat in Parliament, and who was regarded as second only to O'Connell in popular estimation. He rested his claims to represent the County of Louth on his great and successful exertions to secure the triumph of civil and religious liberty in the return of Mr. Dawson; while the remaining candidate on the Liberal side was Mr. Richard Montesquieu Bellew, brother to Sir Patrick Bellew, of Barmeath, whose hereditary connexion with the county, and identification with its interests, pointed him out as a fitting representative. The disunion created by so many candidates standing on the same side, was fatal to the popular cause, and Mr. Dawson had for his colleague Mr. M'Clintock, while Messrs. Sheil and Bellew experienced the mortification of having mutually defeated each other.

The constant shiftings of the political kaleidoscope produced new combinations in Louth. The faithful, and to the last, highly popular member, Mr. Dawson, having died, created a vacancy which was quickly filled by Mr. Sheil. He was this time returned without opposition. When addressing the electors, he strongly eulogised the conduct of Sir Patrick Bellew, who might have supported his brother as a rival candidate; but Mr. Sheil was paid the high compliment of being unopposed, and the Bellews became still more endeared to the people of the County of Louth.

At the next general election, after the passing of the Reform Bill, other changes in the representation occurred. The alterations in the elective franchise placed the borough of Dundalk, as well as the County of Louth, in the hands of the Liberal Party; and a Registry Club was established in Dundalk, of which William Brett, Esq., was secretary, for the purpose of attending to the admission of Liberal freeholders under the Reform Act, and also the selection of representatives of popular feelings as members. The Club having, in 1832, the expectation of being able to return Mr. Sheil for the Borough of Dundalk, he wrote to Mr. Brett a letter, declining the honour, on the ground of being obliged to reside chiefly in Tipperary. He continued as follows:—

"But when I find that the County of Louth has, in the persons of Messrs. Fitzgerald, Bellew, and O'Reilly, three candidates on the Liberal side, and that, by my retiring from Dundalk, one of them may stand in my place, and thus prevent a recurrence of the fatal divisions of which the county was before a victim, I have the consolation to think that in the step which I have adopted I not only do not impair, but, on the contrary, materially promote the general interests."

After strongly recommending Mr. O'Reilly to be selected for the borough, and his (Mr. Sheil's) intention of becoming a candidate for the County of Tipperary, he concludes:—

"I have, while Member for the County of Louth, endeavoured to do my duty to the best of my ability; and, by a constant attendance and unremitting vigilance over its interests, supplied any absence of higher qualifications to do any public service. I retire, carrying with me a deep regret that my political connexion should be determined with a place with which I have been, I trust, most honorably linked, and bearing with me the consciousness that, in the whole course of my political conduct in Parliament, I have not, in a single instance, deserted from the path which my constituents, seconded by my own conviction, desired that I should pursue.

"Believe me,

"Very truly yours,

"RICHARD LALOR SHEIL.

"William Brett, Esq., Dundalk."

The gentlemen indicated by Mr. Sheil were adopted by the Club; and Mr. M'Clintock, whose services would undoubtedly have procured him the support of the Conservative Party, not being desirous of re-election, retired from Parliament. Thomas Fitzgerald, Esq., of Fanevalley, and Richard Montesquieu Bellew, Esq., were elected Members for the County of Louth; and William O'Reilly, a member of the Irish Bar, put in nomination for the Borough of Dundalk. His return, however, was opposed. The Hon. Captain Jocelyn, whose family had so long been the patrons of the borough, would not relinquish it without a contest, and the issue was stoutly battled for. At length the Reformers carried the seat, and Mr. O'Reilly was declared Member for the Borough of Dundalk. A melancholy occurrence, which occasioned loss of a life, happened at this period. A glazier's boy, named Macbeth, on Saturday evening, foolishly ran through the crowded streets of Dundalk, shouting "Jocelyn for ever!" This, of course, produced counter-cheers from other youths, who cried "O'Reilly for ever!" Upon this Macbeth drew forth—not a dagger, but an equally murderous weapon—the knife he used in his trade, and stabbed one of the boys to the heart. He instantly died; and the infuriated slayer attacked, and severely wounded, another. The police soon conveyed him to gaol, and he was tried at the ensuing assizes, convicted of manslaughter, and sentenced to three years' imprisonment.

Mr. Fitzgerald, the newly elected county member, devoted himself with great zeal, and considerable ability, to his Parliamentary duties. He was of the ancient race who earned the high compliment of being more Irish than the Irish—*Hibernis ipsis Hiberniores*, and having acquired considerable property in the West Indies purchased an estate in the County of Louth, and resided at the beautiful seat of Fanevalley. That he felt proud of the position in which he was placed may be seen by the following letter, addressed to Mr. Brett:—

"Dublin, 30th December, 1832.

"MY DEAR SIR,—Although I am aware that your zeal and patriotic exertions on a late occasion may be traced to that public spirit, which has ever marked your conduct in support of the independence of the county, still, as one of the individuals who, in consequence, has been raised to a distinguished station, I cannot divest myself of a personal feeling, nor the necessity of offering you my sincere thanks on the occasion. Be assured it is a very grateful duty I perform, as it embraces an acknowledgment, as well to a meritorious public officer as to a gentleman for whom I always entertained a high regard. I intend setting off in the course of to-morrow to take my family to London. When I am there settled in harness I shall let you know; and hope to hear from you occasionally during the session, with such information as may be useful to me in the discharge of my duty. I need not, I hope, assure you that my inclination will always keep pace with what I owe to my constituents, in attending to the suggestions of the humblest amongst them to the utmost of my power. I hope they are all sensible of this.

"Believe me to be, &c.,

"THOMAS FITZGERALD.

"Wm. Brett, Esq., Dundalk."

The questions then discussed in Parliament were of the deepest interest to every man in the community. Parliamentary and Municipal Reform had a rival agitation in Ireland—Anti-Tithes. This embraced the whole kingdom, and produced disastrous collisions between the troops and the people at Gurtroe, Newtownbarry, Carrickshock, and other places. The distressed state to which the Protestant clergy were reduced by the withholding their means of support, was pitiable. Unwilling often to put forth the power of the law, many suffered uncomplainingly, and hoped the Legislature would speedily settle the question. They sold their books, and articles of furniture to preserve life, and their families underwent severe privations. At length a measure was passed into law, which reduced the Church Establishment in Ireland very considerably. The four Archbishoprics were diminished one-half, and the eighteen Bishoprics reduced to ten. Tithes were changed into rent-charges, a fourth abolished, and the landlord was responsible for the remaining three-fourths, which the tenants pay in addition to their rent.

During this period Ireland was visited by the dreadful scourge cholera morbus, and Dundalk suffered severely. The prompt measures adopted by the skilful medical practitioners, had the effect of subduing this destructive malady. The old

Charter School formed a commodious hospital, and the treatment adopted saved the lives of many patients.

The health of Mr. Fitzgerald, M.P., soon gave way. His devotion to his constituents caused him to take part in the important debates which nightly occurred during the passing of the Coercion Acts introduced by Lord Grey, in 1833. The anxiety he felt for his country was intense. Writing to one of his constituents, he says:—

"London, 16th February, 1833.

"We are all in consternation with the dreadful measures intended for unfortunate Ireland, as brought forward last night by Lord Grey. I was in the House of Lords, and I was really shocked when I heard them. I hope the country will express strong disgust, by petitioning against them while it is in the power of the people to petition. We are not without hopes that the English members will not join in this horrid attempt against us, and that we may be able to make the Ministry feel the atrocity of the measures. We shall take the earliest opportunity of expressing our sentiments on it, and probably this may arise on Monday night."

His close and unremitting attention in Parliament undermined his constitution, and, to the great grief of his family, and the Irish public, this popular representative died in 1833.

About the same time another distinguished Irishman, long connected with the neighbourhood of Dundalk, and for many years member for the county, shuffled off this mortal coil—the Right Hon. John Foster, formerly a Member of the Irish House of Commons, who filled the chair as Speaker to the time of the Union. He strenuously resisted that measure, and delivered one of the most argumentative speeches against it. When the Act passed, he was elected one of the representatives of the County of Louth in the Imperial Parliament; and the British Government, aware of his talents, and experience in Irish financial affairs, appointed him Chancellor of the Irish Exchequer. He was succeeded in this office by Sir John Newport; but it was abolished on the amalgamation of the Irish Exchequer with that of Great Britain. Mr. Foster, though a man of cultivated mind, entertained strong prejudices, and was steadily opposed to the removal of the Catholic disabilities. He was raised to the peerage by the title of Lord Oriel; and, on his death, his son succeeded to the estates, and enjoyed the triple peerage of Ferrard, Massareene, and Oriel.

Although by the measure of Emancipation the Catholics were placed on an equality with the Protestants, all places of trust and power remained in the hands of the lately dominant sect. Parliamentary and Municipal Reform was needed; and England led the way. Ireland had her turn.

Toward the end of the month of October, 1833, there arrived two members of the Irish Bar, in Dundalk, whose coming excited considerable anxiety, and some share of apprehension. These legal functionaries were the Commissioners, appointed by the Government, to enquire and report upon the state of Municipal Corporations in Ireland. They were William Elliott Hudson and Matthew Richard Sausse. The former, a barrister of considerable experience, deeply read in municipal law, brother of the Very Reverend the Dean of Armagh; the latter, a gentleman of high intellectual attainments, who has since reached the elevated rank of Chief Justice of Ceylon. This inquiry occupied several days; and all persons capable of giving information respecting the Corporation, and willing to come forward, were examined. The various charters conferred upon the town by successive monarchs, and the by-laws made from time to time by the body corporate, were inspected. Conveyances, Corporation books, rates of tolls, returns of harbour dues, treasurers' accounts, in short, everything relating to the Corporation was minutely investigated, and a voluminous report prepared. The fate of the Corporation was sealed. It transpired that the entire property with which the Corporation was entrusted had long passed into other hands; and the report of the Commissioners conduced to the extinction of the Corporation. This was effected by the Act 3rd & 4th Vict., c. 108. The town is now under the vigilant care of Commissioners, appointed pursuant to the Act 9 George the Fourth, c. 82, who levy an annual tax for the expense of lighting, paving, and watching the town.

The death of Mr. Fitzgerald having created a vacancy in the representation, the Liberal party desired to return a gentleman whose high character, devotion to the cause of the tenant farmers of Ireland, and tolerant views, pointed him out as a proper person to represent any constituency—Mr. Sharman Crawford. He declined to stand for the county. The Liberal electors then offered the seat in succession to Mr. Faithful Fortescue, and Mr. Lee Norman, either of whom would do honour to their choice; but these gentlemen were not ambitious of the proffered place. As a last resort they turned to one who would have been earlier sought, but he was known to be averse to the turmoil and bustle of public life—Sir Patrick Bellew, Bart., of Barmeath. He possessed high rank, was Lord Lieutenant of the County of Louth, with the prospect of having the ancient title of Lord Bellew restored (which has since been fulfilled). He was prevailed upon to stand; and the Conservative party selected the Hon. Mr. Foster, son of Lord Ferrard, Massareene, and Oriel, to oppose his return.

The polling was well contested at both sides; but the Bellews carried the struggle, and Louth was represented by two brothers, descended from one of the most ancient and respectable of the Anglo-Norman families of the Pale. Dundalk, also, changed its representative shortly after this. Mr. O'Reilly resigned, and the electors of the borough resolved to follow the example previously set by the county, and offered to return Mr. Sharman Crawford. They were more successful; and his presence in Dundalk was hailed with acclamation.

There were some rumours of a contest; and Mr. Talbot Glascock arrived from Dublin and made a speech in the streets of Dundalk; but meeting no prospect of support, he speedily retreated. One of the Jocelyn family was looked for; but as no member of that house came forward, Mr. Sharman Crawford was returned unopposed.

In 1837 Her Gracious Majesty Queen Victoria ascended the throne. This year Dundalk was revisited by the fearful scourge of the cholera morbus. The charitable and humane feelings of the inhabitants, always ready to assist in the preservation of life, caused every effort to be made to prevent the spread of infection; and here all were personally concerned. The philanthropist—the man of the world—the old and young—the religious and the indifferent—the brave, the timid, the strong, the weak—men of every rank and condition, felt they were assailed by an enemy more dreadful than the old foemen of the Pale, or the Scandinavian rovers. The Faculty exerted themselves with that courage, and skill, which, to our mind, entitles an eminent physician to as high a reward from the public as is conferred upon a successful general or statesman. If superior genius, and deep study, and great experience, enables the general to win victories in the field, or the politician in the Senate—by the same means is the physician able to baffle disease, and snatch the victim from the jaws of death. The physicians of Dundalk did battle against the cholera; and, after a stout conflict, freed the town from its ruthless ravages. One of them fell a victim; and his name ought not to be forgotten—Dr. Fitzpatrick. His fellow-townsmen evinced their sense of his merits by erecting a monument to his memory. This is not a solitary instance of the fearless devotion of the medical practitioners of Dundalk to a sense of their duty to their fellow-creatures and profession, or of the appreciation by the townspeople of their untimely fate.

CHAPTER XXIII.

FROM THE SUCCESSION OF QUEEN VICTORIA TO THE YEAR 1852.

For some years after the succession of Her Most Gracious Majesty, in 1837, the Earl of Mulgrave was Lord Lieutenant of Ireland. He was happy in his official colleagues, for Lord Morpeth, then Chief Secretary of State for Ireland, and Captain Drummond, the Under Secretary, were equally bent on conciliating the Irish people, and making them contented subjects of the Queen.

In the Spring of 1839, Lord Mulgrave, then Marquess of Normanby, resigned, and was succeeded in the Viceroyalty by Lord Fortescue. The great popular agitation, at this period, was for the Repeal of the Legislative Union between Great Britain and Ireland. O'Connell, whose first public speech, in 1800, was against the Union, took part in the agitation,* which was very general in 1810, when the Dublin Corporation petitioned for the Repeal.

* *Popular History of Ireland*, vol. iii., p. 72.

In 1822 notice of a motion on the subject of Repeal was given in the House of Commons, when Mr. (afterwards Sir Robert) Peel inquired "if the honourable mover could seriously ask the House to violate that solemn compact?" The agitation, having, in 1832, assumed a formidable shape, and between thirty and forty members being pledged to support it in Parliament, on opening the Session of 1833, King William the Fourth, in the speech from the throne, expressed surprise and indignation at the efforts made to disturb the Union. The Coercion Bill, popularly termed the Algerine Act, was passed to give a great discouragement to this movement, in consequence of which the agitation for Repeal was suspended. The question at length was brought by O'Connell before Parliament, in a speech of five hours' duration; a brilliant debate followed. Mr. Spring Rice* replied to O'Connell. He dwelt on the corruption and inefficiency of the Irish Parliament, the tendency of two Legislatures to produce separation, and the giant strides of Ireland in prosperity since the Union. Mr. (now Sir) Emerson Tennent followed on the same side: Sheil supported O'Connell. Sir Robert Peel displayed his usual ability in replying to Sheil. His quotation—"Repeal the Union—re-enact the Heptarchy"—was considered very apposite. O'Connell replied; and the numbers were—for the motion, 40; against it, 525. O'Connell then established the Precursor Society, the avowed object of which was to see if Ireland would obtain equality with England under the Union.

In 1841 the County Louth Meeting, to address the Queen and her illustrious Consort, on the auspicious event of the birth of the Prince of Wales, was held in Castlebellingham,

* Now Lord Monteagle.

in the month of December. The attendance was a proof of the loyalty of the County of Louth, and all passed off with unanimity and devotion to the Sovereign of the United Kingdom. In this year Sir Robert Peel became Prime Minister, and Earl De Grey, Lord Lieutenant of Ireland. The agitation for the Repeal of the Union was regularly organized. The Loyal National Repeal Association formed; Repeal Missionaries sent into every parish, and monster meetings held throughout the country.

In 1842 New Year's-day was celebrated by a crowded Repeal meeting at Dundalk. It was supposed not less than from sixty to seventy thousand persons attended. The crowds flocked in from the neighbouring Counties of Armagh, Down, and Meath. O'Connell, at this time Lord Mayor of Dublin, was accompanied to the meeting by Messrs. Boylan, Markey, Caraher, and other Repealers, and the chair was taken by Berkely B. Stafford, Esq. O'Connell made a most powerful speech, and, at the banquet which followed, nearly 600 persons sat down. To the toast of "The People—the True Source of Legitimate Power," the Rev. Mr. Marmion ably responded.

It was not by the overwhelming power of numbers alone that O'Connell sought to procure the favourite object of his aspirations. He was desirous of establishing the necessity of Repeal by argument, and conviction, and brought it forward in the Corporation of Dublin. Alderman Butt, a distinguished member of the Irish bar and of the Dublin University, discussed the question on the negative side. On a division the numbers were—41 in favour of, 15 against, the Repeal of the Union.

During the Summer many monster meetings were held, and more than once Dundalk and its vicinity witnessed these popular demonstrations.

On Thursday, 28th June, 1843, a memorable one took place at Castletown. It was, in every sense, a monster meeting. A person writing immediately after stated:—"It is utterly impossible to convey even a faint idea of the glorious and spirit-stirring scene that was enacted on the occasion, or adequately to pourtray the enthusiasm, the determination to succeed in effecting the mighty objects which they assembled to advance—that animated the men who participated in this truly great demonstration." For some days previously the most active preparations were made to give the meeting *eclat*. Houses were decorated with green boughs, and at the entrance to Dundalk a substantial triumphal arch was erected. Another was placed at Haggardstown, within two miles of Dundalk, with a bust of O'Connell holding the keys of the Irish Parliament House. Another extended across the main street of Dundalk, on either side of which was the Queen and Prince Albert; and, near the place of meeting, was an arch surmounted by a portrait of O'Connell. The view from the platform was most extensive and picturesque, and the newspapers estimate the numbers assembled at the immense congregation of 300,000. The chair was filled by Richard De Verdon, Esq., ex-J.P., and Messrs. Molony and Cartin acted as secretaries. O'Connell made a popular speech, promising that Repeal of the Union would give household suffrage, enable the Irish to get rid of the English National Debt, of poor rates, and tithe rent-charge—that it would recall the absentees, and Ireland would then be governed by Irishmen. He contended the Orangemen were as much interested in the Repeal of the Union as he was. Declared there should be no conflict with them. If they chose to petition against it, they had a perfect right to do so. He wished for no triumph at the expense of any class. He wanted to have all Irishmen for Ireland, as well as Ireland for all Irishmen. Such is a brief summary of his speech.

A dinner took place in an apartment in Dundalk, most tastefully fitted up for the occasion. At the entrance, the letters "V. R.," surmounted by a crown, were represented by gas-lights. Galleries were erected at either end of the apartment, and thronged with ladies. Several suitable inscriptions were placed in front of these galleries:—"Long Reign Victoria, Queen of our Affections;" "The Ladies of Louth: Erin's Brightest Gems," &c.

The chair was taken by Nicholas Markey, Esq. Now that we know how events have turned out, the speech which O'Connell made on that occasion is very memorable. On his health being proposed, he said:—"The majestic scene we witnessed to-day—the thousands upon thousands of rational, determined men—the steadiness with which they accumulated—the facilities with which they passed through the streets, each respecting the other, and accommodating him—the quietude, that spoke emphatically even by its silence—all that scene has filled me with a seriousness approaching to sadness; it has made an awful impression on my mind; it speaks to me, trumpet-tongued, of the approach of that great crisis which is to determine the fate of Ireland for centuries—the approach of that period when it will depend altogether on the manner in which we comport ourselves whether Ireland shall be once more plunged into misery, or elevated into the dignity of an independent nation. The slightest portion of rashness would ruin the entire cause; the progress of that steadiness I admire will bring us to success."

It is very likely O'Connell was sagacious enough to foresee that a time might come when he could not control the enormous physical power of the multitude; and to have held millions of undisciplined men, submissive and peaceful, as he hitherto was able to do, was a singular proof of his possessing that spell upon the human mind which proclaimed him an extraordinary man. He continued the monster meetings, and one was announced for the 8th October, at Clontarf, the battle-field on which Brian Boroihme conquered the Danes.

The Government proclaimed the meeting; and O'Connell, dreading a collision with the troops, took prompt measures, and prevented any assemblage. Then ensued the State Trials; the conviction and imprisonment of the great Tribune, and the other "martyrs;" the reversal of the sentence by the House of Lords, with the triumphal procession—a great ovation; but nothing could restore the crushed spirit, the broken heart.

Apparently O'Connell lost nothing of his energy; but his mind was worn with anxiety. The party known as "Young Ireland" were for more warlike measures than accorded with his views. He still agitated for the Repeal by peaceful means.

Tuesday, July 1, 1846, witnessed another great political demonstration in Dundalk. The popular electors were resolved to displace Mr. Redington from the representation of the borough; and Daniel O'Connell, junior, the youngest son of the great Emancipator, having consented to stand, a banquet was resolved on, to allow him to make his *debut* in Dundalk. There was an immense assemblage. All shouted for "Young Dan.," for "The Liberator," for "Repeal," and "Old Ireland;" and, amid the crash of musical instruments from a number of brass bands, the waving of banners, and the shouting of thousands, the demonstration took place. As many of the Town Commissioners as a carriage-and-four could accommodate, attended; and along the streets of the town a vast crowd lined the route. O'Connell addressed the populace at the Market-place, in his usual style, and, having concluded his harangue, proceeded to Cartin's Hotel, Clanbrassil-street, where the banquet took place. Dr. Coleman presided, and a very large party of clergy and laity assembled. O'Connell thus introduced his son to the notice of the electors:—"It may be said that it is presumption on my part to offer a son of mine to the electors of Dundalk, but it cannot be denied that I give, at least in this instance, a great proof of the sincerity of my respect for the undoubted truth, and sterling patriotism, of the electors of this town." When the health of Mr. O'Connell, junior, was proposed, that gentleman promised "allegiance to the cause of Repeal—never for a moment will the cry for Repeal be relinquished, or our exertions be decreased." He was subsequently withdrawn, and a talented young barrister, Mr. Torrens M'Cullagh, elected in his stead.

We have no temptation to dwell upon the history of the famine years. In Dundalk, as elsewhere, an awful amount of destitution prevailed. Want, and woe, and death, stalked through the streets. By day, the sun shone on ruined and desolated homesteads; by night, darkness wrapped in its gloomy pall many a starved and shrivelled form. The population was fearfully decreased; the stalwart man was bent; premature age fell upon, and crushed, the light heart of youth. The gay laugh, and merry jests of the Irish people, were hushed, and there was silence everywhere, as when the Angel of Death smote the armed host of the Assyrian.

The respectable and wealthy inhabitants of this town, did all they could, to mitigate the horrors of these fearful years; but, with business at a stand-still, a population unemployed, credit and confidence vanished, it was hard to do much. The spread of contagion was arrested by the skill of the medical profession, and Drs. Browne and Martin laboured night and day. Unhappily, one fell a victim to his duty. Dr. Laurence Martin, a young and promising physician, was cut off in his 32nd year, and the inhabitants testified their sorrow for his loss by the inscription on the tomb they raised to his memory.

As soon as returning prosperity gave opportunity for improvement, Dundalk rapidly advanced. It was not merely by agricultural industry, so extensively carried on around and about the town; but trade and manufactures absorbed a considerable portion of the labouring population. A good deal of employment was given by the formation of the Dundalk and Enniskillen Railway. The Act for incorporation of this company passed on the 21st July, 1845. On the 15th February, 1849, eighteen miles—from the junction with the Dublin and Belfast Railway, at Dundalk, to Castleblayney—were opened, simultaneously with the line of that company from Drogheda to Dundalk. This at once opened up markets previously inaccessible for agricultural produce, and proved of great commercial advantage to Dundalk.

CHAPTER XXIV.

FROM THE YEAR 1852 TO THE VISIT OF HIS EXCELLENCY THE EARL OF CARLISLE TO DUNDALK, IN 1859.

We approach the close of our labours. Modern history relates more to men than measures—records the struggles of chiefs of parties for succession to power—the rise and fall of those units of which Cabinets are composed. Our history has been brought from remote times—amidst the stormy vicissitudes to which the town of Dundalk was exposed, unto the peaceful reign of Queen Victoria. Through the self-reliance, the energy, and enterprise of the inhabitants, we have seen this town—often desolated by war, and, in recent times, by the visitations of pestilence and famine—rise, phœnix-like, from its ashes, and flourish more vigorously than ever. The words of Mr. Dargan, the great Irish promoter of industrial efforts, seem to have struck root here:—"I have heard a great deal about the independence that we were to get from this, that, and the other source; yet I have always been deeply impressed with the conviction that our industrial independence depends on ourselves. Simple industry, and careful exactness, would be the making of Ireland. We have, it is true, made a step, but perseverance is indispensably necessary for eventual success."

In 1852, the County of Louth was once more the battle-field of a contested election, and the town of Dundalk agitated by the strenuous efforts of the rival candidates and their supporters. On the Liberal side, as it is termed, stood Mr. Chichester Fortescue and Mr. Tristram Kennedy; and on the Conservative appeared a formidable competitor for senatorial honours, John M'Clintock, Esq., of Drumcar, a large landed proprietor in the county, of high family and noble connexions. His personal character, and leading position, secured him such chance of success as rendered his return extremely probable; but the exertions of his opponents were not to be defeated, and, at the close of the poll, the numbers were:—

Mr. Chichester Fortescue, . .	1,152
Mr. Tristram Kennedy, ...	995
Mr. M'Clintock, ...	884

The former were declared duly elected.

Two years later, Mr. Fortescue, having taken office as one of the Lords of the Treasury, rendered his seat vacant; and, as he offered himself for re-election, a new candidate appeared to oppose him—this was John Macnamara Cantwell, Esq., of Dublin, a solicitor by profession, of acknowledged talent, a powerful and fluent speaker, and, for years, a devoted supporter of Daniel O'Connell. This formed his claim to popular support, and the Roman Catholic clergy promoted his canvass, Mr. Fortescue's friends had need to be active. Mr. Gernon, a talented and energetic member of the Irish Bar, published some letters which did efficient service to the cause of Mr. Fortescue. His family, and their numerous connexions in the County of Louth, supported the Fortescue interest; and, notwithstanding the active and strenuous exertions used to return Mr. Cantwell, and his own business qualities, which peculiarly recommended him for a seat in Parliament, he was defeated by a majority of 154.

In 1854, an event occurred which caused very general sorrow in Dundalk—the death of Viscount Jocelyn, M.P. for Lyme Regis. This young and promising officer was eldest son of the Earl of Roden. Born in 1816, his lordship, at the early age of twenty-five, married the Lady Frances Elizabeth Cowper, youngest daughter of the fifth Earl Cowper, a lady who united every grace of beauty to a highly cultivated mind. Two sons and two daughters were the issue of this marriage, which was sadly severed by the decease of Lord Jocelyn, on the 12th August, 1854.

Everyone felt for the affliction of Lord Roden. He is and ever has been, a strong politician—a Conservative from principle, and most consistent in his avowal, and most manly and straightforward in the maintenance of these principles. In the British empire parties form a necessary, we might almost add, a wholesome element in the social state; and when men honestly and steadily adhere to their party, and maintain their principles, they are entitled to respect. If mutual toleration was more practised, and the great moral axiom, "Do unto others as you would they did unto you," oftener observed in deeds than in words, we would have less uncharitable sentiments, and un-Christian conduct, than the history of our country unhappily records.

Dundalk made great advances in appearance and material prosperity since the visit of Sir Walter Scott, in 1824. A period of twenty years worked wonders. The celebrated Mr. Thackeray—the modern Fielding—a novelist of great and deserved popularity in the present day, visited the town in 1843, and thus describes it:—*

"The stranger can't fail to be struck with the look of Dundalk, as he has been with the villages and country leading to it, when contrasted with places in the south and west of Ireland. The *coach* stopped at a cheerful-looking *place*, of which almost the only dilapidated mansion was the old inn at which it discharged us, and which did not hold out much promise of comfort; but, in justice to the 'King's Arms,' it must be said that good beds and dinners are to be obtained by voyagers."

Mr. Thackeray was struck with the grave old church and the superb new chapel, copied from King's College Chapel at Cambridge. He visited, with pleasure, the factory of Mr. Shekleton, whose industry and skill seem to have brought the greatest benefit to his fellow-townsmen, of whom he employs numbers in his foundries and workshops.

---

* *The Irish Sketch Book*, by Thackeray, 1852.

At Mr. Shekleton's factory we found all kinds of iron work in the progress of formation, from the powerful steam-engine to the smallest key; and in every direction was the clank of hammers, the ring of metal upon anvil, the roaring fire, the clamour of busy men. Here, in the words of Thackeray:—"Steam boilers are hammered, and pins made by a hundred busy hands. There was an engine-room where the monster was whirring his ceaseless wheels, and directing the whole operations of the factory—fanning the forges, turning the drills, blasting into the pipes of the smelting houses; he had a house to himself, from which his orders issued to the different establishments round about. One machine was quite awful to me, a gentle Cockney, not used to such things; it was an iron-devourer, a wretch with huge jaws and a narrow mouth, ever opening and shutting, opening and shutting. You put a half-inch iron plate between his jaws, and they shut not a whit slower or quicker than before, and bit through the iron as if it were a sheet of paper."

At the general election in 1857, there were contests in county and town. Mr. M'Clintock, defeated in 1852, was prepared to renew the struggle, and this time with better assurance of success. Mr. Montesquieu Bellew also entered the lists, supported by the powerful influence of Barmeath, while the tenant-right candidate, Mr. Tristram Kennedy, relied on the votes of the tenant farmers, and Mr. Fortescue on his long and faithful services. The result must have been exceedingly gratifying to this gentleman, as also to his excellent brother Lord Clermont, the former representative of the county. The votes were—Mr. Chichester Fortescue, 1,376; Mr. M'Clintock, 1,057; Mr. Bellew, 894; Mr. Tristram Kennedy, 406.

Mr. Fortescue and the Conservative candidate, Mr. M'Clintock, were therefore declared the sitting members.

Meanwhile, Mr. Bowyer, who had represented the borough since 1852, was not allowed a walk over. The former opponent of Mr. Fortescue, Mr. John Macnamara Cantwell, undeterred by his defeat in the county, resolved to contest the town, and supplant Mr. Bowyer. We have mentioned who Mr. Cantwell was, and it is right that we should inform the reader of Mr. Bowyer's antecedents. He was eldest son of Sir George Bowyer, Bart., of Radley Park, Abingdon,* and was called to the English Bar by the Benchers of the Middle Temple, in 1839. Mr. Bowyer soon displayed talents of a high order, united with great literary industry. He published a *Dissertation on the Statutes of the Italian Cities*, *Commentaries on the Constitutional Law of England*, and on *The Modern Civil Law*. When, in 1850, the distinguished Catholic Prelate, Dr. Wiseman, was created a Cardinal, and Archbishop of Westminster, and Lord John Russell wrote his *Durham Letter*, which set England and Ireland in a blaze, Mr. Bowyer published a learned work on *The Archbishop of Westminster, and the New Hierarchy*, which recommended him as a fitting representative for the Catholic electors of Dundalk, and he was returned in 1852. His intimate acquaintance with Italian questions caused him to be always listened to with attention in the House; and his zeal for the Popedom, to lose no opportunity of advocating the rights of his Holiness. Mr. Cantwell had no chance of unseating him, and only polled 39 votes, while Mr. Bowyer had 133. Dundalk was visited by his Eminence Cardinal Wiseman, during his visit to Ireland in 1858. He was accompanied by Lord Bellew from Barmeath; and his entrance into Dundalk on Friday, 3rd September, 1858, was one of the greatest public demonstrations ever made

* Since succeeded to the baronetcy, on the death of his father, in 1861.

by the inhabitants of any town in Ireland. Through Clanbrassil-street, Park-street, Anne-street, and Dublin-street, as far as the railway station, a considerable distance, nearly every house was wreathed in flowers and green leaves, making quite a floral fête, while gay banners, with words of welcome, floated on the breeze. A triumphal arch, erected opposite the Market-place, was surmounted by a banner, with the Irish *Cead Mille Fealthe*, and the windows of the adjacent houses displayed flags of every size.

His Eminence was met by a well arranged procession, headed by a band, and composed of various trades, whose orderly and respectable appearance elicited much praise. He was escorted by Lord Bellew, Mr. Bowyer, M.P., the Rev. E. L. Clifford, Very Rev. Dr. Russell, the distinguished and accomplished President of Maynooth, and many others, while the devoted people drew his carriage themselves.

On proceeding to the beautiful Church of St. Patrick, ample preparations had been made for the ceremonies of the day. Within the sanctuary was a chair of state, occupied by his Grace the Primate. The arrangements were of a costly character. His Eminence, on his arrival, was received by the Very Rev. Dean Kieran, P.P. of Dundalk, and a number of other distinguished ecclesiastics. A procession was then formed, after which the ceremonial prescribed by the Roman ritual, for High Mass in presence of a Cardinal, succeeded. After the Gospel, his Eminence preached a learned, fervent, and eloquent sermon; and, having given his benediction, went to the house of Dean Kieran. Thence the party drove to Mr. P. Russell's, where the Primate, the other Roman Catholic bishops of the province, Lord Bellew, Mr. Bowyer, the High Sheriff, and various high personages were invited to meet him. He next visited the Convent of Mercy and the schools attached, where 800 female children were awaiting him, and presented an address. He listened most kindly to the simple homage of these little ones, addressed a suitable reply, and returned to the mansion of Mr. Russell.

In the evening, his Eminence was entertained at a public banquet, in the Court-house, at which over 200 persons were present. Previous to the commencement of the banquet, addresses were presented from the clergy of the Roman Catholic archdiocese of Armagh, and from the Town Commissioners, representing the Catholic laity of Dundalk. Their address was as follows:—

"MAY IT PLEASE YOUR EMINENCE,

"We, the Catholic inhabitants of Dundalk, approach your Eminence with feelings of the most profound respect and veneration for your character as a prince of the Church. We are deeply sensible of the high honour conferred on our town by the visit of a man so distinguished as your Eminence, and gratefully acknowledge the kind consideration which has induced your Eminence to accept the invitation of our venerated and beloved pastor, Dean Kieran. We joyfully and heartily welcome your Eminence to Dundalk, as Catholics, recognising the unyielding champion of our religion, whose brilliant and powerful eloquence, and bright example, have won so many triumphs for truth, and done so much to reconstruct the ancient glories of Catholicity in England. As citizens, we bid your Eminence welcome, acknowledging the talented and accomplished scholar, whose world-wide fame sheds lustre on our nation—whose master mind, travelling the whole range of the sciences, has rendered them subservient to the illustration of the principles of revealed religion. In these days of progress and enlightenment, when science, with giant strides, is conquering time and space, and most minds are strained to keep pace with the rapidity of discovery, we are proud to be able to point to your Eminence as holding the foremost place among the great men of your time, and showing to the world that the most exalted piety, and the most profound theological learning, with the most thorough devotion for the Church, are not inconsistent with the successful cultivation of every branch of secular knowledge. We pray God to bless and protect your Eminence, to guide your actions, and strengthen your efforts in aid of our holy religion."

To this very appropriate address his Eminence replied:—

"You will allow me to be very brief, in simply thanking you, very sincerely, indeed, for the expression of your kind feeling. I know that there can be no stronger bond between men than that of common faith; and, therefore, though I am not a stranger amongst the Catholics of Dundalk, I rejoice to have an opportunity of fulfilling a promise, long since made, that the very first occasion that brought me to the shores of Ireland would, at the same time, conduct me within the walls of Dundalk. It has been a great gratification to me to witness what I have seen to-day, and to have assisted at the celebration of Divine service within your noble church, so beautifully decorated and finished. The presence of your venerated Primate, and of so many other prelates and clergymen, on this interesting occasion, must have been as gratifying to you all as it has been a source of the greatest pleasure to me. Again I thank you, most sincerely, for the kind expressions contained in your address."

A superb banquet followed, at which the beloved Roman

Catholic pastor of Dundalk, Dean Kieran, presided. After the usual loyal toasts, the Dean, in proposing the health of the Cardinal, said, "his visit to the town would form a bright epoch in its history;" and, in the course of an eloquent reply, his Eminence said:—"I shall always retain a vivid remembrance of my visit to your town; and, in future, I shall always have one temptation to resist, and that is—when perplexed and anxious, harassed and annoyed on every side, I will be tempted to say, 'I will run off to Dundalk.'"

In 1859, the representation of the county was again contested. The Whig Party determined to return the two members, while the Conservatives felt they had an equal claim to send both members representing their views on political matters. Accordingly, in addition to Mr. M'Clintock of Drumcar, they put forward Frederick J. Foster, Esq., whose family, long resident and respected, had fair claims to seek the suffrages of the freeholders. The result, however, was not consonant to their wishes; for, though Mr. M'Clintock was supported by a much more numerous constituency than on any former occasion—1,138 votes being recorded in his favour—he was left in a minority, while Mr. Foster, in sporting phrase, was "no where." The numbers polled were:—

Mr. Fortescue, ...	1,379
Mr. Montesquieu Bellew, . . .	1,208
Mr. M'Clintock, ...	1,138
Mr. Foster, ...	23

For several days, in the middle of July, 1859, Lord Roden's park, at Dundalk, was invaded by a busy tribe of workmen, and the sound of hammer, and saw, and other implements, disturbed the quietude of many a lonely glade. Soon other sounds succeeded—the lowing of innumerable herds, the crowing of a multitude of cockerels, the bleating of flocks of sheep, the neighing of horses, denoted that some great event in connexion with the exhibition of stock was about to occur. And, true enough, numerous rows of blanketed bulls, of carefully groomed well-fed cows, and plethoric swine, were to be seen. There were also every species of fowl—Cochin-Chinas, Dorkings, Bramaputras, and Black Polish, that by their incessant clamour seemed to challenge immediate inspection.

The implement department, too, was most deserving of notice. Here were exhibitions of Irish manufacture, which proved there were heads to plan and hands to work equal to the best in any country. Dundalk, happily, possesses a triumphant spirit of industry, that woos and wins employment to its workshops. All her busy population needs is the opportunity of showing what strong hands and fertile brains can achieve for country and for town.

On Wednesday, July 27th, 1859, the Royal Agricultural Society's Cattle Show took place at Dundalk. This great national exhibition was held in Lord Roden's demesne, a place admirably suited in every respect, affording ample space for the display of agricultural produce, animate and inanimate, while its proximity to the Dublin and Belfast Junction Railway, was a strong recommendation for its selection. The show ground was divided into two great sections of timber sheds; each cattle shed 150 feet long by 15 feet wide. Those for agricultural implements were of the same length, and 20 feet wide. The show, both of stock and implements, was of a most superior description, and the local committee of the society were indefatigable in their exertions to secure success, which the result fully sustained. His Excellency, the Earl of Carlisle, K.G., Lord Lieutenant, arrived from Barmeath, where he had been the guest of Lord Bellew. His Excellency,

Lord Bellew, Lord Monck, and the Viceregal party, were received by the Earl of Erne, president of the society, Lord Cloncurry, the Hon. Mr. Talbot, and other gentlemen of the council. His Excellency having inspected the cattle show, proceeded to the Court House, where an address from the Town and Harbour Commissioners was presented to him. It was read by Mr. M'Ardle, Chairman of the Town Commissioners:—

"May it Please your Excellency,

"We, the Commissioners of the Town and Harbour of Dundalk, beg respectfully to give your Excellency a sincere and hearty welcome to our ancient town. With warm feelings of loyalty and attachment to the British Throne, we greet your Excellency as the representative of our illustrious and beloved Queen, under whose benificent reign we enjoy the blessings of independence and freedom. We also welcome your Excellency as a nobleman in whose person are combined those sterling qualities which so peculiarly fit your Excellency for the high and important office of Chief Governor of Ireland. We cannot but revert to the happy and auspicious occasion which has led to your Excellency's first visit to the town of Dundalk, the grand National Exhibition of the Royal Agricultural Society of Ireland, in honour of which are assembled those of every class, from the high and noble who direct and govern the national affairs, to the citizen and mechanic employed in giving practical effect to the designs of art and science; the peer and peasant—the rich and poor of Ireland, England, and Scotland, associated in this great and noble undertaking—the development of Ireland's national resources—her native industry, and the products of her fertile soil. We rejoice to be able to welcome your Excellency to a country in which the spirit of industry happily prevails, and which has, of late years, so greatly advanced; and we feel proud to think that our countrymen generally have directed their exertions to progress, and have attained a distinguished position in everything connected with agricultural improvement. We sincerely wish your Excellency long life and every happiness.

(Signed)
"E. H. M'Ardle, J.P.,
"Chairman Town Commissioners.
"S. J. Turner, J.P.,
"Chairman Harbour Commissioners."

His Excellency thus replied:—

"Gentlemen,—I beg to return the Commissioners of the Town and Harbour of Dundalk my cordial thanks for their assurances of attached loyalty to the Throne of these realms, as well as of considerate courtesy which they have been pleased to use towards myself. I entirely partake in the feeling of satisfaction which you have gracefully expressed, that my first visit to this ancient and historic town, and this fair and thriving district, should have occurred on an occasion which has brought together, on the adjoining sward, so splendid an exhibition of the material progress of Ireland, and so harmonious a fusion of class, occupation, creed, and race—to witness and appreciate her still expanding resources, her matured, but not stagnant energies. It is my sincere hope that the town and neighbourhood of Dundalk may amply share in the bounties and blessings which I trust that a merciful Providence has in store for the entire country."

At the banquet which followed, over which Lord Erne

presided—when his Excellency's health was drunk, in returning thanks he alluded to the ancient fame of Dundalk, in his usual eloquent and happy manner:—

"On an occasion like the present, I may be allowed to say, that the spot for the exhibition appears to me to have been this year most happily chosen, under these umbrageous trees, in which we were clustered to-day, within easy reach of railway communication, close to an important town, whose very name shows its ancient origin. Dundalgan—the old fort of Dalgan—which witnessed, so far back as 1001, the warriors of the great Brien Boroihme, and many conflicts of Irish chiefs; and even then the county was no stranger to agricultural pursuits, because, it is specially recorded, that an army destroyed the grain and tillage of the plain. Then, afterwards, as the border land of the Pale, it was often the scene of exploits in which Scot and Anglo-Normans were mixed; and though we cannot precisely boast, at the present day, that feuds, and war, and bloodshed have disappeared from the earth—as witness the fields of Magenta and Solferino—yet, we may thankfully acknowledge, that the show-yard of Dundalk, as we saw it to-day, with its long lines of stalled cattle, and its well-filled sheds of peaceful implements, afforded a gratifying and delightful contrast, both to the barbarous broils of the old Septs, and to the more scientific, yet more deadly, massacres of modern warfare."

With this graceful summary of the events of Dundalk we close our narrative of its history.

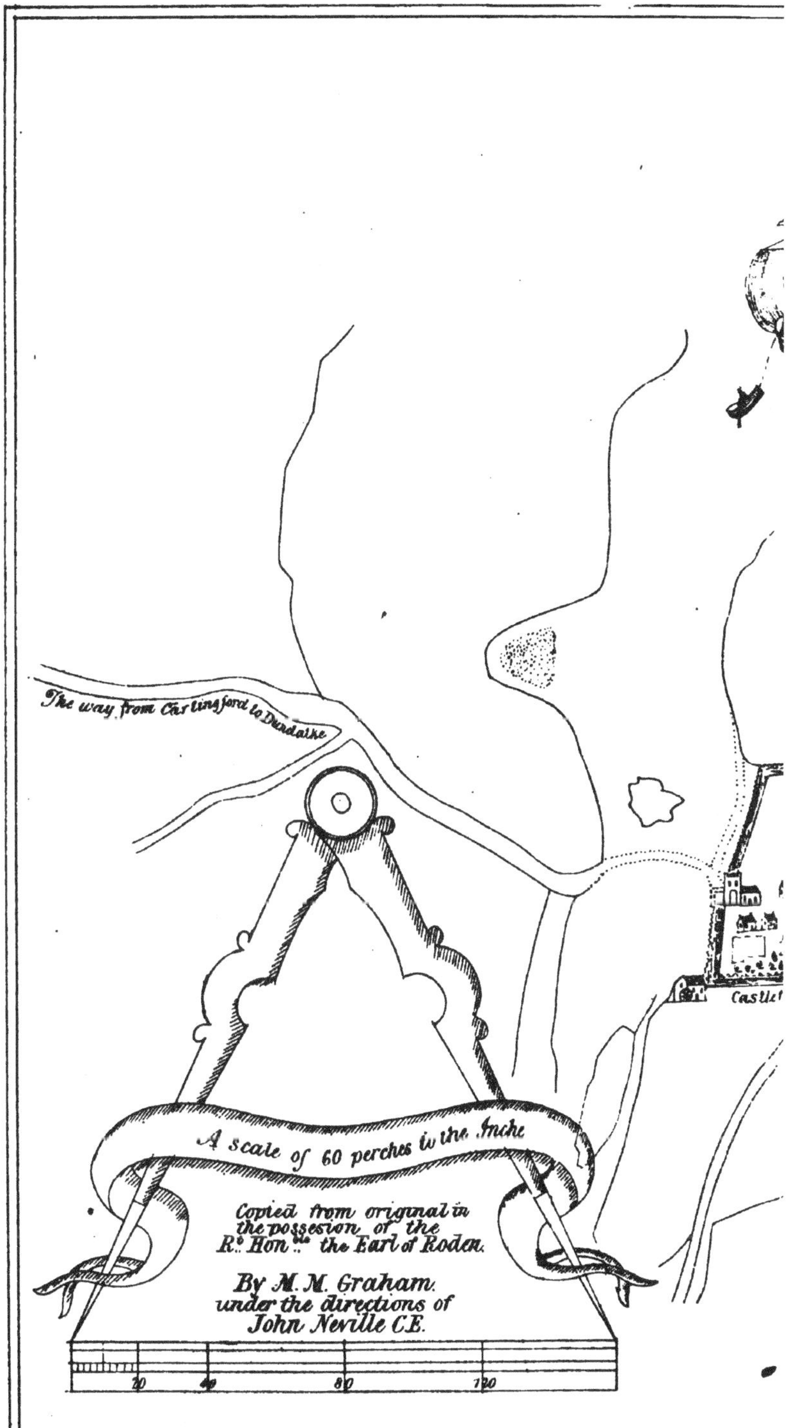

The way from Carlingford to Dundalke
Castle
A scale of 60 perches to the Inche
Copied from original in
the possesion of the
Rt. Honble the Earl of Roden.
By M. M. Graham.
under the directions of
John Neville C.E.
20
40
80
120

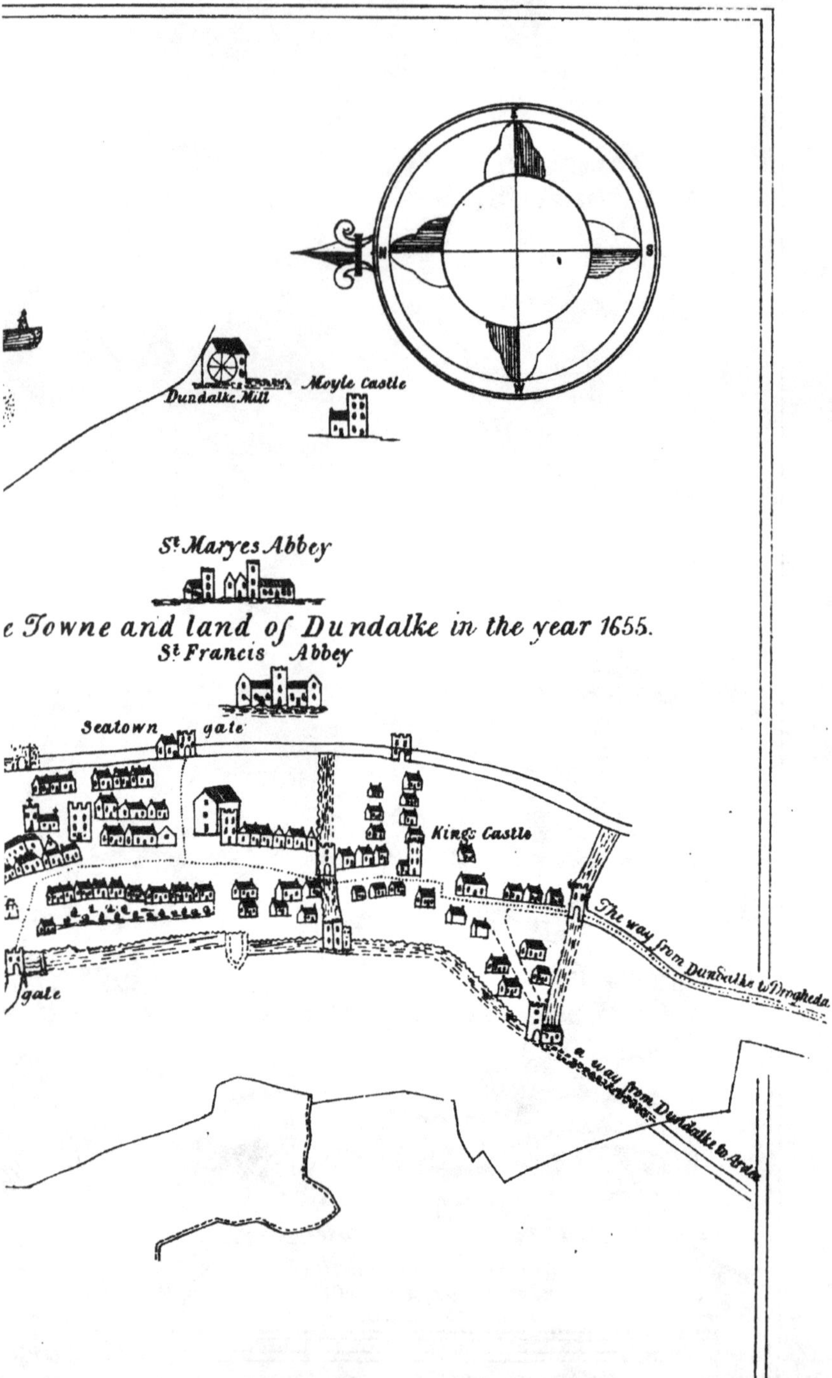

N
S
Dundalke Mill
Moyle Castle
St Maryes Abbey
e Towne and land of Dundalke in the year 1655.
St Francis Abbey
Seatown gate
Kings Castle
The way from Dundalke to Drogheda
gate
a way from Dundalke to Ardee
Forster & Co Lith. Dublin

TOPOGRAPHICAL AND TRADITIONAL

HISTORY OF DUNDALK

AND ITS ENVIRONS.

WHEN Dundalk became the frontier town on the northern Marches of the Pale, strong walls and other defence works protected the garrison; but the mail-clad knights and strong-armed squires who guarded them have passed away, and the walls which sheltered them have alike perished.

The most ancient of the maps, which, through the kind liberality of the Earl of Roden, we are able to place before our readers, is that prepared by Symone Garston, under a commission from Benjamin Morsley, Surveyor-General, A.D. 1655. According to this map the town appears in the form of a parallelogram, lying north and south, environed by walls, and defended by towers. The only gates marked on the map are the Castletown-gate on the west side, and the Seatown-gate on the east; but there are clearly many more:—one on the north, facing where the bridge now stands; two more beneath towers, on the east side; and two on the south—one on the road from Dundalk to Drogheda; the other on the road to Ardee. The town also appears intersected by a wall from east to west, with a castle and gate in the centre, and a castle at the west end. There is also the King's Castle marked on this map; and lying east of Seatown-gate two abbeys—St. Francis's Abbey, which was the Grey Friary erected by Lord John De Verdon in the reign of King Henry the Third, and St. Mary's Abbey. Further east is marked Moyle Castle; and near the shore, Dundalk Mill. No streets are named on this map.

The second map shows the town of Dundalk in 1675. The wall, we perceive, extended from the bridge round the west side; and, on the north, from the bridge tower along the river, towards the old Bowling-green; here it turned eastward, as far as Seatown. On the west a town trench is marked, and several streets. The shape of the town is pretty much as at present, built north by south; and a stone cross stood at the junction of Longstaff-lane and Shop-street. This map clearly lays down the site of Lady Hamilton's house, of St. Nicholas's Church, Mortimer's Castle, the Sessions House, and several gates—Bridge-gate, Blind-gate, and Seatown-gate. High-street appears the principal street of the town, extending from Mortimer's Castle, at the junction of the roads to Drogheda and Donaghmore, to William Shewall's house, near which the cross stood. Shop-street appears a continuation of the Cow Market. Seatown is marked on this map; and the names of old proprietors of tenements are given.

The third map, which, as well as the two former, Mr. Moore Graham has reduced, under the directions of Mr. Neville, the County Surveyor of Louth, shows the town of Dundalk, with Seatown, as laid down by Robert Richardson, in 1680. We find the town extending north by south in a tolerably horizontal line, from Upper-street to the bridge. Few streets are marked on this map. At the junction of the Atherdee and Drogheda roads is Upper-street, which, on the other maps is called High-street. There appears a castle, most

A plan of the Town of

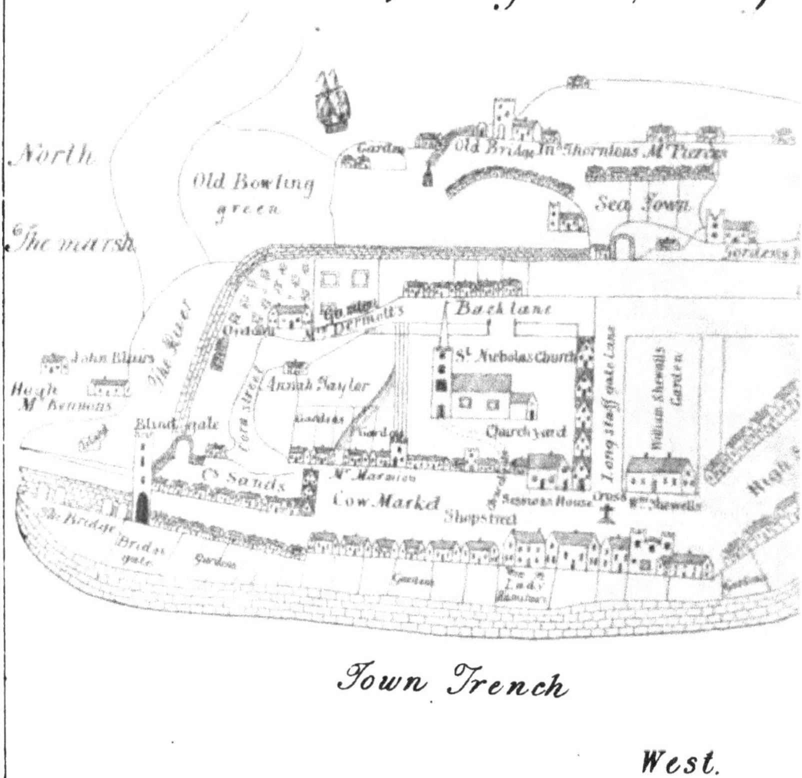

Reduced to 2/3 the size of the Original
under the directions of John Neville M.R.I.A.
by M. Moore Graham.
May. 1863.

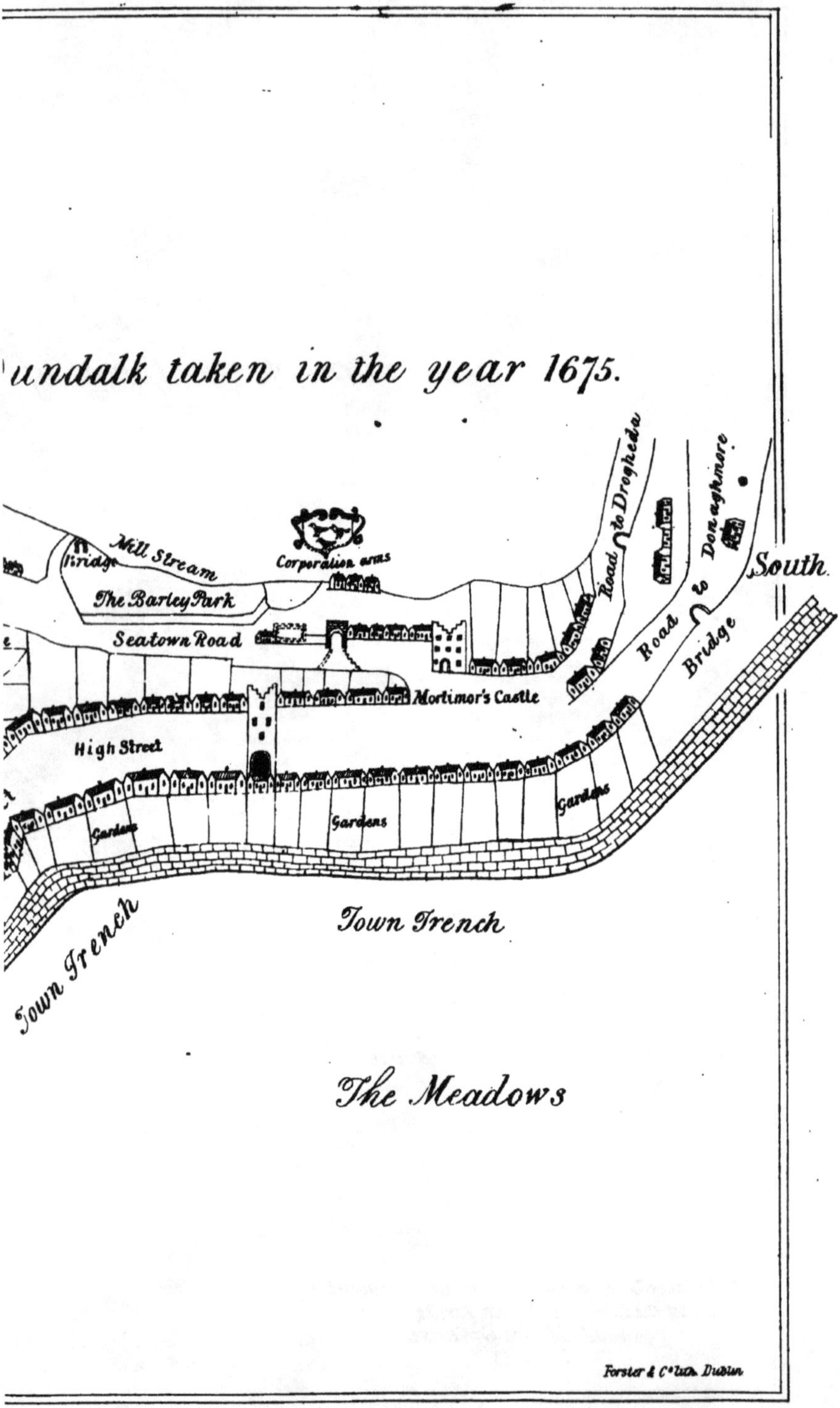
undalk taken in the year 1675.
Road to Drogheda
Road to Donaghmore
Bridge
Mill Stream
Corporation arms
The Barley Park
Seatown Road
Mortimor's Castle
South
Road to Bridge
High Street
Gardens
Gardens
Gardens
Town Trench
Town Trench
The Meadows
Forster & Co lith. Dublin

probably that hitherto called Mortimer's Castle; then a long street, intersected by a wall with a tower, and Warren's-gate; this street leads to Cow Market, on the east side of which stood the church and Seatown-gate. From the Cow Market two streets diverge—one terminated by the Water-gate and the bridge (from this a street branches to Castletown-gate); the other terminated by Blind-gate.

The town wall on this map extends from the gate on the Atherdee road, along the west side, to the bridge; then from Water-gate to Blind-gate on the north, continuing eastward.

There are two Seatown gates marked on this map—that nearer the sea called Seatown-gate; the other, further south, Upper Seatown-gate. In this district we find St. Leonard's Abbey; while the Grey Friary is the abbey marked west. The Commons lie to the east, and border the sea. According to this map, Sir John Bellew's property appeared mingled with that of Lady Dungannon in every direction.

The buildings constituting the Franciscan Friary were very extensive, reaching from Chapel-lane to where Mr. Shekleton's steam mills were erected. Mr. Shekleton enclosed in his yard a spring well, over which was a neat stone crypt; of which Mr. O'Kearney, the distinguished Irish archæologist, gave the following particulars:—

"The well attached to the monastery at Seatown was dedicated to St. Peter, and was a place much resorted to in the olden time by pilgrims, but was not in much repute in my time. The patron of Seatown was held on St. Peter's day; and a truly gay meeting it used to be. The garland was a great pole, as tall as the mast of a sloop, adorned with ribbons, coloured kerchiefs, flowers, &c., having on the top a handkerchief, full of gingerbread, and a dozen pairs of plaid worsted garters; these were the prizes intended for the couple who were adjudged the best performers on the fantastic toe; and the winners were always as proud of the prize as the successful competitors were of yore at the Olympic games. The pole, or garland, was usually planted in the centre of the area, opposite the church gate; and the managers of the sports never omitted to smooth and soap the pole; and the attempts of boys and young men to climb the pole, for quarters of gingerbread, were very ludicrous. The inhabitants of Seatown had their bonfire on St Peter's night."

In the interesting series of papers on ancient monasteries in Ireland, contributed by the learned and distinguished Rev. Mr. Meehan to *Duffy's Hibernian Magazine*, under the title of "Noctes Lovenienses," we find the following account of the Franciscan Friary of Dundalk:—

"It was founded by John De Verdon, and one of the first destroyed by Henry the Eighth. In 1616 nothing remained but the bell tower, and that was sadly dilapidated.*

"The entire of the sacred edifice, with its appurtenances, three or four acres of meadow land, were held by John Brandon, a most respectable denizen of Dundalk, whose grandfather got a lease of the property in the time of King Henry. The said John Brandon waited on me" (Father Mooney, Provincial of Irish Franciscans at Louvain, *loquitur*) "and said he scrupled holding without the consent of the friars. I therefore laid the whole matter before John Cassell,

---

* We are indebted to the accomplished Civil Engineer, John Neville, Esq., for the photograph of this tower.

a native of Dundalk, and syndic of the convent, who, by authority from Rome, allowed him to retain the walls and four acres, on conditions: firstly, to renounce all claim whenever the Franciscans would claim it from him; secondly, he should not sell or alienate any portion of the premises without the consent of our brotherhood; thirdly, he should not suffer anyone to do injury to the place, but save it from decay; fourthly, he would give something annually to our friars, out of the rents he received from the land. Brandon agreed to these conditions, and, indeed, he has been faithful to his word. Such conduct deserves to be recorded, and who knows but this poor testimony to true worth may meet the eyes of some of his posterity."

It is stated that the part of Dundalk near the junction of Ann-street and Dublin-street is built over a lake, called, in Irish, "Loc-aen-la," or "The Lake of One Day," *i.e.*, it sprung up in a day; and that on some future day—which, we trust, will be after the artistic New Zealander's sketch from London-bridge of the ruins of St. Paul's, this lake will burst forth and submerge Dundalk. An hotel, called the "Lough-aen-lo Tavern," was kept here, in the seventeenth century, by an innkeeper named Kelly.

Lady's Well, at the southern extremity of Dundalk, on the Dublin road, was a famous place of pilgrimage; on the 15th of August, and, the preceding eve, crowds of people from Louth, Armagh, Cavan, Meath, and Monaghan, used to assemble there, to perform a station in honour of our Blessed Lady.

There is a tradition that Cromwell received a scar, which marked his face, at Dundalk. The account communicated is as follows:—

"When in Dundalk, Cromwell, with his staff, went to the ford, where the bridge was subsequently built, to water their horses; Lord Plunkett, ancestor of Lord Louth, one of the Royalist officers, who was in the neighbourhood, enlisting men for the Confederate army, was riding at the same time, and his horse wishing to drink brought him to the same ford. Seeing the reflection of Cromwell's star in the water, he determined, if possible, to kill him; and not being sufficiently near to reach him with his sword, flung the naked blade at his head, which gashed Oliver's prominent nose. A rush was instantly made, but the Royalist escaped by means of subterranean vaults, leading into Lord Roden's demesne. A large reward being offered for his apprehension, Lord Plunkett was traced, by a faithless servant named Taaffe, and betrayed. He was instantly seized, and brought captive to Castlecumberland, originally Mortimer's Castle, and latterly occupied as the china and delft warehouse of Thomas Byrne, merchant. They found Cromwell's wounded nose was undergoing surgical treatment. Here several of the Parliamentary officers were suggesting a variety of cruel deaths, in order the sufferer might select the most painful for their prisoner. Cromwell, however, was too brave a man to adopt any of their savage plans, and intimated that he would leave the selection of the final event to Lord Plunkett himself. On demanding how he wished to die, the captive replied boldly:—

"'With my good sword in my hand, and any two of your officers before me ready to execute your orders.'

"This reply so gratified the Lord Lieutenant that he spared Plunkett's life, on condition that there should always be an Oliver in the Plunkett family."

But it is rather opposed to the strict truth of this story

that the name of Oliver was common to the Plunkett family long before the event herein detailed could have happened.

DUNDALGAN.

The remarkable earth-work, occupying the entire crest of the hill above Castletown, and which gives the name to the subject of our history, is one of the finest specimens of the habitations of the early Irish chieftains. These duns, or forts, partook more of a military than a simply domestic character; for they are invariably surrounded with one or more intrenchments, to afford protection for the inhabitants and their flocks against the incursions of foes, bent either on the capture of the fort or the cattle, if the object of invasion was a cattle raid. The name cannot, with any certainty, be traced. It has been supposed to be derived from the Irish words, *Dun-dealg-fin*, from a pillar-stone in the neighbourhood, being called the *dealg*, or brooch, of Fin MacCumhal, the celebrated Irish commander; but, unfortunately for this hypothesis, the name was applied anterior to the days of Fin MacCumhal. This dun forms a conspicuous object from all parts of the country, and consists of an extensive circular mound, the flat surface of the top measuring about 550 feet in circumference. Outside is a deep fosse; on the east a quadrangular intrenchment, with rampart, fosse, and counterscarp; on the west a similar intrenchment, of semicircular shape, but smaller. It is supposed the tide once flowed to Dundalgan, and that it is on the very spot, once washed by the waves, the town is built; hence called Traballyٍ, the Town of the Strand. The summit of the fort commands a fine view—on the north, the Fews mountains; on the east, O'Reilly or Brefni's country; on the south, the Collon and

Dublin hills; while west lie the highlands of Carlingford and Mourne, with the harbour and town of Dundalk, surrounded with mansions and well-wooded lawns.

From the great size of Dundalgan it is fair to assume it belonged to some potent chief, and tradition assigns it to Cuchullin, the most renowned knight of the Red Branch, who lived in the reign of Conor MacNessa, King of Ulster. Among the Irish MSS. in the collection bequeathed to the Royal Irish Academy by the late William Elliott Hudson, Esq., are two volumes, entitled *Books of Battles*, the compilation of a learned Irish scholar—Mr. O'Kearney; and in the second volume is a very entertaining Irish MS., partly translated by Mr. O'Kearney, "The Education of Cuchullin, Son of Subhaltach." In the first volume of the same valuable collection is a very ancient tale, called "The Great Breach of Muigh Muirthemne; or, the End of Cuchulain;" by which it appears that after slaughtering a prodigious number of the men of Ireland, he fell covered with wounds, and was placed by his faithful Laoidh with his face to the foe, and his weapon in his hand, against a pillar-stone, called Carrig an Compan.

Mr. O'Halloran* says;—"With us chivalry flourished from the remotest antiquity. There were five orders of it—four for the provinces, and one confined to the blood royal; and so highly was this profession respected among us, that a prince could not become a candidate for the monarchy who had not the Gradh-Gaoisge, or order of knighthood conferred on him." The education was befitting a *preux chevalier*. At the early age of seven the future knight was taken from his nursery, instructed in philosophy, history, poetry, and genealogy; the use of arms, and morality. By his vows he was to

* *Vide Reliques of Irish Poetry*, by Miss Brooke, p. 9.

be the protector of innocence, and the punisher of the guilty. He was not to reveal his name or his country to any uncourteous knight, who demanded the information as a right. He was to yield to no menace, or decline any encounter; and even when mortally wounded was turned always to face the foe."

The fatal place where Cuchullin fell is called Lochan-an-Chloidheamh, or the Lake of the Sword, on the side of the road near Raheady. It would, of course, be out of place in this work to introduce all the wild legends connected with the great fort of Dundalgan, in which Cuchullin, and Para Buidhe MacScodin, who threw down the stones at Ballymacscanlan, and thereby formed the cromlech called the Giant's Load, played the chief parts; but we must not forget that it is said an incalculable amount of treasure is buried somewhere adjacent to this mound, under the charge of an invisible cat; and it forms a condition precedent to the discovery of the treasure, that the cat must be shot with a silver bullet. This is not an isolated case of superstition connected with the feline race. Cat pillar-stones were at one time oracular in Ireland; and witches always had black cats for familiars. On the summit of the mound is a modern castellated mansion. An inscription over the doorway informs us it was "Erected by Patrick Byrne, Esquire, of Castletown, for his Grand-nephew, Patrick Byrne, Esquire, of Seatown, 1780." This edifice has recently undergone alterations, and now forms a handsome structure, the property of T. V. Dawson, Esq.

CASTLETOWN.

THIS place was commonly called Castletown-Bellew. A castle is said to have been erected here as early as A.D. 1297, which was occupied by Edward Bruce in A.D. 1316; but the present edifice was more probably that referred to in the following enactment of a Parliament held at Naas, 19 Edward the Fourth:—"Richard Bellew, Esq., has built and furnished a tower in the Castletown of Dundalk, on the borders of the Marches of the County of Louth, and intends to build another tower anew in the said town. Enacts, that he shall receive and take twelve pence in every plow-land in the County of Louth, for building the same."

The necessity of having strong defences was, at this time, well proved. At a Parliament held in Dublin, A.D. 1429, before Sir John Sutton, Knight, Lord Deputy, it was declared:—"Likewise, forasmuch as the County of Louth and the subjects of our lord the King dwelling therein, for the greater part, are destroyed and desolated by the Irish enemies and English rebels of our lord the King, by the default of castles and towers in the said county, in resistance of the said rebels and enemies, to the great decay of said county. It is agreed and assented that every subject of our lord the King, who, within the said county, buildeth anew a castle or a tower upon the border thereof in five years; that is to say, in length of xx. feet; in breadth, xvi. feet; in height, xl. feet; that the Commons of the said county shall pay to the said person who will build such castle or tower x. pounds in the aid of the building, assessed off said county."

These castles formed the defence of the Pale, and required

to be strongest in the vicinity of Dundalk. The boundaries of the Pale, as it was held in 1515, are thus given:—*

"The Englysh Pale doth stretch and extende from the towne of Doundalk to the towne of Derver, to the towne of Ardye, allwaye on the lyfte syde, leving the merche on the ryght syde, and so to the towne of Syden, to the towne of Kenlis (Kells), to the towne of Dengal (Dangan), to Kylcoke (Kilcock), to the town of Claune (Clane), to the towne of Nasse (Naas), to the Bryge of Cucullyn (Killcullen-bridge), to the town of Ballymore (Ballymore-Eustace), and soe backward to the towne of Ramore (Rathmore), and to the towne of Rathcoule (Rathcoole), to the towne of Talaght, and to the towne of Dalkey, leveing allwaye the merche on the ryghte hande from the sayd Doundolk, following the sayd course to sayd towne of Dalkey."

This castle was of great importance in olden times. It commanded the pass to Dundalk, called in Irish *Cloghan Dealgna*, or the ford at Dalgan. This was the great battle ground between the Anglo-Normans and Irish for several centuries—guarded on the west by the strong castle of the Bellews at Castletown—on the east by the Moyra pass, near Faughart. The sea then allowed but a narrow approach to the town on the north side. It was long before the *Droghid mor* or the great bridge was built; a strong current flowed by the ramparts to Little Mills and Dunnelong, enclosing the land as an island, and leaving an unflooded space on the north, called to this day *Islanmor*, or the great Island. This marsh was crossed on the west by a tochar, which still gives

* *State Papers*, pt. iii., vol. ii., p. 22.

its name to the field adjoining Lord Roden's demesne on the west.

Castletown, as appears in our drawing,* was a strongly-built edifice, consisting of four stories in height, with machicolated battlements. The old towers are in good repair, and some of the rooms very spacious. It is situated on the north side of a hill, about a mile west of Dundalk; and having mounted to the roof we enjoyed an extensive view of the Bay of Dundalk, Slievegullion, and the Carlingford mountains. It was anciently defended by strong outworks, and witnessed some fighting in the wars of the Confederate Catholics. The descendants of the original founder resided here for generations. Close beside this feudal pile is the mansion of J. Eastwood, Esq., and the tastefully arranged grounds, and well-kept lawn, bespeak great love for the beauties of nature.

The Bellews of Castletown were ennobled by patent, Nov., 1686, James the Second having created John Bellew, Esq., of Castletown, near Dundalk, County Louth, Baron Bellew of Duleek, in the County of East Meath, and also a member of the Royal Privy Council for Ireland.†

There are some venerable ruins in the churchyard of Castletown chapel, called in Irish, *Teampul Dun-Dealgan*. The east gable appears perfect, and clad in its garment of ivy, shelters an altar about six feet long, and three broad, supported by masonry three feet high, with the inscription round the border of the covering slab:—

"Sir Walter Bellew, Priest, erected this Altar in honor of St. John Baptist, the first of January, Anno Domini 1631."

---

* From a photograph by John Neville, Esq., C.E., M.R.I.A.

† *O'Callaghan's History Irish Brigades*, vol. i., p. 151.

Forster & Co. Lith. Dublin

CASTLETOWN, DUNDALK.

Beside it is a stone in the gable, two and a-half feet from the ground, which evidently was used to support the sacred vessels belonging to the altar.

Around are scattered many head-stones, marking where

"The rude forefathers of the hamlet sleep."

One large monument denotes the last resting place of Captain Patrick Byrne, of Castletown, who died in 1791. A white marble slab in the wall of the mausoleum bears the following inscription, written by the weather-beaten mariner for his monument:—

"Neptune's waves and Boreas' blast
Have tost me to and fro,
Until now I am come at last
To harbour here below;
Where I hope my bones will be at rest
Until the judgment-day shall be.
O, good Christians, who read this,
I beg you will pray for me."

Unluckily the sculptor has not preserved the rhyme, so the reader must exercise some ingenuity in reading the inscription so as to preserve the metre.

A short distance from the village of Castletown is Tobar-Ronain, or St. Ronan's Well. It was frequented by thousands of pilgrims from the neighbouring counties, and many from the remote parts of Ireland, on the festival of St. John the Baptist, who was the patron saint of the parish. Many miracles, it was said, used to be performed there. It was not an unusual thing for this well to gush forth suddenly, and cover the little meadow on which it stands, and the adjoining road, with water, several feet deep, in a few minutes. Mr. O'Kearney states he was an eye-witness of this on one occasion.

The patron, or rather fair, was also held, on the 24th of June, at Castletown. It was finally suppressed by Rev. John Connery, C.C., Dundalk.

BALLRICHAN CASTLE.

About two miles from Dundalk are the ruins of the Castle of Ballrichan, consisting of an oblong keep, with a spacious court, enclosed by strong walls. This evidently was a place of great strength, and is commandingly situated on a tongue of land, called the Peninsula of Ballrichan, washed by two streams that unite in the Castletown river. From this we behold Slievegullen looming high to the north the boldly perched tower of Castleroch to the west, and Castletown, with Dundalgan, to the east. Wright, in his *Louthiana*,* says:—"There is a subterraneous cave, and a spacious vault under it, which seems to have had some communication with a sally-port, directing towards the banks of the river, which are here very steep and high."

CASTLE ROCH.

This spacious specimen of ancient feudal power, of which we give a drawing,† covers the summit of a rocky hill to the west of Dundalk, and was one of the frontier castles of the Pale. The area enclosed by the ramparts is of irregular shape, more angular than circular. The greatest extent is eighty yards

* Book xi., p. 8.

† From a painting in the possession of Mrs. Henry T. Dix.

long and forty wide. Opposite the main keep, built in the style of the reign of Henry the Third, in which the lord of the castle kept his state, was a tower of defence, wherein the garrison had quarters, and beneath is a sally-port, from which they could spread death among their assailants. We find, in *Newenham's Antiquities of Ireland*, a short account of this castle, which states that it was held during part of 1649 for Charles the First, but finally taken and dismantled by the Parliamentary forces. The name, obviously derived from its site, Castle Roch, or the Castle of the Rock, tradition assigns to its fair foundress, Rose Verdon, who, according to the popular belief, married into the Bellew family. There is, however, a very romantic legend, assigning the cause of the connexion with the Bellews to the union of a Bellew with a lady of far higher rank than Rose de Verdon—namely, the divorced Queen of John, King of England; and, as it appears from the most able and accurate work on heraldry ever compiled, *Burke's Peerage*, that King John married, first, Avisa, daughter and heiress of William, Earl of Gloucester, *from whom he was divorced*, thus far there may be grounds for crediting this romantic tale.

FAUGHART.

ABOUT two miles north of Dundalk, on the summit of a hill, is an artificial mound composed of earthwork, raised to the height of sixty feet,* in the form of the frustrum of a cone. The locality is called Faughart, and was a place of importance on the north frontier of the Pale, and the theatre of great

---

* *Wright's Louthiana*, pt. i., p. 9.

events recorded in our history. There has formerly been an octagonal building on the top of this mound; but whether a tower, or parapet, there are not sufficient remains left to determine. Mr. Wright, in his *Louthiana*, supposes it was originally a funeral monument, and afterwards used as a beacon or fort, either as an outpost to defend the frontier, or to signal the approach of an enemy. It was well adapted for either purpose; and, situated on the confines of the county, near the formidable Bealach-an-Moirie, or Moyry Pass, was very probably used as a watch-station. Near this mound are the ruins of an ancient church, surrounded by a very densely populated grave-yard. The blending of chapel walls and tombs attest the sacredness of the spot; and the interest of the visitor is increased, when he is told, that close by was born Saint Brigid, in A.D. 453; and here lies buried the mutilated remains of Edward Bruce, the last crowned King of Ireland. He was slain in the valley beneath, in the battle on St. Callextus's Day, 14th October, 1318; and his severed head formed a ghastly gift for the King of England.

The ruins of the old church show a very primitive order of architecture. They are now little better than broken walls; and, save in the hammered windows, show little traces of workmanship. The date of their erection is unknown. Tradition assigns them to the time of St. Brigid; and that this church, called Teampul-aird, was built by her before she founded her great nunnery in Kildare, in A.D. 480. A portion of the building now standing is evidently of later date than the part to the west. Archdall in his learned work* informs us that St. Monenna erected a nunnery here in the year 638, wherein she presided over a hundred and fifty virgins; but resigning the

* *Monast. Hib* p. 464.

government to Orbila, or Torvila, she built a nunnery for herself at Kilslieve, in the County of Armagh. The same authority mentions a monastery here for Regular Canons, in honour of St. Brigid; but it must have existed in very remote times. The church, in after years, was that for the parish in the diocese of Armagh. It is now a mere shell—few of the walls standing, and these devoid of any architectural beauty.

The well dedicated to St. Brigid lies a little to the north of the church, and is protected by masonry of a very primitive character. Immense crowds were accustomed to resort to the Patron of St. Brigid; but these reunions, having quite degenerated from their primitive spirit of piety, were prohibited by the Catholic clergy throughout Ireland, and are now quite obsolete. A leafy ash stands sentinel over the entrance to the well, and casts a soothing shade over the hallowed spot. In another part of the churchyard the pedestal of a cross, with the aperture for the shaft, is to be found. Within the ruined walls a place is assigned as the grave of Edward Bruce; but no monumental stone enables the visitor to discover it. Mr. Marmion* mentions that, in 1824, Sir John Macneill, who was born in this neighbourhood, tried to ascertain whether the remains of Bruce were interred here, and opened the supposed resting-place of the monarch; but desisted, not wishing to distress the feelings of those whose relatives were buried beside, and who seemed to consider it desecration to disturb their remains.

The fact of no stone marking, with suitable precision and respect, where Edward Bruce lies buried, called forth the following letter from one of his countrymen, which we wish may enlist the sympathy of our readers:—

---

* *Hist. Maritime Ports*, p. 280.

"THE NEGLECTED GRAVE OF EDWARD BRUCE.

" *To the Editor of the Belfast Morning News.*

"DEAR SIR,—As a constant reader, I have noticed in your useful paper, the *Morning News*, an advertisement for a subscription to erect a monument to the memory of the great Sir William Wallace—no doubt a good thing, and creditable to the Scotchmen who desire to honour the great patriot; will they take a look at the neglected grave of the brave Edward Bruce, brother of their King, Robert Bruce, a cotemporary, and as valiant a man as the great Wallace, now without a mark of interment—the stone for that purpose having sunk into the earth, or the surface swelled up, so that it is now almost invisible? There could be no difficulty in getting permission from the O'Roddy family to erect something over the grave of the great hero, Bruce. I understand they are a liberal kind of people, who would throw no obstacle in the way; also, that it was the O'Roddy of Bruce's day that waked and interred him. A manuscript writing, stating this, is now in the possession of Mr. O'Kearney (the well-known Irish linguist), of Dublin. If you would be so kind as to give this a place in your next publication it might induce the Scotch to do something in remembrance of their departed countryman, which is the wish of your obedient servant.

"A TRUE SCOT.

"Oct. 6, 1856.

["'A True Scot' makes a suggestion which his countrymen should well consider. The graves of the departed great should always command the jealous attention of the survivors.—ED. *Morning News*."]

This elicited a letter from one of the Roddy family—Mr.

Brien Roddy, builder and architect, of Ballybay—who at once expressed his readiness to facilitate the object of the writer, and his desire to give his professional services, on being furnished with a drawing of the intended monument. The subject, however, was not taken up with the spirit of the "True Scot." There was no meeting called, or committee appointed, or subscriptions collected; and the grave of Edward Bruce still remains unhonoured, and, save to a few, quite unknown. Mr. O'Kearney, above alluded to, has furnished us with the following:—

"The head-stone that marks the grave of Bruce is called *Clar Saengal* in Irish. I think it should be *cloch*, not *clar*. The word *saengal* appears to be *sean*, old; and *ceal*, a cell; so *saengal* signifies the stone of the old church or cell. I have been informed by old members of the Roddy family that this stone, at a distance of about three feet from the top, becomes forked. Superstitious virtues are attributed to this stone which emanated from no spirit of Christianity."

KILNASAGGART.

THIS ancient historic spot is not far from Faughart, on the borders of the County Louth, near its junction with Armagh, and in the parish of Jonesborough, in that county. The name signifies "the Church of the Priests;" and all that now remains to bear out this reverend title are some traces of ancient sculpture and a pillar-stone. Mr. O'Kearney has communicated to us a description of this stone, which he says is about six feet in height and four in width, having an inscription incised in old Irish characters upon its front, while on the back are twelve crosses, each different in form, and surrounded by a circle, indicating the seal of a church dignitary. The inscription Mr. O'Kearney thus translates:—"In this place I, Ternoch, of Magh-oicer (the name then of Kilnasaggart), pray by the authority of the Keys of Peter the Apostle." He adds:—"St. Ternoch, who consecrated Kilnasaggart about the middle of the sixth century, was Abbot, at one time, of the Church of Kilmore, of Moy-Ealta. His festival was held on the 17th of November."

The accomplished and painstaking Rev. Dr. Reeves, Secretary R.I.A., has published an account of this inscription in the *Ulster Journal of Archæology*,* with a well-executed drawing, displaying both front and back views of the pillar-stone. The inscription, as given in his paper, does not correspond in all respects with that copied by Mr. O'Kearney. Dr. Reeves describes it "a good deal obliterated by time; but some of the letters, which are large and deep, are very plain, while the rest, which are not so well incised, are with difficulty deciphered." The reverend writer subjoins this collateral Latin translation, for which interpretation he adds, to his own acknowledged ability as a Celtic archæologist, the distinguished name of the late Dr. O'Donovan:—

"TON LOCVM
HVNC CON-
SECRAVIT
TERNOCVS
FILIVS CERAN
SIT SVB PATROCINIO
PETRI APOS
TOLI"

* Vol. i., p. 221.

In the neighbourhood is the famous Pass of Moyry, so frequently the scene of strife between the Ulster troops and the forces of the Pale. Carefully executed engravings of the numerous objects of interest to the Irish archæologist, in which this county is peculiarly rich, are given in *Wright's Louthiana*, accompanied with descriptive notices, which are not altogether reliable for accuracy.

STATISTICAL
ACCOUNT OF DUNDALK.

HAVING traced the history of the town from its foundation, and noticed its ancient topography and traditions, we next proceed to glance at its present condition.

The following is from the pen of Dr. John Browne,* who has been one of our most able and active coadjutors while preparing this work for the press:—

"The town of Dundalk is situated on the east side of the coast, forty miles north of Dublin, in a pretty extensive valley or basin, formed of an alluvial deposit, and almost on a level with the sea. On the north, and extending towards the north-west it is enclosed by the mountains of Cooley, Ravensdale, and Forkhill, at a distance varying from two to five miles. Towards the south and west the country is slightly elevated, presenting an undulating surface, which is remarkably fertile. About a mile from the harbour it is enclosed on the east by an extensive bay, having a flat, sandy shore of

---

* "Medical Report of the Dundalk Destitute Sick Society, together with a Sketch of the Medical Topography and Statistics of the Town and Parish," by John Browne, M.D.—*Dublin Journal of Medical Science*, First Series, vol. xv., p. 410.

some miles in extent. The ground between the town and coast is extremely flat, and appears, at a period not very distant, to have been an entire swamp. The river of Castletown passes the northern extremity of the town, embanked for a considerable distance on both sides by a level mud deposit, which is washed by the tide; into this the sewers of the town empty themselves, though very imperfectly.

"The geological structure of the surrounding mountains is granite, skirted by hornblende and primitive greenstone; the rest of the country is chiefly occupied by clay slate, with limestone occurring in detached districts. The latter is generally of a bluish colour, abounding in many places with fossil shells, encrinites, &c."

Owing to its geological position the ground on which the town rests, and a large portion of the parish, are consequently wet; the atmosphere is rather humid; and rain falls pretty frequently. When he wrote in 1839 the town was greatly crowded. He says:—

"The town is composed of two principal streets, running north and south, and east and west, respectively; and three others of minor importance, together with a number of lanes and yards, which are kept in a most filthy condition, densely inhabited by the poor. The number of houses in 1837 amounted to 1,851; at which period the population numbered 14,300, including the suburbs; and exclusive of these, 10,078. Since then the town has undergone many improvements."

We find the population in 1841 stated at 10,782, inhabiting 1,798 houses, which decreased in the ten years ending 1851 to 9,995 inhabitants and 1,679 houses; and in 1861, population 10,404, inhabiting 1,868 houses."*

In addition to the foregoing particulars we may add, it is a maritime town, and borough sending one Member to the Imperial Parliament. The town lies in the Barony of Upper Dundalk, County of Louth, and Province of Leinster; and has an area of 450 acres. The names of the principal streets, as may be seen by reference to our map, are Anne-street and Dublin-street, which lead into Park-street. At the end of this street we find a block of houses forming Francis-street, Earl-street, and Crow-street. Pursuing Earl-street we reach the open space of Market-square, in which stands the Court House. Taking the northerly course we pass through Clanbrassil-street into Church-street. Here the new Catholic Church of St. Nicholas and a School-house form the angle of Bridge-street and Meetinghouse-lane. Retracing our route by Clanbrassil-street we pass the Protestant Church and the Court House, and reach Crow-street. Here Roden-place is seen, with the spacious Roman Catholic Parish Church; next, Jocelyn-street, Seatown-place, and Barrack-street, leading to the Cavalry Barracks; bounded on the east by the shore of Dundalk Harbour. Following the Shore-road we reach the Quays, and mark the recent improvements effected in this portion of the suburbs, especially the new Fair-green—a tract of about eight acres, rescued from the flow of the tide by the energy of Dr. Browne, and the engineering skill of the County Surveyor (John Neville, Esq.), whose name is most appropriately given to the spacious roadway leading to the

---

* *Thom's Directory.*

bridge. This ground has been freely given by the Earl of Roden. The broad streets, with the many excellent buildings which constitute the Court House; the Bank of Ireland, National, Belfast, and Savings Banks; the handsome Commercial Buildings; the churches of various congregations; the shops, marts; the harbour, with the vessels and steamers, give the visitor the idea of a thriving town, occupied by an industrious and enterprising population. Here is food for every palate—abundance to gratify every disposition. An agriculturist will be delighted with the state of tillage, the improved breed of stock, and the excellent farming implements used in the locality—for which the Louth Farming Society has done much. The mercantile eye will examine the commercial industry, and note the import and export trade carried on by commercial enterprise, aided by the appliances of railroads and steamboats. The benevolent eye will glance approvingly over the well-managed Poor-house, the County Infirmary, and Gaol. The lover of the picturesque will mount one of the neighbouring hills, or, perhaps, the old Fort of Dalgan, and survey a rich and varied landscape. The historic eye beholds the princely O'Neill—the chivalrous Bruce—the haughty Essex—the valiant Mountjoy—the brave King William—the high-minded Cornwallis—and courteous Carlisle. All have visited Dundalk. Hitherto the townspeople thought little of their ancient district. They did not know the proud memories associated with their town; or, if they did, went by their old historic scenes with indifference. We trust our labours have done something to prevent the growth of such feelings; and shall rejoice to find the youth of Dundalk making their history part of their education; and, as they traverse the streets, remember they are walking upon storied ground. We agree with the American who said:—

"It is hard to feel such memories slipping away day by day. It is a sad experience when you go by old historic scenes and realize first that the busy world around you has swallowed up your sentiment so that it ceases to kindle, and your eye wanders over them as the veriest common-places of the day."*

Having done our duty to the past, we must now perform our part to the present, and give an account of the various religious, educational, charitable, administrative, and commercial establishments in Dundalk.

THE PROTESTANT CHURCH AND SCHOOLS.

The Protestant Church of St. Nicholas is a grave, reverend-looking building, with an old ivy-mantled tower of moderate altitude, and a well-proportioned, copper-sheathed spire, pointing from earth to heaven. Brewer† has preserved the name of the architect—F. Johnston, Esq. He, however, was only the restorer; for, about a hundred years ago the church was destroyed by fire, and the registers consumed, which we lament —having thereby failed to procure information our account, on many points, is far from being as full as we wished.

The notions of church building in the days of this restoration were not as they are now. The consequence is, the Church of Dundalk has little to recommend it save a richly-coloured antique painted window, the unfading tints of which transmute the light of day into a glorious radiance, symbolic of the light of Heaven. This beautiful ancient window is thus inscribed:—

---

* *Fresh Gleanings*, by Marvel.

† *Beauties of Ireland*, vol. ii., p. 323.

"ST. ANDREAS FACIOLANUS, E PUO,*
EX NOBILI CORSIONORUM FAMILIA
NATUS VIR PROPTER EXIMIAM CHARITATEM
ET MAUSUETUDINE POPULUM REFUGIUM
ORPHANUM PATER VIDUARUM SPONSUS
VULGO ESTIMATUS; ITA OMNIA OMNIBUS FACTUS
MIRACULI CORRUSCANS, PRÆDICTA MORTIS
DIE PYSSIME OBYT 1373."

There are a number of mural monuments on the walls around the Communion Table, pathetic records of departed worth. One is to the memory of the last Earl of Clanbrassil, who died in 1798; another to his sister Anne, Countess of Roden, obiit 1802; one to the Hon. John Jocelyn; and, in the transept, one to Lady Harriet Jocelyn, sister to the present Earl of Roden. Near the Communion Table is the monument erected to the memory of Rev. Elias Thackery, late Vicar of Dundalk, who is held in most affectionate remembrance by the inhabitants of every religious denomination. In this part of the church is a stone inscribed with the name and virtues of Susanna, wife of Rodolph

---

* Evidently a contraction of "*Episcopus;*" "*populum*" contracted for "*populorum.*" The inscription may be thus translated:—

"St. Andrew Faciolanus, Bishop—
Sprung from the noble family of Corsini—
A man universally esteemed for his boundless charity;
And on account of his mildness the refuge of the people,
The father of orphans, the spouse of widows;
So he was all (things) to all (people).
Renowned by his miracles—having foretold the
Day of his death—he died in the odour of sanctity, 1373."

Lambert, S.T.P., Vicar of this church, who died on the feast of St. Paul, 1707, aged 40.

The vestry is a small apartment attached to the church. In this is an inscription:—

"ECCLESIA HÆC TEMPORIS ET BELLI INURIA PENITUS DIRVTA FORMA NOVA ET ELEGANTIOR INSTAURATA FUIT ANNO CHRISTI 1707.

"RODOLPHO LAMBERTI, S.T.P.,

"VICARIO.

"HENRICO BUSH,
GEORGIO ION, } CUSTODIBUS."

Outside the vestry window is an old tomb, erected in memory of more than one, as *jacent* and *corpora* indicate; but only one name is legible—Thomas Field. The words *presbyter* and *capella fundator* imply his sacerdotal character. The date is 1536. There are a number of other ancient monuments in the churchyard; but the hand of time has pressed so heavily upon them, that, although we took great pains to decipher them, we did not achieve much success. We made out the dates of a few. One large tomb has the following, in a double row of letters around the covering slab:—

"HERE under lyeth the body of John Mortimer, of Dundalk, Alderman, who deceased the 8th day of May, Anno Domini, 1534, unto whose soul be mercy."

In the centre of this slab is a richly chiselled coat of arms, with a hand bearing a star at the tip of the fore-finger.

In the corner of the churchyard, near the sexton's house,

is a large tomb, erected to the memory of Agnes Galt, sister of Robert Burns, the glorious national poet of Scotland, to whom a pillar is dedicated, from the circumstance of his kindred clay resting here.

When Mr. Thackeray, the eminent English author, visited Dundalk in 1842, the Vicar of the town was his namesake—Reverend Elias Thackery; and, in the account of the visit published in *The Irish Sketch Book*,* the author gives this graceful and faithful portrait of the Vicar, since gone to render an account of his ministry:—

"I was so lucky as to have an introduction to the Vicar of Dundalk, which that gentleman's kind and generous nature interpreted into a claim for unlimited hospitality; and he was good enough to consider himself bound not only to receive me, but to give up previous engagements in order to do so. I need not say that it afforded me sincere pleasure to witness, for a couple of days, his labours among his people; and, indeed, it was a delightful occupation to watch both flock and pastor. The world is a wicked, selfish, abominable place, as the parson tells us; but his reverence comes out of his pulpit and gives the flattest contradiction to his doctrine, busying himself with kind actions from morning till night—denying to himself, generous to others—preaching the truth to young and old, clothing the naked, feeding the hungry, consoling the wretched, and giving hope to the sick; and I do not mean to say that this sort of life is led by the Vicar of Dundalk merely; but I do firmly believe that it is the life of the great majority of the Protestant and Roman Catholic clergy of the country."

---

* *Titmarsh's Irish Sketch Book*, vol. ii., p. 187.

The author then describes the schools under the Vicar's care:—

"We went from the church to a school which has long been a favourite resort of the good Vicar's; indeed, to judge from the schoolmaster's books, his attendance there is almost daily; and the number of the scholars some 200.

"We found a large room with sixty or seventy boys at work. In an upper chamber were a considerable number of girls with their teachers, two modest and pretty young women; but the favourite resort of the Vicar was, evidently, the infant school—and no wonder. It is impossible to witness a more beautiful or touching sight."

The children sang a little hymn, and it deeply affected the listener.

"It was the first time I had ever heard it, and I do not care to own that it brought tears to my eyes; but I think I will never, while I live, forget that little chorus; nor would any man who has ever loved a child, or lost one. God bless you, O little happy singers! What a noble and useful life is his who, in place of seeking wealth or honour, devotes his life to such a service as this! And all through our country, thank God! in quiet, humble corners that busy citizens and men of the world never hear of, there are thousands of such men employed in such holy pursuits, with no reward beyond that which the fulfilment of duty brings them."

We were not able to procure a list of the incumbents, from any quarter. The following are the names of a few of the Vicars of Dundalk, which the present Vicar kindly furnished us. The old records of the parish, he informed us, were burned, which prevented a more complete list:—

Rev. Mr. Bowes.
Rev. Mr. Hamilton.
Rev. Mr. Montgomery.
Rev. Elias Thackery.
Present Vicar—Rev. Marcus Rainsford.

DUNDALK GRAMMAR SCHOOL.—"There is some doubt as to the origin of the Dundalk Endowed School. It is alleged that the endowment was made, in 1725, by Lord Limerick, afterwards Earl of Clanbrassil, in consideration of certain commons in Dundalk, on which he had some claim, being given up by the Corporation."—*Report of the Endowed School Commission*, 1858.

The Earl of Roden, the present representative of the Earl of Clanbrassil, is the Patron of the school. The annual endowment is £50 Irish, and the local rates are paid and the premises kept in repair by the Patron.

The Master's house and the school-rooms, with the dormitory, were probably erected in 1725, and the dining-room (in the rere) subsequently. In 1830, Dr. Darley, the then Master, built the dormitories over the dining-room. The Lodge was "annexed" by Mr. Stubbs, and the borders of the play-ground extended in the time of Dr. Brough. In the garden, which is an English acre in extent, there is a ruin, said to be part of an old monastery. The field adjoining the garden is held by the Master, and is used as a cricket ground.

The early history of the school is involved in obscurity; and it is perhaps impossible to give a complete list of the Masters who have presided over it. The first Master, whose name the writer has ascertained, is Mr. Murray. His son was Dean of Ardagh, and his brother Provost of Trinity College, Dublin. Of the next Master, Maurice Hawkey, the name remains, and nothing more. He was succeeded by the Rev. G. Tinley, an Englishman, who had previously been Assistant Master in the Carrickmacross Grammar School. He appears to have been appointed about 1786, and to have resigned in 1814, when appointed to the living of Faughart. The ferule was next wielded by the Rev. J. H. Stubbs, A.M., the present Rector of Dromiskin, who resigned, in 1825, in favour of the Rev. Dr. Darley. Dr. Darley worked the school with great success; and, on his promotion to the Dungannon Royal School, in 1830, took with him sixty-two boarders from Dundalk. Dr. Darley is now Rector of Cootehill. Since 1830, the Mastership has been held by the Rev. Dr. Brough, Dr. Boyd (both now in the colonies), the Rev. Dr. Goslett (promoted, in 1858, to the Drogheda Grammar School), and Mr. Price, the present Master.

The Patron has recently (1860) established a medal (the *Roden* Medal), to be competed for annually. The names of the Roden Medallists, of the Præfects, and of the first pupil in the order of merit, for each year, are posted up in a conspicuous part of the school-room. The lists commence from 1860.

THE INCORPORATED SOCIETY'S SCHOOL.—These schools were formerly known as the Protestant Charter Schools. They had their origin in the Society incorporated in 1733, on the petition of the principal nobility, clergy, and gentry of Ireland, for the purpose of maintaining "a sufficient number of English Protestant schools, wherein the children of the Irish natives (might) be instructed in the English tongue and the fundamental principles of true religion." The trust of the charter was to maintain English Protestant schools in Ireland, for instructing the Roman Catholic children, and other poor native Irish, in the English language, writing, and arithmetic; in housewifery or trades; in the Holy Scriptures, and especially in Protestant principles. The funds were augmented by bequests and donations; and, from 1733 to 1784, these schools always were noticed by each succeeding Viceroy in his speech at the opening of the Irish Parliament, and in almost every address in reply. It appears that some grave mistakes were made in the statements of the Society, as to the numbers frequenting their schools, which was discovered by Mr. Howard, the philanthropist, during a visit he paid to Ireland in 1784; which induced the Irish House of Commons to bring the subject before a committee. The result was—Mr. Howard's complaints were fully sustained, and several Masters were dismissed.

By the Report of the Endowed School (Ireland) Commission we find that, in the years 1775–6, children of the Roman Catholic religion alone were admitted to these schools; and it was not until 1803 this rule was modified, in order to admit Protestant pupils Efforts were made, from time to time, to induce the children of Roman Catholics to attend; but this proving quite hopeless, the Parliamentary grants dwindled down from £19,500, in 1826, to £5,750, in 1832, when they were finally withdrawn.

The landed estate attached to the Dundalk Institution was the first held by the Incorporated Society. Few years elapsed after the incorporation before Mrs. Anne Hamilton, mother of the Earl of Clanbrassil, bequeathed an estate of about 360 statute acres, in the County of Down, and a house in Dundalk, for the support of a school. In 1738, this was conveyed to the

Incorporated Society. At first it was a boarding school for girls; but, in 1835, this was altered, and now it is an excellent boarding and day school for boys. In 1839, the Vicar, Rev. Elias Thackery, anticipated the present mode of testing fitness for the civil and military services, by introducing the election of children on the foundation of the Institution by a competitive examination. The election is restricted to children of the districts in which the Society possess estates. No child is eligible who has been previously attending any school of public legal foundation—such as National and Workhouse Schools. The candidates are required to be between the ages of twelve and sixteen years, and to have attended a Scripture school for at least twelve months prior to examination. Those successful are educated and supported for four years; and, according to their efficiency at the end of that time, a portion of them may be continued in the Institution two years longer. While they remain they are required to attend the service of the Established Church; but members of any Protestant denomination are eligible as candidates. There is always a rivalry for these foundation scholarships, which is the best test of the value attached to them. Boys intending to compete are, for some time previous to the examination, in active preparations for it; and apply to what are termed "grinders," in order to acquit themselves with success. The teachers whose pupils succeed in distancing their companions receive certificates, which establish their reputation, and induce boys to frequent their schools, and board with them while preparing for the subsequent examinations. The pupils educated in the Dundalk Institution have been eminently successful in obtaining and retaining good situations, which naturally causes this school to be well attended.

The Head Master receives £100 per annum, with salaries

for Assistants; the house and grounds rent free, with fuel and other allowances.

At the EDUCATIONAL INSTITUTION, DUNDALK, the present Head Master is Mr. John Turner, who has the aid of a most efficient staff of tutors. This Institution, which is under the patronage and superintendence of the Incorporated Society for Promoting English Protestant Schools in Ireland, provides accommodation for upwards of one hundred boarders, of whom forty-four are educated and maintained on the foundation. There is also accommodation for a large number of day pupils.

The course of education, both commercial and mathematical, embraces the Holy Scriptures, and English generally, including drawing, surveying, mapping, use of the globes, &c., &c. The drawings of the pupils reflect credit on Mr. Chapman, the Drawing Master.

A deputation from the Board, consisting of Fellows of Trinity College, Dublin, and other gentlemen of high literary standing, visit the Institution annually, and test the progress of the pupils by a most searching examination.

Inclusive Terms—Parlour Boarders, £32; Hall Boarders, £24 per annum.

On the religious and moral training of the pupils the greatest care is bestowed, not only by the Head Master and his Assistants, but also by the Catechist of the Institution, the Rev. Marcus Rainsford, Vicar of Dundalk, who lectures once a week on the Holy Scriptures.

The Institution is situated in a most healthful locality; the dormitories are spacious and well ventilated, and the play grounds extensive—all calculated, in an eminent degree, to promote the health and happiness of the pupils.

ROMAN CATHOLIC CHURCHES, CONVENTS, AND SCHOOLS.

In 1704 the Catholics of Dundalk had no chapel within the town. Mass was then, and for years afterwards, celebrated in an apartment; neither did the priest reside within the borough. In 1750, the building of a commodious chapel was commenced in Chapel-lane (taken down in 1850, and the National Schools built on its site); and in 1756, Mr. George Byrne, of Seatown, Dundalk, brewer, one of the most extensive import merchants in the town, erected therein a fine altar and tabernacle,* and over it placed a splendid painting of our Lord's crucifixion, purchased by him in Italy, and presented to the people of Dundalk.† Some years afterwards, a black marble tablet was placed at the Gospel side of the altar, which continued there until the chapel was pulled down; and upon it was the following inscription:—

"This altar was erected, in honour of God, by Mr. George Byrne, Merchant, of Dundalk, who departed this life on the 16th January, 1769, aged 61 years.

"Requiescat in Pace."

---

* A portion of the tabernacle and some of the candlesticks were, in 1847, transferred to, and are now used in the chapel attached to the Convent of the Sisters of Mercy, Seatown, Dundalk.

† This picture, being too large for the new Church of St. Patrick's, was sold by auction after the consecration of St. Patrick's Church, and purchased by Mr. Patrick James Byrne, of Lisnawilly, a member of the family of the donor. It is now to be seen, having been restored at much expense, in Lisnawilly House; and the black marble tablet, with the inscription, is attached to the wall underneath the picture.

In 1834 the Catholics of Dundalk, and their respected Parish Priest, the Very Rev. Matthew M'Cann, D.D., purchased the site of their present splendid Church of St. Patrick. The plan for the erection of this structure, to cost about £25,000, was obtained from Mr. Thomas John Duff, architect, of Newry, and the works commenced; but little progress was made beyond the foundations, base of the columns, and some few feet of the walls, during the lifetime of Dr. M'Cann. He died in the latter end of the year 1836, and the Very Rev. Dr. John Coyne, Parish Priest of Tandragee, was, in 1837, appointed his successor. On taking charge of the parish he devoted his best efforts towards the completion of the church. Such was his zeal, his persevering industry, and indefatigable exertion, the building was pushed forward with great rapidity. During the ten years of his parochial administration this magnificent church was finished, and over £25,000 expended on it.

The Very Rev. Dr. Coyne died in February, 1848, and a meeting of the Catholic inhabitants of the parish of Dundalk was speedily held in the parish church, for the purpose of expressing their sincere and heartfelt regret for his loss. Nicholas Martin, Esq., Chairman of the Town Commissioners, presided, and James Byrne, Esq., was appointed secretary; and, on the motion of Michael Kelly, Esq., J.P., seconded by Peter Russell, Esq., J.P., and carried unanimously, it was resolved:—"That the Catholic inhabitants of the parish of Dundalk record to-day their deep sorrow for the loss with which it has pleased God to grieve them, by taking away their late venerated pastor, to whose ceaseless and successful efforts they are indebted for the erection of their splendid church, and whose services to religion cannot be sufficiently estimated."

A strong feeling was expressed by the meeting that a

testimonial of the gratitude entertained for the services of Dr. Coyne, as well as reverence for his memory, should be raised to commemorate his exertions; but it was ultimately determined that the best monument was *the church itself*. It was resolved to proceed with the decorations; and these, under the auspices of Rev. Dr. Coyne's respected successor, the Very Rev. Dean Kieran, were soon completed. Dr. Kieran did much to aid in these embellishments; and the result is, the Roman Catholic Church in Roden-place fully testifies the earnest devotion of the people of Dundalk. It is built in the Gothic style of architecture. The front facing the entrance is of granite, highly wrought; and the fine arched doorway and embattled octagon towers, rising on either side, impress the beholder, even before the wonders within meet his gaze. The interior is of great extent and exceeding beauty. Here the workmen of our day emulated the piety of departed ages, and proved that there is yet in the land the same zeal for God's honour, and man's spiritual progress, that, in former years, threw splendour over the Island of Saints. The roof is spanned by lofty arches, supported on pillars, which divide the nave from the lateral aisles, and behind the altar, formed of Caen stone, is a magnificent painted window, illustrated with scenes from the Bible.

THE CHURCH OF ST. NICHOLAS.—In February, 1859, the erection of a second church in the Parish of Dundalk was considered essential, and the site of the present new Church of St. Nicholas, in Bridge-street, was obtained. The plan of Mr. John Murray, of Dundalk, architect, was approved of; and the tender of Mr. Arthur Hammond—£3,000 for the completion of the church—was accepted.

On the 25th August, 1860, the Church of St. Nicholas

was consecrated. The total cost of it, including purchase of site, has not exceeded £4,000.

Here, also, is a painted window, though of less elaborate design than those in St. Patrick's. Yet no one can enter the Church of St. Nicholas without feeling grateful to the mediæval art which produced those glorious combinations of artistic skill.

The following list of parish priests of Dundalk is communicated by Patrick James Byrne, Esq.:—

"1704.—In 1704 the Very Rev. Dr. Mathews was parish priest of Dundalk, and continued as such for many years.

"1735.—In 1735 the Very Rev. Dr. Dowdall was parish priest of Dundalk; and during his administration of the parish the chapel was built in Chapel-lane, where now the National Schools stand.

"1760.—The Very Rev. Dr. Markey, a most learned divine, educated at Sorbonne, was appointed parish priest of Dundalk. He died about the year 1770. His successor was—

"1770.—Rev. Michael Verdon, D.D.

"1776.—Rev. Michael Taaffe, D.D.

"1787.—Rev. Philip Levins, D.D. This was a most learned divine. He was parish priest of Ardee previously to his promotion to Dundalk. Dying 1st June, 1794, aged sixty-seven, he was buried in the churchyard of Dysert, near Barmeath.

"1794.—The Very Rev. James Martin, D.D., was appointed Dr. Levins' successor. He was a learned divine, educated at Rome, and a distinguished scholar. He was the son of Mr. Patrick Martin, and brother to Mr. Thomas Martin, of Dunmahon Castle.

"Dr. James Martin was elderly when appointed to the parish of Dundalk; and an old man when he died in 1806.

"His father, Patrick Martin, of Dunmahon Castle, lived to the great age of 109 years; and his brother, Mr. Thomas Martin, who was great-grandfather of Richard Byrne, Esq., J.P., of Rosmakea, reached 106 years.

"1806.—The Very Rev. Dr. Maginnes M'Ardle succeeded Dr. Martin as parish priest of Dundalk. He was descended from the Maginneses of Iveagh, in the County of Down, of which county he was a native. He continued parish priest of Dundalk until 1819, when—

"1819.—The Very Rev. Dr. Matthew M'Cann (uncle to the present Member for Drogheda) became parish priest. He was a man of letters and a most accomplished gentleman. We have seen he commenced the beautiful parish church of St. Patrick's. On his death, in 1836, the parish priest of Tandragee—

"1837.—The Very Rev. Dr. Coyne, succeeded Dr. M'Cann. We have already mentioned his services to religion. He died in 1848, when—

"1848.—The Very Rev. Dr. Kieran, the present parish priest, succeeded Dr. Coyne. We hope it may be a long time before the future historian of Dundalk records the name of the Dean's successor; unless, indeed, his elevation to a mitre caused the vacancy."

Dominican Monastery.—The Catholic inhabitants of Dundalk, besides the large chapel erected in 1756, and so embellished by Mr. George Byrne, had also, at the entrance to the town, a small Dominican chapel.

The Dominican Priory of St. Malachy, in the County of Louth, was founded in 1305, in the town of Carlingford, by

Richard De Burgo, Earl of Ulster. It was destroyed at an early period of the persecutions that raged against the Catholic religion. Its ruins to this day attest its antiquity and importance. By letters patent, dated at Westminster April 22, 1588, Edward the Sixth granted to Sir Nicholas Bagnall the entire house and site of the Friars Preachers, called the Black Friars of Carlingford; and again by letters patent, dated 18th February, 1611, James the First granted to Arthur Bagnall, Esq., all that the late monastery or late dissolved house of Preaching Friars, called the Black Friars of the Town of Carlingford, and the site, circuit, precinct of same, with the appurtenances.

On a partial relaxation of the Penal Laws, in 1775, this priory was established in Dundalk, with all its rights and privileges. The Rev. Father Thomas, O.P., Prior.

In the year 1756 the following friars were professed for the ancient convent of St. Malachy:—Father Dominick Thomas, Prior; the Rev. Stephen O'Carney, Rev. Jacob MacMahon, and the Rev. Patrick Davitt.

The succession of Dominican fathers in the priory of St. Malachy, Dundalk, from 1775, has been uninterrupted down to the present time:—Rev. Fathers Thomas, Kelly, Quinn, Maguirk, Crawley, Duffy, and the present universally-respected and learned Very Rev. Patrick Dunne, D.D., under whose auspices a very fine and spacious Dominican church is being raised, adjoining the old edifice, at a cost of about £6,000.

St. Mary's College, Dundalk, under the patronage of his Grace the Primate, and the kind protection of the Very Rev. Dean Kieran, P.P., and V.G., occupies the premises of Mr. Read, at one period agent to the Earl of Clanbrassil; and the main building was Mr. Read's dwelling.

The object of the Marist Fathers in opening the above establishment under the sanction of the local clergy is, to impart to the children and young men who will be entrusted to their care, such a religious and literary education as will enable them, in after-life, to discharge their duties to God and to society. The fathers endeavour to attain this important object by remaining with the children during the hours for school and recreation, and by devoting their best energies to the moral and literary improvement of their pupils.

Besides English grammar, elocution, poetry, history, geography, and all the other branches of an ordinary English education, the *course of studies* embraces book-keeping, arithmetic, practical geometry, and algebra. The Greek and Latin languages are taught on the most approved methods.

No children are admitted into the college but such as have attained the age of seven, and learned to read and write at some other school. They also require a written or verbal recommendation from their parish priest.

The terms for all out-door students are moderate—£5 per annum; and £1 additional per annum for those who wish to learn French. The parents or guardians of the children are required to provide them with books, paper, and all other school requisites.

The children attend Mass and Vespers in the collegiate chapel on Sundays and holidays, and also Mass every Thursday at nine o'clock.

As the fathers of the Society of Mary devote themselves to the home and foreign missions, they also admit and board in their house a limited number of novices, who receive instructions in philosophy and theology.

The parent house of this Order is at Lyons; and the zealous fathers seek to carry the Gospel to the savage nations of Oceanica, and the Indians yet inhabiting portions of the American continent. We were much pleased with the school and play-ground; and when the proposed accommodation is completed, the number of novices taken to board will be about fifty.

The annual examination and distribution of prizes took place on the 15th and 16th July, 1863. The Very Rev. Dean Kieran, V.G., P.P., with his accustomed kindness, presided during a long examination, at which the proficiency of every pupil was thoroughly tested. On the following morning, after Mass, he addressed the students and many of their friends, who were present, on the advantages of education, and especially on the necessity of early religious training. He concluded by giving some kind and affectionate advice to the students as to their conduct both at college and during the vacation, and then distributed prizes to those amongst them, who had distinguished themselves during the past year. Several of the local clergy were present on the occasion with the fathers of the community.

Convent of Sisters of Mercy.—It is a singular proof of the vitality of the Catholic Church to find a Convent of Nuns occupying portion of the site of the Priory of St. Leonard's, founded by Bertram de Verdon seven hundred years ago.

In January, 1847, the Commissioners of Excise advertised for sale, in London, the Excise premises in Dundalk, being portion of the Abbey ground in Seatown. The Rev. Dr. Coyle, Parish Priest, was desirous the Catholic poor of Dundalk should experience the pious and charitable ministrations of that excellent community, the Sisters of Mercy, and this advertisement attracted his attention. Through his solicitor,

P. J. Byrne, Esq., he sent in a sealed tender for the purchase. His offer, £1,805, was accepted upon the 19th January, 1847, and the house intended for the Convent was soon busy with the throng of workmen, making all requisite preparations for the reception of the Nuns. On the 27th October, in the same year, it was pronounced ready; and, at once, four Sisters, from the parent house, in Baggot-street, Dublin, founded the Convent of Dundalk. They lost no time in making their presence useful to the poor, whose servants it is their pride to be. On the 8th November school opened; but the school-room was so small only thirty pupils could be accommodated. This, of course, was merely temporary. Four school-rooms, of size more in accordance with the large hearts, and devoted purposes, of the good Sisters, were building; and their zeal was such, no sooner was one roofed, than (not waiting until the walls were plastered, and the necessary furniture procured) they turned the workmen out, and the children in—borrowed from the church a number of seats, and taught as many scores of pupils as they hitherto counted units. When their school-rooms were completed, in less than twelve months from their occupation, they counted nearly 500 pupils. The funds for this most beneficial work was supplied by the exertions of the excellent successor to the Rev. Dr. Coyle, the present estimable pastor, Dr. Kieran.

The immediate wants of the poor being first attended to, the education of the wealthier classes required their next care. In 1852 two large school-rooms were added, and about fifty pupils of the higher class instructed.

In July, 1857, Mr. Regan, a respectable inhabitant of Dundalk, desirous of testifying his sense of the services of this valuable community, caused a beautiful Gothic chapel to be added to the Convent, at his own expense; and, at present, the Nuns are enlarging the house, in order to accommodate more of the sisterhood, and thereby increase their usefulness.

They visit the sick poor of the town, the patients in the County Infirmary, and the inmates of the Gaol. They now number seventeen. One has gone to receive her reward since they founded the Convent of Dundalk. The average attendance in the National School, under the care of the Sisters, is 350. They also contrive to maintain ten destitute orphans in a small orphanage. This is mainly achieved by a monthly collection for the sick and orphans, contributed by the charitable inhabitants of Dundalk.

A Conference of the Society of St. Vincent De Paul is established in Dundalk; and the members visit the poor without religious distinction—thereby displaying true Christian charity.

THE NATIONAL SCHOOLS.—The National School, No. 1, which was that first established in Dundalk, is attached to the chapel of the Dominicans, who, faithful to the traditions of their order, devote themselves to imparting instruction to the youth of the humbler classes. The other Schools, Nos. 2 and 3, occupy the tasteful and admirably arranged building designed by John Neville, Esq., C.E. It is in the later English style; and is not only ornamental outside, but lofty and spacious within. We were much pleased with the zeal and ability of Messrs. Moley and Mohan, the Masters. They were both surrounded by about 150 boys of the district. The attendance is the best proof of the skill of the teacher, and the character of the Masters of the National Schools of Dundalk is deservedly high.

The Female National School is, as we have already seen, under the care of the Sisters of Mercy, with an average attendance of 350.

HISTORY OF DUNDALK PRESBYTERIAN CONGREGATION.

The earliest historical notice of this ancient and respectable congregation dates from the time of the Commonwealth, when no less than 130 Independent ministers followed in the train of the great Protector's armies, and settled in all the leading towns and villages of Ireland. In 1655 there were altogether 150 Protestant ministers in our land receiving State endowment, in sums varying from £80 to £200 per annum (sums corresponding to nearly £800 and £2,000 in the present day), of whom 130 were Independent; 12 Episcopalian; and 6 Presbyterian. The minister of Dundalk—the Rev Joseph Bowesfield, an Independent—received from the public Treasury the sum of £110 a-year. How long Mr. Bowesfield remained minister, or by whom he was succeeded, or at what period the congregation became Presbyterian, is not clearly known; but we know from our historical records that, up to the Revolution, Presbyterianism increased rapidly in Ireland; and that, in 1702, there were no less than 140 Presbyterian congregations, organized into 9 presbyteries, and annually convened in synod.

In the year 1710 the synod of Ulster—which, in the case of the Dundalk congregation, extended its jurisdiction into the province of Leinster—resolved to send out nine ministers to preach the Gospel in Irish to the Irish-speaking population —one of whom was the Rev. Patrick Plunket, minister of Glasslough, County Monaghan, grandfather to the late celebrated Lord Chancellor Plunket, and great-grandfather of the present Right Rev. Thomas Lord Plunket, Bishop of Tuam. In 1717 there were three additional ministers appointed, one of whom was the Rev. Patrick Simpson, of Dundalk, and also three probationers. This minister must have held a high position in the church about this time; for Dr. Reid informs us—"that the synod agreed to erect a school for teaching to read Irish in the Town of Dundalk, to which each presbytery was to contribute a certain sum; and they further resolved to print editions of the Catechism and a short grammar, in the Irish tongue." All these measures were carried into execution; but some of them not till the following year—1718. The Rev. Patrick Simpson was allied to the M'Neill family, whose descendants still reside in the district. We may mention, as a piece of local history, that two brothers, named Malcolm and Archibald M'Neill, officers in the army of William the Third, landed in Dundalk in 1688, fought the great battle of Ballymascanlon, and succeeded in taking the castle, which was formerly occupied by the Scanlons, a Celtic family, who were afterwards driven into exile. William the Third gave those brothers the castle, with a portion of land, for ever, as a reward for their gallantry and valour. Soon after their settlement, they brought over from the island of Islay two Presbyterian ministers—the Rev. Patrick Simpson and the Rev. Mr. Drummond—one of them to settle in Dundalk, and the other beside Scanlon Castle, where Malcolm M'Neill built a Presbyterian church, on the site of which now stands the parish church of Ballymascanlon. Malcolm soon died, and was buried in the graveyard beside this church. The Rev. Mr. Simpson married the sister of his excellent patron, but they had no family; and he received besides a farm of forty acres, at Mount Pleasant, on the site of which now stands the residence of the present Sir John Macneill—one of Ireland's greatest engineers—son of Torquil Park Macneill, to whom the property was left by the minister of Dundalk.

Archibald M'Neill, the other brother, gave £100 towards building a meeting-house in Dundalk. This old house stood in a lane between Bridge-street and Linenhall-street; and was sold by the congregation in 1839, when the present new church was opened. It is an interesting fact that, in the year 1826, the descendants of Simpson and Drummond, who still inhabit the island of Islay, visited this country for the purpose of instituting inquiries after their ancestors, who had left the land of their birth 120 years before to preach the Gospel in Ireland. Mr. Simpson died in 1760, at the patriarchal age of ninety-nine, and is interred in the Ballymascanlon graveyard, beside his successor in the congregation, the Rev. Mr. Drummond, who died on 3rd July 1778. Mural tablets have been placed over their graves, with now almost illegible inscriptions.

The Rev. Mr. Bryson—of whom we know nothing—succeeded Mr. Drummond, and died at Dundalk. He is also buried at Ballymascanlon. The Rev. Mr. Lindsay was minister of Dundalk in 1798; but the political troubles of the time led him to emigrate to America. His successor was the distinguished linguist, the Rev. Dr. Neilson, who was ordained in April, 1799. It was necessary at this period that the minister of Dundalk should be able to preach in the Irish tongue; and the family traditions affirm that the new minister applied himself so assiduously to the study of Irish as to be able in a fortnight after his ordination, to address his audience in that difficult language. Dr. Neilson is still well known by his Irish grammar, which is, perhaps, one of the very best extant; and was equally distinguished for his abilities in general classics. He was appointed Professor in the Belfast Academical Institution in the year 1816; and almost the latest news that he heard upon his death-bed was his appointment to the more important Professorship of Greek in the Glasgow University. There is no doubt, whatever, that Dr. Neilson was a Unitarian in his doctrinal sentiments, though he was anything but controversial, and confined himself, in his pulpit addresses, to that dry, didactic moralism which always characterized the Arian party in the synod. The Neilson family joined the Remonstrants in 1830. The Rev. James Neilson, of Downpatrick, County Down, brother of the Dundalk minister, was also a distinguished linguist, and maintained for many years one of the best classical schools in the North of Ireland, at which the great majority of the Roman Catholic youth in the North were prepared for their collegiate course. The only surviving minister of the Neilsons is the Rev. Samuel Craig Neilson, son of James, minister of the Downpatrick Unitarian meeting-house, who is also distinguished for his scholarship. We should mention that the late William Neilson, Esq., elder in Mary's-abbey, Dublin, was a son of Dr. Neilson, of Dundalk.

The next minister of Dundalk was the Rev. Mr. Davidson, a native of Bangor, who remained until 1825, when he became the minister of a Unitarian chapel in London, which died out under his ministry. He is four or five years dead. It is evident that the Dundalk congregation was not entirely exempt from that Unitarian element which entered, in larger or smaller proportions, into the composition of many of the northern congregations before the year 1830. The following extract from the minutes of Dundalk session throw some light upon this point:—

" A meeting of the Presbyterian congregation of Dundalk was convened in the meeting-house after Divine service this 11th day of October, 1829, to decide upon the question—

Whether or not we shall adhere to our connexion with the Synod of Ulster? when it was resolved—'1st. That we, as a congregation, do not wish to separate from the Synod of Ulster, or withdraw from its care; 2nd. That we hereby appoint James Dickey, Esq., elder, to attend the meeting of the presbytery of Armagh, to be held at Markethill, on Tuesday, the 13th inst., to vote according to the above resolution. Joseph Andrew Neilson, M D., acting session-clerk."

The Arian element, however, lost its power under the ministry of the Rev. William Cunningham, who was ordained in 1825, and died of consumption in 1827, at a very early age. This young minister was one of the most devoted and successful in the Synod of Ulster. His ministry left a hallowing influence behind, and many of the Dundalk members still speak of the promising and pious youth with tears in their eyes, and can recall some of his soul-stirring sermons and addresses. He was a native of the County Derry, and had a poetic and elegantly cultivated mind, so as to remind many of the sainted Robert Murray M'Cheyne. After his death, the Rev. James Beatty, who was born in the neighbourhood of Clogher, County Tyrone, was settled over the congregation. It was during his pastorate that the beautiful new church was erected, at an expense of over £3,000. Mr. Beatty's labours are still fresh in the memory of the congregation. He was cut off in the prime of life, by typhus fever, and is interred beside the church he so ably assisted to erect; and his sorrowing flock have erected over his remains a very handsome monument, with an entablature which tells of his life and labours, and his lamented death. He was twenty-four years minister of Dundalk; and died in December, 1851, aged fifty-one. His successor, the Rev. William M'Hinch, was a native of Donaghadee, County Down, and was ordained in the year 1852. It is only two years since the grave closed over the remains of this talented and devoted minister of Christ, who died, like his predecessor, of fever caught in the discharge of his pastoral duties. The present minister, the Rev. Robert Black, formerly of Ballycopeland, on the Ards coast, is a native of County Monaghan, and is well fitted, by his talents and piety, to sustain the cause of Presbyterianism in the frontier line of Northern Protestantism.

The Dundalk Presbyterian congregation, under the pastorate of its present minister, the Rev. Robert Black, erected, during the year 1862, a manse, at the cost of £600, in the Ladywell field, where a fine plot of land—five statute acres—was granted in perpetuity, by the Earl of Roden, to trustees, for the benefit of the congregation, at the same rent paid for it by tenants at will. They have also built a schoolhouse in the rere of their church, capable of accommodating 100 children, at an outlay of £200. School was opened in it in May, 1863, with 55 children on the roll, which was placed under the care of the National Board of Education.

WESLEYAN CHAPELS.

There are two houses of Divine worship, of Methodists, in Dundalk, which are handsome buildings, eligibly situated. One is attended by the Primitive, the other by the New Methodist Connexion.

THE COURT HOUSE.

This truly classic building stands in Market-square, and is well worthy of being the Temple of Justice for the capital of a county. The portico is similar to that of the Temple of Theseus, at Athens, with Doric columns rearing their massive bulk from base to cornice. The interior contains the usual distribution of court-houses—jury rooms, &c.; and we were struck with the superiority it presents to many buildings of like purpose with which we are acquainted. The gallery, containing the jury-box, has been judiciously lowered, so as to bring that important body within reasonable distance of the Bench, and the Judge is not now obliged to strain his neck while addressing them. The room appropriated for the deliberations of the Grand Jury is 35 feet long, by 25 feet wide, and of proportionate height. Every facility is given for the progress of business, and the presence, when necessary and fitting, of the public. A portrait of Her Majesty adorns this room—presented to the County of Louth Grand Jury, in 1851, by Thomas Fortescue, of Ravensdale Park, M.P., now Lord Clermont, a nobleman universally respected and esteemed.

THE COUNTY GAOL.

The County Gaol is situated in a fine, healthy locality. This commodious and well-arranged prison was built from the plans furnished by John Neville, Esq., C.E. It is adapted to carry out the separate and silent system. Attended by the intelligent Governor, Mr. Lamb, we went through the various wards, and into many of the cells, of this building, which we found in a highly creditable state.

The Board of Superintendence meet on the first Friday of every month. The present officers connected with the Gaol are:—Inspector—E. H. Croker, Esq.; Governor—Francis Lamb, Esq.; Protestant Chaplain—Rev. Marcus Rainsford; Roman Catholic Chaplain—Rev. John Tandy, C.C.; Presbyterian Chaplain—Rev. Robert Black; Physician and Surgeon—E. G. Brunker, M.D., F.R.C.S.I.; Apothecary—Mr. Francis Scott.

DUNDALK POOR LAW UNION.

THE area of statute acres in this Union embraces 104,434, in the Counties of Louth, Armagh, and Monaghan. The Electoral Divisions number 19. The Poor Law Valuation, on 29th September, 1861, amounted to £101,699. During the year ended on 29th September, 1861, the number of persons relieved indoor was 1,434; outdoor, 622. The cost for indoor paupers was £1,938; outdoor, £330; and it speaks well for the management of the Union that the poundage of expenditure, on valuation, did not exceed eightpence. The present Board of Guardians and officials are:—

Chairman—Right Honourable Lord Clermont.
Vice-Chairman—Sir John J. Robinson, Bart.
Deputy Vice-Chairman—Michael Kelly, Esq.
Clerk and Returning Officer—Mr. James Murphy.
Master and Matron—John Gill and Anne M'Donell.

CHAPLAINS.

Established Church—Rev. Joseph G. Rainsford.
Roman Catholic—Rev. John Marmion.
Presbyterian—Rev. Robert Black.

Medical Officer—John Gartlan, M.D.
Relieving Officer—John Daly.

MEDICAL OFFICERS OF DISPENSARY DISTRICTS.

Barronstown—William Pollock, M.D.
Carlingford—Thomas Barber, M.D.
Dromiskin—Joseph Callan, M.D.
Dundalk—John Browne, M.D.
Louth—Matthew Kearney, M.D.
Ravensdale—William Ponsonby Deverell, M.D.

The Workhouse is built on Ballybarrack Hill, the site of which was given, rent free, by Lord Clermont. The Government advanced £9,100 towards the expenses of building. It is capable of containing 920 inmates, and was opened on 29th September, 1850. The Institution appears well managed, and the inmates are employed in industrial pursuits—such as spinning, weaving, shoemaking, tailoring, embroidery, and in agricultural operations. If this would teach our poor people improved habits of farming, and such knowledge of trades as would be of use in their daily life, the country would bear the burthen of poor-rates with more patience, and pay them with more willingness than at present.

THE COUNTY LOUTH INFIRMARY.

This admirable Institution is situated on the elevated ground at the southern outlet of the town, and is a substantial, well-built edifice, erected by subscription. The original County Infirmary was opened in 1755, but increasing requirements demanded a more suitable structure; whereupon the benevolent inhabitants caused the present house to be built. It cost over £3,000, and was opened, in 1835, for the reception of surgical and medical cases. Here the most scrupulous attention is paid to the patients. There are separate wards for males and females—the former containing accommodation for thirty, the latter fifteen beds. The institution, as appears by the abstract of accounts from 6th January, 1862, to 5th January, 1863, is supported by—

	£	s.	d.
A County grant of	750	0	0
Government grant of	85	15	2
Interest from private fund, . .	11	11	0
Subscriptions and donations, . .	54	2	0
Constabulary patients, . . .	3	8	4
Incidentals, ...	4	3	0
Balance on foot of former account, .	129	18	3
Total, . . .	£1,038	17	9
The disbursements for same period, .	952	3	2
Balance, . . .	£86	14	7

The medical department is under the charge of E. G. Brunker, Esq., M.D., whose high professional and personal worth is duly estimated, not merely in Dundalk, but throughout the country. He is ably seconded by the resident Apothecary, Mr. Scott; and the arrangement of the wards attests the care and attention of the Matron, Mrs. Clarke. The Treasurer and Secretary is A. Shekleton, Esq.; and the economical manner in which the money is expended may be best judged from the annual reports.

Patrick Byrne, a worthy representative of the Irish bards, lately expired in this Infirmary. He was blind, like his distinguished predecessor, Carolan; but the loss of sight, perhaps, rendered his sense of hearing more acute, and in no way interfered with his ability as a first-rate performer. His talents and high character gained him the esteem and regard of those who possessed his acquaintance; while his social qualities, his gifts of song, and minstrelsy, secured him a friendly greeting, not only in his native land, but in the sister kingdom. He was taken ill at Sibthorpe's Hotel, in Dundalk; and, suffering from bronchitis, his friends removed him thence to the excellent County Infirmary, where the attention of Dr. Brunker, and his assistants, secured him every care that skill could suggest. The hour, however, for his term of life to close was at hand; and he resigned his spirit into the hands of his Maker on the 8th April, 1863.

LITERARY INSTITUTIONS.

Previously to the year 1844 there had existed a Literary Society in Dundalk, supported by an annual subscription of one guinea from each of the members. One of the chief promoters of this society was the Rev. Elias Thackery, Vicar of Dundalk; and the Rev. James Beatty, Presbyterian Minister, was Secretary. This society seems to have confined its labours to the purchase of books and the formation of a small library, which was kept in a room in the Free School. From causes now unknown the number of subscribers gradually diminished; and it ceased to exist as a Society about 1844, when it was proposed to form a Mechanics' Institute. Thereupon the Secretary, together with the surviving members, generously offered to hand over to the custody of the Committee of the Mechanics' Institute their books, amounting to nearly five hundred volumes. The offer was accepted, and the books then obtained formed the nucleus of the present Free Public Library.

In 1844, when Mechanics' Institutes were extensively spread over this and the sister countries, the idea of forming one in Dundalk, on the plan originated by Dr. Birkbeck, was taken up by Mr. Andrew Inglis, foreman of Mr. Shekleton's foundry, and Mr. Holland, manager of the Gas Works.

On the 3rd of June, 1844, a meeting, at which John Straton, Esq., presided, was held, for the purpose of taking the subject into consideration; and having been fully approved of at a subsequent meeting, the "Dundalk Mechanics' Institute" was formed. Rules and regulations were adopted for its government, and a Committee, consisting of twenty-one members, a President, four Vice-Presidents, a Secretary, and Treasurer, were appointed. The following is the list of the first Committee:—

President—John Straton, Esq.

Vice-Presidents—Robert Haig, Thomas Coleman, Dr. Brunker, Patrick Wynn.

Committee—Dr. Gartlan, Alexander M'Donald, John Moony, J. M'Nugent, Peter Runde, Richard Dunphy, John Merron, Alexander Graham, Andrew Inglis, William Falkiner, Patrick Denvir, John Holland, Patrick Clark, William Henderson, William Banbury, Dr. Martin, John Dockery, William Robson, Richard Berry, James Renfrew.

Dr. Browne, Secretary; John Coleman, jun., Treasurer.

During the first year 195 members were enrolled, and in the second year sixty were added to its numbers. In 1848 there were 211 members in connexion with the Institute, which was the largest number ever reached. From that period the number of its adherents gradually diminished, so that, in 1853, it might be said to have ceased to exist; and on its ruins was erected the "Literary and Scientific Institute," which existed for some years. At this period the library, which had been handed over by the Committee of the Mechanics' Institute, consisted of upwards of 2,000 volumes, chiefly works on science and general literature.

About this time an Act had been passed by the Legislature giving power to Town Commissioners *in England* to form and support free public libraries for the people out of the municipal rates; and shortly after its enactment, mainly through the instrumentality of Chichester Fortescue, Esq., M.P. for the County of Louth, the provisions of this Act were extended to Ireland, of which Dundalk was the second town in this country to take advantage.

Accordingly, in the year 1857, a Free Public Library was formed in Dundalk, to which the books of the Literary and Scientific Institution were transferred. The library consists, at present, of upwards of 3,000 volumes. It is open every evening from six till ten o'clock. It is very advantageously circumstanced, having, in the new Exchange Buildings, two most commodious rooms—one for the books of the library, and the other, a large, well-ventilated reading room, lighted with gas, and freely open to the public. This room is well supplied with newspapers and periodicals. Books are lent out to persons living within the limits of the borough at the small charge of one penny per week.

Besides the Free Public Library, there are "The Young Men's Christian and Literary Association," presided over by J. Barton, Esq.; and "The Young Men's Catholic Association," of which the Very Rev. Dean Kieran is the President.

The former meets every Thursday evening in the Market

House, when essays are read and discussed, on religious, literary, and scientific subjects; and the latter has a room in the Exchange Buildings, where the members have a small library, and meet every evening.

THE DUNDALK PRESS.

The year 1829 witnessed the establishment of the first newspaper in Dundalk. Previously the public events of the County of Louth were announced in the Drogheda and Newry papers; but in 1829 an intelligent gentleman, named Brett, encouraged by liberal contributions from influential individuals, started a journal called *The Louth Free Press*, in Dundalk. For some time it was published twice each week; but having become anything but a prosperous speculation, was reduced to a weekly issue; and, after a brief struggle, ceased altogether. The papers now in circulation are *The Newry Examiner and Louth Advertiser*, established in 1830, P. Dowdall, proprietor—published Wednesdays and Saturdays—advocates the improvement of the condition of tenant farmers—agricultural and commercial industry; and is of liberal politics.

The Dundalk Democrat, established in 1849, proprietor, J. Carton—published Saturdays—advocates the rights of Ireland and the Irish; and is strongly opposed to Whig policy.

The Dundalk Express, established in 1860, proprietor, G. M'Carthy—published Saturday—advocates the just rights of the people, and is uninfluenced by sectarian or political parties.

LOUTH HORTICULTURAL SOCIETY.

THIS useful society for the promotion of the choicest embellishments of green-house and garden, was instituted in 1856, under the appropriate presidency of the Right Hon. Lord Clermont, and the following Committee:—Major the Hon. A. G. F. Jocelyn; John Murphy, Esq.; Acheson Thompson, Esq.; Patrick James Byrne, Esq.; Travers Wright, Esq.; A. Blackburne, Esq.; Peter Russell, Esq.; William Skelton, Esq.; Rev. Somerset L. Townsend, D.D.; Robert Haig, Esq.; William Ruxton, Esq.; William Woolsey, Esq.; Myles Taaffe, Esq.; Richard Macan, Esq. Hon. Sec. and Treasurer—Mr. John Farquharson.

The list of members testifies the general approval of the objects of this society, so conducive to develop refined tastes, and add to the intellectual enjoyments of all who love "The Scriptures of the Earth," as flowers have been truly designated.

DUNDALK HOUSE.

DUNDALK HOUSE, anciently the residence of the Earl of Clanbrassil, now part of Lord Roden's estate, is nearly opposite the church, and situated in a very extensive demesne, finely wooded. The house has undergone many alterations, and was formerly much larger than it stands at present. None of the rooms are remarkable for size, but contain a number of interesting portraits. Here is the picture of Anne Hamilton, daughter of Lady Mordaunt, and sister of the celebrated Earl of Peterborough. Also there looks down from the walls the intelligent face of James Hamilton, of

Tollymore. Beside them, the venerable aspect of Harriet, Countess Dowager of Clanbrassil, who died 10th June, 1792, having reached the ripe age of fourscore and six years. She survived, for nearly half a century, James, Viscount Limerick, afterwards Earl of Clanbrassil, who died in 1758. There is a fine portrait of the present Earl of Roden; and on the walls are a number of prints and family pictures. King William the Third, and his Queen, Mary, look solemnly from their frames. Some of the furniture is of antique formation; a chair is marked 1742. Overhead are bedchambers with stuccoed ceilings, and ancient chimney-pieces. It is said King William the Third rested here, after his journey from the North, when on his conquering way to the Boyne Water.

In the hall of Dundalk House we noticed a very tasteful marble urn, with the inscription:—

IN REMEMBRANCE
OF THE MANY VIRTUES
OF THE HONORABLE GEORGE JOCELYN
THIS URN WAS ERECTED,
WHO,
TO THE INEXPRESSIBLE AFFLICTION
OF ALL WHO HAD EVER KNOWN HIM,
DEPARTED THIS LIFE 10TH MARCH, 1798,
AGED 36 YEARS,
LAMENTED, BELOVED, AND ESTEEMED.

In the grounds, beneath a shady tree, is a monument in the Italian style—a vase on a pedestal, inscribed:—

Θ . Κ
ΚΛΑΝΒΡΑΣΣΙLLΟΣ
ΜΟΝΘΕRΜΕRΩ
ΦΙΛΩ ΗΑΤΤΑΤΩ
ΜΝΕΙΑΣ ΧΑΡΙΝ.

The Earl of Roden informed us this tasteful memorial was erected by the Earl of Clanbrassil in honour of his dear friend, the Marquess of Monthermer, son of the Duke of Montague.

LOUTH FARMING SOCIETY.

THE importance of placing sound agricultural knowledge within the reach of all classes, and affording the most demonstrative proofs of progress by competitive examinations, caused a Farming Society to be established in the County of Louth, in the year 1817, one of the earliest formed in Ireland. After doing much service in its day, it was succeeded by the present society, established 3rd February, 1830, for the encouragement of agriculture, rural improvements, and domestic economy, in the County of Louth and County of the Town of Drogheda. According to the excellent rules of this society, its qualification for membership comprises all persons residing within the district, or possessing property within it. The subscription is twofold:—Two guineas a year give a right to be elected to the general committee, or any other office of the society; and one guinea a year entitles the subscriber to be a general member, to vote upon the general concerns of the society, and to be on any local committee. To ensure the exclusion of all topics likely to disturb the harmonious working of the society, Rule No. 12 provides:—"No conversation on religion, or general or local politics, shall, on any account, be permitted." A spring and autumn general meeting is held, when premiums are awarded for "the improvement of agriculture, breeding of cattle, planting, and improved domestic economy, cleanliness and comfort in cottages, horticulture, and also for the encouragement of industry and good behaviour among servants and labourers in husbandry."

More important subjects than are embraced in this 19th Rule could not occupy any body of Irishmen. Rescuing the poorer tenants and farm labourers, from the wretched hovels in which they drag on a miserable existence—inducing habits of industry and good behaviour, in place of idleness and dissipation, are labours worthy of a Farming Society having the welfare of the country in view; and we wish this rule was generally adopted throughout Ireland. That excellent nobleman, Lord Clermont, has set an example in supplying the farm labourers with cottages containing several rooms, which, with a quarter or half rood of land, are let for a trifle.

The regulations respecting the ploughing match, held at Newtown Darver, 4th February, 1863, afforded all classes a fair field for competition:—

"First Class.—Open to all farmers, farmers' sons, or hired ploughmen in the service of members of the society, living in any barony of the county, who have obtained premiums at any previous ploughing match of the society.

"Second Class.—Open only to farmers and farmers' sons who have never obtained premiums at any previous ploughing match of the society.

"Third Class.—Open only to hired ploughmen in the service of members of the society, who have never obtained premiums at any previous ploughing match of the society."

In addition, the Royal Agricultural Society's prizes of £2 and £1, to the best and second best managers of ploughs in the entire field, called forth the skill and energy of all those whose position debars them from the more costly premiums of the society.

We learn from the efficient Honorary Secretary, Alexander

Shekleton, Esq., that the society is very well supported. The annual amount of subscriptions is about £120, and of this sum about £80 is annually paid in premiums. The list of members for the year 1862 bears the respected names of all the principal noblemen and gentlemen of the district; and that blending of creeds which is so desirable in this country, where religion, "the sacred name of religion," to use the words of the celebrated Father O'Leary, "has too often been a wall of separation to keep men asunder."

The following account of the last general meeting of this society, held in July, 1863, bears sufficient proof of the important service conferred by its working upon the agriculture of the district around Dundalk:—

"LOUTH FARMING SOCIETY.—1863, JULY 24.

"The annual show of this society was held on this day, and, although the quantity of stock, farming implements, &c., exhibited were not on a large scale, it was admitted that the quality was very superior. The principal exhibitors in live stock were Lord Clermont, C. S. Fortescue, M.P., Sir A. Bellingham. In agricultural implements, Mr. James Shekleton's attracted general attention for the large display and high quality of the articles. Mr. Kearney also exhibited a very superior class of ploughs, &c., and got first prize for a drill plough. The Messrs. Russell, millwrights, were awarded first prize for a portable steam threshing mill, which was very much admired for its compactness, working powers, &c. In the stock, Lord Clermont was awarded first prize, in Class A, for an entire horse, for swine, a four-year-old bull, five hoggets, and five one-year-old ewes, &c. J. T. Dickie, Esq., Clonaleenan, won first prize for a beautiful coal-black colt, two years old, intended for breeding purposes. Sir A.

Bellingham was awarded one prize in Class A, for a one-year-old bull, a magnificent-looking animal for its age; a one-year-old heifer, very beautiful; and a milch cow. R. Byrne, Esq., J.P., received first prize in the second class, for a splendid two-year-old heifer, and a three-year-old milch cow; also for a sow and her young. T. Bradford, Esq., of Carnbeg, first prize in Class B, for one and two-year-old heifers, and for turkeys, geese, and a pair of ducks. Mr. Doran, of Glyde Farm, besides other prizes, got, in Class B, first and second prizes for milch cows. In the evening, the friends of the society sat down to an excellent dinner, supplied by Sibthorpe, of the Commercial Hotel, in his usual good style, where, after discussing the viands provided, the usual toasts were proposed, and the proceedings terminated in a most satisfactory manner."

TRADE AND COMMERCE.

Built on the margin of the sea, Dundalk possesses the advantage of a harbour, and the Irish Parliament voted considerable sums of money for its improvement. In 1767, £2,000, and £400 a-year for eight years, was granted for this end. It appears to have been expended in constructing a rampart from the Soldier's Point towards the Black Rock, which effectually prevented the sea flowing over and submerging the land known as the Southern Marsh. According to *Wright's Louthiana*,* "the town is very advantageously situated for a most extensive inland trade, and the port is very safe for shipping. The bay has good moorings at all times of the moon, in four to upwards of eight fathoms water, with

* Published in 1747.

very good land-marks, either for bringing up or making the harbour; and in crossing the bar at high water, on ordinary neap tides, there is from 15 to 18 feet water. Besides many other good qualities, the bay abounds with all sorts of fish customary in the Channel. No true account of this port being to be met with, I have been tempted to say more in this place than perhaps was required."

In the reign of her present Majesty, the 3rd & 4th Vict., c. 119, was passed. The Act provides for the regulating, preserving, and improving the port and harbour of Dundalk, and a sum of £20,150 has been expended under the direction of the eminent engineer, Sir John Macneill. The river has been straightened, a dredging machine of 17-horse power purchased, and ponts constructed. The present channel, from Soldier's Point to the Bar, has been deepened by the dredging machine, and improved by the abolition of several weirs, so that vessels drawing 16 feet of water can come up to the quays. The course of the channel is well defined, and efforts are directed to improve it still more.

Within the Bar, on the south side, a lighthouse, 45 feet high, has recently been erected, on the screw-pile principle, which much facilitates the safe progress of ships, and a fog-bell gives warning during the prevalence of these dangerous vapours. There are 22 licensed pilots belonging to the port. The income, arising chiefly from tonnage and ballast dues, amounted, in 1860, to £8,000. The Harbour Commissioners at present are:—President—The Right Hon. the Earl of Roden. Chairman—Robert Haig, Esq., J.P. Hon. Major Jocelyn, W. Robson, Michael Kelly, J.P.; P. Wynne, J.P.; Richard Verdon, H. Backhouse, E. H. Macardle, James Shekleton, J. Farrell, J. C. Duffy, S. Brown, J. E. Caraher, J.P.; James Murphy, and J. O'Hare, Esqrs. Solicitor—

Patrick James Byrne, Esq. Engineer—Mr. Cahill. Secretary—Mr. Thomas J. Pooler. Harbour Master—Mr. John Lawless.

The Steam Packet Company have built a large warehouse, and expended a considerable sum in improving their quay; and the line of quays, recently extended by Mr. Russell, has much shortened the distance between the lower portion of the town and harbour. In Mr. Marmion's valuable work,* a full account of the commerce, tonnage of vessels entering inwards and clearing out of this port, and other details, is given, and to this work we refer the reader for the most carefully-written particulars relative to the trade of Dundalk. We must be more brief in our summary. Steamers ply regularly to Liverpool, taking about 150 tons each trip, chiefly oatmeal, wheat, barley, oats, butter, bacon, lard, hams, eggs, linens, flax, and other articles, computed at 23,400 tons annually, besides horses, cows, sheep, and pigs, averaging 650 each trip, and 72,150 annually. The imports, which consist of Indian corn, flour, groceries, box and bale goods, amount to about 18,200 tons annually.†

In former years, when Irish manufacture was more general than at present, the linen trade was carried on here. Lord Dungannon, the proprietor of the town (temp. Charles the Second) fostered this branch of native industry, and a Linen Hall was built in Bridge-street. Then the bleach-greens of Ravensdale were in full operation; but now no produce of the loom gives a snowy aspect to the landscape, or diversifies the emerald hue of the plains. In later years, we have seen, the efforts of Primate Boulter established a cambric factory here,

---

* *History of the Maritime Ports of Ireland*—"*Dundalk*"—pp. 288–298.

† *Thom's Official Directory for* 1863, p. 1088.

and the extensive ranges of building, now occupied as Cavalry Barracks, was built for the weavers employed.* The Parliament granted bounties for the encouragement of this branch of industry, which gave the name of Parliament-square to the locality.

We hoped to find some traces to account for the decline of this concern, which started under such favourable auspices, but in vain. We then directed our inquiries, suggested by the *Ulster Archæological Journal*, to ascertain whether the French weavers were Huguenots; and if so, whether any clergyman accompanied them; but the only person able to give us any information was an old man, named Flanagan, whose recollection was much impaired by time and disease. We ascertained from him that he worked as a weaver, towards the close of the last century, where the Barracks now stand. His mother was a Frenchwoman, daughter of Stephen Gidleau, who had come over with many others. Stephen Gidleau was a Huguenot; but his wife was a Catholic, and had some brothers priests in France. No clergyman came over from France, and the workmen attended the Protestant Church. The girls from this factory attended Lady Anne Hamilton's School.

In 1811 a company was formed for erecting a butter crane and corn stores in Dundalk; and, in pursuance of the deed of co-partnership, the stores in Quay-street were built, at a cost of £7,000, and vested in three trustees for the benefit of the shareholders. The present trustees are Messrs. Gillichan, Patrick James Byrne, and J. A. Haig. Mr. Byrne's family supplied many eminent merchants to Dundalk. Mr. William Byrne, by will, dated 3rd December, 1768, left large legacies

* *Marmion's Maritime Ports*, p. 288.

to the poor of this town; and Mr. Henry Byrne was also an extensive merchant.

The distillery formerly worked by Messrs. Malcolm, Brown, and Co., and now in the hands of an excellent man of business, Mr. Haig, produces whiskey held in high repute.

The Messrs. Russell have a rectifying distillery; a sugar bakery, erected so far back as 1784; and Mr. Maxwell was extensively engaged in this trade.

Mr. Wynne's brewery does a fair share of work.

The extensive foundry, engineering establishment, and farming implement factory of Mr. Shekleton, affords constant employment to a great number of tradesmen and labourers. The tobacco manufacture is also carried on under the enterprising energy of Mr. Carroll. There are also tan-yards, salt works, and malt houses. In this branch of industry considerable business was done some years ago by Mr. Peter Cahill. He has since transferred his operations to Dublin, where, we understand, he has realized a handsome fortune.

Close to the district of Seatown is a gigantic windmill, considered the largest in Ireland. Its sails have been idle for many a year, and it has a dilapidated appearance, as if too old for work. Its duties are now performed through the agency of steam, which is employed in the corn and flour mills. Dundalk also possesses several soap manufactories, and one for starch. There are also rope walks and a pin factory. The embroidery of cottons and muslins affords considerable employment to the female population in this district. The milling business is not confined to the town; for at Chanonrock, Waterlodge, Scotchgreen, and Philipstown, are extensive flour mills. The last named was built by the late Mr. James Kieran, at an outlay of £30,000. This gentleman was a most enterprising merchant, and embarked very extensively in foreign trade. Owing to his efforts, the flags of almost every European nation floated over the Dundalk waters. The Russians sent their hemp, flax, and tallow; Sweden and Norway, bar-iron and timber; Holland, seeds and bark; Portugal and Spain, the wines of these countries. The stars and stripes of the great American Continent occasionally flaunted on the breeze; while the British colonies furnished produce to the vast stores of the Messrs. Kieran. About the year 1808 Mr. William Kieran started the victualling trade; and, for the three succeeding years, the greater part of the contracts for supplying the navy of Great Britain with beef and pork was made up in Dundalk. The trade was afterwards less extensively carried on by Messrs. Hogg, Martins, and Fitzpatrick, Anthony Marmion, John Chambers and Co., John Robinson, and others.*

A considerable improvement appears to have lately taken place in the labouring class. "The inhabitants," writes Dr. Browne, in 1838, "are variously employed in the common operations of labour, as handicraftmen, or in trade; and many appear to subsist without any means of permanent support. Being possessed of no manufactures, to give constant employment to the poor, with the exception of a large foundry, distillery, and pin factory, then lately established, many of the poor, during the summer months, suffer much privation. The food of these classes consists chiefly of salt fish, milk, potatoes, and oatmeal. Fuel is rather scarce. The dress of the men is commonly coarse frieze. A great amount of wretchedness then prevailed, owing to want of employment, of education, moral culture, and the

* *Vide Marmion's Maritime Ports*, p. 290, in which this subject is fully treated, and from which our information is derived.

early and ruinous habits of intoxication" We rejoice to say there is not the same amount of destitution now. The introduction of railways into this district has opened many avenues for energy, and commercial enterprise, and unites men of all opinions. "Commerce," as has been well observed, "tends to wear off those prejudices which engender animosity. It unites men by one of the strongest ties—the desire of supplying their mutual wants. More than anything, it disposes towards peace; for without public tranquillity commerce cannot exist."*

The railways already connecting Dundalk with various parts of Ireland are, the Dublin and Belfast Junction Railway, incorporated by Act of Parliament in 1845, of which H. M. Bourne is Secretary; D. J. Rowan, C.E., Resident Engineer; Thomas Cowan, Traffic Superintendent; and Henry Harden, Locomotive Superintendent. The Dundalk and Enniskillen Railway, which commenced working in 1852, is now merged in the Irish North Western Railway, of which the Earl of Erne is Chairman; Thomas Edwards, Secretary; John Dawson, Traffic Manager; John Stokes, C.E., Resident Engineer; and F. Pemberton, Locomotive Superintendent.

The projected Railway to Greenore will connect Dundalk with the deep water at Greenore, from whence steamboats are intended to ply to Holyhead and Liverpool.

DUNDALK STEAM PACKET COMPANY.—Daily Sailings to and from Liverpool. Directors:—Major the Hon. A. Jocelyn, Chairman; E. H. Macardle, W. Robson, B. Brabazon, Thomas Coleman, P. Hegarty, P. Wynne, J.P.; Michael Kelly, J.P.; James M'George, Newry; J. Porteous, Manchester; F. N. Osborne, Julianstown, Drogheda; James

---

* *The New Review*, vol. i., p. 381.

Latimer, Drogheda; Thomas Carroll, Dunleer; John Townley, Tullyvin, County Cavan. Secretary, William M'Master. The half-yearly balance sheet of the company for six months, ending 31st July, 1863, showed net gain, £5,644 6s. 5d.; the receipt from Irish ports for freights, £16,606 17s. 0d.; for passengers, £1,348 10s. 10d. Owing to the daily sailings the expenses were heavy.

COMMERCIAL BUILDINGS.—A public exchange, corn exchange, markets, and other public buildings, having been very much required in this town for many years, the Dundalk Exchange and Market Company was formed in 1856, for the purpose of supplying these desirable objects.

The Company accordingly purchased the old gaol premises, at an expense of £2,000, and proposed to erect thereon a corn exchange, a public exchange, and news-room, with other commodious rooms attached, for public purposes; as also fish, poultry, egg, vegetable, fruit, and general markets, which, on a moderate calculation, would pay four per cent. on the proposed capital of £5,000.

The Earl of Roden, Lord Clermont, Mr. M'Clintock, Brown and Co., and the principal inhabitants of Dundalk, and its vicinity, took shares in this company, and proceeded to erect the exchange, market, and other buildings. Before they were completed, however, a new joint stock company, called The Dundalk Commercial Buildings and Market Company, Limited, was formed in the year 1861, and opened in July, 1862, capital—£7,000, in 70 shares of £100 each; of which P. J. Byrne, Esq., is Solicitor, and Charles M'H. Denvir, Esq., Secretary.

The object of this undertaking was the completion of the exchange, market, and other buildings of a public nature, partly erected, at a cost of £7,045, on the site of the old gaol premises, by the late Dundalk Exchange and Market Company.

The parties interested in the late company, who went security to the Bank, were now the absolute owners of the concern; but did not seek any undue benefit; and were solely actuated by a desire to carry out this important project, and prevent the premises being diverted to any other than the public purposes for which they were intended, and are so admirably suited. The shareholders in the first-named company renewed, and largely increased their subscriptions to the new company; and the capacious Commercial Building in Dundalk is a lasting monument to their spirit and patriotism. The Exchange, Commercial News-room, Free Library, &c., are a credit to Dundalk.

DUNDALK CHORAL SOCIETY.

A CHORAL society was established in 1862 in Dundalk, under very favourable auspices. President—Major the Hon. A. G. F. Jocelyn. Committee — Messrs. Tipping, Neville, J. Shekleton, Supple, W. R. Rogers, jun., P. J. Byrne. Treasurer—M Kelly, J.P. Honorary Secretary—Mr. J. Caulfield.

This society owes its institution chiefly to Mr. Caulfield, Professor of Music, and Organist in Dundalk. He is well supported by honorary and performing members; and concerts are given twice each year, in Spring and Autumn. We extract from that ably-conducted journal, *The Irish Times*, the following account of the success of the Dundalk Choral Society:—

"Nov. 4th, 1863.—The sixth concert of this society came off at the large hall of the Commercial Buildings with much *éclat*. The room was beautifully fitted up for the occasion. On a raised platform, neatly carpeted and hung round with festoons and banners, were placed two powerful-toned piano-fortes. The young musical talent of Dundalk were composed of at least fifty of the finest ladies and dashing young gentlemen in Louth; and appeared to no disadvantage in performing with the trained professional talent brought from Dublin to shed a halo on the entertainment. These latter were the Misses Barry; Mr. and Mrs. J. Caulfield; and the prince of concertina players—Mr. Scates. But on the border town of the cold North they found amateurs that would grace any professional boards; and they must have felt the sweet warbling of the beautiful soprano that rang in melody through the spacious hall—a credit to Dundalk enterprise, as a model of Irish talent—and the fine tenor of our young townsman could not fail to fix their attention. The music selected was of the most popular description; and those, who had the pleasure of hearing the style in which the "Minstrel Boy" was executed, will wish for another treat, so richly and deservedly applauded. The beautiful National Anthem was sung in a manner to entrance royalty itself; and our gracious Queen would be sure to enjoy it in her royal palace. We trust it will yet be encored in her Irish palace. The body of the Hall, which was admirably arranged, and festooned with the consular flags of different nations; flowers and exotics in costly vases, supplied by the generous owner of Lisnawilly House, P. J. Byrne, Esq., was filled by the nobility, gentry, and merchants of this rich town, and county, with a large attendance of the officers of the gallant 4th Dragoon Guards, who are mostly subscribers to this useful society, presented a *tableau* not often to be witnessed in a provincial town. On the whole the display of beauty, talent, and musical acquirements, reflects the greatest credit on the committee of management, the stewards, decorators, and the clever young leader—Mr. James Caulfield. It is to be hoped that such re-unions, comprised of all sects, classes, and disinterested intellect, will be adopted in every town in this beautiful island, where a suitable room can be procured to bring out nature's choicest gift—music—the soothing spirit that allays all our sorrows, and settles all petty prejudices."

The town possesses that valuable institution, which enrolled its millions of disciples through the energetic zeal of the great apostle of temperance—Father Mathew—a total abstinence society. The clergy of various creeds give this great movement their support. The Rev. Joseph G. Rainsford is President, and Messrs. William M'Murray and Richard Gray, Secretaries, of one "Total Abstinence Society;" while the Rev. Dean Kieran is President of another, called "The Catholic Total Abstinence Society."

The manly sport of cricket is not neglected. A cricket club has the advantage of the Presidentship of Major the Honourable Augustus Jocelyn, with M. Kelly, Esq., Vice-President. There is, likewise, the Dundalk Band, of which Mr. F. F. Campbell is Secretary.

The Clerk of the Peace is Thomas Bourne, Esq. *The Collector of Excise* is Charles Dudgeon, Esq.; *Supervisor*, T. A. Bentley, Esq. *The Surveyor of Income-tax*, Thomas Tarleton, Esq. *Customs*—Collector, Joseph Barrett, Esq.; Clerk, Mr. Connelly. *Coast Guard*—Inspecting Commander, Captain Cerjat, R.N. *Consuls*—United States, Sweden and Norway, John E. Caraher, Esq.; Prussia, Joseph Farrell,

Esq. *Registrar of Marriages*—Dr. Browne. *Distributor of Stamps*—Patrick Russell, Esq. *Agent for Lloyd's*—Joseph Farrell, Esq. *Commissioners for taking Affidavits in Law Courts and Chancery*—Patrick Russell, William Robert Rogers, jun., and Richard Needham, Esqrs. *Acknowledging Deeds by Married Women*—P. J. Byrne, Esq. *For High Court of Admiralty and Special Bail*—P. J. Byrne, Esq. *Post Office*—Postmistress, Miss Parks; Clerk, Mr. M'Murray; Assistant, Mr. Davison. *Day Mail* to Dublin, Drogheda, &c., box closes at 2·45 p.m.; *Night*, ditto, at 10 p.m. *Day Mail* to Derry, Enniskillen, Belfast, Newry, &c., at 10·5 a.m.; *Night*, ditto, at 8·40 p.m. The pillar receivers are cleared half-an-hour previous.

MEMOIRS OF EMINENT PERSONS CONNECTED WITH DUNDALK.

We think some biographical sketches of eminent persons, connected with Dundalk, ought to have place in our volume. We find our feelings quickened, and thoughts stirred, by visiting localities famous in story, and reverence the places in which the steps of the good, and wise, have worn foot-prints. There are human beings so dead to the promptings of veneration for such places, they would see, in the Pass of Thermopylæ, only a gap for cattle, and feel no fervour among the ruins of Iona. We do not ambition such readers. We would enlist the sympathies of those who reverence Faughart as the birth-place of St. Brigid, and respect Dundalk as the native place of Richard FitzRalph, Archbishop of Armagh, whose deeds are briefly noticed in our Annals. There are, doubtless, many others in the long line of creation, from the early times to the eighteenth century, deserving of being held in remembrance, but our space does not admit doing them full justice; so we confine our sketches to a few, who, within our own recollection, have earned distinction for this locality. It will be, we trust, a pleasing change to turn from descriptions of the battles, sieges, visitations of famine, contested elections, and other catastrophes recorded in the *Annals of Dundalk*, to the careers of men who climbed the heights of fame by the path of duty, and the exercise of the faculties with which God gifted them. Some passed their lives in retirement, in deep study and research, and do not present any very striking, or prominent points of view; but they teach the useful lesson that, in whatsoever lot a man's life is cast, he may gain distinction, and take his place among the best and noblest; and, without going out of the sphere in which he commenced, he may make for himself a name—honoured while living, and held in reverential regard after his death. This was the case with the

MEMOIR OF REV. WILLIAM NEILSON, D.D., M.R.I.A.

This eminent clergyman was born 12th September, 1774, the fourth of seven sons. His father, Rev. Moses Neilson, D.D., was Presbyterian Minister at Redemon, Co. Down, and enjoyed the reputation of being the best instructor of youth in the north of Ireland. This was of great use to a schoolmaster. On the master the character of the school mainly rests; and, as man is by nature imitative, we cannot be surprised if the sons of such a father were desirous of emulating his fame, and gaining renown as preceptors. This undoubtedly was the case with William, who showed an early aptitude for the study of languages, especially the Greek. His proficiency soon qualified him for the important office of tutor. While yet a mere youth he became an assistant in his father's school, and wrote an English Grammar, which was extensively used through the Province of Ulster. It held its ground, although deemed rather too philosophical, until superseded by the grammar of Lindley Murray.

Having received a first-class education under his father's care, William Neilson proceeded to the College of Glasgow, to prepare himself for the ministry. Here he remained two years, and displayed such superior intellectual acquirements as gained the highest prizes. The best proof of his merit may be found in his becoming licensed by the Presbytery of Antrim in his 19th year; and in 1797 he was ordained Pastor of the Presbyterian Congregation of Dundalk. Here he lived on most friendly terms with his brother clergymen of all denominations. Sincerely impressed with the great spirit of Christianity, he had charity in his heart and on his lips; avoided controversy, and preached moral discourses that went home to every hearer.

While residing in this town he conducted a large boarding and day school, which was attended by pupils of every religious denomination; and it was a legitimate boast for the Principal to record, every year, his young students taking honours in the Protestant University of Dublin, the Roman Catholic College of St. Patrick's, Maynooth, and the Presbyterian Universities in Scotland.

Meantime his pen was not idle. In 1804 appeared his Greek Exercises, on much the same plan that the equally celebrated English schoolmaster, Arnold, adopted for his Latin Exercises. The want of a more methodical Greek Grammar than those in use being felt, the Rev. William Neilson supplied the deficiency; and these books are highly esteemed to this day. The heads of the Glasgow University felt called upon to recognise the services this quiet and unobtrusive Pastor of the Congregation of Dundalk rendered classic literature, and conferred on him the degree of Doctor of Divinity.

Having done so much to promote the study of the English and the Greek languages, Dr. Neilson bethought him another language, not inferior to either, was daily fading from the land—the venerable Gaelic of Erin. The sweet mother tongue was rarely heard amid the green hills, and on the wide plains around Dundalgan;* and those who understood it, neither spoke it with precision, or read with due accent. The cause of this decline of our national language was easily accounted for. The incessant exertions to break every Celtic tie, which bound the Irish to their native land, included the extirpation of language, as well as literature and laws; and, when the native population grew ashamed to speak the language of their sires, we cannot wonder at its general disuse. The study of our native tongue is not overlooked in the Catholic University of Ireland; and the recent publication by that Institution of the *Lectures on the Manuscript Materials of Ancient Irish History*, by the late Professor O'Curry, is a practical proof of earnest desire to promote this hitherto much neglected study.

The value of this language, and the necessity, nay, the duty, of every one proud of the name of Irishman, of having some acquaintance with it, is thus stated by the Rev. Dr. Neilson in the preface to his Irish Grammar:—"That the Irish is the best preserved dialect of the ancient and extensive Celtic language is allowed by the most liberal and enlightened antiquarians. To the general scholar, therefore, a knowledge of it is of great importance; as it will enable him to trace the origin of names and customs, which he would seek in vain in

* *Father O'Molloy's Address to his Countrymen.*

any other tongue. To the inhabitants of Ireland it is doubly interesting. In this language is preserved the venerable annals of our country, with as much fidelity as is usually found in the primitive records of any nation; while the poetic and romantic compositions, with which the Irish manuscripts abound, afford the finest specimens of elegant taste and luxuriant imagination."

The Grammar was published in 1808. It had a high character, which it has not lost, though the Grammar of the late Dr. John O'Donovan is far more comprehensive. The language must have been very generally understood at the close of the last century; for the Rev. Dr. Neilson was fond of preaching in Gaelic.

In connexion with the preaching of his Irish sermons, an amusing incident occurred to Dr. Neilson, in 1798, when many persons traded on their exhibitions of extreme loyalty, and sought to parade themselves before the Government of the day as informers, or, at least, as vigilant watchmen of their neighbours. Dr. Neilson, about that time, had occasion to visit his aged father, and to officiate in his church; and he embraced this opportunity for delivering one of his Irish discourses in Redemon. Due notice having been given, a large assemblage of all denominations attended. Shortly after the commencement of the service, a lieutenant of yeomanry entered, with about a dozen of his soldiers, who, finding all the pews filled, stood on the stairs leading to the pulpit. At the conclusion of the service the lieutenant arrested Dr. Neilson, and seized his manuscript, on the charge that he had been preaching treason and sedition—although neither the officer, nor his his men, understood a single word of the discourse; and although it was universally known that Dr. Neilson and all his family, whilst they entertained liberal and progressive views in religion and in politics, were staunch loyalists, but kept aloof from all extreme parties, and seldom mingled in the arena of religious or political strife. Having been marched to Downpatrick gaol, he was permitted by the Governor to dine and sleep at the house of his brother, who became responsible for his appearance next morning. On entering the Sessions Court he was called upon, first, to read his sermon, and then to translate it into English, as no interpreter could be procured. It was, like all his addresses, a plain, practical, moral discourse, inculcating piety, good-will, and peace. The charge being dismissed, and the Doctor released, he addressed the Bench, with a quiet, humorous smile:—"Gentlemen, you have depended on myself for the correctness of the translation; you might as well have taken my own word as an assurance of my loyalty."

The fluency with which Dr. Neilson spoke, as well as wrote, the Irish language, made him very popular with the peasantry around Dundalk. His kindly disposition, and philanthropic exertions on all occasions that demanded their display, made him a favourite with all classes; and his general ability, his acquaintance, not merely with various European, but Oriental languages, rendered him well known to the most eminent scholars of the age. In conjunction with his brother, the Rev. James Neilson, of Downpatrick, he contributed many excellent articles to the *Classical Journal*, and maintained friendly critical, and philological controversies with some of the renowned *literati* of Europe.

But the connexion which so long, and happily, subsisted between the Rev. William Neilson and Dundalk, like all things earthly, was not to endure. In 1818 he was invited to become Principal of the Classical Department, and Professor of Hebrew, in the Belfast Royal Academical Institution. We make no doubt he did not sever the ties which linked him with Dundalk without deep pain; but, conscious that his services in Belfast were likely to promote the cause next to his heart, after the service of the ministry—the cause of education—he stifled his feelings, and obeyed the call of duty. At the Belfast Institution his great learning, and energetic zeal, contributed to raise that establishment to the eminence it has so justly attained. He was also an excellent musician, and attached to the exquisite melodies of his country, he established and fostered the Irish Harp Society, in Belfast, for the Blind. Another sphere for his exertions was open. He was sought for in the University of Glasgow as Professor of Greek; but his days on earth were numbered. He had a violent rheumatic fever, which caused mortification and death. His career of earnest devotion to the service alike of God and man terminated at Belfast, after a short illness, on the 26th April, 1821, before he completed his forty-seventh year.

The funeral procession, which accompanied his remains from Belfast to the old family burial place at Redemon, was a convincing proof of the universal sorrow felt for his loss. It is supposed that not less than fifteen thousand persons, of all creeds and classes, attended his remains to the grave.

It is an affecting close of this sincere tribute, to the memory of one who served his country in the lot of life in which God placed him, to state that, on the death of the Rev. Dr. Neilson, his aged father, then nearly blind, resolutely took his post. He taught the classes in the Belfast Institution until his son's successor, the learned Rev. Dr. Hinks, was able to remove from the Seminary of Fermoy, County Cork, in which his labours for the cause of classical education are still gratefully remembered, and to take the place in the Belfast Institution, so ably filled by the Rev. William Neilson.

Dr. Neilson left a son and daughter. The former adopted the honourable profession of solicitor, and became the head of the firm William Neilson and Son, Abbey-street, Dublin; now efficiently represented by James Neilson, Esq., married to Mary, eldest daughter of William Corban, Esq., of Bettyville, County Cork. Miss Neilson married the late Dr. S. H Sloane, who held a high position in his profession in the City of Cork, where she still resides; and to her affectionate solicitude for her revered parent we are indebted for some of these details. The late eminent Queen's Counsel, Joseph Neilson, who was successively Assistant Barrister of the King's County, and County Longford, was his nephew; and the Rev. Samuel Craig Neilson, and his brother, whose name combines those of the greatest commanders of the age, both on land or wave—Wellington Nelson—are also nephews.

MEMOIR OF THOMAS COULTER, M.D., M.R.I.A.

Among the distinguished natives of Dundalk no one has higher claims to notice, for zeal in the acquisition of knowledge, or services rendered to science, than the object of this brief memoir. Truly of him has an eminent son of science, the Rev. Dr. Robinson, thus eloquently written:—* "It is an old saying that science has its martyrs as well as religion; we may add, that it has its Forlorn-hope as well as war—urged to the adventure by loftier and nobler impulses, encountering in its pursuit even a greater amount of suffering and danger—but too often unnoticed and unrewarded. Its heroism is of too high an order to be appreciated by vulgar minds. The wise and good, who alone value it, are compara-

* *Biography of Dr. Coulter*, by Rev. R. Robinson, D.D., from *Report of the R.I. Academy*. *Vide* Proceedings R.I.A., vol. ii., p. 553.

tively few and powerless, and the triumphs which it achieves are not in unison with the evil tendencies and passions which unhappily predominate among mankind. Therefore it finds, in the Present, neglect, perhaps scorn or contemptuous pity of the folly which wasted on such unprofitable pursuits the powers that, if otherwise directed, might have commanded wealth, rank, and power. But the Present, ere long, becomes the Past. All of its glittering array, which is not based on the eternal and immutable principles of virtue and truth, moulders into dust; the stream of time, in its flow, washes all that is earthy from the ruin, and leaves, in imperishable brightness, the grains of gold and gem which it contained—the treasures of the Future."

In the vicinity of Dundalk, this wanderer into the regions where science can best be tracked, was born A.D., 1793. He had the misfortune to lose his parents in his childhood; but an attached uncle supplied their place, and, under his care, the boy grew strong and intelligent. When the time arrived for cultivating the fertile mind Dr. Neilson's school was established in Dundalk, and Thomas Coulter had the advantage of the instructions of this excellent teacher. He soon became a favourite pupil. When the learning and diligence of the Rev. Dr. Neilson had prepared him for the university, he entered Trinity College, Dublin, and had the good fortune to be placed under the care of the late eminent Dr. Lloyd, whose high scientific attainments, mild and gentle deportment, modest, unobtrusive worth, survive in his distinguished son, the present Vice-Provost. Dr. Lloyd was not slow to fathom the depths of his pupil's mind. He soon perceived the gleams of rich ore that betrayed the wealth concealed, and directed the student to pursuits best calculated to develop his resources. In chemistry, physiology, entomology, and botany, Coulter went a-head of his fellow-students; and already, during his student days, his collection of Irish insects, and mosses, laid the foundation of his future fame. His love of science was gratified by a visit to France; and in Paris he made dried collections of the botanical productions of the *Jardin des Plantes*. Switzerland has great charms for the botanist. We have witnessed the delight of men, far advanced in years, at finding rare specimens beneath the snow-drifts on the Alpine peaks. Here Coulter spent three or four years, and his labours were incessant. The results appear in the memoir on the Dipsaceæ and his Herbarium, which, including the Mexican and Californian plants, contained the enormous number of about 150,000 specimens. While at Geneva he formed an intimate friendship with a kindred botanist, the late Professor De Candolle, who was an extensive collector.

When Coulter re-visited his native place, in 1824, the man of thirty was very different from the slim, yet active boy, who showed such talent at Dr. Neilson's school. His figure was tall and well-proportioned; he had a pleasing, animated, and agreeable countenance, great strength, and dexterity. He possessed, also, high courage, and that ready presence of mind which is best gained by traversing the great glacial seas, and precipitous passes, of the Alpine or Polar regions. Like the eminent English naturalist, Waterton, whose *Wanderings* show his zeal and courage in the pursuit of *his* favourite science, Dr. Coulter sought the great Southern American Continent as the field for his botanical researches. He became medical attendant of the Real del Montè Mining Company, in Mexico, and soon was employed in collecting specimens of the Mexican Flora. Some idea of the extent of his collection may be formed from his presenting to the Botanic Garden of Trinity College, Dublin, through his friend the Rev. Dr. Lloyd, plants of seventy varieties of *Cacti;* and he sent a like present to Professor De Candolle, for the Botanic Garden at Geneva. One of these, the *Cereus Coulteri*, a tall-growing species, was named in his honour.

He did not find the Mexicans pleasant neighbours. "Here," says the Rev. Dr. Robinson, whose graceful narrative forms the basis of this memoir, "there was found neither probity nor peace. The English companies were regarded as legitimate objects of plunder; and several of those whom they employed retired, in sickness or despair, from their posts."

But it was not mere love of gain, or the post he filled, that attracted Coulter to this unhappy country. He had need to be there for the sake of science; and stay he should, no matter in what position—so it was almost immaterial whether he was called simply "Doctor," or "Captain of the Mines." He filled both posts; for he actually took charge of one of the principal mines—the Veta Grande. A person not possessed of the same extensive range of knowledge, and with it his indomitable energy and perseverance, would have shrunk from this responsibility, or failed in the duty. Not so Thomas Coulter. His scicntific tastes found a new field to range over, and he quickly acquired all the knowledge needed for the mechanical part of the work. Under his care the mine became productive; and, had he been fairly dealt with, would have yielded to him, as to his employers, considerable profit. But these were hard, selfish, worldly men, who used his talents, and denied him his fair recompense; so he departed from among them, and went to California. The strange, perilous, adventurous life of the wanderer in that region has, latterly, been made familiar to the inhabitants of these remote isles, by the spirited novels of Captain Mayne Reid, and the pleasant *Recollections* of Frank Marryatt and other travellers. Coulter experienced adventures to fill volumes. He braved the tomahawk of the Indian, the rifle of the trapper, the revolver of the Mexican, the knife of the Californian. With the thermometer at 140° he traversed the sandy wastes; and neither dangerous reptiles or formidable freebooters stopped his progress. Such exertions could not fail to produce great results. The *Pinus Coulteri*, from the mountain of Santa Lucia, near the mission of San Antonio, in lat. 36°, within sight of the sea, at an elevation of 3,000 or 4,000 feet above its level, preserves his name in many collections in England, and this, his native land. It is a tall-growing pine, having cones a foot long, and six inches in diameter. In addition to his immense Herbarium, he formed a collection of nearly 1,000 specimens of wood, of various descriptions, with specimens of the foliage and inforescence of the parent trees.

Having thus fulfilled his mission, so to speak, he turned his face to the East, and prepared to return to his native land. Our frame, like all that is earthy, is not durable; and time and travel dealt hard blows on the strong and sinewy form of Thomas Coulter. He reached London with his precious cargo, and dreamt of the pleasure he would have in reading his journal, and laying his botanical manuscripts before his friends; but the old adage—

"There's many a slip
'Twixt the cup and the lip,"

was unfortunately exemplified in his case; for, in his journey from London to Dublin, the box he brought in safety so many thousand miles, containing these valuable writings, disappeared, and was lost. All that remains from his pen is the account of Upper California, contained in the fifth volume of the *Journal of the Geographical Society*, and some communications to De Candolle and Mr. Lambert. The preservation of his Herbarium then was his chief care. It became the property of Trinity College, Dublin; and the duty of arranging it was, most properly, confided to the collector. This formed the employment of Coulter's declining years. His constitution, much impaired by his labours, was evidently breaking up; and the energy with which he worked at his specimens, showed he was conscious there was no time to spare. He did not live to perfect the undertaking. The European part was finished, and some progress made in the American specimens, when death put a bar to further work; but the carefully prepared memoranda of each remaining package rendered the completion comparatively easy. He died in 1843, at the age of fifty years, deeply lamented by all who knew him.

MEMOIR OF LAWRENCE MARTIN, M.D., M.R.C.S.

Few natives of Dundalk will read without interest the brief memoir we have compiled of this eminent, yet unobtrusive, member of a highly distinguished profession. His frank guileless nature made him a general favourite, and his early loss was deeply felt.

Lawrence Martin was younger son of John Martin, of Dundalk, merchant, and Arabella, daughter of Richard Dowdall, Esq., grand-daughter of Sir Andrew Aylmer, Baronet, of Balrath Castle, County Meath; lineally descended from the ancient Anglo-Norman family of Hussey, of Weston, and the far-descended O'Neills of Clanєboy. He was born in Dundalk, in the year 1815, and educated under the careful superintendence of the Rev. John R. Darley, A.M., then Principal of the Dundalk Endowed School, now Rural Dean, Rector of Drumgoon, and Incumbent of Dernaclish, near Cootehill, in the Diocese of Kilmore. The distinguished Arctic navigator,

Sir Leopold M'Clintock, was a pupil at this school during Lawrence Martin's schooldays.

Soon as his boyhood ripened into youth young Martin resolved to devote himself to the study of medicine. There was much in this noble profession to awaken his sympathies and recommend itself to his disposition. He gloried in the triumphs which the Dublin school of medicine gained. The skill of Collis, and Cusack, of Crampton, Carmichael, and other eminent surgeons, made him ambitious to belong to the same high calling. His native town reared many eminent medical men. The two brothers, John and Robert Skekleton, acquired the highest reputation. John was a distinguished anatomist, prematurely removed by a dissecting wound. His memory is preserved by a bust placed in the Royal College of Surgeons; Robert still survives, having served his country as an army surgeon. Dr. Alfred M'Clintock ably sustains the credit of Dundalk among the Dublin physicians, while the local practitioners are among the best of the profession.

Having studied in Dublin and Edinburgh, Mr. Martin visited Paris, and availed himself of the advantages which the scientific schools of that great capital afford. Having passed his examination with credit, and obtained his diplomas in the respective Colleges of Surgeons of London, Glasgow, and Dublin, he received an appointment as assistant surgeon in the Royal Navy, which opened for him a new and extended sphere of action. While with his ship on the Canadian station Dr. Martin became endeared to his brother officers; and all who associated with him became impressed with the genial spirit amongst them. He was thoroughly practical. His philanthropy showed no sickly sentimentalism. He was religious without ostentation. When he discharged a duty, or performed a kindness, it was done silently; and his firmness of purpose, when united to the gentleness of his nature, formed a marked contrast. His superiors in rank admitted him to the closest friendship; and he proved that the Irish character is not deficient in any one quality requisite to make a man thoroughly respected.

Thus qualified for private practice, Dr. Martin's friends induced him to settle at home; and he naturally selected his native place as the fitting field for his labours. The respectability of his connexions,* together with the confidence reposed in his professional skill, soon procured him practice; and his *confreres* in Dundalk, who are distinguished for high intellectual and professional attainments, entertained a sincere respect for the mental and social qualities of their young colleague. With that noble expansiveness of soul which teaches that all men are brothers, and that generous sympathy of heart which no difference of religious belief can weaken, these gentlemen welcomed among them one whose high attainments they well knew would prove a source of benefit to the afflicted, and of advantage, in point of social intercourse, to themselves. Having had, as we already observed, very extensive opportunities, Dr. Martin turned them to the best account; and his acquaintance with languages and history, especially that of the country of his birth and his affections, was considerable. He directed all to practical aims; and among the faculty there was none more zealous for the establishment of an organization which would insure the thorough independence of his high and noble profession from any sordid dictation, whether Legislative or Governmental. In this feeling he met ready and hearty response from his brethren in Dundalk.

---

* His sister married the highly esteemed Clerk of the Crown for County Louth, P. J. Byrne, Esq., of Lisnawilly.

In 1845 Dr. Martin was appointed one of the two medical officers of the Dundalk Poor Law Union, having for his colleague the present Dr. John Browne. Perhaps, if he was to have selected from the whole list of the faculty of the United Kingdom—wide and distinguished as that list is—a kindred spirit, his choice would have been Dr. John Browne. Few men possess so high a capacity for business. Active in mind and body, he never allows his faculties to rust—self-reliant, and of proud independence, he never fears to speak the truth; and, on looking into a man's heart, if he there finds honesty of purpose, and a desire to do right, gives him credit for good intentions, and cares nothing about his politics or religion. Devoted to his profession, Dr. Browne has long enjoyed a considerable practice; and, anxious to elevate the working classes of Dundalk, laboured to establish a Mechanics' Institute in the town. His efforts, for a time, were successful. In the notice of the Literary Institutions* of Dundalk, which he has kindly contributed, we find his exertions afforded a copious spring where the sons of toil might slake their thirst for knowledge. From want of perseverance, the Mechanics' Institute did not endure; but Dr. Browne was not to be diverted from his purpose by mutations of fortune. Upon the ruins of the Mechanics' Institute, was upreared the Literary and Scientific Institute, which he fondly hoped would reflect credit on Dundalk, and foster a spirit of intellectual progress among the townspeople; but their ambition for mental improvement was not equal to his. Fortunately, at this period, the Act empowering Towns Commissioners to form and support Free Public Libraries for the People, originally confined to England, was extended to

---

* *Ante* page 319.

Ireland; and, ever on the alert to elevate the character of his humble fellow-townsmen—to induce them to unite industrial with intellectual pursuits—to demonstrate how harmoniously they blend and improve each other—Dr. Browne set to work, and, happily, found among the Town Commissioners many sharers in his benevolent projects. The result we have seen in the establishment of the spacious and excellent Free Public Library, founded in 1857, and now containing over 3,000 volumes of standard works, with a reading room, supplied with newspapers and periodicals. Here the men, who earn their bread with the sweat of their brows, enjoy refreshing food for the mind after the heat and fatigue of the day. Dr. Browne's exertions did not rest here. We are informed it is mainly owing to him the extensive Fair Green, which promises to be a place of healthful recreation, as well as a useful adjunct to the town for commercial purposes, has been placed in its present accessible state; and we believe it is mainly owing to his energy and public spirit, the volume on which we are engaged owes its completion.

There was soon arduous work for Doctors Martin and Browne. The year 1847 was a memorable one in the annals of Ireland. Everywhere stalked through the land sickness and death. Along the margin of the sea, into the lanes bordering the quays, through the crowded alleys, and wretched hovels of the poor of Dundalk, fever spread rapidly. This was a fearful enemy to contend against; but boldly and bravely was it combated. Side by side, like the Roman brothers of old, fought Doctors Browne and Martin. Both had the same kindly dispositions, the same active spirit of philanthropy, the same love for the poor. The following graceful notice of Dr. Martin's efforts to relieve the patients is equally applicable to Dr. Browne:—

"Many and many a day have we observed Dr. Martin, with unvarying punctuality, paying his visits to the temporary Fever Hospital—not flying visits, but protracted visits—during which the humble victims of poverty and disease had the full benefit of his skill, his care, his concern. In truth, for so short a practice, never was there a physician more universally respected, and, what is a higher fame, more beloved by the poor, among whom he was as generous in making pecuniary bestowments as in giving professional advice. His condescension had no affectation about it; it sprang from the deep source of a good heart, which felt for, and sympathised with, the sorrows of the poor and the forlorn.

"Many of the observant friends of Dr. Martin, had, for some time, apprehensions of a premature termination of his earthly existence, from the humane chivalry with which he devoted himself to the counteraction of a fearful epidemic. He not only attended the ordinary class of fever patients, but hunted the epidemic, in all its varied forms, through foul and narrow ways, and into lanes and alleys, where, amid noisomeness, and in a pestilential and congenial atmosphere, it had hid and burrowed. Amid these dens of foulest misery, from morning till night, his time, for the last two years, was constantly occupied—with gentlest tenderness and earnest zeal devoting his superior professional abilities, and often giving his pecuniary assistance to suffering creatures, who had nothing but gratitude to return, and whose sorrowing countenances, and sobs and tears, proved how deeply they felt the loss of their benefactor."

The end was near at hand. With an earnestness which admitted of no self-regard, Dr. Martin went about doing his work until he caught fever; and, though all that devoted care and deep solicitude for a beloved colleague could suggest, was tried, human aid availed not, and he died on the 14th November, 1847, in his thirty-second year, of typhus fever, caught in the zealous discharge of his duty, while attending on the sick poor of the town. Well might the writer of his obituary say:—

"Were he a mere traveller on life's highway, who, wearily plodding, had fulfilled his course, we would feel for him a passing regret; but it is hard to see the angel of death cast his shadow upon one yet young, so richly endowed with all that makes our life on earth so beautiful, who had already entered on a path lit by hope, where fresh laurels were gathering round his progress, and bright promises beckoned him on his way. But, if the religion of the heart deserves a recompense—if a life directed by the purest and kindliest feelings of our nature, pass not without some requital here, the martyr of charity is sure to receive, hereafter, a reward nobler than all that this world can bestow. Though many in the town had not been apprised of Dr. Martin's death, before an advanced hour on the following Monday, the funeral, on the morning of that day, was most respectably and numerously attended, by the clergy of all denominations, the members of the Doctor's high-minded profession, who seemed deeply grieved, and our townsmen of all creeds and classes. The most affecting tribute to the worth of the deceased, who had never made for himself an enemy, was in the melancholy of all, and in the unrestrained and bitter lamentations of the poor.

"One who had talents to command respect, and qualities of heart to ensure esteem; warm and devoted in his domestic affections, true and cordial in his friendships; a philanthropist in his sympathies; in a word, a good man has passed from amongst us—Dr. Martin is no more."

The inhabitants of Dundalk took prompt action to testify their sense of his loss.

Immediately after his death the inhabitants of all denominations—Protestants, Catholics, and Presbyterians—determined on erecting a monument to his memory; and in the churchyard of Haggardstown, within two miles of Dundalk, a lofty pillar of cut stone, with a weeping figure at top, was built at much cost, and the base bears the following inscription:—"Erected to the memory of Lawrence Martin, M.D., by the Inhabitants of Dundalk, in commemoration of his worth as a Citizen, a Friend, and a Physician. He died on the 14th of November, 1847, aged 32 years, of typhus fever, caught in the zealous discharge of his duties while attending on the sick poor of the town." *

PERCY FITZGERALD, ESQ., M.R.I.A.

Biography is a most valuable adjunct to history. While the latter is conversant with mankind in masses the former traces them in detail, and enables us to form a truer estimate of character and conduct than possibly can be learned from the general features of history. It is the energy of individuals

* On the tomb adjoining over Dr. Martin's remains, is the following inscription:—"Here lie the remains of John Martin, of Dundalk, merchant, who died on the 27th July, 1839, aged 53; and his wife, Arabella Dowdall, daughter of Richard Dowdall, and grand-daughter of Sir Andrew Aylmer, Bart., who died on the 7th of September, 1846, aged 60 years; also their two sons, Dr. Lawrence Martin, who died on the 14th November, 1847, and Nicholas Martin, of Dundalk, merchant, who died on the 13th October, 1851, aged 43 years."

that stamps an impress upon society; and, if there is not latent energy in the man, no amount of school, or college training, will raise him above the ordinary level. The subject of our present memoir is an example of that energy—of that strong purpose, resolute will, and manly self-reliance, which has earned him already a high and solid reputation in the literary world.

Mr. Percy Fitzgerald is younger son of the late Thomas Fitzgerald, Esq., M.P. for the County of Louth, whose devotion to his Parliamentary duties injured his health, as we have noticed.* He was born in Fane Valley, and passed the age of infancy and childhood amidst the charming scenery of his paternal home. When sufficiently grown to be sent to school Stonyhurst, in Lancashire, was his destination; and the mysterious ecclesiastics, who are adepts in the witchcraft whereby the followers of Loyola captivate the human understanding, were his preceptors. Stonyhurst boasts a respectable antiquity. Originally built by the Sherbournes, it was afterwards occupied by one of the Dukes of Norfolk, from whose representatives it was purchased by Mr. Weld, of Lulworth Castle; and when the Jesuits were driven from the Colleges of Bruges and Liege, Mr. Weld, remembering, with gratitude, the lessons he received from the Fathers of St. Omer's, received them into his house and heart, embraced them and their order, became an ecclesiastic, and bequeathed them this property. To the eyes of the pupil there was something solemn in the aspect of the stately old house, with its wide entrance, and large basins of water, the unruffled surface displaying stagnant tranquillity. The Pendle Hills loomed darkly against the sky, and the rivers Hodder and Ribble, fringed with

---

* Page 238.

many a goodly tree, flowed leisurely through the valleys beneath.

Among the preceptors young Fitzgerald found pious and devoted men, who considered they best served their Divine Master by instructing the young, and, by precept and example, inculcated piety and learning. They combined, with a well-regulated zeal for religion, sound common sense, and an earnest desire to fit their pupils for the parts they would be called upon to sustain in the battle of life. The fellow-pupils of young Fitzgerald were chiefly English Catholics of the highest rank; and the Howards, Stourtons, Cliffords, Talbots, Welds, Withams, Whitgreaves, of a former generation, mindful of the care bestowed, sent hither their olive branches for culture beneath the same guiding hands. Many Irish Catholic youths also received instruction, and formed those intimacies that often lead to most lasting ties. Acquaintanceship with brothers sometimes involves meeting sisters; and Lord Byron has left his impression of the peculiar fascination of an English Catholic lady in Aurora Raby:—

> "She was a Catholic too, sincere, austere,
> As far as her own gentle heart allowed,
> And deemed that fallen worship far more dear,
> Perhaps because 'twas fallen. Her sires were proud
> Of deeds and days, when they had filled the ears
> Of nations, and had never bent or bowed
> To rival power; and, as she was the last,
> She held their old faith and their feelings fast."

On his return to Ireland the young student of Stonyhurst entered Trinity College, Dublin; and, after the usual course, took his degree. He determined to adopt the law as his profession, and was called to the Irish Bar, in Michaelmas Term, 1855, and shortly afterwards appointed one of the Crown

Counsel on the North-East Circuit; which we hope is but a step to more lucrative advancement.

His literary attainments quickly procured him introductions to some of the leading celebrities of the day, and, what was better still, regular connexion with first-class periodicals. He has been a constant contributor to Dickens' *Household Words*, *All the Year Round*, *Temple Bar Magazine*, the *Dublin University Magazine*, *London Society*, and other serial works. But it is with Lawrence Sterne, the Tristram Shandy of English literature, Mr. Fitzgerald takes his stand as an author. "The world," he says,* "has been a little rough with the Rev. Lawrence Sterne, sometime Vicar of Sutton, Cuxwold, and other places. It has worked itself into prodigious heat on this score; protests it has been taken in as by a reduced respectability, going round furnished with letters and a well-got-up tale; and now, through the public prints, cautions well-meaning and benevolent persons against being imposed upon by sham sorrows and maudlin tears." He vigorously takes up the case of the poor clergyman. "It is not," he says, "a little cruel of the strong, vigorous writers of our time to lean thus heavily on, perhaps, the best scholar that Rabelais ever turned out." Alluding to Thackeray's scalping "the poor clergyman" in his Lectures on the English Humorists, Mr. Fitzgerald writes:—"The strong, vigorous Fielding of our own day—whose fine common-sense style has a fresh, healthy ring, and positively clears the air—has dealt very hardly with Mr. Sterne. He has stood up to him fearlessly, as it were, in a round of the old English manly sport, and, in the language of the ring, has punished the reverend gentleman

* Sterne in the "Stereoscope," *Dub. Univ. Mag.*, vol. lv., p. 542.

severely." Mr. Fitzgerald contends Sterne has been misunderstood; that "we know no more of him than did our great grandsires, who lived in his day, and even of his company (and famous company it was); and yet they who met him at the wells of Scarboro', at the York races, at what was then termed 'The Spa,' and at the Baron de Holbach's intellectual *soirées*—in short, wherever men of wit and quality did congregate—could weep and whimper over the old Monk and his snuff-box—over Moulins, Maria, and the rest of them." And, in order to clear his reputation from the accumulated mud and taint which has impaired its brightness, Mr. Fitzgerald applied his vigorous mind to setting forth *Sterne and his Day*, in a manner to rescue him from the slough into which he was rapidly sinking. A good idea of his style may be formed from the opening passage:—

"The accounts of Sterne's life that have hitherto been presented to the public seem to be poor, meagre outlines—the scaffolding and bare poles of a life, rather than the rich and fully furnished memoir which it is the fashion of the age to allot to every British worthy, of whatever calibre. When such go down to join the sacred family dust a diligent rummage of their private written effects is appointed to some skilful literary workman, and honour is paid to the lamented remains by voluminous publications of all his despatches, notes, letters, and letterets; his invitations to dinner—his acceptances of the same; his acknowledgments of money; together with even the precious autograph which enclosed his mite to the Society for the Endowment and Support of Destitute Farriers' Widows. And when such materials are slack it may be fairly and justifiably turned into a memoir of the friends and acquaintances of the immediate subject of the memoir, and the superfluous space filled in with their letters and communications."

Mr. Fitzgerald had many qualifications for the task he voluntarily undertook—extensive knowledge, a keen sense of humour, large acquaintance with fashionable life, and that enthusiastic respect for his hero which sweetens every labour undertaken in his cause. This has given Mr. Fitzgerald's work that pleasant aspect which ensures the reader's attention.

In 1862 Mr. Fitzgerald was elected a member of the Royal Irish Academy.

SIR JOHN MACNEILL, M.R.I.A., LL.D., F.R.S.

Macneill is one of the oldest Celtic names of Ireland and Scotland, and, in the latter country, the clan was located in Knapdale, Argyle, where they became hereditary constables of Suen Castle. Nial, the ancestor of the MacNials of Barra, was named in a charter dated temp. King Robert the Bruce. The clan settled in the isle of Barra during the reign of the Scottish King James the First, 1421. The chiefs of this ancient house intermarried with the daughters of Clan Ranald, Cameron, MacLeod, and others in the West Highlands.

The M'Neills were originally of Irish origin. The Chieftain of Barra, according to the *Encyclopædia Brittanica*,* had a very considerate custom. It is related that when the Chief dined, a horn was sounded from the battlements of the castle tower in Barra, and a herald proclaimed:—"Hear, O ye people, and listen, O ye nations! The Great M'Neill of Barra, having finished his meal, the princes of the earth may dine." Their castle of Kismul was reckoned impregnable.

* Vol. ii., page 280.

A warder kept watch night and day, and no one was allowed admission, save by the authority of the chief. The branch of this house from which has sprung the distinguished engineer whose fame, as a native of Dundalk, we desire to connect with its history, settled here fully two hundred years ago. We find it stated that two brothers, Malcolm and Archibald MacNeill, who held commissions in the army of William the Third, landed at Dundalk in 1688, and fought a battle at Ballymacscanlon, then the property of an Irish family named Scanlon. The Scanlons being driven from their castle, it was granted by the king to the brothers, as a reward for their valour.

Mr. D'Alton found, in the churchyard at Ballymacscanlon, the tomb of one of these soldiers of William the Third. It was inscribed:—"Tombstone of Archibald MacNeill, son of Loughlan MacNeill, of Tirfergus, in Kintyre, Scotland, who died February 6th, 1696; as also the body of Grisell MacNeill, spouse to Malcolm MacNeill, of Ballymacscanlon, who died April 11th, 1714; also the body of Malcolm MacNeill, of Ballymacscanlon, who died 28th day of June, 1731, in the 63rd year of his age. Also the body of Kitty MacNeill, who departed this life 22nd July, 1755, aged 45 years. Also the body of Malcolm MacNeill, Esq., who departed this life 27th February, 1781, aged 69 years."

This gives us almost a genealogy of the family for one hundred years. They possessed considerable property in this parish, and a very beautiful seat called Mount Pleasant. Here, towards the close of the last century, was born the subject of this brief memoir. Devotedly attached to scientific pursuits, he selected the profession of civil engineer for his avocation, and studied under the most distinguished professors. The fame of Brunel and Stephenson fired his ambition, and stimulated his energies. When the wonderful improvements in locomotion were covering England with lines of rails in every direction, Ireland was sure to profit by the example.

What vast benefits are conferred by railroads! The opportunities of travel induce a love of locomotion; and, in the variety of stations on life's journey, we lose much of the limited views, and prejudices, of the locality in which we were brought up. The heart and mind expand. We find that, however we may differ on some points, there is a great field for cultivating opinion and affections common to all, in which prejudice can make no progress, and where party feelings have no place. The first line opened in Ireland was the Dublin and Kingstown, which was the only Irish Railway used for many years. Then came the Ulster Railway, opened for traffic in 1841; and the engineering skill of John Macneill was soon employed upon the Dublin and Drogheda Railway, which was opened for traffic on the 24th May, 1844. It was upon this occasion the honour of Knighthood was conferred upon the successful engineer, by the Lord Lieutenant, Earl De Grey. And the *History of Drogheda*, by Mr. D'Alton, contains a valuable topographical and historical account of the interesting locality through which the rails are laid. A wider field for Sir John's scientific skill was then opened. The Dublin and Belfast Junction Railway Company was incorporated, by Act of Parliament, in 1845, and he was appointed engineer. It is upon this line the Boyne Viaduct, perhaps the most stupendous work in Ireland, and second only to the celebrated bridge over the Menai Straits, in boldness and engineering skill, is constructed.

The Boyne bridge is ninety-five feet above high water, admitting tall-masted vessels to pass under it without impediment, and shows three openings of 264 feet for the central, and 138 feet each for the sides respectively, the entire length of the lattice beam being 540 feet, with a depth of 22 feet 6 inches. At the north side of the river, three great semicircular cut stone arches, and at the south 12, form the approach to the viaduct, which, taken in its *tout ensemble*, must be admired as a successful combination of architectural taste with engineering skill.

This wonderful work will long preserve the name of this eminent engineer. He has earned much renown for his success in railway bridges. In the *Encyclopædia Brittanica** we find the following notice of the improvement he effected in the bridge rail:—

"Another example of the bridge rail was applied by Sir John Macneill on the Great Southern and Western Railway of Ireland, weighing 92lbs. per yard. It is laid on cross sleepers, into which it is notched by machine the whole breadth of its bearing; and thus the gauge is accurate. The cross sleepers are about two feet six inches apart, and the total bearing does not exceed sixty square inches per yard run, or one-third of the Great Western system. Yet the rail does not crush the timber, partly because it does not deflect, and partly because it crosses the fibres of the timber."

He has thus been connected with many of the important lines of Ireland. Sir John Macneill was elected a Fellow of the Royal Society, a Member of the Royal Irish Academy, and Professor of Practical Engineering in Trinity College, Dublin. He resides much at his beautiful seat, Mount Pleasant, near Dundalk, where we hope this brief outline of

* Vol. xviii., p. 755.

his eminent career may prove the high estimation in which we regard this distinguished native of the vicinity of Dundalk.

SIR F. LEOPOLD M'CLINTOCK, R.N.

This distinguished naval officer was born, in 1819, at No. 1, Seatown-place, Dundalk. His grandfather, John M'Clintock, Esq., of Drumcar, represented Enniskillen and Belturbet in the Irish House of Commons, and married, in 1766, Patience, daughter of William Foster, M.P. for the County Louth, and first cousin of John Foster, Speaker of the House of Commons, and afterwards created Lord Oriel. The youngest son of this marriage, Henry, entered the army as cornet in the 3rd Dragoon Guards. He married Elizabeth Melesina, daughter of the Venerable George Fleury, D.D., Archdeacon of Waterford. On the retirement of Lieutenant M'Clintock from the Dragoons, he obtained the office of Collector of Customs at Dundalk, which he held for the long period of thirty years. Several children were issue of this marriage. One has obtained a most eminent position in the medical profession in Dublin—Alfred H. M'Clintock, M.D., F.R.C.S.I., ex-Master of the Rotunda Lying-in Hospital. Another, T. Ernest, is an Assistant Commissary-General, and at present on service at the Cape of Good Hope; while he whose fame shed such brightness on the family name, and whose career is so well adapted to illustrate the family motto—*Virtute et labore*—has won his knighthood in a manner to disprove the assertion of Edmund Burke, that "the age of chivalry is gone."

The subject of our memoir was educated at the Dundalk Endowed Grammar School, under the care of the Rev. Dr. Darley; and, having selected the naval service, he entered, as a first class volunteer, in June, 1831, on board H. M. S. *Samarang*, then at Portsmouth, under orders for the South

American station. The young sailor passed his examination on the 23rd October, 1838, and, on the strong recommendation of Sir Charles Hotham, for the assistance he rendered towards the recovery of H. M. ship *Gorgon*, stranded at Monte Video, M'Clintock obtained his lieutenancy, 29th July, 1845. He was appointed to the *Frolic*, 16 guns, in the same year, and was stationed in the Pacific until 1847, when this vessel, on her return to England, was paid off. Determined to acquire a thorough knowledge of every branch of his profession, he applied himself diligently to master the various details of nautical science taught in the Royal Naval College, Portsmouth, especially steam navigation, which has latterly been superseding the sails. He found soon a new field of action in a region very different from the sunny waters of the Pacific.

The bold experiment of seeking the North-west Passage through the Polar Seas had been repeatedly tried without success, and great anxiety, respecting the expedition under Sir John Franklin, was felt. The first searching voyage for the missing navigators was decided upon—the command given to Sir James Ross, and among the officers were Lieutenants M'Clure and M'Clintock. This voyage occupied 1848–9, and was fruitless. No traces of Sir John Franklin's ships were discovered. Another Arctic expedition went forth in 1850–1, under Captain (now Admiral) Austin, in which Lieutenant M'Clintock served. This had no better success than the first; and having been promoted to the rank of Commander, and put in command of the screw steamer *Intrepid*, M'Clintock set forth again northward, in company with the *Resolute*, commanded by Captain Kellett, R.N., in 1852. This expedition was commanded by Captain Sir Edward Belcher, C.B., on board the *Assistance*. There was also the *Pioneer*, commanded by Lieutenant Osborne. In company with the *Resolute*, the *Intrepid* sailed to Dealy Island, where they wintered. They were the only ships that ever reached Melville Island, excepting the *Hecla* and *Griper*, of the renowned Captain Parry. During this expedition, M'Clintock outstripped all his brother officers, by the length of his sledge journeys. He performed the wonderful feat of traversing 1,400 miles in 105 days, being an average of 13⅓ miles a day for 105 days. Some notion of the labour undergone in this journey may be formed from the fact that ninety-five consecutive days were spent in dragging the sledge. The supply of game during this journey also proved very abundant; and the service owes much to the subject of this memoir for the improvements he effected in this mode of exploration. The objects of this searching expedition were twofold—to ascertain the fate of Sir John Franklin's expedition, also the safety of the Arctic navigators M'Clure and Collinson. M'Clure was discovered, and taken on board the *Resolute* by Captain Kellett, with the crew of the *Investigator*, which was abandoned; but no tidings were heard of Collinson, who was left to his fate, when, in the autumn of 1854, the four ships under Belcher's command were abandoned in the ice, and that commander, with the officers and crews, sailed home in the *Phœnix* and *North Star*, from Beechey Island. One of the abandoned ships, the *Resolute*, alone and unaided, got released from her icy moorings, and was found adrift in the Atlantic, picked up by the Americans, who refitted and restored her to the British Admiralty. In a letter, written to the Admiralty from Cork, shortly after his arrival in 1854, Sir Edward Belcher writes thus positively respecting the fate of the crews of the *Erebus* and *Terror*:—"I feel satisfied that no reasonable being in this expedition, with brains free from the delusion of interested motives, will venture to suggest that our unfortunate countrymen ever passed the meridian of Beechey Island after the spring or autumn of 1846." It is rather unfortunate for the correctness of this strongly-worded assertion, that a reasonable being of the expedition, with brains wholly free from any motives save the dictates of a sound judgment, not only suggested, but proved, that Franklin did the very thing this dictatorial officer considered impossible. But we must not anticipate. On the return of Belcher's expedition, M'Clintock was promoted to the rank of Captain, 21st October, 1854.

Collinson returned in safety on 6th May, 1855, from Behring's Strait to Cambridge Bay, and back, a distance of 4,000 miles; and this completed the Government searching expeditions. The Government allowed a book, by Sir Edward Belcher, to bear the title, *The Last of the Arctic Voyages.* It failed to satisfy the public, who longed for some result after so large an expenditure of money and risk.

But a few days after the return of Sir Edward Belcher, Dr. Rae announced that he received, in the spring of 1854, intelligence from Esquimaux of the destruction of the *Erebus* and *Terror* off King William's Island, and of the miserable fate of the crews, at Montreal Island, near the mouth of the Fish River. This report, on inquiry from the Hudson's Bay settlements, conducted by Messrs. Anderson and Stewart, was corroborated by the production of various articles from the missing ships. *No trace of writing, however, nor any vestige of the remains of the deceased navigators, could be found;* nevertheless, the Admiralty adjudged a reward of £10,000 to Dr. Rae and his companions for *ascertaining the fate of Sir John Franklin's expedition!* As yet, however, there was no authentic intelligence; and it was consistent with the statements of the Esquimaux that many of the officers and men might be alive—so Lady Franklin, and many another anxious wife, hoped on.

Although every expedition heretofore planned to discover the fate of Sir John Franklin, and the crews of the *Erebus* and *Terror* had failed, each attempt served to indicate how the failure occurred; and Captain M'Clintock was of opinion that a successful effort might yet be made. Scientific men agreed the expeditions, hitherto, had taken too northerly a course, and that, if portions of the neighbourhood of the North Magnetic Pole, yet untraversed, were visited, it was nearly certain that buried copies of Sir John Franklin's and Captain Crozier's journals would be found. These, it was expected, would narrate what had befallen them and their crews, and afford details of much scientific importance. The commercial value of previous Arctic voyages had been very great. The cod fishery of Newfoundland, the Greenland whale fishery, the fur trade of Hudson's Bay, and other important results, had been achieved. These considerations, in addition to the anxious desire to learn the fate of our missing ships and crews, were ably brought before the Royal Irish Academy by the Rev. Professor Haughton, in 1857. His object was to induce that influential body to present an address to the Premier, Lord Palmerston, praying him to give the consent of her Majesty's Government to the use of the *Resolute*—in an expedition resolved upon by Lady Franklin, wife of the commander of the missing vessels—and of such Government stores as might be requisite for the full and efficient equipment of that expedition. This resolution, seconded by the Right Hon. Joseph Napier, M.P. for the University of Dublin, was unanimously adopted. The address was forwarded, and also a similar one from several influential inhabitants of New York, to the Admiralty; but both were unproductive—the answers alleging the hopelessness of any beneficial result.

When the ceaseless solicitude of Lady Franklin caused her to devote her means to purchase Sir Richard Sutton's screw yacht *Fox*, 177 tons burthen, and to fit it out, in order to ascertain the fate of her beloved and gallant husband, as the Government declined on the ground that, "after so many failures, they would not be justified in risking the lives of brave men in a hopeless case," she selected Captain M'Clintock to take the command. He thus relates the circumstance in the able and interesting work published by him, describing the discovery which left no doubt of the fate of the commander and crews of the *Erebus* and *Terror*:—*

"On the 18th April, 1857, Lady Franklin did me the honour to offer me the command of the proposed expedition; it was, of course, most cheerfully accepted. As a post of honour, and of some difficulty, it possessed quite sufficient charms for a naval officer who had already served in three consecutive expeditions, from 1848 to 1854. I was thoroughly conversant with all the details of this peculiar service, and I confess, moreover, that my whole heart was in the cause. How could I do otherwise than devote myself to save, at least, the record of faithful service, even unto death, of my brother officers and seamen? And, being one of those by whose united efforts not only the Franklin search, but the geography of Arctic America, has been brought so nearly to completion, I could not willingly resign to posterity the honour of filling up even the small remaining blank upon our maps."

---

* *A Narrative of the Discovery of the Fate of Sir John Franklin*, p. 4

How ably and successfully he achieved these two objects are best disclosed in the work just quoted. It must suffice, in this meagre outline, to state that the *Fox* sailed from Aberdeen on the 1st July, 1857. She was roughly handled by the climate during the winter of 1857–8, being locked in ice off Melville Bay, in lat. 76° N., on the coast of Greenland, and for eight months she drifted southwards, until finally released from the ice in lat. 63° N. Captain M'Clintock seized the first opportunity to get from Baffin's Bay to Pond Inlet, thence to Beechey Island, through portion of Peel Strait, and over the previously unnavigated waters of Bellot Strait. This expedition enabled M'Clintock to lay down the unknown coast-line of Boothia, southward from Bellot's Strait, to the Magnetic Pole—to delineate King William's Island, and prove the existence of a channel from Victoria Strait, north-west, to Melville or Parry Sound. This is now known as M'Clintock's Channel.

The sledge journeys of 1859, as the Rev. Professor Haughton justly observes, prove that the chief had trained his pupils after such a fashion as threatened to endanger his own claim to the sledge-champion's belt. The mileage result was, on an average, eleven miles per diem. Captain M'Clintock travelled 910 miles in 79 days; Captain Allen Young, 940 miles in 81 days; and Lieutenant Hobson, 770 miles in 74 days. This showed sledge racing almost as close as a well-contested Derby. In these journeys dogs were employed as well as men; and the proportion of weight was 200 lbs. per man, and 100 lbs. per dog, as the maximum. Each party consisted of four men, two officers, and six dogs.

Captain M'Clintock generously assigned to Lieutenant Hobson the examination of the west coast of King William's Island, where his idea that traces of the missing ships would be found, proved fully sustained. He himself explored the east and south coasts of this island, and the estuary of the Fish River, while Captain Young completed the survey of Prince of Wales' Land.

At Point Victory, on the N.W. coast of King William's Land, Lieutenant Hobson, R.N., found a record of the missing crews. It was dated 28th May, 1847, and mentioned, "Sir John Franklin, commanding the expedition, and all well."* The central part of this was written and signed by Lieutenant Gore; but round the margin of the paper on which he wrote the words of hope, "all well," another hand traced the sad lines:—

"April 25, 1848.—H. M. ships, *Terror* and *Erebus*, were deserted on the 22nd April, five leagues N.N.W. of this, having been beset since 12th September, 1846. The officers and crews, consisting of 105 souls, under the command of Captain F. R. M. Crozier, landed here, in lat. 69° 37′ 42″ N., long. 98° 41′ W. Sir John Franklin died on the 11th June, 1847; and the total loss by deaths in the expedition has been, to this date, 9 officers and 15 men.

(Signed) "JAMES FITZJAMES,
"Captain H. M. S. *Erebus*.

(Signed) "F. R. M. CROZIER,
"Captain and Senior Officer.

"And start on to-morrow, 26th, for Back's Fish River."

The interesting narrative of Sir Leopold M'Clintock describes the discovery, on the 30th May, of a large boat, 28 feet long, and 7 feet 3 inches wide, with marks which showed

* *Vide Fate of Franklin*, by M'Clintock, p. 284.

her British built. Portions of two human skeletons were in the boat. Here, also, were five watches and several articles of clothing, some small books, a Bible, which bore evident traces of having been much read, and passages marked that, no doubt, served to solace the seamen in their last sad hour. Spoons and forks, with the crest of Sir John Franklin, and those of other officers, were also found; and these memorials being carefully preserved, the expedition set forth homeward bound. The *Fox* reached Blackwall Dock on 23rd September, 1858. The relics were deposited by the Admiralty in the United Service Institution; and, in the words of the gallant M'Clintock, they "now form a national memento—the most simple and most touching—of those heroic men, who perished in the path of duty; but not until they had achieved the grand object of their voyage—the discovery of the North-West Passage."

Immediately on the return of the *Fox*, Captain M'Clintock reported to the Admiralty the result of his search, and the reply acknowledged he gave the first authentic account of the fate of Sir John Franklin. Their Lordships were also pleased to recognise his period of service in the *Fox* as so much sea-time, thereby giving him so much seniority. And then, from every quarter, honours thick and fast were showered upon the distinguished seaman. The first and best tribute was the address from the officers and crew of the *Fox*, witnesses of his conduct, and sharers of his danger. His fellow-townsmen of Dundalk were ready to testify their pride at his career; and on the 31st of October, 1859, a very pleasing ceremony took place in that town—the presentation, in the County Court-house, of an address to Captain M'Clintock from his fellow-townsmen, and other friends in its vicinity. This most cordial and complimentary expression of admiration and esteem, was accompanied by a massive silver salver, and claret jug of the same metal, of elegant design and beautiful workmanship. In his reply, he spoke of this expression of congratulation being peculiarly gratifying to him, as emanating from Dundalk, the place of his nativity, and from those among whom the early years of his life were passed.

The metropolis of Ireland speedily followed the example of Dundalk. A preliminary public meeting, summoned by the Lord Mayor, was held in the Mansion-house, "for the purpose of presenting a suitable testimonial to Captain Francis Leopold M'Clintock for the great services rendered by him to science during his Arctic voyages, and for discovering the fate of Sir John Franklin, as well as to congratulate him on his safe return to his native country." The meeting was highly influential. Among the speakers were Lord Talbot de Malahide, Rev. Professor Haughton, F.T.C.D., Captain Sir Robert Hagan, R.N.; Dr. Corrigan, Mr. Whiteside, M.P.; Alderman John Reynolds, the Right Hon. Joseph Napier, Sir Patrick O'Brien, &c. A committee of twenty-one gentlemen was formed to collect subscriptions, and the result showed their zeal for the work. In little more than a month, on Tuesday, 27th December, the National Address was presented. The Round Room of the Mansion-house contained an array of rank, beauty, and worth, of which any man might be proud.

The Lord Mayor said:—"It was his pride and privilege to hand him the address, emanating from a meeting composed of the rank and intelligence, not merely of the City of Dublin, but from all parts of Ireland. It was to be observed that was a meeting composed of gentlemen as opposite in their political and religious views as are the poles themselves asunder; but all uniting in harmony to pay a tribute of honour where honour was so justly due."

Mr. L. E. Foot, Vice-President of the Royal Dublin Society, then read the address; and Captain M'Clintock, having read a very eloquent and expressive answer,

Dr. Corrigan, President of the College of Physicians, in moving a vote of thanks to the Lord Mayor, addressed the meeting in a speech of such power, and beauty, that we make a few extracts. Alluding to the ease with which Lady Franklin found gallant men ready to assist her, he said:—"Had Lady Franklin to call for volunteers? No. Had she but asked for them she would have had volunteers, not alone from our own isles, but from every sea-coast in Europe, and from the whole length of America. Is it detracting from the merits of the brave Captain and crew of the *Fox* to say that thousands would have taken their places? Certainly not. This only shows how proud they must feel that they were selected. But the thousands of heads, and hearts, and hands offered thus would not suffice for Lady Franklin's last effort. She needed head, and heart, and hand, combined in one—a head to judge and decide promptly—a heart to feel as her own did—and a hand to grapple with every obstacle that might arise; and she found them all combined in our countryman, whom we have the honour to have here with us to-day—a man that might be typified in our own national emblem, the shamrock:—

"'A type that blends
Three much-sought friends,
Head, heart, and hand, together.'"—(Cheers).

From the address presented on this occasion we make the following extract, as it succinctly records the chief Arctic services of Captain M'Clintock:—

"While the actual result of your expedition is patent to

the comprehension of all, we should not appreciate it as it deserves, did we not glance at your labours and services introductory to its accomplishment. We deem it a pleasure to recognise your last Arctic Expedition as the *fourth* in which you have been engaged, the three preceding having been in the service of the Crown; to call to mind that you have passed *six winters* in the Polar ice, during which time you have travelled between *five and six thousand miles on foot* within the Arctic circle (the laborious employment of 416 days), of which more than 2,000 miles have been in the geographical exploration of coast line; that you organized and improved sledge travelling to such a degree as to enable you to extend your journey from five hundred miles, on your first expedition, to one thousand four hundred in your third."

The interesting work published by Captain M'Clintock—*The Voyage of the Fox in the Arctic Seas; a Narrative of the Discovery of the Fate of Sir John Franklin and his Companions*—met with wonderful success. The first impression, of 10,000 copies, was sold in a short time. It is stated that 7,000 copies were engaged before the work appeared; and learned bodies sought for the honour of including Captain M'Clintock among their distinguished members.

The Dublin University conferred on him the degree of LL.D. The English universities, also, their honorary degrees. In January, 1860, the Court of Common Council agreed to grant "the freedom of the City of London, in a box of British oak, of the value of fifty guineas, to Captain F. Leopold M'Clintock;" and "that the thanks of this Court be given to the officers and crew of the yacht *Fox*, for the bravery and self-sacrifice which distinguished the conduct of all those who accompanied Captain M'Clintock as volunteers upon this patriotic service."

Mr. C. Reid, F.S.A., in proposing the resolution, sketched, in most masterly style, and with consummate ability, the history of Arctic navigation, and the great services of Captain M'Clintock.

On the day of presenting the freedom of London, the Lord Mayor entertained a numerous circle at the Mansion-house, assembled to do honour to the gallant seaman. Her Gracious Majesty testified her sense of his services by conferring on him the honour of knighthood—and never were spurs more bravely won. A more substantial token of the nation's gratitude was a Parliamentary grant of £5,000 for the officers and crew of the *Fox*. This was brought forward in the House of Commons by Sir F. Baring, supported by the Right Hon. James Whiteside, and approved of by Lord Palmerston and Mr. Disraeli.

The scientific societies of Dublin—the Royal Dublin Society, and the Dublin University Zoological and Botanical Society—were not slow to do honour to the renowned Arctic navigator. The former of these societies not only voted him an address, which was presented to him by the Lord Lieutenant—as President of the Society—but had his bust sculptured in marble (by Kirke), and placed in the Society's magnificent museum, which he had so largely enriched with Esquimaux relics, and with specimens of Arctic geology and natural history.

In May, 1860, the gallant object of so much public favour was again employed in the Arctic region. He commanded H. M. S. *Bulldog*, commissioned for sounding the North Atlantic Ocean, between the Faroe Islands, Iceland, Greenland, and Labrador, with a view of testing the practicability of connecting Great Britain and the Western Continent by the electric telegraph. The object achieved, the *Bulldog* returned; but had to put into Killibegs harbour in a crippled state. It appears that, by laying down the telegraph wire on this route, the extreme length of any one submarine cable would not exceed 500 miles.

In the spring of 1861 Sir Leopold was appointed to H.M.S. *Doris*, then in the Mediterranean. While in command of this vessel the Eastern tour of His Royal Highness the Prince of Wales occurred, and the *Doris* formed the Royal escort in the Turkish and Greek waters. On the return of the *Doris* to Devonport, in December, 1862, she was paid off.

During the visit of the Channel Fleet, under Admiral Dacres, to Dublin Bay, in September, 1863, Sir Leopold M'Clintock was an active member of the Committee engaged in giving the fleet a hearty Irish welcome. Those who had the good fortune to examine the magnificent specimens of naval architecture which the *Black Prince* and *Warrior* displayed could not fail to be impressed with the wonderful change in the navy of late years, and the conviction that discoveries in science are effecting revolutions on sea as well as land. At the banquet given by the citizens of Dublin to the officers of the Fleet, the health of Sir Leopold was thus proposed by one of Ireland's noblest peers:—

Lord Talbot de Malahide said:—" My lords and gentlemen, the Lord Mayor has imposed a duty on me which I feel much pleasure in discharging. It is to propose a toast, the health of a friend of mine, whom I see at the other side of the table—Sir Leopold M'Clintock. We all know the great service he has rendered both to science and humanity, and he also raised the character of the navy, with which he is connected, as the promoter of both. We know the great distinction he attained in that voyage to the North Pole, which, we may say, has determined the question of the north passage, and in which he discovered the relics of Sir John Franklin. We know the great obligation we are under to him, and wo, in this country, feel quite a national pride at having so distinguished a sailor as our countryman. (Applause.) I shall not go into any further details, but beg you to drink in a bumper the health of Sir Leopold M'Clintock."

The toast was duly honoured.

Sir Leopold M'Clintock, who was warmly applauded on rising to respond, said:—"My Lord Mayor, my lords, and gentlemen, I hardly know how to thank you sufficiently for the favour you have done me in proposing my health; and I feel quite at a loss to express my sense of gratification and gratitude for the manner in which it has been received. I derive gratification in another sense from the toast you propose, inasmuch as you offered to our naval guests an admirable illustration of your enthusiastic feelings of patriotism, loyalty, and public spirit. My naval friends know that the calls of duty often take us far beyond the reach of special correspondents, and for a lengthened period of time, yet no sooner are our acts made public than they are carefully investigated by thousands of our countrymen, who never lose an opportunity of bestowing on us the most liberal praise. I think this is a most convincing proof that our glorious navy still retains its ancient and well-earned popularity; and I attribute the high honour you have conferred on me this evening to this cause, as well as to the indulgent favour of the citizens of Dublin. It is true that the *Fox* was not a national vessel; she was not under the Admiralty, nor in the navy. Her mission was not war—it was humanity. But the teaching which enabled me to conduct her was all derived from the navy. (Applause.) And, as naval men, we all bear in remembrance Lord Nelson's memorable prayer—that after the battle humanity should be the predominant characteristic of the British navy. (Applause.) Again, gentlemen, I thank you all very heartily."

Sir Leopold was not long allowed to remain unemployed. On 16th November, 1863, he was appointed to the command of H. M. S. *Aurora*, a new steam frigate of 35 guns, under orders for service in the Channel. And here we conclude our memoir, perfectly satisfied that whensoever, or wheresoever, Great Britain needs a sailor to defend her flag, to sustain her honour, and uphold her fame, she will find no one of her gallant blue jackets more prompt, more faithful, or more true, than this chivalrous knight and distinguished Irishman, whom we proudly claim as a native of Dundalk.

APPENDIX.

LISTS OF OFFICIALS.

DUNDALK CORPORATE OFFICERS.

	BAILIFF	DEPUTY BAILIFF	RECORDER
1692	George Walker	...	William Shaw, Esq.
1693	Viscount Dungannon	George Walker	
1694	Ditto	Joel Hoey	
1695	Ditto		
1700	John Smith		
1703	Viscount Dungannon	Roger Bury	
1705			
1706	Blaney Townley		
1707	Hon. Henry Tenison	William Tuigh	
1708	Frederick Hamilton	Jeremiah Patterson	
1709	Jeremiah Patterson		
1710	Nicholas Price	Jeremiah Patterson	
1711	Hans Hamilton	Ditto	
1712	Frederick Hamilton	Ditto	
1713	Jeremiah Patterson	...	R. Jones, Esq.
1714	Frederick Hamilton	Ditto	
1715	Nicholas Price	Stephen Marmion	
1716	Hans Hamilton	Ditto	
1718	Ditto	William Johnson	
1719	Michael Ward	John Shewell	
1720	Jeremiah Patterson		
1723	Thomas Fortescue	Ditto	
1724	Hans Hamilton	Ditto	
1725	Thomas Fortescue	...	Faithful Fortescue, Esq., in room of R. Jones, deceased.
1726	Ditto	David Clifford	
1727	Michael Ward	John Shewell	
1728	Thomas Fortescue	W. Mercer	
1729	Ditto		
1730	William Mercer		
1760	Isaac Read		
1761	Visconnt Jocelyn	Isaac Read	
1762	Isaac Read		
1763	Rev. R. Stuart, D.D.	Isaac Read	
1764	Isaac Read		
1765	Thomas Read		
1766	Isaac Read	Thomas Read	
1767	Thomas Read		
1768	Isaac Read		
1769	Thomas Read		
1770	Isaac Read	Ditto	
1771	Thomas Read		

DUNDALK CORPORATE OFFICERS—*continued.*

	BAILIFF	DEPUTY BAILIFF	RECORDER
1772	Isaac Read	Thomas Read	
1773	Thomas Read		
1774	Isaac Read	Ditto	
1775	Thomas Read		
1776	Isaac Read	Ditto	
1777	Thomas Read		
1778	Isaac Read	William Pitman	
1779	Thomas Read	Ditto	
1780	Isaac Read	Ditto	
1781	Thomas Read	Ditto	
1782	Right Hon. James Earl of Clanbrassil		
1783	William Pitman	...	A. C. Macartney, Esq.
1784	Earl of Roden		
1785	Ditto	Ditto	
1786	Ditto		
1787	William Pitman		
1788	Earl of Roden	Ditto	
1789	Ditto	Ditto	
1790	Arthur C. Macartney		
1791	Robert Browne		
1792	Henry Doyle		
1793	Robert Browne		
1794	Henry Doyle		
1795	Robert Browne		
1796	Henry Doyle	Robert Browne	
1797	Robert Browne		
1798	John Straton		
1799	Hon. John Jocelyn	...	Henry Doyal, Esq.
1800	John Straton		
1801	Hon. & Rev. P. Jocelyn		
1802	Hon. John Jocelyn		
1803	Hon. & Rev. P. Jocelyn	Tobias Purcell	A. C. Macartney, Esq., in room of H. Doyal, Esq., deceased.
1804	Hon. John Jocelyn	Ditto	
1805	Hon. & Rev. P. Jocelyn	Ditto	
1806	Hon. John Jocelyn	Ditto	
1807	Hon. & Rev. P. Jocelyn	Ditto	
1808	Hon. John Jocelyn		
1809	Hon. & Rev. P. Jocelyn	Leonard Bigger	
1810	Hon. John Jocelyn	Ditto	
1811	Viscount Jocelyn		
1812	Hon. John Jocelyn	Ditto	
1813	Viscount Jocelyn		
1814	Hon. John Jocelyn	Ditto	
1815	Ditto	Ditto	
1816	Viscount Jocelyn	...	Walter Steel, Esq.
1817	Hon. John Jocelyn	Ditto	
1818	Viscount Jocelyn		
1819	Hon. John Jocelyn	Ditto	
1820	Matthew Forde	Ditto	
1821	Walter Steel		
1822	Hon. John Jocelyn	Ditto	
1823	Walter Steel	Ditto	

DUNDALK CORPORATE OFFICERS—*continued.*

	BAILIFF	DEPUTY BAILIFF	RECORDER
1824	Matthew Forde	Leonard Bigger	
1825	George Foster		
1826	Ditto	...	Frederick Shaw, Esq., elected in room of Walter Steel, Esq., deceased.
1827	Walter Newton	George Forster	
1828	George Foster		
1829	James Nicholson Frood		
1830	Robert Burke		
1831	James Nicholson Frood		
1832			
1833			
1834			
1835	William Samuel Hill		
1836	James Nicholson Frood		
1837	William Samuel Hill		
1838	James N. Frood		
1839	J. J. Bigger		
1840	Ditto		
1841	Ditto		

LIST OF MEMBERS FOR THE BOROUGH OF DUNDALK IN THE IRISH HOUSE OF COMMONS.

1559	Christopher Moore and Patrick Stanley.
1585	Richard Bellewe; Thomas Bath; John Stronge.
1613	William Cashell, Gent.; Richard Tulleis, Gent.
1624	Peter Clynton, Gent.; Oliver Cashell, Gent.
1639	Oliver Cashell, Gent.; Nicholas Smyth, Gent.
1642	Francis Moore, Esq., *vice* Cashell, expelled 22nd June, for the Rebellion.
1644	John Stoyte, Esq, *vice* Smyth, deceased.
1644	John Hatch, Esq., *vice* Moore, deceased.
1661	Wolston Dixie, Esq.; Nicholas Comber, Esq.
1692	William Shaw, Esq.; Thomas Percivall, Esq.
1695	Kilner Brazier, Esq.; Thomas Percivall, Esq.
1703	Henry Bellingham, Esq.; James Somerville, Esq.
1707	Richard Tisdall, Esq., *vice* Somerville, deceased.
1713	Henry Brooke, Esq.; Henry Bellingham, Esq.
1715	James Hamilton, Esq.; Henry Brooke, Esq.
1719	Hon. Henry Moryson, *vice* Hamilton, Viscount Limerick.
1721	James Tisdall, Esq., *vice* Moryson, deceased.
1727	Thomas Fortescue, Esq.: Hans Hamilton, Esq.
1727	John Hamilton, Esq., *vice* Hamilton, deceased.
1757	James Fortescue, Esq., *vice* J. Hamilton, deceased.
1761	James Smyth, Esq.; Robert Waller, Esq.
1761	David La Touche, Esq.
1758	William Henry Fortescue, Esq.; Robert Waller, Esq.
1769	James Smyth, Esq.
1771	James Sheil, Esq.
1776	Robert Waller, Esq., and William Cunningham, Esq.
1781	Robert Lindsay, Esq., in room of Sir Robert Waller, deceased.
1783	Viscount Jocelyn, and Hon. George Jocelyn.
1790	Same Members Re-elected.
1796	Hon. George Jocelyn, having accepted Office, re-elected.
1797	Hon. George Jocelyn, and Hon. John Jocelyn.

The following have been Returned since 1800:—

1801	Isaac Corry, Esq.
1802	Richard Archdall, Esq.
1806	John Metge, Esq. On the acceptance, by Mr. Metge, of a Government appointment, Park Crawford Bruce, Esq.
1808	Thomas Hughson, Esq., in room of Park Crawford Bruce, Esq., who had accepted a Government place.
1812	Frederick William Trench, Esq., in room of Thomas Hughson, Esq., deceased.
	John Metge, Esq., in room of Frederick W. Trench, Esq.
1813	Lyndon Evelyn, Esq.
1818	Gerard Callaghan, Esq.
1820	John Metge, Esq. (March).

1820	George Hartopp, Esq., in room of John Metge, Esq., who accepted a place of profit under the Crown (June).
1824	Sir Robert H. Inglis, Bart, in room of George Hartopp, Esq., deceased.
1826	Charles Barclay, Esq.
1830	John Hobart Craddock, Esq.
1831	James Edward Gordon, Esq.
1832	William O'Reilly, Esq.
1834	William Sharman Crawford, in room of William O'Reilly, Esq., resigned.
1837	Thomas N. Redington, Esq.
1841	Same Re-elected.
1847	William Torrens M'Cullagh, Esq.
1852	George Bowyer, Esq., D.C.L.
1857	Same Member Re-elected.
1859	Same, now Sir George Bowyer, Bart.

CLERKS OF THE CROWN, AND COMMISSIONS, AND KEEPERS OF ALL THE WRITS, BILLS, FILES, RECORDS, AND ROLLS FOR THE COUNTY OF LOUTH, IN THE TOWN OF DUNDALK.

1553	Michael Cusac.
1576	Thomas Dillon.
1593	Zachery Peers.
	John Talbot.
1597	Nicholas Berford.
1609	William Bradley.
1615	Said William Bradley and Robert Dixon.
1615	Robert Gale.
1627	John Darnell and Henry Mawdsley.
1644	Thomas Eustace, and Alexander Eustace.
1657	Bartholomew Hussey and Richard Ward.
1660	John Eustace and Maurice Eustace.
1677	Robert Aicken and Arthur Podmore.
1680	David Aicken and Arthur Podmore.
1722	Paul Whichcote.
1761	Hugh Carmichael.
1794	John Pollock.
1826	Arthur Hill Cornwallis Pollock.
1846	John Maher.
1856	William Horan.
1857	Patrick James Byrne, the present Clerk of the Crown.

MEMBERS OF THE COMMONS HOUSE OF PARLIAMENT ELECTED FOR THE COUNTY OF LOUTH.

1559, Jan.	Nicholas Taaffe, Esq., Ballybragan; Edward Dowdall, Esq., Glasspistol.
1585, April	Roger Gernon, Esq., Gernonstown; William Moore, Esq., Barmeath.
1613, April 15	Christopher Verdon, Gent., Clonmore; Richard Gernon, Gent., Stabannon.
1634, June 30	Sir Christopher Bellew, Knt., Castletown; Christopher Dowdall, Esq., Killaly.
1639, March 2	Sir Christopher Bellew, Knt., Castletown; Sir John Bellew, Knt., Wylystown.
1642, August	Philip, Lord Lisle, Dublin; Colonel Laurence Crawford. Both Bellews expelled 22nd June, 1642, for the Rebellion.
1644, May	Hon. Francis Moore, Esq.; Gerard Moore, Esq., Ardee. Lord Lisle and Crawford absent in England without leave.
1661, April 9	Sir Thomas Stanley, Knt.; Henry Bellingham, Esq., Gernonstown.
1695, Aug. 26	Sir Henry Tichbourne, Knt., Beaulieu; Thomas Bellingham, Esq., Gernonstown.
1703, Sept. 12	Thomas Bellingham, Esq., Gernonstown; Henry Tennison, Esq., Dillonstown.
1710, May 29	Sir Henry Tichbourne, Knt. and Bart., Beaulieu, *vice* Tennison, deceased.
1713, Oct. 30	Richard Tisdall, Esq., Ardee; Stephen Ludlow, Dublin.
1715, Nov. 9	Hon. Robert Moore, Ardee; Richard Tisdall, Esq., Ardee.
1727, Oct. 11	Faithful Fortescue, Corderry; William Aston, Esq., Beaulieu.
1741, Oct. 28	Henry Bellingham, Esq., Castlebellingham, *vice* Fortescue, deceased.
1745, Oct. 17	Wm. Henry, Esq., Reynoldstown, *vice* Aston, deceased.
1756, Oct. 27	Thos. Tipping, Esq., Beaulieu, *vice* Bellingham, deceased.
1761, May 5	Wm. Henry Fortescue, Esq., Reynoldstown; Anthony Foster, Esq., Collon.
1761, Dec. 22	James Fortescue, Esq., Ravensdale Park, *vice* Fortescue, for Monaghan.
1767, Nov. 18	Stephen Sibthorpe, Esq., Newton, *vice* Foster, Lord Chief Baron.
1768, July 19	John Foster, Dunleer; Jas. Fortescue, Esq., Ravensdale.
1776	Right Hon. James Fortescue and Right Hon. John Foster.
1784	Right Hon. John Foster and Thomas James Fortescue, Esq.
1785	Right Hon. John Foster, Speaker of the House of Commons, and Thomas James Fortescue, Esq.
1790	Same Members Re-elected.
1796	Right Hon. John Foster; Wm. Charles Fortescue, Esq.

Members for Co. Louth, since the Union:—

1800	Right Hon. John Foster, and William Charles Fortescue, Esq.
1806	Right Hon. John Foster, and Hon. Lord Viscount Jocelyn.
1807	Same Members Re-elected.
1812	Same Members Re-elected.
1818	Same Members Re-elected.
1820	Hon. John Jocelyn, and John Leslie Foster, Esq., LL.D.
1826	Alexander Dawson, Esq., and John Leslie Foster, Esq., K.C., LL.D.
1830	Alexander Dawson, Esq., and John M'Clintock, Esq.
1831	Richard Lalor Sheil, K. C., and Sir Patrick Bellew, Bart.
1833	Thomas FitzGerald, Esq., and Richard Montesquieu Bellew, Esq.
1835	Sir Patrick Bellew, Bart., and Richard Montesquieu Bellew, Esq.
1837	R. M. Bellew, and Henry Chester, Esqrs.
1841	R. M. Bellew, and Thomas Fortescue, Esqrs.
1847	R. M. Bellew, and Chichester Fortescue, Esqrs.
1852	Chichester Fortescue and Tristram Kennedy, Esqrs.
1854	Re-election of Mr. Fortescue, consequent on his acceptance of Office.
1857	Chichester Fortescue, and John M'Clintock, Esqrs.
1859	Chichester Fortescue, and R. M. Bellew, Esqrs.

LIST OF ASSISTANT BARRISTERS (NOW CHAIRMEN OF QUARTER SESSIONS) FOR THE CO. LOUTH.

1798	William Calbeck.
1803	Arthur Chichester Macartney.
1820	Francis Hamilton.
1830	Richard Moore, K.C.
1839	William M'Dermott.
1840	Michael O'Shaughnessy.*
1848	Henry Baldwin, Q.C.; Robert Andrews, LL.D.†
1849	John Finlay, LL.D.
1854	John Perrin.
1857	David Lynch, Q.C.‡
1859	John Leahy.§
1863	David Richard Pigot, jun.

---

* Now Chairman of Quarter Sessions for Co. Clare.
† Now ditto for Co. Donegal.
‡ Now one of the Judges of the Court of Bankruptcy and Insolvency.
§ Now Chairman of Quarter Sessions for West Riding, Co. Cork

INDEX.

CPSIA information can be obtained
at www.ICGtesting.com
Printed in the USA
LVHW101928170422
716440LV00004BA/307

9 783752 592948